ELLA RUBY SELF is a Sh
nestled against the rise of the
an MA in Literature and Creative Writing graduate.

Ella is currently in the first year of her PhD, looking at how folk stories are inherently intertwined with the natural landscape. Stories inspired by nature, myth and folklore have always been a large part of her life, and you can often find her up on some distant edge, lost in the woods, in abominably cold water or under big moorland skies with a notebook in her pocket and a head full of day dreams.

Abraxus Elijah Honey is her debut novel.

Follow Ella on Twitter/X @local_sea_wytch

ABRAXUS ELIJAH HONEY

ELLA RUBY SELF

Northodox Press Ltd
Maiden Greve, Malton,
North Yorkshire, YO17 7BE

This edition 2024

1
First published in Great Britain by
Northodox Press Ltd 2024

ISBN: 9781915179555

This book is set in Garamond Pro Std

This Novel is entirely a work of fiction. The names,
characters and incidents portrayed in it are the work of the
author's imagination. Any resemblance to actual persons,
living or dead, events or localities is entirely coincidental.

For my family, both blood and chosen,
who have wandered so far,
and taught me so much

ERself

part one
the shallows

I
then.

Somewhere past the horizon.

Do you hear the roar of the sea, m'boy? Do you feel its power, its gentleness? Do you understand that it is benevolent and cruel? The sea is many things, m'boy. It changes like the currents and like the tides. It will tear apart the cliff walls, and reshape the sands and rock into new land.

We are but fragile things upon it, m'boy. Men talk of taming the sea, ploughing it in their handsome boats of oak, collecting its riches and making them their own. They do not understand the sea at all. They seek only to conquer, to gain, to take. To try and tame the sea and make it your own is akin to trying to catch lightning in a bottle. All that power held in one place? No, m'boy. It would destroy you.

Lie down. Close your eyes. Do you hear the water around you? Listen to the ship, listen to how she moves with the tide. She knows she is brittle, fragile. And yet, she dances over the waves like a petrel through a storm. Have faith in her m'boy, she will not let us fall to the depths. Sleep. Let the sea rock you. Listen.

Do you hear the song of the sea, m'boy?

ABRAXUS ELIJAH HONEY

No place for the living.

It shouldn't have been sunny. There shouldn't have been calm waters. The day shouldn't have had a cool breeze that played over the long grass, nor gentle blue skies that stretched over the graveyard and out over to the horizon. She didn't want any of these things. If the world could act as a mirror for the tempest of her mind, as the sea was acting as a mirror for the sky, then the cliffs would have torn themselves apart. The sea would have become slate grey and wild. Wind would have screamed, and she would scream alongside it. But instead, she now had to weather the storm *inside*, rather than out.

Idly, she thought that it might make things easier. If nature was allowed to cry out its feelings over the land, then she could join in. Maybe it wouldn't make her feel so alone. Because that's what she was now. Alone. Clinging to a broken piece of wood that had once been part of a beautiful ship, tossed about in the unforgiving waves of her own grief. And the want, the *need* to let go and fall into that cold, black depth was overpowering. The siren song of those dark waters called to her, and she could feel the insidious tide rising.

The gravestone before her was new, its carved inscription clear: indelible words that could only be erased by time and the bitter sea winds. Distantly, she was aware that she was kneeling, her dress that had cost more than she could afford dirtying at the hem and knees. She couldn't bring herself to care. It hardly mattered now anyway. The dark ocean within roared.

ELLA RUBY SELF

Let go. Succumb.

She reached out, and brushed cold fingertips along the first word chiselled into that black rock. A name that could never be spoken again without a deep inflection of sorrow. A name that had once brought such joy to her, and now only left her feeling empty and cold. She wanted to say it, to feel the name on her lips again. She didn't. The breeze drifted through the tall grass instead, murmuring quietly and not understanding her grief.

A different sound then pierced through the fugue of her mind. A soft sniffle, the gentle snap of fabric caught in the wind. She closed her eyes for a moment and stilled the black ocean inside. That last little bit of wood she clung to would have to keep her afloat for a while yet. She couldn't drown, not now. Opening her eyes, she took a breath, and another, and stood.

Not alone. The voice sounded so like him that she had to push down a cry. And yet, as much pain as it caused her, she forced herself to listen.

Not alone, she agreed with it.

Her two boys stood in the shelter of the Reverend's arms, his long black robe rippling behind him. Tias was crying silently. Eli was stony faced, his eyes shuttered. *They need you. Hold on.*

She knew it was the truth. 'I'll try,' she said to no-one. Or, at least, no-one living. She resolutely stepped away from the grave, from the fresh earth that covered it. She opened her arms, and pulled her sons toward her. 'Go home,' she said softly, 'I will follow.'

'But–'

'Go.' She said it forcefully, but not unkindly.

The Reverend put his hands onto the boys' shoulders, and guided them away from their mother, promising to walk them home and sit with them until her return. He told her to take as long as she needed. She nodded gratefully, but knew that if she did as he requested, she would likely not come home ever again.

As the three figures disappeared down the soft rise of the graveyard's hill, she turned toward the cliff edge, protected by a low stone wall. The sea was deceptively calm, its waters a rich sapphire, shot through with patches of green. It was beautiful. And how she hated it. The anger she felt then was terrifying. An all-consuming wave of fire and acid. Something was trying to claw out of her chest, a beast with fangs and claws and an evil eye. She let it loose, and her own voice became its roar. Her words were snatched away by the wind, stronger here over this precipice. Her old language, dormant but not forgotten, rolled from her tongue and the words tasted bitter. She spat them out, and more rose to replace them.

After a time, she came back to herself. The beast was sated, her throat raw. The sea remained unchanged, glittering on the crests of waves as it broke along the shoreline. She turned her back on it, and marched away.

The Depths.

They heard.
   Something old awoke below.

II
now.

Ink.
November, 1815.
Tias.

'Tias, go and find your brother.'

'I don't know where he is. I'm busy.'

'Well, that's the point of going to find something, *cariad*, so you know where it is.'

'I'm *busy*.' Tias resolutely did not move from the small writing desk, his notebook open in front of him. The open pages were slowly being covered in his cramped, sloping handwriting. Ink spattered his hands, creating new constellations of freckles and blackening his fingertips. Tias reached up, raising his hands above his head, stretching out the cramped ache that had settled between his shoulder blades.

He had been working on this particular page for over three days now, and it was still barely half-way complete. The weather had kept him inside today – thankfully – so he'd had a good few undisturbed hours working on this particular spread. The storm petrel, sketched in light pencil, stared balefully up at him from the rough paper. He'd completed the sketch yesterday, and was now in the process of writing down everything he could remember about this particular seabird. It was important to get it all down correctly. It had been one of his father's favourites.

'Tias.' His mother said, taking a tone that brooked no argument.

'How can I find something when I don't even know where to

start looking?' Tias asked, resignedly standing up and cracking his knuckles. He dragged his feet on purpose as he moved over to the steep ladder that led down into the main, and only, room of the cottage.

'Don't do that.' Ffion had her back to him, sitting at the table and wielding a needle and thread like a sword. Tias caught sight of a ragged and faded shirt, a large rip along the sleeve.

'That's more stitching than shirt.' Tias observed facetiously.

Ffion sighed heavily, holding up the garment. 'Goes through more shirts than the whole village.'

Tias jumped the bottom two rungs, an old habit left over from childhood. He inspected his own shirtsleeves, rip free but, like his hands, spattered with ink. Surreptitiously folding them up, Tias walked over to his mother and stood behind her, inspecting the shirt. It looked to be in an even more sorry state up close.

'That's going to have to do,' Ffion said, laying down the needle. 'This will have to last him until next spring.' She deftly folded the newly mended shirt and stood up to return the needle and thread to the small box kept on the mantelpiece. The fire crackled gently.

'Do I have to go look?' Tias tried one last time. 'He'll come home eventually, when he's hungry or cold or...' He trailed off, wilting slightly under the hard look Ffion was directing at him. Tias looked out of the window, and listened to the wind roar outside. It sounded cold.

'Take this.' Ffion nudged a scarf into Tias' hands, hand knitted and smelling faintly of woodsmoke. 'I need to talk to you both.'

Someone had poured cold water down Tias' back. The last time that had been said to them was when his father's boat had been found splintered against the rocks a mile down the coast.

Taking the scarf, he wrapped it around his neck, fingers fumbling a little. His mother reached over and gently cupped his face, her hands rough and calloused but comforting. She said nothing, but Tias understood. *Everything was alright. This isn't like last time.*

Tias managed a smile, drops of the cold water still resolutely clinging to his neck. 'I still don't know where to look.' He said quietly.

'Follow the noise. I think you'll know when you're close.' Ffion said, soft amusement glinting in her eyes.

Blood.
November, 1815.
Eli.

The jeering had reached a deafening pitch, becoming louder than the wind. Or at least, louder in Eli's ears than the wind. The knees of his trousers were sodden. One of them felt ripped, and he could already hear his mother's disapproving tone. Eli spat, and pushed himself to his feet.

'Say that again,' Eli said, voice brittle. He shifted his feet slightly, widening his stance.

'Again? Why Eli, I thought I had made my point. But if you insist ...' Thomas looked around at the small group gathered around the pair, gauging reactions. 'I said that your–'

He never finished the sentence, his words broken off by Eli's fist connecting with the older boy's cheek. Thomas spun and roared his anger, bringing a hand up to touch the small cut that now slashed red across his face. He snarled and lunged for Eli, who sidestepped and kicked out hard at the back of Thomas' knees. The other boy stumbled into the ring of onlookers, hands reaching out to catch and then push him back into the impromptu ring.

'Try that again and I'll–'

'Then don't say things like that.' Eli said.

'Crow told us not to lie. Lying is a sin.' Thomas spat back. 'I'm only telling the truth.'

It was Eli's turn to snarl, baring his teeth as he felt the sick heat of anger lick up the inside of his chest. 'It is not!' Without further warning, he threw another punch, connecting messily with Thomas' shoulder, rather than his chin, which he'd been aiming for. Eli paid for his mistake by taking a returning hit to his temple. He staggered backwards and fell hard on his back, the jeering loud in his ears.

Get up, whispered the wind.

Stay down, called the shouts.

He felt more than saw Thomas come to stand over him. Eli rolled over and clambered to his knees. He curled his bruised and scraped knuckles into fists, pulling up handfuls of damp grass. He waited for the inevitable pain that was about to descend, and tried to scrape together enough will to at least stand.

'Hey!' An unwelcome reprieve. Eli closed his eyes for a moment, and desperately hoped the voice didn't belong to who he knew it to be. 'Leave him alone!'

'Look who's come to save you, Eli!' Thomas crowed, sick delight dancing behind his eyes.

Eli managed to pull himself back to standing, and squared his shoulders. Sure enough, Tias was standing just inside the ring, looking determinedly at Thomas. Eli hoped that Thomas would take the clenching and unclenching of Tias' jaw to be a sign of anger, rather than the nervousness he knew it to be.

'Tias, go home,' Eli said flatly. His brother's eyes twitched over Thomas' shoulder to Eli himself, taking in the split lip and the bruises that were already blackening across his face.

This time, true steely anger coloured Tias' words. 'Leave him alone.'

Thomas looked slightly taken aback at the shift in Tias' tone. Eli took vindictive pleasure in it. Regaining his brash composure, Thomas took a threatening step towards Tias, who, to his credit, did not back away. Eli groaned internally: he didn't have it in him to fight on two accounts.

'Why?'

'Why – what?' Tias said, looking confused.

'Why should I leave him alone?' Thomas put a mock puzzled expression on his face.

Eli shook his head slightly behind his tormentor's back. *Don't.*

'I'm only helping spread the good word of the Crow,' Thomas continued, 'or do you not listen during his sermons, Tias, when your family even shows up? Too busy scribbling pointlessness in that book of yours, I expect.' A round of soft laughter met that last statement, and Eli decided that once he was finished with Thomas, everyone else here would be sporting some form of injury.

Tias had gone still, his hand dipping into his pocket, where Eli knew the latest notebook would be nestled. His brother seemed to draw a little strength from the binding, as he straightened once more and said, 'I still don't understand. Perhaps you could elaborate for me?' The cynical politeness that coated Tias' words made Eli want to simultaneously laugh and hit him.

'He's a liar.' Thomas said. 'All I said was the truth, that you, Tias, are entirely abnormal, obsessing over those books, and that your mother is unnatural, possibly even a witch.'

Tias' face had gone white, and Eli felt the anger roar up in him once more. He tackled Thomas from behind, sending the pair sprawling onto the wet grass. Eli managed to get several good hits in before he felt hands capture his arms and pull him forcefully away. He turned quickly, ready to thrash whoever had dared pull him off Thomas, and came face to face with his brother.

'Come on!' Tias grabbed Eli's wrist and began to run from the circle.

Eli twisted in his grip, yelling his frustration, 'No, Tias, stop, he has to pay–' but it fell on deaf ears. Eli stumbled over his own feet, nearly sending both of them to the ground. He saw that Tias was not about to let him go and beat Thomas to a bloody mess, so instead put his energy into something currently more productive: running.

They were out of the church yard gates and into the street before they heard the sound of shouting and footsteps following them. 'Tias, where are we going?' Eli asked, his heart beating a tattoo against his ribs.

'Away,' Tias gasped, seemingly incapable of any more than a single word response.

Eli scanned the streets as they ran, seemingly pell-mell, through them. 'There!' It was his turn to pull Tias by the wrist, dragging them through a gap between the bakery and a cottage, and onto the road beyond. Eli skidded around a corner, let go of Tias and threw himself over an old wooden gate. Tias scrambled to follow, the end of the scarf he was wearing catching slightly on a rusty protruding nail.

The meadow they found themselves in was overgrown, the grass reaching their waists. Without warning, Eli grabbed the back of Tias' collar and pulled him down into the grass. 'Eli, what–'

'Be quiet.' Eli let go of Tias' collar and flattened himself to the earth. The sound of shouting and footsteps got louder, and Eli could distinctly make out Thomas' voice above the others, taut with rage and frustration.

Tias turned to look at Eli, eyes widened slightly. In turn, Eli raised a finger to his lips. The footsteps and shouting receded, moving off back down into the village.

The tension rolled off Eli, and he flopped down face first into the sodden grass with a groan. Then he yelped as Tias' fist hit him squarely on the arm.

'What was that for?' Eli glared at his brother, rolling over onto his side and rubbing the new sore spot.

'You know better than to pick a fight, especially with Thomas Gillet.'

'Did you hear what he said? I wasn't going to let that pass!'

'You shouldn't rise to it, Eli! That's what he wants.'

Eli, for what felt like the fifth time that day, clambered to his feet and offered a hand to Tias. 'I wasn't going to let that pass,' Eli repeated quietly.

'I know,' Tias sighed, and then yelped as Eli yanked his hand out from his grip, sending him sprawling backwards into the grass.

Eli doubled over laughing, whilst his brother glared up at him from the floor, wet clumps of grass now sticking out of his hair. The glare softened after a moment, and Tias got up, mumbling, 'I probably deserved that.'

'Yes, you did. I've been punched enough today, I don't need more from you.'

'Are you alright?' Tias' voice had softened as he took in Eli's less than composed appearance.

'Fine.' Eli saw the disbelief in Tias' face, and then amended, 'Alright, my lip hurts and I'm going to be covered in bruises for the foreseeable future and Mam is probably going to kill me because these trousers are now ripped. Again.' Eli looked down sadly at the tear adorning the cloth at his knee. 'Come on. Let's go home.' Together, they walked toward the gate, climbed over it, and headed off down the road that led them to Roseate Cottage.

Thread.
November, 1815.
Ffion.

Ffion pinched the bridge of her nose as her two sons walked in through the door. Tias was covered in damp strands of grass, and the scarf that was wrapped loosely around his neck had a hole torn through at one end. *At least he was better presented than Eli*, she thought dully. The boy was covered in bruises, and an ugly split lip demanded her attention immediately as she laid eyes on his face.

Before Ffion could open her mouth to begin reprimanding him, Eli jumped in first with a hasty, 'It wasn't my fault.'

'Oh?'

'Really.' Eli shifted slightly in the doorway, fingers twisting the dirty cuffs of his shirt. 'He said that... that...' Eli trailed off, now looking at the floor. Ffion sighed, knowing that his avoidance of her gaze wasn't out of guilt for his actions, but rather that whatever had been said had upset Eli greatly.

She reached out and gently pulled her son into the cottage, leading him over to the scrubbed wooden table at the centre of the room. Tias shut the door quietly behind him, cutting out the increasing noise of the wind and sea.

'Who said what, Eli?' Ffion asked, her voice softer as rough hands turned Eli's head toward the light.

Eli mumbled something unintelligible, trying to shift his head down to avoid his mother's gaze.

'It was Thomas.' Tias spoke up from by the fireplace, over which a large blackened pot had been placed, a soft herby aroma drifting from the contents within. 'He said you were a witch and I was "abnormal".' Tias' voice was even as he spoke, but Ffion heard the undercurrent of tension permeating his words.

'Thomas Gillet?' Ffion asked, standing and fetching a small

bowl and cloth.

'Yes.'

'Eli, I told you to stay away from him. He does nothing but antagonise you, and time and time again you give him the satisfaction of a rise.' As she spoke, Ffion filled the bowl with fresh water from the bucket they kept underneath the workbench, and moved back toward the table.

'But he shouldn't say things like that!' Eli's voice had risen, hurt and anger colouring the words. 'They're not true.'

'I know, *cariad*. But you must try and ignore him.' Eli flinched away as his mother brought the now dampened cloth to his lip, blotting away the blood that was clotted there. 'We know he's wrong. That's all that matters.' Ffion said gently, now wiping away some of the mud crusted under Eli's nails.

'And Thomas is also an idiot, so anything he says can probably be taken with a sack full of salt, let alone a pinch.'

'Tias!' Ffion worked hard to keep the amusement out of her voice, wringing out the cloth.

'Well, if we're talking about the truth, and how important it is to tell it, that's all I'm doing,' Tias said, deadpan.

Eli snorted at his brother's words, and then promptly schooled his expression as Ffion turned a disapproving eye on him. 'I just – I just wanted him to *stop*. And he wouldn't.' Eli's voice was quiet, the unspoken apology hanging in the air between them.

Ffion wrung out the cloth again, and placed it down on the table. She reached over and pulled Eli towards her. After a moment of tenseness, he sank into her embrace, one hand curling slightly in the loose fabric of her shawl. '*Fy machgen dewr, ffôl.*' My brave, foolish boy.

'Mam...' Eli groaned, relinquishing his hold on the coarse, homespun cloth. Two bowls of stew clattered onto the table, and Ffion looked up to see Tias fetching a third from the pot over the fire. Today's bread and spoons were already set out.

Eli immediately pulled his bowl toward him, grabbing a hunk of bread out of Tias' hand and liberally dunking it in the thick broth. Tias reached over and cuffed the back of Eli's head, causing him to choke slightly.

'Behave,' Ffion said mildly.

A gentle quiet fell through the cottage, the only sounds the increasing howl of the wind outside and the distant crash of the winter sea against the cliff faces, and the more immediate noise of spoons against crockery. Ffion gazed out the little window as she ate, watching as the early darkness moved in across the sky. Winter was always a more difficult time in Porth Tymestl, with the seas too rough to allow for a catch every day, and the small coastal village buffeted almost daily by storms that blew off the Irish and Celtic Seas. This winter had hit particularly hard, however. Ffion couldn't recall the last time she'd seen the sky unmarred by banks of thick, slate grey clouds. The catch was dwindling too, partially due to the inclement weather conditions keeping the boats firmly in the small harbour. It was nothing to worry about though, she was sure of that. They had plenty of reserves from the summer, and could call inland to the markets if they got truly desperate.

'What did you want to talk to us about?'

Ffion was pulled from her thoughts by Tias' question, asked thickly through a mouthful of bread. Eli's head shot up, his spoon suspended halfway between his bowl and his mouth. Anxious eyes flicked between Tias and his mother, and Ffion could tell that Eli was experiencing exactly the same thoughts as Tias had earlier.

'I'm travelling inland,' Ffion said, noticing how her sons' shoulders dropped fractionally, 'and I plan to be away for a while, perhaps a little longer than two weeks.'

'Why?'

'There are some... affairs that I need to put in order here. And I thought I could travel back past the market towns.'

'Affairs?' Tias asked, stew forgotten before him.

Ffion felt the deep, black ocean pulling her into its currents again. She took a steadying breath, and listened for that long gone voice, letting it pull her back into shallower, more manageable waters. 'To do with Jo – your father.' Ffion looked down at her bowl, and tried to see the chipped pottery through tear-clouded eyes. The sound of a chair scraping across the stone floor forced her to look up. Eli was retreating from the table.

'Eli–'

'I hope they can be sorted easily,' Eli said softly, before he all but ran for the door and wrenched it open. The fire flickered from the sudden blast of cold air. The door slammed shut and Eli disappeared into the darkening afternoon.

Ffion buried her face in her hands, barely noticing Tias' gentle touch on her shoulder. 'I'll go find him. Don't worry.' The door opened again, the fire danced, and once more all was empty silence. Ffion wept into it.

III
then.

A net of salt water.

There was once a fisherman who lived in a city made of marble and ivy. Tall towers of gleaming white stretched up to the skies, winding vines of verdant green wrapping around them. During the day, the city kept its inhabitants safe from the hot, relentless beat of the sun. The streets were often quiet, the heat of the midday sun too much to bear for longer than an hour. At night, however, the city came alive. The white towers, home to the thinkers and philosophers, glowed with bright candlelight. Markets sprung up along the wide streets, and under colourful silk canopies, spices, cloth and curios changed hands.

The fisherman had little time for the intrigues of the city. He loved his birthplace, but the love he held for the sea was more. This city of marble and ivy was built atop tall cliffs of chalk and limestone. Long, twisting stairways were cut into the soft rock, and these led down to long quays and harbours of wood. The fisherman commanded his own ship, a handsome boat of stone-pine with two masts and four vast canvas sails. The sails were a bright cobalt and seaweed green, and when the ship danced through the waves, its sails appeared to be part of the water itself. The fisherman took pride in his vessel, and out of all the other ships docked below the city of marble and ivy, its wood shone the brightest.

The sea called to the fisherman as a lover would call to

their soulmate. Its soft whispers drifted in through the open windows of the fisherman's small house at night. He found beauty and awe in its stillness, in its rage and its lawlessness. All men became equals upon the sea, for there was only one master out there, and it did not work in mortal terms of life and death. The fisherman spent more and more time on the sea, or else working on his ship. The meagre crew under his command spoke of him in hushed voices around mugs of wine after their job was finished for the day. Of how the fisherman seemed with every passing day to become more like the sea they sailed on. Of how he would not always answer a call from another crew member, but rather stare off out at the horizon with something akin to longing on his face.

As time passed, the fisherman lost more of his crew to other vessels. And as more time passed, the fisherman became strange. He did not seem to eat or sleep as other men needed to. His bed was hardly slept in, and his house remained unlit during those bright, market nights. If someone were to look over the cliff edge, however, they would spy the small flickering of a fire, tinted green from saline soaked wood. The sand of the beach became his bed, and the gentle wash of the waves his lullaby. The fisherman would stand for hours at a time, waist deep in the surf and merely stare out across the horizon.

And then one day, the fisherman disappeared. Only two people in the entire city of marble and ivy noticed his vanishing; his erstwhile first mate and the one who at one point may have called him a lover. His ship no longer was docked at the cliff side quay. The cobalt and seaweed green sails no longer embraced the horizon visible from those tall towers.

Deep below, a man who was once a fisherman, hung suspended in the water. He neither sank like his ship had, nor floated to the surface like carrion. His hair and coat drifted around him, his eyes closed. His mind sang softly out into the water around him. The sea heard the song, and listened. It had never heard anything quite like it before, and found it beautiful, but melancholy.

The man who had once been a fisherman hung in the water, in something like sleep. The sea held him gently in its embrace, and then, after a time listening to that strange song, a time in which the man's city had grown, fallen and become nothing more than ruins, let him go.

The tang of salt water filled his nose. And the man who was once a fisherman breathed again for the first time in a century.

IV
now.

Hail.
November, 1815.
Tias.

The hail outside pounded down upon the streets, small balls of ice bouncing and ricocheting off the cobbles. At first, he'd thought it was just another heavy rainfall, and was relatively content to bear it and make it back to Roseate Cottage. But then the storm had started in earnest and Tias had felt it *sting* against his exposed face and hands. Porth Tymestl didn't tend to get hail all that often, and a part of him wanted to remain outside, watching, cataloguing and locking the sensation away for a notebook page later. However, the sharp pinpricks of pain were becoming worse as the wind found its voice and began to howl. Perhaps finding shelter was the more sensible option.

He'd slipped and skidded down the street to the nearest building he could find. The Five-Pointed Compass' windows had been lit up from within, doing a roaring trade with fishermen docked by the weather. Tias all but collided with the door in his haste to get inside. It swung open easily, and the warmth that embraced him felt like a solid thing, a soft wall of comfort tinted with the smell of a wood fire and drink. Chatter and laughter filled the room, permeated by the clink of mugs against tables.

'Boy, shut that door!' One of the patrons at the table nearest to Tias called out, accentuating his words with a slightly unbalanced wave of his hand. Unfortunately, it was the hand that was holding the man's mug of ale, causing it to spill over the floor and onto his lap. Tias turned and forced the heavy door closed against the storm whilst the man swore and his companions laughed.

Tias leaned against the jamb for a moment and surveyed the room. The Five-Pointed Compass was one of the few buildings in Porth Tymestl that had more than one floor. As far as Tias knew, the owner, a man known enigmatically as Stooger Smythe, had kept building storeys onto the original building. Rickety stairs led upward to four rooms that were available to travellers, and Tias had heard rumours that Smythe himself lived in the attic above them.

The bar was a low-ceilinged room, an old stone fireplace set into the wall at one end. Small, boxed windows were placed seemingly at random around the room, the meagre light they let in obscured further by small pieces of driftwood or off-casts of netting placed in the deep sills. Lanterns hung from more pieces of sea rope, suspended from the bare rafters. When Tias and Eli were younger, their father used to take them to The Five-Pointed Compass late at night. Whilst John Kincarran had drank an ale or two with the crew of his fishing vessel, Tias and Eli had wandered around the inn, craning their necks to look at the array of lanterns that hung above them. Smythe had an incredible collection of them; ones that had pinpricks worked into the metal so that constellations of light dotted the walls and ceiling, ones that had panels of coloured glass, even ones made from silk or paper painted in bright red, green and gold. Tias had once asked the barkeeper where he had got them all from, only to receive the unhelpful answer of, 'All over, my boy. From as far away as the horizon, to as close to home as the next valley over.'

'Matthias?' Tias looked over toward the bar, where Stooger Smythe was busily pulling drinks for his patrons. He waved him over, handing a foaming mug to a man whom Tias recognised as one of his father's old crewmates, Medwyn. The fisherman walked past, carefully avoiding Tias' eyes.

A lot of the fishermen do that now, Tias thought idly, as he picked his way through the mass of people towards the bar. *They don't know what to say to a boy who also lost one of their own.*

'I thought it was you!' Smythe leaned over the bar and ruffled Tias' hair. 'Haven't seen you in an age, lad.'

Tias did his best to not reach up and straighten his hair. 'Sorry, Smythe.' He floundered for something else to say. He didn't really have much reason anymore to frequent the inn; the trips had stopped once his father had died.

Smythe seemed to read this, and picked up the fallen conversation for him. 'How's your Mam? And Eli? Heard he was in a scrap the other day.' Smythe raised an eyebrow, but his eyes gave away a hint of amusement.

'Does everyone know?' Tias groaned. Apparently nothing Eli had ever done, not once in his life, had been kept quiet.

'The Gillet boy – Thomas? He's been going 'round saying that he was set upon by the savage Kincarran lad. His father was in 'ere yesterday, talking about it. Or raving more like it, once he'd downed three mugs of this stuff.' Smythe pulled a quarter pint tankard from under the bar and filled it with a rich, golden liquid. He passed it over to Tias.

'Smythe, I haven't any money...'

'Ah, don't worry yourself about it lad, you look half frozen. *Mae hi'n bwrw hen wragedd a ffyn.' It's raining old wives and sticks.*

'Hail, more like.' Tias said. He took a sip of the ale, savouring the rounded, sweet flavour it left behind.

'Well, that's something new.' Smythe sounded surprised. 'It hasn't hailed in Porth Tymestl, for, oh, I can't remember how long.' His eyes drifted to a spot just behind Tias. He turned, looking for what Smythe was staring at, but only found one of the small windows. Behind the pane of rough glass, the sea swirled agitatedly.

'Smythe?' Tias said.

Smythe's blue grey eyes snapped back to Tias, 'My apologies, lad.' Tias was just about to ask Smythe what had distracted him, but Smythe quickly asked, 'Now, what did that Gillet boy do to deserve a beatin'?'

Tias immediately launched into the story, glad to have someone to listen to him about Eli's somewhat tedious behaviour. Smythe proved a good audience, his attention focused solely upon Tias, even as he continued to pour and serve drinks for the steadily changing crowd around them. '–and I *know* that Eli is going to finish what he started at some point, especially because both he and Thomas don't know when to leave well enough alone. And also because Mam is away.'

'Ffion's away?'

Tias nodded, 'For at least two weeks. She said there was some business she had to take care of inland. With her family.' He added.

'Who's looking out for you two then? Crow?' Smythe was the only adult that Tias knew in the village who called the Reverend by his nickname, given to him by the children of Porth Tymestl due in part to his hooked and rather beaky nose, and in part to the long flowing black robes he perpetually wore.

'No, Mam trusts us to look out for each other,' Tias said. 'She's left whatever money she could with us, and enough food to last.'

'Still,' Smythe began, 'it doesn't feel right, leavin' you two alone up there. Especially with the storms an' all.'

'We're fine, Smythe. I mean, I might kill Eli if Mam is away for longer than two weeks; he's taken to just leaving his things out wherever he wants.'

Smythe laughed, 'Well I'd better check on you in a week then, make sure there's not a corpse.'

The conversation after that guttered like a candle flame in the wind. Smythe moved away down the bar and disappeared down a trap door into the cellar, cut out from the rock of the cliffs that the inn was built on. Tias pulled his notebook from his pocket, and lost himself in the pages. The storm petrel page was finally completed; he'd finished it the morning of his mother's departure, nearly three days ago. The blank pages afterward called to him, and he wondered what creature or phenomena would fill up the next spread. He thought about trying to capture the hail, its sensation on his skin, the noise it made as it fell. Another mug of ale appeared at his elbow as he was sketching out the cobbles that lined the streets.

Stone.
November, 1815.
Eli.

The hail was starting to get on Eli's nerves. It had started not too long ago, and he'd been forced to take shelter in the cavern and wait it out. He watched as the small droplets of ice hit the beach, making the sand jump slightly on impact. Whilst the cavern provided shelter from the elements, it did not protect him from the cold. Gusts of frigid sea air swirled through the gap in the cliffs, creating a soft, if eerie, whistling sound. Eli debated whether or not it was worth building a fire. Their supply of driftwood hung, netted, on a system of ropes and improvised pulleys to keep it above the high-water mark that ringed the top of the cavern in a faint green tinge.

Despite the inclement weather, Eli had insisted on going down to the beach today, dragging an unwilling Tias behind him. The sky had been overcast, and both of them had to bundle up in several layers of scarves and cloaks, but there had been no sign of the hailstorm that was now raging outside. Tias had left shortly after arriving at the cavern, complaining of numb fingers. He had kept fumbling with a chunk of chalk, dropping it onto the sandy floor below. A half-finished drawing of a flatfish covered one of the walls. Eli wondered vaguely if his brother had managed to find shelter to wait out the sudden storm, and then slightly jealously wondered if it was warmer than where he was currently.

Pulling his cloak closer around his neck and shoulders, Eli scrambled up onto the natural shelf of rock at the back of the cavern and curled into one of the corners. A few pieces of old sacking lined the shelf, keeping some of the cold from seeping up through the seat of his trousers. From his position, he could watch the storm pound on and the waves crash against the shore. The world had shrunk into grey sky and grey sea, viewed through a long and scar-like opening in the rock. It seemed to Eli in that moment, that nothing else existed beyond this small vista. *Tua'r Môr* Bay was the less frequented of Porth Tymestl, *Angorfa* Beach getting most of the small village's foot traffic. The harbour and boat sheds on *Angorfa* Beach was the beating heart of Porth Tymestl, and to that end, *Tua'r Môr* Bay was superfluous; a stretch of shoreline only accessible by a steep and winding cliff path and only really useful for a rare fine summer's day when picnics were to be had.

Eli supposed he should hate *Tua'r Môr* Bay, the same way his mother did. He'd found splinters of his father's fishing vessel at the very far end of the beach. Eli still had the forearm sized piece of wood that bore part of the ship's name. It was in an old sea chest under his bed. His mother had expressly forbidden Eli or Tias coming down to *Tua'r Môr* Bay after that. Tias had obeyed for a few weeks, but Eli had broken the new rule within days. He didn't believe what his mother did; that the sea itself was vicious, that it was solely responsible for taking his Da away. Eli had always found comfort in the vast expanse of water, in the notion that he was so small in comparison to the world that lay just over the horizon. His father had loved the ocean, and it remained the strongest connection to him that Eli could find. Part of him felt a little guilty that he could revel in potentially two weeks of his mother being away, allowing him to come down to the bay whenever he liked. But a much larger part of him found he couldn't care all that much, not when there was that splintered window with its wild view beyond for him to look at for hour upon hour.

The hail continued for another hour, increasing and decreasing in strength intermittently. Eli did end up building a small fire, the flames flickering green from the salt infused wood. Eventually, the sky cleared from a dark grey to slightly lighter shade and the hail changed to rain and then into a soft drizzle. The horizon was lost under the haze, and the beach took on a more spectral feel, shapes rearing up out of the mist unexpectedly. Eli let the fire burn down slowly and emerged from the impromptu den of his cloak. He had hoped that once the storm had passed, the sun might make an appearance and burn away any of the clouds remaining. He'd have to settle for the watery and pale imitation that lurked behind the cloud cover instead.

Leaving the fire to die down into embers and ash, Eli jumped off the shelf and headed out onto the beach. He felt the mist settle against his face and into his hair. Taking a moment to pull in a deep breath of saline tainted air and listening to the crash of the waves, Eli then set off down the stretch of sand to the far end of the beach. Knowing that he'd most likely regret it later, Eli kicked off his boots and rough woollen socks and buried his toes into the freezing sand. He knew *Tua'r Môr* Bay like the back of his hand, which rock pools were likely to have the best fish, which parts of the cliffs could be climbed somewhat safely for a better view, where the tide tended to rise higher or lower than other parts of the bay. He walked diagonally across the beach, heading toward the surf. The frigid water against his bare skin made him gasp, but it was quickly followed with a smile. Wading through the water, Eli let his attention wander as he scanned the horizon and the rest of the sandy coastline intermittently.

He would have missed them if he hadn't been looking for one of his favourite places to watch gannets plummet into the sea below. The mist seemed to distort the view, shapes that he knew were familiar seemed uncanny somehow, although he could still place them more or less accurately from memory. However, these new shapes he had no recollection of at all.

A little more than halfway from the water, two parallel rows of what appeared to be posts driven into the sand reared up. They were all at odd angles, leaning and curving towards each other, some nearly meeting in the middle of the gap between the two rows. Eli left the surf and walked slowly up the beach, trying to figure out what they were. They were much taller up close, towering over Eli, at least double his height. The posts were weathered, covered in clutches of barnacles and seaweed, dripping rainwater dismally onto the sand below. It looked like they had been there for a lifetime, but Eli couldn't remember these posts being in this spot even last week. Reaching out a hand, he gently pressed the tips of his fingers against the damp surface. He recoiled slightly; the posts looked like they should be made of wood, they had similar colouration. But the surface was slick and somewhat slimy, nothing like the soft springy dampness of wet wood at all.

Thoroughly confused, Eli circled the group of posts, counting them. There were twenty-two in each row, and they stretched back towards the cliffs. At the far end of the row, the posts seemed to get a little smaller. On a whim, Eli bent down and dug his hands into the sand around the base of one. It seemed to be sunk into the sand far deeper than he had originally thought. It also seemed to curve more, and Eli had to dig a little more horizontally to uncover more of the post. After a few minutes, Eli realised he wasn't going to get very far with just his hands and by himself. The wind was picking up again, although most of the rain and hail seemed to have passed. He shivered, sat down and leaned against one of the posts to pull his boots on. It didn't shift at all under his weight. Standing, he made a mental image of where this new oddity was in relation to the cavern, and set off back the way he came. Perhaps Tias would have a better understanding of what these posts were.

ELLA RUBY SELF

Summons.
November, 1815.
Smythe.

Stooger Smythe looked out over the ocean. He let the early winter wind play over his face, whipping his hair about his shoulders. The sea below him was an uninviting grey. The hail had eased a few moments before, settling into a mist that resembled the sea frets that blew over the Celtic sea in summer.

The stone was a comforting, cold weight against his palm. Across the smooth surface he had etched his message, scratching it with a splinter of sea slate. It had been so long since he'd had to use a stone, and he wondered distantly whether it would work. The ocean was vast after all, and he was calling to a singular life upon it.

Without thinking about it any longer, Smythe reached up and cast the stone over the side of the precipice, watching it tumble through the air and hit the water with a distant splash. The ripples it caused were swallowed almost immediately by the rolling waves.

Smythe turned away from the sea and headed back inside. Far below, the currents carried a message far away.

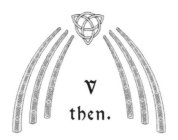

∀

then.

The life below.

They could not recall a time before. They were not aware of not existing. They had just always been. And would continue to be. Below the wild surface, they swam with the current, against it, diving to depths unimaginable to the mind of man, or cavorting in the warmer shallows. They were wholly of the sea.

Whilst they existed just outside human comprehension, traces of them could be found everywhere. Small and large across various pieces of parchment, a child's drawing in the sand, in countless sailor's fables and tall tales. The human mind is an extraordinary thing, but it often only comprehends what it wants to. These creatures belong in the realm of stories and of dreams. But that is not to say that dreams do not spill, that stories do not take elements from real life and transmute them into something that can be safely classed as fiction.

Despite the tales told, the warnings scrawled across countless maps, they serve humanity. Gently guiding ships into harbours, funnelling a catch towards a net cast below. They are the guardians of the water, and all that floats upon it. Their master is uncaring to their servitude to man. The master sleeps deep below, in the hadal region of the ocean. Full control is handed to them, and they choose, in their benevolence, to help the flotsam of mankind cast out onto the sea. They swam in the first ocean of the world, and will swim in the last.

Do not be afraid. Here there be monsters.

The life upon.

The ripples of the message reached him from far away. His ship slowly navigated the icebergs of Baffin Bay, towering chunks of pure diamond and sapphire cast upon the ocean. The ropes creaked from the cold, and the sails were crusted with a film of ice crystals. The ice chattered incessantly around him, a constant noise of cracks, of monumental shifting. Ice glare had him surveying the landscape through squinted eyes; everything was a blazing blue and white. He leaned upon the foredeck railing, looking out over the water. He listened to the ripples and was troubled by what he heard.

He went below, and after a moment of consideration at the row upon row of maps and charts shelved on the wall of the cabin, he pulled one down and unrolled it. He weighted down the corners with the detritus on his desk and studied the map. Three thousand, one hundred and thirty-two nautical miles to the destination of his summons. He gathered up the map, and pulling his coat closer around him, left the warmth of the cabin.

The ship responded to his touch, and he grasped the wheel, and he gritted his teeth against the freezing wood underneath bare palms. His heading changed, the bowspirt now pointing steadily south-east. The sea below the prow was mirror-like and for a dizzying moment, he couldn't tell if he sailed upon the sky instead.

VI
now.

Bones.
November, 1815.
Tias.

'Are you sure?'

'Tias, I swear if you ask me that one more time–' Eli said exasperatedly, shifting the two shovels he'd liberated from the rundown outhouse, so they settled more comfortably against his shoulder.

'Alright, alright, I just wanted to check.' Tias clutched his notebook and pencil to his chest as he and Eli traversed down the steep cliff path down to *Tua'r Môr* Bay. He knew it would probably be more prudent to store it in his pocket so he could keep his balance better over the wet stone and dirt, but he couldn't quite bear to let go of the familiar binding. Eli had insisted that he bring the book down with him, so Tias could make a note of his apparent discovery the other day.

Eli had returned to Roseate Cottage out of breath and with a wild look in his eyes. For a moment, Tias thought he'd managed to get himself into another fight, until Eli had blurted out his slightly nonsensical story about the new posts on the beach. Tias had listened with mild incredulity and confusion. He had no recollection of anything like Eli was describing on *Tua'r Môr* Bay. They had discussed the subject well into the evening, over Eli's invention of the night for dinner. Later, sitting around the fire with the darkness pressing in upon the windows of the cottage, Tias had wondered whether or not the story was some elaborate scheme Eli had concocted just to get him down onto the beach again. But the look on his brother's face had been so fervent, so genuinely excited that Tias dismissed the notion quickly.

That night was another loud one. The wind buffeted the coast and screamed through the gaps where the shutters didn't quite reach the wall. Tias lay awake for a while, listening to nature rip itself apart. He must have fallen asleep at some point, as the silence woke him. He was so used to waking to the sounds of rain or gale that the quiet outside disconcerted him for a moment. Eli was still asleep, blankets tangled around him and one socked foot sticking out from underneath them. Tias slipped out of bed and down the ladder, rekindling the fire and placing a pot of porridge over it to warm through for breakfast. Opening the shutters, he noticed that the weather was the best it had been for days. The blue sky was trying valiantly to break through the weak cloud cover, and the sun was just visible. The wind was merely a susurration through the long seagrass, and overhead a gull turned and pinwheeled.

Tias turned away from the window, smiling. Deciding to prolong his good mood, he climbed back up the ladder and stood over his brother's bed. Gently gripping the edge of the blankets, Tias waited a moment to see if Eli would stir, and when he didn't, he ripped them off.

'*Cer i uffern!* Go to Hell!' Eli sat up and promptly threw his pillow at Tias, who ducked, laughing. It sailed over the bannister edge and hit the kitchen table below with a soft *thwump*.

'Don't let Crow hear you say that, you'll be scrubbing the church floor for a month,' Tias said, still grinning. 'Get up, breakfast is nearly ready.'

Eli had declined to speak to Tias all the way through breakfast, but when they reached the small gap in a crumbling dry-stone wall that demarcated the start of the cliff path down to *Tua'r Môr* Bay, that excitement had returned to Eli's eyes and he had animatedly begun describing where his discovery was. The beach was empty again; the rest of the village was making good use of the weather today, and *Angorfa* Beach and harbour was a distant hub of activity. Tias could just see from the cliff path the specks of white, and some of colour, that showed Porth Tymestl's fishing fleet were out in full today. Once they were down on the beach, Eli pulled his boots off and stowed them in the long grass that grew at the base of the cliff. He handed one of the shovels to his brother and headed out towards the tide. After a moment, Tias copied him. He revelled for a moment in the feeling of cold, wet sand on his bare feet, listening to the muted crash of the waves and the call of the seabirds. For just a moment, breathing in the sea air and closing his eyes, Tias had never felt more at peace with the world around him.

Eli was already calf-deep in the surf, shouting at its coldness. Tias plunged in after him, wading and kicking up arcs of water. Eli leaned over, seemingly inspecting something in the sand below. He suddenly straightened and threw a cupped handful of water at Tias, who yelled and tried to leap out of the way. He didn't manage it, and was now soaked.

'Revenge for this morning,' Eli said, shooting his disgruntled brother a sly look.

'Fair enough. Truce?'

'I'll think about it.'

Tias rolled his eyes and tried to wring out his shirt as best he could. 'So, where is this mysterious discovery of yours then?'

'This way,' Eli said, walking back to shore, 'it's near where we watch for the gannets, remember?'

'Vaguely, aye.' They walked for a while in silence. 'Hey, Eli..?'

'What?'

'Why are you *so* interested in them?'

Eli thought for a moment, then said, 'So after I found them, I didn't come straight home. I went to ask a few people if they'd seen them and what they were here for. I asked Old

Man Morgan and the Griffiths and also Crow, and *here's the thing*. They all thought they'd been there for ages. Old Man Morgan said he could remember them being put in. Apparently, there's something similar they use on bigger beaches, called "groynes". Stop the sand shifting or something.'

'Could they have always been there? And we're just not... very observant?'

Eli just looked at him. 'Tias, we both know that we could walk this beach blindfolded and still know *exactly* where everything was.'

'Yes, you're right,' Tias conceded. 'So, everyone thinks they've always been part of the bay?'

'*Exactly*.'

Tias was quiet again, thinking. That was indeed very peculiar, and he certainly had no memory of anything man made on this stretch of sand. Eli moved on, slightly ahead of his brother. The sun had finally managed to break through the cloud cover, and Tias felt its meagre warmth play gently across his face. It caught in the copper of Eli's hair, and made the water below them glint. He saw them before Eli even had to point them out.

Exactly as Eli had described, two parallel lines of posts stuck vertically up from the sand. Eli had rushed on, chattering excitedly, the words coming back to Tias in snatches; 'Knew it... told you, look–'

Hurrying to catch up, Tias looked up at them, head already full of questions. Eli had thrust the point of his spade into the sand, and was now circling in between the posts, running his fingers lightly over the surface. Tias did the same, and then pulled his hand away, hastily wiping his fingers on his trousers. 'Doesn't feel like wood, does it?' Eli said.

'No...' Tias steeled himself, and pressed the flat of his hand against the nearest post again. Slippery, as Eli had described last night. Certainly not sea-weathered wood, but definitely old. The discolouration was enough to tell Tias that. He paused for a moment, and then ran the tips of his nails down the post. The motion made him cringe, and he took his hand off it. 'It's porous.'

'What?'

'Come here, look,' Eli came over and looked at the post Tias was examining. 'Feel it.'

Eli did, and then made a face. 'That's not particularly pleasant.'

'No,' Tias agreed, 'but did you feel it? It's pitted with really small holes.'

'What's your point? All the rock around here is like that. From the tide, right?'

Tias looked closely again at the post. 'Y-es...' he said slowly, 'but I don't think it's rock, Eli.' He could feel his brother looking at him, but instead of turning to him, Tias grabbed one of the shovels and said, 'Show me which one you started to dig around.'

The sand around the post Eli indicated bore no mark of disturbance, wiped clean by the night's high tide. 'It kind of went down and then along,' Eli said, unhelpfully demonstrating with a motion of his hand.

'Right,' Tias said. 'Get your spade.'

By Tias' estimate, they had dug for about a half hour before he hit something solid. They had followed one of the posts as it curved downward and along, just as Eli had vaguely described. Tias looked up at his brother, who had anticipation shining in his eyes. Together, they hurriedly dug around whatever it was below them, and exposed something rounded and off-white.

'What is it?' Eli asked, confusion lacing his voice.

'I'm not sure, a – a column maybe?' Tias said. He knelt down into the damp sand and began to excavate around the thing with his hands, piling the sand at his side. After a moment, Eli did the same, wiping the grain off it to better expose it to the light. If it was a column, it seemed to have been broken into pieces. It was about as wide as the length of Tias' forearm, and looked to be nearly double that in diameter. Another chunk could be seen just through the edges of the hole they'd made around this one. The post itself seemed to curve, and seemed like it could once have been attached to the round. Eli looked thoroughly perplexed. He canted his head to the side, brows furrowed.

Understanding hit Tias like a wave. He felt his breathing pick up slightly, and his thoughts went strangely blank. It couldn't be. He heard Eli from what felt like the other end of the bay, '... is it? Maybe we should dig further down and – Tias?'

Tias felt a hand on his shoulder. He looked up. 'I think...' He trailed off. It felt too impossible.

'Tias, *what*?' Eli insisted.

'I think it's a spine.'

Chalk.
November, 1815.
Eli.

Tias had shown him. He'd drawn it out on a page of his precious notebook. Eli still couldn't bring himself to believe him. He stared down at the rough drawing now adorning the wall of the cavern. Tias was pacing, frenetically. The chalk in his hand had stained his palm and fingers a strange, ashy white. He stopped every now and then to make an addition to the drawing, sketching quickly and muttering.

Eli sat up on the ledge, Tias' notebook still open in his lap. Beside him was a piece he'd broken off one of the posts and the central column. Aside from the difference in colouration, they appeared to be made of exactly the same material. Bone.

'Remember when one of Old Man Morgan's sheep wandered off the side of the cliff?' Tias had said, as they walked back to the cavern.

Despite the bizarre situation he'd found himself, Eli couldn't help but smile. It wasn't really funny, except it kind of was. One minute the sheep had been there, bleating and pulling up grass. The next it wasn't.

Tias whacked him on the arm. '*Concentrate*. Anyway, remember we found it about two months later? Just by the crab-pool?' Eli nodded, remembering how big the crabs had gotten after having access to an easy meal. 'It was picked clean, just a skeleton. You wanted to keep the skull.'

'I still think it would have looked good over the doorway.'

'*Eli.*'

'Sorry, continue.'

'The bones there felt exactly the same as this does,' Tias held up one of the pieces they'd taken. 'Therefore, we can conclude it is bone of some sort, although it feels strangely lighter than I'd expect of something that size.' Tias had continued in this vein until they got back to the cavern, where he'd grabbed a chunk of chalk and started to sketch on the wall.

'Tias..?' Eli began.

'Hm?'

'Could it have just been, I don't know, a whale or something that got beached?' Only one whale had ever managed to beach itself on the sands of *Tua'r Môr* Bay. Tias and Eli had only been seven when it happened, but despite his young age, Eli could still remember the mournful noises the creature had made as it slowly suffocated. It had been one of the only times he could remember the entire village's population gathering together in the small chapel to discuss what was to be done with the whale. Eli and Tias had been left in the care of Smythe, but Eli had managed to sneak away whilst Smythe distracted Tias with a book and listened at the door. His Mam and Da had fought particularly hard to try and save the beast. In the end, it died before a decision was made, and the oil and meat and fat were syphoned and hacked off, sold to the market towns inland.

'I thought the same thing, at first,' Tias said, still drawing, 'but we would have seen it alive first, and there is no way a whale could decompose that fast.' He fixed Eli with a close look. 'You've been down here nearly every day you could manage without Mam finding out, right?'

Eli nodded sheepishly.

'And I even joined you on some of those days, and I know for a fact that I never saw, nor heard a whale.'

'But then... *what is if?*'

Tias grinned, slightly manically. 'I have absolutely no idea.'

Looking over at the wall, Eli saw a swirl of coils, of reptilian scales and fins. Long, needle like teeth and whip like tails. It seemed that Tias had drawn an entire bestiary of imaginary sea creatures on the rough stone wall. He traced one of the long, looping coils with his eyes until it made him dizzy. The cold, smooth weight of what could only be part of a gigantic rib sat neatly in the palm of his hand.

Sails.
December, 1815.
Abraxus.

The port would be in view soon. The message stone had been very specific about which one to harbour in. The wilds of the Celtic Sea would have made light work of any other ship against the towering and jagged rocks of the Welsh coast, but his vessel took it in her stride, making a tempest into a dance.

The coastline itself didn't particularly look like anything he hadn't seen before. The small fishing village was nestled atop the cliffs, cottages hunkered down against the ferocity of the ocean wind. A small, thick-walled harbour sat at the bottom of one side of the cliffs, the incline much less steep than the others that boxed the village in on two other sides. The lights of the village flickered dimly against the dark sky that seemed to bore down upon it.

The stars were veiled that night, and the wind had a bite to it that spoke of deepening winter. He guided his ship closer to the shoreline, training his weathered eyes on the beaches. All seemed quiet for now, the night's silence only permeated by the gentle lap of the waves against the shore. In the distance, he vaguely heard loud chatter from the village, carried to him out on the ocean by the prevailing wind. He took a moment to listen to the mother tongue of the village, and made a note to adjust his own speech accordingly. No use in scaring the inhabitants with words they couldn't understand.

Beneath him, the currents swirled. The ship creaked lowly, and he ran a placating hand over the wheel. He adjusted his course minutely to catch a small current that ran the length of a longer, less accessible bay, and the sails swung, the fabric snapping quietly. The village drifted out of sight, leaving behind only the pure darkness of the sea at night. He found himself missing the still mirror of Baffin Bay, how the stars would be reflected up at him from the velveteen surface of the water.

He made port in a natural harbour, just as the message stone had specified. Letting down the sails and casting the anchor overboard, he went below and gathered up his belongings into an old sea chest, battered and rusted at the metal hinges, and a weathered leather bag which he swung up onto his back. Muttering a soft goodbye to his ship, he lowered a gangplank to the rocky side. The sea murmured its approval as Abraxus Elijah Honey strode inland.

VII
then.

Branwen's will.

Inland was a strange place. He was still getting used to the sound of the wind through the leaves of the towering trees, rather than the shriek of it over the ocean and up the cliff walls. Of course, he'd seen green before, but nothing quite like this. The forest was verdant, and seemed to breathe deeply as he walked along the rough trail. He had the strangest notion that it felt kinder, more benevolent than his home element. Leaf litter and moss created a springy carpet beneath his feet, and he felt as though he was walking on air, rather than the earth below. The distant chatter of a bird, one he couldn't name, broke through the green quiet.

John had spent most of his life by the sea. Listening to it roar at night, revelling in the salty spray that danced over his face when he was cast about on the waves. The years of calluses on his hands attested to a hard life, but not one that he had ever given up. It had felt so wrong to turn his back upon that wet, wild expanse and march along the path that would take him into the lush valleys, but, as he told himself each night when he found himself missing the lullaby of the tide, it was necessary.

Porth Tymestl was prospering. The catch that came in each day was bountiful, with plenty of extra fish to send inland to the markets and make a pretty penny for the families that resided upon the cliffs. However, with so much to sell, the town had decided to spread its connections further afield. Flood one place with too much and the prices would drop again. And so, after many hours spent in discussion in the barroom of The Five-Pointed Compass, John had agreed to head inland and see if any of the villages of the vales would enter into a trade agreement. It was no secret that John Kincarran was the best fisherman to come out of Porth Tymestl for an age, and that his amicable manner and rough good looks were sure to catch the interest of smaller landlocked villages looking to do business with their countrymen on the coast.

So far, John had tried three different settlements, each reliant on farming. They had all listened to the fisherman with polite disinterest and then promptly sent him elsewhere, offering him better luck at the next village. They all already had trade agreements with other, larger port towns. He was beginning to lose hope in what seemed like a pointless quest. It was an innkeeper at the third town who had pointed him in the direction of *Dyffryn Cernunnos*. 'You might try the next valley?' He had said, wiping down the bar after the evening's drinking had settled down into sleepy contentment. 'They're all usually quite keen for more connections to the outside.'

'Isolated?'

'You could say that, aye.' There had been something in the innkeeper's eye that John had not fully understood, but now as he looked down onto the small settlement nestled in the valley below, he realised that it had been amusement.

The settlement – for he wasn't really sure that he could call it a *village* – was small, barely more than a dozen cottages and no land cleared around them for farming. It was as if *Dyffryn Cernunnos* had simply grown up with the trees of the forest. John stood on the brink of the valley, looking down and weighing his options. He could try his luck down in this tiny outpost of a village, or he could return home and claim the entire trip as a waste of time. In the end, it was the music that persuaded him. Drifting up through the trees, a soft melody reached him. It was light and floating, as if the wind had simply decided to pick up a harp and try and play its own sound. He didn't realise he was moving toward it until he tripped over a root growing directly into the path.

The main entrance of *Dyffryn Cernunnos* was beautiful; two huge willow trees that had been cleverly laced together when saplings, in order to make them grow into a natural archway. Woven between the branches of the willows were pieces of glass, and scraps of brightly coloured cloth. They twinkled and fluttered in the gentle breeze. John lingered in the archway for a while, just out of sight of the cottages. The main street of the village was nothing more than hard packed earth that wended through the trees that grew up around it, and was alive with people and colour. Chatter filled the air, as did the smell of something delicious cooking over a central fire pit. His mouth watered, and he took a few more hesitant steps forward.

The inhabitants of *Dyffryn Cernunnos* seemed to be celebrating something. It seemed like the entire village was out, dressed in their finery. Rich greens, reds, blues and yellows adorned the skirts of the women and the waistcoats of the men. Several people were dancing, fast-paced with a heavy beat that John found himself tapping his foot to. The wind melody had changed seamlessly into something that sounded more earthy.

A voice at his shoulder made him jump. He spun around and came face to face with potentially the oldest woman he had ever seen. Her face was deeply tanned from a life under the sun and sky, and prominent lines creased at the corners of her eyes and mouth. She spoke again, and with mild panic, John realised she was speaking the old language. 'I'm sorry,' he started, 'I don't–'

The woman barked something at him, and then pointed a finger at the ground imperiously. The message was clear. Sit.

John sat.

The old woman hobbled away, toward the fire pit. She tugged

on the sleeve of a bear of a man, murmured something to him and pointed. John waved feebly. The man came over, the old woman clinging to his arm.

'Well met, traveller,' said the man, his accent thick. 'We don't often get visitors here. I am Tudwr. Who might you be?'

'John Kincarran.' John said, looking up at the man from the floor. Tudwr studied him for a moment, and then proffered his hand to John. He took it and gratefully stood. 'I'm sorry, I didn't mean to interrupt.'

Tudwr waved a hand, 'Not at all, you caught us at a good time. This time of year is beautiful, is it not?'

'Yes, I suppose it is,' John said, perplexed. Then to be polite, 'What are you celebrating?'

Tudwr looked surprised. 'The summer solstice, of course.' He looked at John for a moment, appraising him with dark eyes. 'Come, join us. You must be hungry.'

Allowing himself to be led toward the fire, John looked around. The inhabitants of *Dyffryn Cernunnos* were all staring unabashedly at him, their looks ranging from openly curious to hostile. Tudwr sat him down and handed him a hunk of meat, steaming, from over the fire. John began to eat, studying the strange place he'd found himself in. 'Where do you come from, Ifan?'

'Ifan?'

'Ah, my apologies. This is the name that is closest to yours in our tongue.'

'I see.' John looked around, and saw that he had the complete attention of everyone gathered around the fire pit. 'I'm from Porth Tymestl, it's a small fishing village south of here. Perhaps you've heard of it?'

Tudwr shook his head, 'Not many of us ever leave the valley. Tell us about your home, Ifan.'

John passed the next hour describing Porth Tymestl, its beaches, the fishing livelihood, the sea. Many of the people's faces had shown deep interest and amazement when he had told them about the sea. The hostility seemed to lessen as John spoke, and as evening crept over the valley, he seemed to have the entire village hanging on his every word. One of the children tugged on Tudwr's sleeve and whispered something to him.

Tudwr chuckled and leaned over to John, saying, 'She wants to know if the sea really has no trees.'

'It doesn't,' John said, smiling, 'but underneath the waves there are forests of kelp – long stringy water plants. Seals play in them and they make the water a bright green.'

Tudwr related his words back to the young girl, who stared up at John with wonder bright in her eyes.

As the short night moved on toward dawn, John found himself telling tales of the sea, of old fisherman's tall stories about sea serpents and old gods. Tudwr acted as translator for the younger listeners who had not yet learnt any language aside from their mother tongue. As John talked, he noticed that one young woman crept closer and closer to the circle. She kept glancing furtively at the old woman who had first met John outside *Dyffryn Cernunnos*. The old woman resolutely sat with her back to John. Eventually the young woman joined the circle and listened with the same rapt expression that adorned the children's faces.

No lanterns were lit that night, the only light provided by the fire. It cast the woman's long blonde hair in reds and golds, painting shadows in the delicate hollows of her neck and cheeks. As the children around him began to fall asleep, John found himself speaking more and more directly to her. Tudwr had left at some point and joined in the raucous dancing still going on. The dawn lit the forest in soft blues and pinks, the sun having yet to crest over the lip of the valley.

'You tell the most amazing stories.' He blinked. The woman had just spoken to him. Her voice was low. 'I can't help but wonder if they are true. A lake that goes on forever?'

'It's true, I promise you.' John said. He thought for a moment. 'It's the most beautiful thing you'll ever see.'

'I would like to, I think. See it.' She moved closer, sitting cross legged from him. 'Tell me more? Perhaps this way I can see it in my mind first.'

John nodded, and started, 'Well, when the wind catches for the first time in a day and my boat just dances over the waves...'

He left *Dyffryn Cernunnos* with three things. A trade agreement between the forest and the sea, offering each other what their home could not provide. A lock of hair from the woman. And her name. Ffion.

VIII
now.

Frost.
December, 1815.
Tias.

'Eli.' No response. '*Eli.*' Tias tried again, kicking the side of his brother's bed.

All he got this time was an unintelligible groan, and Eli's hand reaching up and out from under the covers to pull the blankets firmly over his head. The message was clear. *Go away.*

'I'm going down to the beach.'

'Again?' Eli stuck his head out from under his pillow where he'd buried it once it had become obvious that Tias was not going to give in so easily.

'Yes, again. Are you coming?' Tias tapped his foot impatiently on the floor, arms crossed and already holding his notebook.

'Maybe later,' Eli said through a yawn. 'We need some more bread. I was going to get some today from Owen.' He rolled over and waved in the general direction of his brother. 'Have fun,' he said vaguely.

Tias gave Eli's bed one last kick for good measure and descended the ladder into the main room of the cottage. He stoked the fire, banking it up for the day, and pulling his cloak around him, set off out into the morning. It was a clear day, the sun shining softly down over the winter landscape. It seemed to Tias that deep winter had been sneaking up slowly over Porth Tymestl, and had only now just sprung its ambush. Frost lay heavily on the grass, glinting like miniature glass beads under the light. It crunched satisfactorily beneath Tias' boots, the cold seeping through the well-worn leather and numbing his toes. The village was already awake and relatively busy, the cobbled streets lined with familiar faces. The fishermen of Porth Tymestl were all hurrying down toward *Angorfa* Beach, matching looks of excited anticipation on their faces. The sea below was a flat, shimmering green, shot through with deepest indigo. Tias took a moment to feel the wind direction, and then smiled. It was the perfect day to be out on the ocean. Perhaps the catch would be yielding today.

A sudden pang of sadness hit him, and for a moment it was like trying to breathe through a chest full of broken glass. It would have been the perfect day for Eli and himself to join their father and his crew aboard Porth Tymestl's only Brixham trawler. To help pull up the nets and watch as the waves passed by beneath the prow. Tias gave himself a little shake; the Brixham trawler was in splinters at the bottom of the sea, and his father was gone. There were other matters now to attend to.

He noticed as he walked that many of the people passing in the street were grouped together, whispering conspiratorially to one another. The daily morning queue outside Owen's small bakery seemed to be one long murmur, voices low and many heads bowed together. Tias caught a few of the words being passed around as he walked by.

'...out of nowhere, I was in there this morning and...'

'Smythe oughtn't to let...'

'...strange looking fellow, I'd stay out of...'

'Boy!' The bellow made Tias stop dead in his tracks. He took a breath, squared his shoulders and turned. Thomas Gillet's father was standing at the back of the line, his wide face red from either the biting cold or anger. Possibly both.

'Yes, Sir?' Tias put all the politeness he could manage into his tone, hoping to diffuse the situation before it rose to a head.

'Where's that brother o' yours?' Aron Gillet was a big man, weathered and scarred from a hard life on the sea where a lot of graft didn't always equate to a lot of profit. His beard seemed to bristle as he spoke.

'At home, Sir,' Tias said.

'Hm. Next you see 'im, tell 'im I want a word.' Aron stood to his full height, towering over Tias. He clutched the binding of his book for comfort.

'Here, Aron, leave off the lad.' Smythe had joined the queue for the daily bread and was standing with his feet planted firmly on the cobbles, arms crossed. Everyone in the line now was silent and watching the scene unfold before them. Alys and Catrin were openly staring; delight on their pointed faces. Tias suppressed the urge to roll his eyes. With those two playing witness to this, all of Porth Tymestl would know of the confrontation by the end of the day. Undoubtedly, in their version, some punches would have been thrown and inevitably one of them would have been in *great distress* at one point.

'Only giving 'im a message, Stooger. Ain't no harm in it.'

'Aye, maybe to *him* there's not. His brother, now that's a different story.' Smythe stared Aron down, daring him to carry on. 'And from what I 'eard, Eli was provoked into it?' Smythe bobbed up and down on the balls of his feet, a mask of sharp innocence placed carefully over his face.

Aron huffed and went even redder. 'Well, that's the sort of tall tales I'd expect to 'ear from a Kincarran. Strange, the lot o' them.'

'That's not true.' Tias said coldly, involuntarily taking a step forward. Smythe reached out and pulled Tias back and took his place, putting him slightly behind the barkeeper. Smythe did not cut an intimidating figure, with his perpetually hunched shoulders and greying hair, but somehow, he seemed to command everyone's attention to him.

Aron was apparently not done, saying with a sneer, 'You'd know all about that, about *strange*, wouldn't you Smythe? I've 'eard what everyone's sayin'. About your new *guest*.'

'I didn't think it was any of your business, Aron, to know the guests at *my* inn.' Smythe said. And then, 'So back off, *twpsyn.' Moron.*

A round of shocked and slightly amused murmurs broke out through the crowd. Aron Gillet was not a particularly well-liked man, and Smythe was known for his razor-sharp tongue. Aron's beard bristled and he sputtered indignantly, giving Tias a hard stare, and turned back around to face the front of the line.

'Maybe that'll give 'em something else to chatter about rather than who's in my guestbook...' Smythe said. There was a bitter note to his voice. The curiosity that had long been the source of many a telling off from his mother stirred in Tias. He tamped it down, offering Smythe a weak smile instead.

Smythe looked at him knowingly, 'Come by The Five later, lad. Perhaps that'll clear up some of those questions cluttering up your head.' Tias nodded his thanks at the offer, and started to move away. 'Where you off to, lad?'

'*Tua'r Môr* Bay,' Tias called over his shoulder.

'I won't keep you,' Smythe said, moving to the front of the line, 'them posts are waitin' for you.'

Tias waved, and headed off down the street toward the meadow that would lead him to the cliffs overlooking the bay. It was only halfway down them that he realised that he had never told Smythe about the posts on the beach, and, he was certain, neither had Eli. Lost in thought, he didn't notice the solitary figure standing on the cliff edge a little way down the meadow, watching Tias' descent as his dark hair whipped around his face.

ELLA RUBY SELF

Bread.
December, 1815.
Eli.

Everyone thought he was a witch. Or a demon. One day he was not there, and now he was. Eli had spent most of his days since the discovery at *Tua'r Môr* Bay on the beach, trailing after Tias. His brother had quickly become obsessed with the giant bones half buried in the sand, going as far as to beg access to Crow's small library he had in the vestry.

Eli was out later that day, having successfully managed to evade Tias and his mission to get him out of bed at some ungodly hour each morning. He loved going down to *Tua'r Môr* Bay, but there were things that needed doing around Roseate Cottage that couldn't be put off any longer. Lack of food, for one. Counting out the small supply of coins that their mother had left behind, Eli pocketed a few and set out into the late morning sun. *Tias would probably be down on the beach already*, he thought as he navigated the frost-slickened cobbled streets.

It seemed that he had missed the morning rush outside Owen's bakery and there was no one waiting outside aside from Old Man Morgan. He smiled vaguely at Eli when he offered him a 'Good morning' and returned to waiting placidly with his hands behind his back. Old Man Morgan was, aptly, the oldest inhabitant of Porth Tymestl, having grown up before *Angorfa* harbour was even fully constructed. Eli and Tias had spent many afternoons with Old Man Morgan, who had offered to watch them whilst their father was out at sea and Ffion was busy with the cottage or village affairs. Eli hadn't seen him for a while, he supposed due to the fact that the man was becoming a lot less spry and a little scattered in his thoughts.

'*Bore da*, lad,' Owen said, sticking his flour-dusted face out of the little hatch in his bakery's wall that served as a counter. 'Be with you in a moment. Here you go, Cynfor.' Owen handed Old Man Morgan a round loaf of bread, still steaming gently in the cold morning air. Old Man Morgan nodded his thanks and with shaking fingers counted out his payment. As he muttered under his breath the figures, Owen rested his elbows on the rough wood of the counter and scrutinised Eli. 'Your brother was past here this morning. Early too.'

'Aye, he was heading down to *Tua'r Môr* Bay,' Eli said. 'Tried to get me to go with him.'

'Good thing you didn't, lad,' Owen said. 'He ran into a bit of trouble with Aron.'

'Aron? You mean Thomas Gillet's father?' Eli felt the creep of worry stir in his chest.

It must have registered on his face somehow, as Owen rushed to reassure him, 'Nothing came of it, Stooger stepped in before Aron did something rash.'

Eli let himself relax, and moved closer to the counter. Old Man Morgan pushed the small pile of coins toward Owen and gave him a vague smile, gathering up his loaf. The smell of the freshly baked bread made Eli's mouth water, and he decided that if the heel off the loaf disappeared mysteriously on the way, well Tias would never have to know. He was just placing his order, when he felt a clawed hand drop onto his shoulder. Old Man Morgan was still standing there, scrutinising Eli through misty eyes. Despite their fogginess, however, Eli thought he saw a moment of intense sharpness in the brown irises. 'Stay away from him, Elias.' He said.

Eli and Owen exchanged a confused look. 'Who, Cynfor?' Eli asked, turning to give the old man his full attention.

'Your brother, for all his wit, does not know when to stop looking,' Old Man Morgan said cryptically. 'I saw his face light up, I did, when Stooger told him to go by The Five later on.'

'I'm sorry, I don't quite–' Eli started, but Owen interrupted him.

'Oh, aye he did, din't he?' Owen turned to Eli, 'After Stooger had dealt with Aron – quite spectacularly, I might add – he told your brother to drop by the inn later on. I didn't hear the rest, but I reckon it was somethin' to do with this new guest up there. The one everyone's been talking about.'

'New guest?'

'Aye, and you'd know about him too if you got up before midday, boy,' Old Man Morgan said, amusement playing on his wrinkled face.

'Arrived last night, far as we can tell,' Owen said, suppressing a laugh. 'Strange fellow.'

Old Man Morgan's face fell back into seriousness. 'Stay away from him,' he repeated. 'Tell your brother too.'

'Why?'

'He's not... natural.' Old Man Morgan spoke low, as if he was afraid that this newcomer would be hiding behind Owen's counter. Owen nodded his agreement, handing Eli his bread.

'Al-right,' Eli said slowly. He counted out the money, dropping it into Owen's hand. '*Diolch*. I'll tell Tias.' He turned away from the counter, walking back down the street toward Roseate Cottage. The conversation played over in his mind, and he wondered why Smythe would tell Tias to come and visit if everyone else was so vehemently opposed to whoever this man was. Absentmindedly, he ripped the crust off the end of the bread and chewed on it thoughtfully as he walked. By the time he'd reached Roseate Cottage, he'd made up his mind. After slicing a few cuts off the loaf and wrapping them in an old cloth, he stoked the fire and pulled on an extra jumper.

The Five-Pointed Compass was usually busiest in the evenings, sailors seeking warmth and drink after a long day out on the water. The sun was already at its zenith as Eli made his way down to *Tua'r Môr* Bay; Tias would surely keep him occupied until then. He smiled. He'd always been far too stubborn for his own good.

Ale.
December, 1815.
Smythe.

'Here, I'll get to you in a moment!' Smythe called down the bar. He shook his head and went back to pulling drinks. It seemed like all of Porth Tymestl had invaded the barroom tonight, in celebration of the relatively good weather holding for two days. Sure, the catch wasn't as good as it could have been, but after a couple of weeks with barely any fish coming up, what they had now felt downright bountiful. The low-ceilinged room was packed and noisy, the little windows having long since steamed up. Soft multi-coloured light from the array of lanterns seemed to mitigate the cramped feeling of the barroom, but the patrons still had to shout to one another to make themselves heard.

Night pressed in against the village, and the wind had picked up again in the last hour, scratching cold fingers against the glass and slipping inside every time the door swung open. Smythe was near rushed off his feet, calls for more ale and bowls of stew increasing as more people crammed themselves into the inn. He was turning away from the hearthside, two steaming bowls held in his hands, and nearly walked straight into Tias, who he had not spotted.

'Woah, careful there, lad!' Smythe brought the bowls up above Tias' head, trying not to spill scalding stew all over the boy.

Tias leapt backward and Smythe saw his lips move, probably an apology, but not one he could hear over the tumult of the room. Smythe indicated the bowls he held with a nod of his head, and then gestured over to the bar. Thankfully, Tias understood, and Smythe watched, bemused, as he seemed to reach backward into the crowd and pull Eli out by the wrist.

Smythe watched the two boys disappear and picked his way

through the barroom, calling out greetings to those who raised mugs of ale at him, or else shouting over the tumult that he'd get to them soon *for pity's sake*. Depositing the bowls down onto a table near the back of the room, Smythe took a second to wipe the perspiration from his forehead and look around. It took him a moment to spot the two lads, but when he did, an amused smile made its way onto his weathered face.

The bar, like the rest of the room, was packed, with people either having claimed their territory over the stools, or else standing around it and leaning against the long wooden expanse. Eli and Tias had managed to slip under the space created by the gap in the bar by which Smythe could access the other side, having lifted the small hatch first. They sat kitty-corner to one another, knees to their chests. Eli seemed to be content in watching the room around him, whilst Tias had his notebook open and was scribbling furiously in it.

'You're in danger of trippin' me there,' Smythe said, kneeling down by the gap. Eli whacked Tias on the arm, as he hadn't looked up from his notebook. Tias shot his brother a dirty look, and reluctantly stowed the book in his pocket.

'Find us a seat and we'll take it,' Eli said, shuffling over to the other side of the bar. 'Is there any of that brandy left, Stooger?'

'Oi, get your paws out of my stock Elias,' Smythe said, laughing. He nodded to Tias, 'You may as well go join 'im, you're not likely to find anywhere else to sit.' He thought for a moment, and then leaned closer, 'And folks here might get a little... twitchy about what we're discussing, if you take my meaning.'

Tias' eyes widened slightly and he crawled through to follow his brother. Smythe lifted the hatch and stepped through. The brothers had made themselves comfortable leaning against the back of the bar. Eli was unashamedly eyeing the barrels that lined the back wall, and Tias had pulled out his notebook again. Smythe looked down at them, and suddenly felt a wave of sepia tinted nostalgia roll over him. The Kincarrans and Smythe had always been close, Smythe having been a long and firm friend of John before he died. And when the weather was good, and John was away fishing for days at a time, Smythe would offer to watch the two boys to give Ffion a little bit of a break. The Five had become like a second home to them. And then John had died and Ffion, understandably, had wanted to keep her sons close.

Smythe shook his head to clear the cobwebs of memory away, and returned to the bar, pulling drinks for the demanding patrons that ranged the length of it. He kept glancing towards the rickety narrow stairs that led to the rooms above, always half hoping to see his new guest standing at the bottom of them. Of course, he didn't make an appearance, and on a more realistic level, Smythe was not disappointed. No point in making yourself into an unwilling spectacle in front of most of Porth Tymestl's population. The night deepened around the inn, and the crowd began to ebb, leaving the comfort of the inn for the safety of their own beds. If the good conditions kept up, then most of the patrons would have an early start to look forward to. Time and tide wait for no man, and certainly no man with an aching head and bleary eyes.

Eli and Tias had made an impromptu nest with their coats and scarves against the bar, out of sight of the remaining patrons lining it. Tias was still determinedly writing, though he kept scrubbing at his eyes as if to stave off tiredness. Eli had leaned back against the bar and was staring off into nothing. Two nearly empty quarter-pint mugs stood next to them; Smythe having poured them both some of the ale that was on tap that night. He had lied and said he didn't have any of the brandy that Eli seemed partial to, not wanting to get into trouble with Ffion when she returned from the inland. Eventually, only seven people remained in the inn, slumped over their tables and conversing quietly. Smythe watched them for a moment, and then when he was sure no one would notice, slunk down to the floor to sit opposite Eli and Tias.

Nudging Tias' foot, Smythe got his attention. It was Tias'

turn to whack Eli, this time in the chest.

'What?' Eli sat up a little straighter, clearly coming out of the thoughts that had sent him thousands of miles away. Tias gestured to Smythe, and all the fog cleared from Eli's face.

'Answers?'

'Aye, I reckon so. Or some at least.' Smythe looked at the boys for a moment, as if appraising them. 'Most people here wouldn't want me telling you about 'im. I'm not even sure if *he'd* want me telling you about 'im. But you two are too curious and stubborn for your own good, and you know about them posts down on *Tua'r Môr* Bay.' He smiled when Eli and Tias looked at each other. 'Aye, I know about them too. And you'd be right in thinking that they aren't wood, Tias.' He held up a hand, as Tias had leaned forward excitedly, ready to bombard the innkeeper with questions no doubt. 'What they are exactly isn't my place to say, truly. I can give you some answers, but not all. There's a man upstairs that has the answers, but whether he'll impart them to you, well, that ain't up to me.'

'Who is he? Everyone is talking about him,' Eli said. 'They're saying he's a bad omen.'

''Course they would,' Smythe snorted, 'ain't got the mind to see him as they truly should.'

Eli and Tias exchanged a confused look. 'What do you mean, Stooger?' Tias said quietly.

'I'll tell you two things,' Smythe said, disregarding Tias' question. 'The first, keep lookin' for answers. Dig, explore and look as much as you can, and don't let anyone stop you, no matter what they say. That's the first part of it. A keen and open mind will get you further than anything else. A dash of adventurousness wouldn't go amiss either. The second thing I will tell you is this.' Smythe stood up and walked over to a small writing desk that made up part of the bar. On the wall next to it were four nails hammered halfway into the wood, keys hanging off all but one of them. Smythe pulled the thick ledger off the desk and brought it back to Eli and Tias. He set it down in front of them. 'Go on.'

Tias reached for it, opening the book slowly. Eli leaned closer. As Tias turned the pages, his eyes scanned down them. Smythe sat and watched.

Over the bar, a stair creaked.

Eventually, Tias made it to the last page that wasn't yet full. With a finger, he skimmed down the page to the last entry there. A date of arrival, payment and length of duration all sat in neat columns next to one labelled "name". 'I will tell you his name,' Smythe said quietly.

'Abraxus Elijah Honey.' Eli breathed.

Tias repeated it, and then looked up at Smythe, 'I've never heard a name like that before, where is he from?'

'Ah, now Tias, I said only two things, and I have given them to you.' Smythe reached over and pulled the ledger back, closing it with a snap. 'Now, back home with both of you, and remember what I said.' Eli and Tias immediately began to complain, but Smythe was adamant. He chivvied the boys back into the barroom, and toward the door. Tias pulled it open, and a blast of icy air sent splinters of ice through Smythe. 'Hurry up and be off with you, you're after making my inn cold.'

Eli and Tias left, making their way into the night and toward home. On a whim, Smythe called after them, 'A third thing! *There are more things on heaven and earth...*'

'*Than are dreamt of in your philosophy.*' Tias called back through the darkness.

'Keep that in mind! *Nos da.*' Smythe closed the door to the inn. Of the seven remaining patrons, only two remained, the rest seemingly having drifted out whilst Smythe was preoccupied. 'Last orders, gentlemen.' The two men, both fishermen, stood, stretched and stumped off toward the door, muttering 'goodnights' to Smythe as they passed. Smythe nodded at them, and locked the door behind them. He returned to the bar and began to clean down the surface, collecting empty mugs as he went.

'You always did have a weakness for the cryptic.' The voice

came from the shadows of the staircase.

'And you, old friend, always had a penchant for lurking in the shadows,' Smythe said. The bottom step creaked and Abraxus stepped into the barroom.

'You should have told them nothing, Smythe. They are inconsequential, and I would rather not have two boys underfoot as I work.' The lantern light caught on the beads in his black hair, making them shine a bright, fiery gold.

'You don't know them.' Smythe pulled a mug out from behind the bar and filled it with ale. He slid the foaming mug over to Abraxus, who took it gratefully and sipped from it thoughtfully. Into the silence, Smythe said, 'I think you would like them, if you met them and gave 'em a chance.' He raised an eyebrow meaningfully.

'Absolutely not,' Abraxus snapped.

Smythe held up his hands. 'Alright. But I won't discourage them.'

'You would do well to not actively *encourage* them.' Abraxus sighed. 'But you seem set upon it.'

'That's the most leeway you've ever given me,' Smythe chuckled. 'I'll drink to that.' He filled another mug and raised it. Abraxus shook his head, but nonetheless raised his own and knocked it against Smythe's. They both drank deeply.

'I think tomorrow I will venture down to the bay, what did you call it?'

'*Tua'r Mór.*'

'*Tua'r Mór...* a fitting name I suppose. The bones have not been disturbed, have they?' Smythe shifted a little under Abraxus' mismatched gaze. 'Of course. Well, I suppose that two skinny boys could not do much harm. I will take a look and then see where the current takes me next.' He drained the rest of the ale, and set it down upon the bar with a thud. Abraxus stood, stretched and muttered, 'I shall have to get used to sleeping on land again.'

'You'll find it doesn't move as much,' Smythe said dryly.

'Hm.' Abraxus made his way toward the stairs, but stopped suddenly with one foot upon the first. 'Why Shakespeare?'

'It seemed fitting, I suppose. And I know that Tias, the taller one, likes it and – *aros eiliad! wait a moment!* You once told me you didn't like his work!'

'I do not. But I pick things up. *The Tempest* was not to my liking at all.'

'No, of course it wouldn't be.' Smythe rolled his eyes. 'To bed with you. I have an inn to put to rights.'

Abraxus nodded, and ascended the stairs, disappearing from view. As Smythe set about collecting mugs from the tables and extinguishing the multiple lanterns, he heard the rattle of a window being opened above. The sounds of a distant song reverberated through the inn a moment later, muffled slightly by the thick beams of the ceiling. Smythe smiled to himself, and began to murmur the words alongside the deep voice emanating from above.

Outside, the sea rolled over in its sleep, muted waves tumbling gently onto the shore.

IX
then.

A forest path to the sea.

'*No good will come of it,*' her grandmother had spat as she'd packed up what little belongings she had.

'*Or perhaps everything good will come of it,*' Ffion responded in her mother-language. Her grandmother had point blank refused to converse with her in what she called 'the common tongue', despite Ffion's insistence that she needed the practise. '*I go not to spite you, but to better myself. I follow where my heart takes me.*'

'*You go where that fisherman fool will lead you. Your heart is here, in* Dyffryn Cernunnos, *not out there.*' She gestured broadly to the slopes of the valley that enclosed them. '*Your heart is with me, is it not?*' Suddenly her grandmother seemed shrunken, and old. She looked at the floor, sadness heavily lining her face.

'*It is,* Nain, *but it is not only that which calls me away.*' Ffion set down the skirt she was carefully folding up, and took her grandmother's hands in her own. She ran her fingers over the twisted and rough knuckles, tanned to a deep nutty brown by years of hard work under the sun. Her grandmother pulled Ffion's hands up to her lips, kissing them softly.

'*I know.*' And then her face hardened again. '*Were we not good enough for you? I have tried to give you everything you could ask for, could need.*'

'*And for that I am grateful* Nain, *but...*' Ffion thought about her next sentence carefully. '*It was always enough to survive, to go to sleep each night content and peaceful. But I cannot settle anymore for content and to merely survive. I desire to see the world, to explore and feel alive once more.'*

Her grandmother's mask of sharp disapproval was back. She slipped her hands out of her granddaughter's and turned aside. *'Go and live then.'*

'Nain...'

'Go. But remember, as a tree stretches upward for the sun, it cannot leave its roots behind.'

Ffion stared at her grandmother's profile, and after a moment, finished packing her belongings. She left the small cabin, ducking under the bright cloth that served as a covering for the entryway. Whilst it felt like her heart was splitting in two to choose between the safety and comforts of home, and the doorstep of the wild beyond, she knew deep down that she had made the right decision. There was nothing else *Dyffryn Cernunnos* could offer her. It had shaped her from a girl into a young woman, breathed the light and life of the forest into her blood and bones, and now was whispering its farewells as she turned toward the path that John Kincarran had arrived by two years ago.

John had become a frequent visitor to the forest vale, bringing with him other people from Porth Tymestl, goods from the sea, and most cherished by Ffion, stories. The trade agreement was strong, and many of dwellers of *Dyffryn Cernunnos* had come to anticipate their sea-faring neighbour's visits. Her grandmother was, of course, excluded from this number, always refusing to speak to the traders, and stubbornly remaining inside her cabin for the duration of their visit.

Tudwr was waiting for her at the archway that led out into the forest. 'You're really going.' His accent was thick and rolling. His dark eyes held a sadness in their depths that Ffion knew too well, and one that stirred guilt within her.

'I am.' She held her head up high, waiting for Tudwr to try and convince her to stay too, that there was nothing else out there for her.

'I will miss you,' he said, and pulled her into a fierce hug. Ffion stiffened at first, and then melted into the warm embrace.

'I'll come back.' She promised, trying to ignore the aching lump in her throat. 'I just have to – to...'

'You have to see.' Tudwr leaned back, and gently tucked a strand of her long blonde hair behind her ear. Ffion nodded. 'I understand.' He released her, sniffed, and then said in a business-like tone, 'You have everything you need? You know the way?'

Ffion nodded, 'John brought me a map when he last visited.'

'Well, you had better go. Don't waste the daylight.' He studied her, 'I wish you all the luck and joy in the world.' Ffion didn't trust herself to speak, and instead pressed her hand over her heart and inclined her head. Ffion resolutely shouldered the pack, and with one last look behind her, delved deep into the forest beyond.

Where green meets blue.

'Heave!' The call was met with many hands reaching over the side of the boat, scarred knuckles and tanned fingers grasping the net and pulling it up. In one well-practised motion, the crew of the *Dawnsiwr y Wawr* hefted the waterlogged net up and over the side. Chatter broke out amongst the crew, many slapping each other on their crewmate's backs. The catch was good, excellent in fact.

'Get it below!' John called. A rush of feet and a flurry of knives later, and the catch was safely sorted and stored below in the hull. John tied off a knot, and headed back towards the rudder. The sky above was a vast, endless blue, cloudless and mirroring the sea perfectly. Spring had given way to summer, and most of the crew were only in their shirtsleeves, some forgoing boots in favour of lighter shoes, or even bare feet. A gentle summer's breeze had brought warm weather down to the coast, and had filled the sails of the fishing fleet. Each day

Porth Tymestl's boats would leave the harbour, jumping and gliding over the waves in their excitement for the open waters. White sails would dot the horizon, and *Angorfa* Beach would be a hub of activity; those who could not sail were left behind to weave new nets, or else repair the old ones, ragged with sea-use. Children would splash and swim in the shallows, the younger ones shrieking in pleasure. The stench of seaweed and fish filled the air, and shining piles of scales dusted the cobbles leading back up to the village.

John grasped the rudder and lifted his face up to the sun. He wished he could remain out on the waves for longer, but the catch wouldn't keep, and there were hungry mouths to feed back home. The horizon called to him, but he resolutely hauled on the rudder and swung the *Dawnsiwr y Wawr* north-east and toward home. The bright red sails snapped in the wind, and with a creaking lurch, the boat took up the breeze and made for port.

The *Dawnsiwr y Wawr* was John's pride and joy. It was Porth Tymestl's only Brixham trawler, and it was by far the superior vessel. The inhabitants of the coastal village had all come together in order to buy it, knowing that it would be an investment that would pay for itself over and over again. It was the purchase of this vessel that had allowed them to seek trade deals further inland, since the catch was so bountiful. The red sails had been a flight of fancy, inspired by the name and also as a mark of superiority over the other vessels. The innkeeper, Stooger Smythe, had been a particularly big advocate for it. And John had been given command of it. There had been little to no contest there, even Aron Gillet, notoriously proud, had conceded that the *Dawnsiwr y Wawr* should be under John's care.

The sight of the red sails coming into *Angorfa* Beach brought up a cry from those ranged along the short harbour walls. A prevailing wind and a sea the colour of blown glass had brought them home quickly, and John smiled and waved at the children who were splashing out into the shallows to meet them. Docking and unloading the catch was made light work by many skilled hands, and John hopped down off the side and onto the harbour wall.

'Afternoon, John!' Cynfor Morgan called from his own vessel. Cynfor was getting to the age where sailing was becoming more of a difficult task, but he adamantly refused to leave the helm of his small boat, the *Esgyll Gwerin*. Many regarded John as Cynfor's protégé, and John did little to discourage the idea. He owed all his knowledge of seamanship to the man, who, despite his growing age, still surpassed John in knowledge and skill. It was Cynfor who had sailed through the natural sea-arch that lay around the headland past *Tua'r Môr* Bay, and which now bore the same name as the boat in which he'd done it, Finfolk.

'*Prynhawn Da*, Cynfor! How goes the day?'

'An excellent catch, my friend. We shall eat well tonight, and there's plenty left over for the next trade with the forest vale. I imagine you'll be going along?'

'Aye, I reckon I will,' John said, and then pointedly ignored the knowing look Cynfor gave him. 'Just for trade, you understand.'

'Of course, of course.' Cynfor ruined the agreement by winking.

John smiled and turned back to his own vessel, securing the mooring lines and reaching up to take down some of the crates of fish that were being unloaded, ready to head to the filleting and salting houses.

'Drinks, Kincarran?' Medwyn called as he carefully knotted up and stowed the net.

'I thought you had to get home!' John called.

'Alright, a drink then. Efa's still in the salt houses.' Medwyn walked down the gangplank and clapped a hand on John's shoulder. 'C'mon, we have to celebrate this catch!'

'Alright, alright! Lead on.' John shook his head, but nonetheless followed his crewmate up through the village. Many people were making good use of the fair weather, and were out in the streets, either heading down to *Angorfa* Beach to help with the newest catch, or up into the village to run various errands. A small thoroughfare of sailors were treading the same path that John and Medwyn were on, heading towards the golden ale and homely comfort of The Five-Pointed Compass. The smell of freshly baked bread rose from the bakery and wafted down the main street, making John's mouth water.

John had expected to be greeted with noisy chatter upon entering the inn. Instead, there was a soft, if slightly uncomfortable, quiet. All eyes swung to John as he stepped inside, and then back to the bar. A young woman with long, golden blonde hair sat on one of the stools, seemingly unaware of the stares she was attracting. 'Ffion?' John stopped dead, the name tumbling from his lips unbidden. She turned, and smiled.

'You told me I should come see the ocean. So here I am.' Ffion's smile faltered a little under John's stare. 'A-assuming I am welcome?' She bit her lip.

John strode over to her, and took her gently by the shoulders. 'You are more than welcome.' And he bent to kiss her. Breaking apart, he rested his forehead against hers, 'I'm so glad you're here,' he whispered. 'I have so much to show you.'

John looked up, and realised that everyone was staring at him. He shifted uncomfortably. 'Well, there's lovely.' Smythe came to his rescue, 'Will you be needing a room, *cariad*?'

'Yes,' Ffion said at the same time John said, 'No.' Ffion looked at him, and John felt a flush creeping up his face.

'I mean, you can stay with me, if you want. Although, perhaps that's not appropriate–'

'I'd love to.' Ffion said, smiling up at him. John relaxed, and sat himself down next to her at the bar. Smythe poured them both a mug of the house ale, and moved away to tend to the other patrons. They had all gone back to their conversations, and John had no doubt they were muttering about Ffion and himself. He found he couldn't bring himself to care. Over the next hour, they talked incessantly together, John expressing his surprise to find Ffion here, and Ffion in turn recounting her uneventful journey to the coast.

Once both of their mugs were empty, Ffion turned in her seat and took John's hand. 'I think I'd like to see this unending lake now.'

Hand in hand, they left the inn and headed back down towards the sea. Ffion could not take her eyes off the great blue expanse, wonderment shining in their hazel depths. After a moment, Ffion tugged on his hand and broke into a run.

John laughed in surprise and ran after her. 'Wait, this way!' He called, and pulled her away from the main street and over a field. Ffion should see the wilds of the ocean in its unbridled glory, not marred with the tang of fish, nor the eyes of the curious. He led her down the steep cliff path that led to *Tua'r Mór* Bay. He reached the sand line, and she halted. 'Here.' He knelt down and gently unlaced her boots. Ffion stepped out of them, and took one step onto the sand. She gasped slightly at the cold, grittiness of it, and then smiled widely.

In a moment, she took off again down the beach, running for the sea. John followed, watching the gold of her hair catch in the late afternoon sunlight. She plunged into the surf, and span, arms outstretched and head thrown back to the sky. John joined her, and scooped her up into his arms. Ffion's face was alight with joy, and tears glinted in her eyes. She reached up and kissed him gently, cupping his rough face with her smooth palm. John sat down, letting the waves roll over them softly. Ffion reached down and ran her fingers through the water, creating little ripples in between the crests of the waves. Together they sat and watched the sun ebb toward the horizon.

'I think,' Ffion said quietly, the murmur of her words melding with the murmur of the tide, 'this is where I was always meant to be.' She looked out over the sea, and then up into John's face. They didn't leave the beach until the light of dawn washed over them, pale and new.

X

now.

Coastline.
December, 1815.
Abraxus.

Porth Tymestl was not what Abraxus had been expecting. When the message had lapped gently against his ship's hull, he had at first thought that the currents would take him towards one of the larger port towns that littered the coastline. Or the capital perhaps. But no, he had found himself washed up on some lonely shore in remote south Wales. 'Why here?' He muttered as he stared out of the small window that was the only source of natural daylight in his inn room. 'What is so important about *here*?'

The sea beyond him sprawled away towards the horizon; a glittering, unknowable expanse. If he remained very still, he could hear the whisper of the tide. If he closed his eyes, the wind whipped his hair around his face, the saline tang wrapping around him. But it was an illusion, just small tricks of the mind and senses to try and convince him he was somewhere he was not. The rough, wooden planks of the room upon which he stood, although they creaked and bowed slightly as he walked, felt too sturdy. They had none of that roll, the motion of the waves translated into whatever was cast out upon it.

Abraxus reached out and hooked the little window catch with a finger, pulling it shut. The call of the wind and tide dissipated immediately, and he was left behind, locked away behind glass and sturdy stone walls designed to keep out the raging of the Celtic sea. The day had dawned cold, blustery and overcast. Sheets of fine rain blew diagonally through the streets, deceptively soaking those through who had braved the cobbled lanes, thinking that it was merely a passing shower. Abraxus couldn't help but admire the stubbornness of the Porth Tymestl fishing crew; despite the weather, many of the ships had left the thick-walled harbour at first light. Smudges of white against a rolling grey sea and flat grey sky marked their progress.

The bar below him had to be empty; he couldn't hear any of the chatter that had wormed its way up to him through the floor from last night. No raucous laughter, nor any slightly drunken singing. He had found juxtaposition in it; after so long being surrounded only by the susurration of the waves and the far-off call of the gull, the sounds of other human life had been somewhat comforting. And yet, he found himself yearning to escape the noise of humanity and disappear again into the sea frets and foam. The odd clatter and snatch of distant humming that he caught could only be Smythe clearing up from the night before, or else getting ready for the onslaught of patrons he was surely going to receive later on.

Five paces towards the door, skirting the single cot, its blankets thrown haphazardly across it, and the small writing desk. Five paces with his back turned to the door, toward the casement and its slice of view beyond. Abraxus traced the path over and over again, the movement providing a blank canvas. He needed to get down to *Tua'r Môr* Bay, find the bones and then think about where to go from there. All his potential planning and half-formed theories were no good to him at all without that touch stone. The question was, how to do it relatively unnoticed by the residents of Porth Tymestl? Thanks to Smythe's meddling he already had two shadows interested in the bones, and, by extension, himself. Abraxus stopped dead in the middle of the room. How did the boys know about the *bones*? From what he had gathered from the innkeeper, the true nature of what had washed up on *Tua'r Môr* Bay had been concealed from Porth Tymestl, as was usually the way with things like this. But Smythe had clearly inferred that both of the boys had seen through the concealment; and that the taller one had even worked out what the posts actually were, despite not knowing where they came from. He pushed the thought away, it was a puzzle for another hour.

Around midday, Smythe knocked on his door, leaving him a modest lunch and word that the cliff paths were particularly empty today. Abraxus thanked him and resolved to walk them after he'd eaten, needing to know the layout of the coastline and the village before he really got to work. Leaving the now empty plate on the small writing desk, Abraxus pulled his long leather coat around him, turning up the salt-stiffened collar. He wound most of the length of his scarf around the lower half of his face – in part to provide some extra warmth, and also to keep some degree of anonymity. His staff, leaning against the desk, he decided to leave behind. It was unlikely he'd need it quite yet. He closed his eyes for a moment and pulled in a long breath, smelling the wood and wax scent that permeated the cabins of his ship.

Despite the inn being clearly empty, Abraxus found himself treading lightly along the corridor. Three other doors lined it, behind each another single room probably identical to his.

'Afternoon,' Smythe said, not looking up from the thick ledger he had open on the gleaming bar.

Abraxus mentally cursed that last step, wanting to draw as little attention to himself as he made his way out into the wind and rain. He nodded to Smythe, pulling the scarf up and over his nose.

'My, what scintillating conversation,' the innkeeper said, deadpan. He looked up, an eyebrow arched. 'You might want to start with the path that goes past the church. You'll get a good view of the Bay, and it'll lead you back 'round behind the village toward *Angorfa*.'

Abraxus raised a hand in silent thanks, earning another eyebrow raise. Smythe shooed him away with a lazy gesture.

The door seemed slightly heavier to pull open; the force of the wind clearly wanting him to remain inside. Abraxus slipped through it, and it slammed shut behind him. The cobbles were slick, and he found the well-worn tread of his boots sliding over the surface as if he were walking on ice, not stone. Narrowing his eyes to peer through the sheets of misty rain, Abraxus spotted the church, its weathervane atop the spire spinning and creaking dismally over the ever-increasing roar of the wind. He walked slowly toward it, grappling to find purchase on the cobbles and walking head-on into the wind. The tall grass of the graveyard immediately soaked through the shins of his trousers, making him grimace each time the wet fabric slapped against his legs. Most of the headstones were weathered beyond reading, some even missing chunks of stone from corners. A few, though, seemed newer than the rest, the smooth stone not yet pitted by coastal weather, the names and dates still legible. Careful not to walk over where the dead lay, Abraxus made his way over to the small gap in the low stone wall that surrounded the church and its graveyard. Beyond it, a well-trodden path wove along the edge of the cliffs, disappearing and reappearing with the undulation of the land. He passed one of the newer graves that sat right on the edge of the graveyard's boundaries, closest to the cliff edge and the sea. The words shone out on the black stone, droplets of water pooling in the curves and angles of the letters.

John Maredudd Kincarran
May 18th, 1771
October 6th, 1815

A minnau, yn flinedig, yn aml
Wedi gorfod dygnu
Yn llwybrau y moroedd

How I, weary, often
Have had to endure
In the sea-paths

Welsh was not one of Abraxus' more commonly used languages, and he took a moment to translate the inscription on the headstone. He smiled faintly when he recognised it, knowing the ancient poem it came from by heart. After all, most muses would recognise themselves in works of art if they saw it hanging on a wall. Abraxus reached out and gently brushed some of the clinging droplets of water off the headstone, sending them cascading down the rock and into the grass. Then, with a sharp movement, he turned away from the graveyard and strode through the gap and onto the coastal path. It had been lined with chalk and gravel, which crunched beneath his feet as Abraxus made his way along it. Whilst the visibility was poor, he could still hear the sea to the west. The coastline here was rugged, and the cliffs a sheer drop to the waters below. Through the gaps in the misty rain, Abraxus spotted small inlets far below, white-grey sand giving way to chunks of rock that must have been shattered under the driving force of the sea and wind. Rickety wooden fencing or tumbledown stone walls protected the path from the precipice, however, as Abraxus drew further and further away from Porth Tymestl, the gaps in these barriers became more frequent and larger. It was clear that the coastal paths weren't traversed all too often.

After an indeterminable time walking – it was now dark, day seemingly having given way immediately to night under the cover of the winter clouds – Abraxus came to a fork in the path. One continued to follow the cliffs, and the other rounded back on itself and toward Porth Tymestl. It was undeniable now that the rain and wind was quickly forming into a storm. Abraxus pulled the scarf closer around his face and turned his back to the increasing gale. The sea below him was roaring its pleasure at being let loose, and Abraxus found himself hoping that the cliffs had the stubbornness to remain strong in the face of such gleeful chaos. Particularly whilst he was atop them. The long, lonely path heading off further along the coastline seemed to beckon him, stretching far across the fields and away. He found himself taking a few unwilling steps forward, until the edge of his boots reached the divide. Just as Abraxus was about to take that deciding step, the distant roll of thunder reached him. His eyes snapped toward the sky, in time to see a far-off arc of lightning briefly light up the dark clouds above. Whilst he might belong to the sea, Abraxus had never been one to ignore messages from the sky.

Resolutely, he turned away and set off down the path that would take him back into Porth Tymestl. The roar of thunder grew louder as he walked, the wind whipping his hair into his face. It was slow going, the elements seemed bent on keeping him on this coastal path. Abraxus stopped for a moment to rest under a stunted and windblown tree, bare of its leaves and crooked. But the branches created something like a bower, and part of a drystone wall had crumbled beneath it, offering a mossy and damp seat. He pulled a tarnished flask from the depths of his coat, and drank deeply. The burn of Smythe's best whiskey warmed him from the inside out, and settled his tidal thoughts. The storm was overhead now, lightning cracking the sky open in luminescent arcs of silver and white. Abraxus took another drink from the flask, stowed it, and carried on walking.

'You sure you didn't go for a late-night dip?'

'Hm.'

'Well, if you aren't going to grace me with actual speech, then go stand by the fire, you look like you went overboard in a tempest.' Smythe flicked the rag he was using to wipe down a glass toward the hearth. The fire crackled merrily, the golden and red flames casting a gentle warmth and light into the inn's barroom.

Abraxus stumped over to it, pulling a chair from a nearby table as he did so. He sat down with a long groan, and then set about pulling off various items of soaked clothes. The seaweed laces of his boots were suitably wet, and as such were a nightmare to try and undo, the fine braided strands slipping through his numb fingers. His long leather coat he set over the back of another chair to dry out.

'Here.' Smythe pushed a bowl of something aromatically herby into his hands, and then bent down to pick up Abraxus' discarded boots. 'Porch?'

'Aye, thank you Smythe.'

'Why you insist on having boots that must be perpetually damp, I'll never know,' the innkeeper muttered as he opened the door and deposited the boots in the little sheltered entranceway.

'Why would I need boots that have to be perpetually dry?' Abraxus countered, sipping the stew straight from the bowl and not bothering with the spoon Smythe had pointedly laid out on the hearthside.

'Sounds like quite the storm,' Smythe said, coming to sit beside Abraxus.

'Hm. This is good.' Abraxus smiled slightly at Smythe's exasperated expression and raised the bowl to his lips again.

'Find anything interesting?' Smythe was persistent.

'In this weather? No, but I did get some idea of the landscape. And some time to think.' Abraxus set the bowl down and leaned back in his chair. Smythe was silent for a while, gazing into the fire. Outside, thunder rolled. Only no lightning had preceded it. Abraxus closed his eyes, waiting. Again, the thunder echoed over the cliffs and valley, and all was still in stormy darkness.

'Is that..?' Smythe began in hushed tones.

Abraxus didn't open his eyes; there was a melancholic confirmation in this lightless roar. 'Yes, it is.'

'*Achub eu heneidiau.*' *Save their souls.* Smythe said quietly. It was as if all the warmth had been pulled from the room. Abraxus sat contemplating the fire, and after three more calls of thunder, sprang to his feet and swung his still-damp coat over his shoulders.

'Where are you going?'

'I cannot – I *will not* sit here and listen to that,' Abraxus gestured wildly out of the window. The little lights of Porth Tymestl seemed to flicker through the driving rain. He strode over to the door, letting the cold seep inside. Smythe was flitting around him, imploring him to wait until the storm had passed, or until it was daylight out. Abraxus stolidly ignored him, lacing his boots up and trying not to grimace at his damp socks.

'Abraxus, please, *listen for a moment*. The path down to *Tua'r Môr* will be treacherous in this weather, you can't help if – *o uffern* what are they *doing*?' Abraxus looked up at Smythe, who was now staring out through the open door. He followed Smythe's gaze in time to see the dim light cast out by a lantern illuminate two figures. Abraxus only saw a flash of a dark blue cloak, before the figures vanished around a corner.

'Smythe, please tell me that was not–'

'It was,' Smythe said grimly. 'I'd recognise that lantern anywhere.'

'The lantern?'

'It was one of mine,' Smythe gestured vaguely above his head to the multitudes lighting the barroom. 'John took a shine to it and asked for it for the bowsprit of the *Dawnsiwr y Wawr*. It washed up on the shore a week after the boat came back to us in splinters.'

Abraxus had a sudden mental image of a lonely headstone atop a cliffside graveyard, lines of ancient poetry etched into the black rock. He looked out into the rain. 'Which way is *Tua'r Môr*, Smythe?' Abraxus asked quietly.

Smythe looked at him, and said, 'Follow the lantern light. I reckon they'll lead you well enough.'

ELLA RUBY SELF

Lightning.
December, 1815.
Tias.

The candle flickered wildly inside the lantern. It cast sporadic shadows over the path, temporarily lighting the cliffside heather in an explosion of constellations. Tias had pulled it down from the mantelpiece, brushing the dust from its surface with the cuff of his shirt. There was still the end wedge of a candle stuck to the pin inside, the wax frozen in droplets cascading down and pooling within the rim. He'd pried it out with his pocketknife, and was about to throw the stump into the late night fire, when Eli had taken it from his hand and disappeared up the ladder to their balcony bedroom. Tias heard the creak of hinges and then the scrape of something being dragged along the wooden floor. He knew that Eli kept a small chest full of keepsakes under his bed, most of the space within it now dominated by the splintered piece of their father's boat.

Now the lantern lit the way for both of them, although they still had to take the cliffside path down to *Tua'r Môr* Bay slowly, the continual rain making the dirt loose and slicing it down into mud. Tias pulled the hood of his cloak closer about his head, and watched his feet. Behind him, Eli slipped and cursed. 'Alright?' Tias called over his shoulder.

'Aye, let's just get down to the shore.' Tias nodded, sending droplets of water flying from the rim of his hood. He knew that they should have really waited for the morning, or at least for the storm to abate somewhat, but the flame of curiosity refused to be dampened.

Tias had been coming back over the meadows from the church when he'd spotted them. Crow had graciously allowed him to use his small personal library he kept in the vestry – 'On the condition that your brother does not put his sticky fingers all over my books,

Matthias. Am I understood?' – for 'research' purposes. So far, it had been a disappointing couple of visits. There was nothing on natural history, nor any science volumes pertaining to the sort of sea creatures that might be found off the coast of Porth Tymestl. The only semi-valuable thing Tias had managed to turn up was a battered and dog-eared book of faerie tales.

The lamp light in the vestry had grown brighter as the storm rolled over the coast, and Tias had dithered between trying to wait it out or making a run for it back to Roseate Cottage. He had chosen the latter, knowing that Eli would worry if he couldn't find Tias, especially in the midst of what was becoming a tempest. As he had slipped and skidded through wet grass, soaking his trousers and boots in the process, an almighty flash of lightning had temporarily lit up *Tua'r Môr* Bay below. In the brief, bright light, Tias had spotted through the curtains of rain a familiar row of posts far down the beach. Except these ones were closer to the water's edge than the others. Tias had frozen, momentarily forgetting the rain, and watched. All was dark again, the sky away to the south-east that strange murky brown that accompanied a twilight storm. A clap of thunder, a moment of reprieve, and then another lighting arc. And there, far below, another set of posts. These were half submerged in tide, the wild waves breaking against them in dark sprays of water. Tias had felt his heartbeat faster. He had run all the way back home.

Tias' feet found sand, and let out a breath he hadn't realised he'd been holding. He heard the soft thumping of Eli jumping down from the small height left between the beach and the end of the path.

'Cavern?' Eli called over the wind, which seemed somewhat diminished now they weren't up on the heights of the cliff-face. The call of the sea, however, was much louder. It swept all other sounds up in it and curled around Tias' head. The tide was on its way out, meaning they wouldn't have to contend with thoroughly wet feet if they decided to take refuge in the cavern.

Tias nodded and gestured with the lantern to follow him. Together, they set off down the bay, bent slightly from the force of the headwind. Eli had given up trying to keep his hood over his head, and let the wind tangle his hair into snarls. Water dripped into his eyes, and he kept reaching up to wipe away the droplets that fell to his lashes.

The cavern offered protection from both wind and rain, although the cold still swirled and eddied in the high irregular corners of the roof. Their supply of driftwood creaked and swung gently to and fro in their handmade harness that kept it above the high-water line. Tias jumped up onto the shelf, setting down the lantern and watching for a moment the patterns the light made on the rough stone walls. Eli had already hoisted down the harness and was stacking the driest pieces of wood into his arms.

'Here,' he said, throwing them up to Tias in one stack. Brushing away the ashes of the last fire, Tias set up a small pyramid of wood inside the stone ring. He pulled a small packet of dried seaweed wrapped in paper from inside his jerkin and set it in the middle. Eli clambered up to sit beside him and passed over his strike light. Within moments, they had a small blaze lit. The strong tang of seaweed and salt filled the cavern, and Tias leaned back against the wall, legs outstretched before him toward the fire in order to dry his boots.

'So,' Eli said, rubbing his hands together over the fire, 'what's the plan?'

Tias remained silent, staring out into the storm through the slash entrance in the rock.

'Oh, for the love of − *please* tell me you actually have a plan? And it wasn't limited to just 'let's go down to the beach and see what happens'?'

Tias shot his brother a look. 'No! I do have a plan, it's just still... in the works.'

'Unbelievable.' Silence fell over them, punctuated only by the sounds of the sea's wild dance, accompanied by the chorus of wind. The occasional burst of lightning lit up the beach beyond. Tias watched as the silver fire ran through the sky, wondering where it would make landfall.

'I think,' he said slowly, catching Eli's attention, 'that we should warm up a little, and then try and find the new bones that I saw from the cliffs. They seemed to just... appear between the lightning. If we're lucky, and in the right place at the right time–'

'We might see what creatures they belong to.' Eli finished.

'Exactly. They're clearly coming in from the sea, but we should be careful if we decide to wade out, the current will be strong in this storm.' Tias shivered, not only due to the cold, but also in excitement. Ever since Smythe had revealed the name of the man who was also investigating the bones, the need for answers had grown ever stronger, more difficult to resist. And now, tonight, as the world tore itself asunder, he might get some. The spiralling, looping coils of the beast he'd drawn on the cave wall was still partially visible. It seemed to ripple across the stone; a trick of an uneven surface and firelight.

'Well, time and tide,' Eli said, standing. 'I'm not getting any warmer, nor drier, so we may as well go. Where do you want to start?'

The cold seemed to have intensified since they were last outside, and Tias huddled deeper into his damp cloak. Eli had gripped the edge of Tias' cloak in one hand to keep them from getting separated. The lantern barely lit up any more than the next two steps before them, the flame dancing so wildly within its metal confines that Tias was sure it was about to go out entirely. 'This way!' He called, and they set off down the beach, heading toward the surf more by sound than sight.

Eventually, one of the new sets of posts came into view, tall and solid in the liquid darkness. Like the first, they were coated in strands of kelp and pitted with limpets. This set was shorter than the others, only twelve posts in a row.

'Now what?' Eli shouted over the furore.

'We wait,' Tias responded simply. 'Count the seconds between the thunder; let's see if we can time it.'

Eli nodded, and moved away toward the nearest pair of bones, running his hand over it.

Tias huddled into the meagre shelter the posts provided, and waited. A flash of lightning, but no thunder. He frowned, wondering if he had somehow missed it over the sea sounds. Eli visibly jumped when the crack of it eventually punctuated the air. 'That's not right...' Tias muttered to himself. Turning his face up to the sky, he watched, anticipation humming through his veins. Once again, the lightning and thunder did not come as a pair, but rather in a seemingly sporadic mismatched pattern. Eli had returned, standing shoulder to shoulder with his brother. He looked unnerved.

'What's going on?'

'I – I'm not sure. I think we should–' Tias broke off abruptly as a figure seemed to appear from nowhere behind Eli. A hand clapped down on Eli's shoulder, and his brother yelped, whirling around and deliberately squaring his shoulders.

'You need to leave.' The voice was not loud, and yet Tias caught every word over the sounds of the storm. In fact, it seemed as if the voice had captured those noises and twisted them and taken them for speech. It rolled like the tide. Tias lifted the lantern higher, illuminating the speaker.

'Who are – ?' Eli started, offence in his voice.

'*Eli,*' Tias hissed, elbowing his brother none too gently in the ribs.

Eli stopped and looked up at the man. '*Oh.* You're him.'

The man muttered something under his breath that sounded distinctly like, 'Damn Smythe.' Abraxus Elijah Honey straightened and reached out a hand again for them. The other was holding a long staff, straight aside from the deep 'C' curve about three quarters down the length.

Eli immediately backed away, pushing Tias with him.

'You need to *leave.*' Abraxus repeated.

'Why?' Sometimes Eli's stubborn streak could be infuriating. However, at this precise moment, Tias found himself silently cheering his brother's hard-headedness. He nodded.

'We aren't doing any harm, we just came to look at the bones.'

Abraxus ran a hand over his face, flicking away the water droplets that clung there. He opened his mouth to respond, but was cut off by a particularly loud rumble of thunder. His eyes snapped to the sea, scanning it. 'I do not have time for this,' he said, and reached out.

'Hey!'

'Get off!'

In one fluid movement, Abraxus had slung the staff over his shoulders, the curve fitting perfectly behind his neck, leaving either side to hang over his shoulders. He then grabbed both Tias and Eli by the backs of their cloaks and had started to drag them away from the shoreline. Eli put up a token struggle, but quickly gave up after he had determined that Abraxus had an iron grip on the wool. After putting a substantial amount of distance between the bones and themselves, Abraxus released their cloaks, propelling them forward. Tias crashed into Eli, nearly sending them both down into the wet sand.

Eli pulled him steady and rounded on Abraxus. 'What are you *doing?*'

'Where is the cave, boy?' Abraxus said coldly. 'I saw the light from it as I crossed the beach. Now, where is it?'

'This way,' Tias said resignedly. Unlike Eli, he knew when he was beat. Abraxus deliberately walked behind them as they made their way toward the cliffside.

The fire was still smouldering up on the ledge when they reached the cavern. Eli climbed up, prodding it with a charred length of wood. Tias, following Eli's example, pointedly ignored Abraxus' presence and pulled down the harness, throwing a few chunks of driftwood to his brother.

Abraxus stood in the entrance, and as Tias joined Eli, the firelight cast his features into flickering relief. The green-golden flame caught on the beads and metal woven throughout his tangle of black hair, some strands tied with seaweed, or else coloured thread. One particularly thick matted lock had a length of thin ships' rope wrapped around it. His coat, Tias noticed with a pang, was not unlike his father's; a sea-stained brown leather, except Abraxus' brushed his ankles. Everything under the coat seemed to be layer upon layer of different fabrics – a dark ochre yellow scarf crossed his chest over the top of a sturdy cord jerkin and loose shirt. The scarf bore a swirl of green and blue patterns embroidered onto it. A thick belt encircled his waist, and Tias caught a glimpse of something burnished and copper hanging at Abraxus' hip as the wind whipped his coat around him. Seeming to notice Tias' intrigue, Abraxus stepped further into the cavern. The shadows glanced off the angles and plains of his face, seeming to cast his features in a dark basalt black.

'Get warm. Get dry. And then we go,' Abraxus said shortly.

Tias beat Eli to it this time. 'Why?'

Abraxus didn't seem inclined to answer.

'We're only curious about what's going on.' He pressed on. 'We don't mean any harm, and anyway, it seems that perhaps we could help each other? Smythe said you knew what these bones were and where they came from, and we know the coast better than any.'

'I do not require help from children.' Abraxus grumbled. He moved over to the wall where the partial drawing of the beast Tias had created was still outlined. With a long finger he traced the curve of the spine. His eyes followed the spiralling form down and over the wall, and Tias noticed that they were two different colours. There was something else about them too, but he couldn't quite put his finger on it. 'Did you draw this?'

'I did,' Tias said.

'Hm.' Abraxus moved away, looking around the cavern. 'A nice den you have made for yourselves.' He came over to the ledge. The edge of it reached his chest, and he leaned his staff against it. A soft clinking noise drew Tias' attention and he saw that at the top of the curve, several strands of coloured thread had been strung; shells, sea glass and two ornate rings hanging off them at intervals. Tias was tempted to reach out and lift it, but knew that he'd probably get an earful from Abraxus.

Eli was still determinedly not looking at Abraxus, but rather staring sullenly over the top of his head and through the entranceway. The silence stretched long and thin, and Tias felt the breaking point approaching. Outside, the sea seemed to have calmed slightly, the waves no longer pounding against the shoreline as if determined to splinter the land apart.

'I'm not going to stop coming down here, you know.' Tias looked at Eli, who was still looking out seaward as if he hadn't spoken at all.

Abraxus sighed, the sound caught between annoyance and understanding. 'You should not. But I know I cannot stop you.' Abraxus looked up at them, a stern expression in his eyes. 'However, to come here tonight was folly. I would strongly suggest that you do not come here during storms, or the night. Those are the times that I need to be here, *alone*, so that I may work, unencumbered.'

'Yes, alright, but what is your work?' Tias said, ignoring the annoyed sound Eli made when he so hastily agreed to Abraxus' conditions.

'That is not for you to know, nor may I remind you, is any of your concern.' And then, quietly and exasperated, 'Despite what meddling innkeepers might have implied otherwise.' Before either of them could complain or question further, Abraxus straightened and studied them both critically. 'Well, have you warmed?' He reached out and patted the edge of Eli's cloak that pooled about him as he sat. 'Enough, I think. Let us go.' He picked up his staff, and beckoned.

Eli looked outraged, but Tias pushed him in the back. He was getting the distinct impression that Abraxus was not a man to be argued with. Eli grumbled, but climbed from the ledge nevertheless. Tias doused the fire with a few handfuls of damp sand, and took up his lantern again.

Abraxus was already outside the cavern, waiting for them. He said nothing, but allowed Tias to take up the lead. Eli stumped along beside him, casting resentful glances over his shoulder every now and then. Tias half expected Abraxus to see them as far as the path back up the cliff, and so was surprised when he stepped onto it himself. He clearly didn't trust them to not double back sneakily when he returned to the bones. And judging by the thoroughly put out expression on his brother's face, that was exactly what Eli had been planning.

The walk back up to the village felt a lot more difficult than coming down, now that he was soaked, cold and tired. Tias found himself stumbling over his own feet a few times, each time finding Eli's hand on his shoulder as a steadying presence. A moment after one of these stumbles, he heard Eli shout and then Abraxus say, 'Careful there, boy.'

Tias turned in time to see Abraxus release his grip on Eli's upper arm, apparently acting as a steadier for his brother. The path had slipped slightly after having torrents of water pour down it, the mud at the very edge giving way underneath Eli's boots.

'*Diolch*,' Eli muttered.

Eventually, they reached the top and the late-night lights of Porth Tymestl glinted invitingly. Tias felt exhausted at this point, legs made of lead and thoughts muzzy. He turned to Abraxus, ready to say something approximating a farewell, when he saw that Abraxus was now taking the lead. He turned and called back to them, 'This way. Quickly now.'

Eli looked at Tias and shrugged; it was clearly a testament to how tired Eli was feeling too that he didn't even argue. Together, they followed Abraxus through the sleeping village. By now, the storm had died down into gusts of winter wind, the rain having been taken off further inland. The lighted windows of The Five-Pointed Compass came into view, and for the first time that night, Tias found himself thanking one of Abraxus' choices. He didn't know if he or Eli had any energy left to try and reach Roseate Cottage on the outskirts of the village.

'In.' Abraxus stood to one side in the little porch, and was about to bring the top of his staff down on the door to knock, when it was flung open.

'You two are lucky that Ffion isn't here, so you'll 'ave to settle for a berating from me.' Smythe said, pulling Tias and Eli inside by their shirt fronts. It was blissfully warm; it wrapped Tias up gently and drew him further into its embrace. Smythe fussed around them, pulling off their wet cloaks and chivvying them closer to the fire.

Eli crumpled onto the hearth, stretching out at full length alongside the fire like a cat.

'Boots.' Smythe said, holding out a hand. He already had placed Tias' at the far end of the hearthside. Eli sat up slowly and pulled them off, casting them haphazardly beside his brother's before lying back down. 'Thank you,' Smythe muttered to Abraxus, who merely inclined his head.

Tias had sat down in a chair that had been placed close to the fire, letting the warmth wash over him and make his thoughts heavy. The door opened and closed quietly behind him.

'When I said search for answers, I didn't mean go out and get frozen in the *middle of a storm*.' Smythe said irritably. 'Tias, surely you have more common sense than to listen to your brother's schemes?'

'Hey, it was *his* idea,' Eli said from the hearthside. 'Can't blame me this time, Smythe.'

Smythe rolled his eyes and then muttered, 'I'll go and sort out one of the rooms for you. Wait here.' He hurried up the creaky stairs to the lodgings above.

'Well, that was an adventure,' Eli said.

'Quite. Eli... are you going to actually listen to anything Abraxus–'

'No. You?'

Tias smiled tiredly. 'No.'

'Glad to see we agree.' Eli fell silent after that as Tias stared blindly into the ruby fire, so different to the light green-gold of the one he had lit hours before. The thunder had ceased its bellow outside. By the time Smythe came back downstairs, both Tias and Eli had fallen into sleep.

From deep under the murky depths of dreams, Tias was aware only for a moment of a voice that rolled like the tide, chanting in a language that no living ear had heard for more than a century, drifting up from the shoreline.

XI
then.

All in the name.

The clatter of a window opening broke the quiet within the cottage. The single room was stuffy, the air oppressive and wet with the scent of blood and sweat. Outside, the late afternoon sun blazed in a crystalline blue sky. Now, with the cottage opened up a little more, the distant sounds of the sea drifted in through the window. The breeze that carried it set the hanging herbs and chimes Ffion had strung from the rafters rustling and clinking.

John turned away from the window, and cast open the door too. Ffion stirred in her sleep, turning instinctively toward the salty air that gently blew over her tired face. Her long blonde hair was haloed about her on the pillow, damp at the scalp and shining. John quietly sat down on the edge of the bed beside her and ran his fingers through it. A peace the like of which he had never felt before was rolling over John, such a depth of contentment that it seemed as unfathomable as the sea that glinted beyond the walls of Roseate Cottage.

A weak, squalling cry did nothing to break the serenity. John stood immediately and crept over to the crib that lay on the hearthstones nearby. He knelt and gently ran one finger along the baby's cheek. The cry settled into a soft whimper, and John reached down and pulled the baby into his arms, trying not to wake his still sleeping brother. Ffion had not been as surprised as John when the midwife Rhian had announced that there were two. Just before Ffion had succumbed to sleep, she had muttered that they should have seen this coming, as they had prepared meticulously over the past few months for their child's arrival. 'Best laid plans,' John had chuckled, gently kissing her forehead.

The baby in John's arms opened his eyes. They were a clear honey-brown, a shade darker than the soft wisps of hair that curled on the eggshell head. John noticed how clear the baby's eyes seemed, how already he was looking and learning. Tiny fingers flexed slightly, and John hooked his little finger into the grasp.

'Someone's enamoured.' John looked up to see Rhian pouring away a basin of water into the little patch of grass beyond the door. She was smiling, a knowing expression on her lined face. John simply grinned a little lopsidedly and returned his attention to his son. 'He's the elder, I believe,' Rhian said.

'How much by?'

'Ten minutes, give or take.'

'Well, that can be something for them to fight over when they're grown, I'd expect,' John said.

Rhian laughed, 'I'll be heading off in a moment, *cariad*. Is there anything else you or Ffion need?'

'I think we've got all we need right here.' John said. 'Thank you, Rhian.' He gently set the baby back down beside his brother and stood. He saw the village midwife to the door, and, on a whim, pulled her into a tight hug. After a moment, Rhian reciprocated, and then pulled away, setting a hand on John's shoulder.

'You know where I am if you need me.' John nodded and watched her turn away and head back down into the village. He left the door open, the sun sinking in the sky, but the temperature not yet dropping to a summer night's chill.

'John?' Ffion was awake, and had propped herself up on slightly shaky elbows. John hurried back over to the bed and sat beside her.

'How are you feeling?' He asked seriously.

She merely looked at him.

'Alright, fair enough. Shall I bring them over?' Ffion nodded, letting John stack pillows behind her so she could sit up unaided. Not taking any risks, John brought the twins over to her one at a time, and then sat alongside his wife.

'You know,' Ffion said slowly, tracing the whorl of one of the baby's ears with the tip of her finger, 'after all that planning we did, and getting everything ready, we never discussed names.'

'You're right, we didn't. How did we forget that?' John said. 'Well, at least this way, we don't have to squabble over a single name. One each?'

Ffion elbowed him as best she could whilst still holding a baby, but amusement shone on her face. 'I always liked the idea of family names – maybe people who aren't here anymore, so that their memory and spirit can live on?'

'I think that is a wonderful idea,' John said. He knew that family and keeping the memory of departed loved ones close was a very important aspect in *Dyffryn Cernunnos*, and if Ffion couldn't be there, then John wanted to honour her heritage any way he could. 'You never met my grandfather, but I think you would have liked him,' John said. Ffion looked up at him, and then gently leaned against his shoulder, listening. 'He was a tall man, and strong. Hands the size of an oar blade, I remember putting mine against his as a child. My fingers barely reached the second joint. Had a temper on him like a summer squall – came out of nowhere and was fierce. But he was so gentle most of the time. He taught me how to sail, how to tie off knots and run up and down rigging like a monkey. He lived in Porth Tymestl all his life, but he always used to say to me, 'John, there might be a world behind us, but out there,' and he'd point toward the horizon, 'out there is where the adventure lies.' He was determined to sail over the horizon, just to see if it could be done.' John quickly dashed away the tears that clouded his eyes.

Ffion rubbed his shoulder and said quietly, 'Sound advice. I think you're right, I would have liked him. What was his name?'

'Elias.'

'Elias...' Ffion said, feeling the name out on her lips. 'Yes, it's good. It... *moves*.' She looked down at the baby she was holding. His eyes were open and were roving about the cottage, settling eventually on his mother's face. They were nearly the same colour as his older brother's, if a little lighter with flecks of deep chestnut around the pupil. Ffion bent down and pressed a kiss to his forehead, murmuring something in her mother language. John hadn't ever picked up the knack for it, but he heard his grandfather's – his *son's* – name in it.

'And for your family?' John asked.

Ffion was quiet for a moment, as if in thought. Then, 'My uncle, I think. He stepped into the role of my father after he died. Provided for me, *Nain* and my mother until the forest took her too. He was... strange perhaps, but I loved him, nonetheless. He'd get up with the dawn and walk for miles, following the sounds of the birds until he either looped back to home, or got hopelessly lost. He used to call me his little goldfinch.' Ffion smiled at the memory.

'I never met him..?' John began softly.

'No. He died a year before you arrived. He was out on one of his walks, and there was a storm and...' Ffion tailed off, eyes misty and distant.

'I'm sorry.'

'His name was Matthias.' Ffion said, looking down at the baby nestled in John's arms. And then the cloud of sorrow lifted from around her as she laughed lightly. 'Matthias and Elias. It has a nice musicality to it, don't you think?'

'Aye, it does.' The little family sat quietly together, their peaceful quiet intermingled with the merest sounds of life; a breath, a sigh. Beyond the window, the sun sank below the horizon, taking the last of the light with it and ushering in a clear and star-speckled night.

XII
now.

Harbour.
December, 1815.
Ffion.

Twenty-one days. Four days of travel bookending her time away, thirteen spent in the soft green peace of *Dyffryn Cernunnos*. The moss had grown over the cracks in her soul, and the gently clinging soil had marked her fingernails and knees. And yet, as Ffion had drawn closer and closer to the coast, she felt the leaf litter and mulch erode from her, swept away by the abrasive roll of the waves and tide.

All too soon, she stood at the overlook, Porth Tymestl nestled below her in the armchair bay. It was a fair day for mid-winter, the sky a pale icy blue with little cloud cover. There was no warmth to the air though, nothing between her and the sapphire sharpness in her lungs. That pine balsam balm had been stripped away, and there was nothing but salt and ragged limpets left.

Far away, upon the indigo sea, several white sails drifted hither and thither, the ship's gleaming wooden prows disappearing beneath the waves and spray. She found herself looking instinctively for the red sails of the *Dawnsiwr y Wawr*. Ffion shook herself mentally and steeled her resolve. She would not have to endure this much longer. Taking in a deep breath, Ffion marched down the heather covered moorside and into the village.

Those who were out on the streets eyed her as she passed, and she felt as she had all those years ago, first arriving in a small, unmapped fishing village. A breeze made up of rumour and whispers followed her over the cobbled streets, snapping at her ankles. It was all Ffion could do not to break into a run and put her sturdy door between herself and the world. As she passed *Angorfa* Beach and the little harbour, she spotted the bent figure of Cynfor Morgan. He sat perfectly at ease at the very end of the harbour wall, his legs hanging over the void. He seemed deep in thought, eyes distant and locked on the sails dancing over the winter's sea. Ffion walked along the curve of the harbour toward home, and raised a hand in greeting when she was in Old Man Morgan's eyeline. He didn't seem to notice her at first, but as she turned away toward the little track that would take her up to Roseate Cottage, she heard her name called in his thin voice.

'Good afternoon, Cynfor.' She said politely, walking back over to the harbour wall. After an infinitesimal hesitation, she stepped onto it and headed toward the still sitting figure.

'*Prynhawn Da, cariad.* It's good to see you back again.' He struggled to rise, but Ffion stayed him with a hand, and sat down next to him. She was careful, however, to sit crossed legged a little further back from the edge than he was. The sea was the calmest she had seen it for a while, flat and reflective. It whispered against the rock of the harbour wall, and Ffion resolutely closed her mind to its siren song secrets. 'How was the forest vale?'

'Beautiful, even in the dead of winter,' Ffion said, allowing herself for a moment to fall back into the lichen. 'It snowed whilst I was there. The quiet is something I shall never forget, how it seems to muffle all other life, and yet itself is *alive*.' She broke off, clearing her throat. 'How's it been with you?'

Old Man Morgan gestured expansively out over the sea. 'Today is good. We 'ad an almighty storm last night though. Not seen one quite like it for a good many year. No snow,' he smiled a little sadly, 'I reckon you got it off the winds.' They sat in companionable silence for a while, until Cynfor said quietly, 'I would 'ave a word with your boys.'

'Oh, *arglwydd*, *Good Lord,* what have they done?'

Cynfor levelled her with an appraising look, the age seeming to lift from his eyes. 'There's a man staying at Smythe's inn.' As Ffion listened to the talk swirling around the newcomer, she had a sinking feeling about where Cynfor was heading.

'They're intrigued by him, aren't they?'

'Aye.' He looked out over the sea, conflict across his weathered face.

'Cynfor? There's something else?' Ffion pressed.

'Aye.' Old Man Morgan said. 'Last night – I was still awake due to the racket the storm was makin', and I saw... well I saw Eli and Tias walking back up from *Tua'r Môr* Bay with this man. Soaked to the bone, the lot of them were. He took 'em to The Five, which I reckon was sensible mind, Roseate is quite the distance from the cliff path. They're home now, I was up with the birds.'

Ffion fiddled with a loose thread on the hem of her travelling breeches. 'And do you think he's... dangerous?'

Cynfor thought for a moment, before saying, 'No. Not dangerous. Just... strange. An' perhaps in a way that is harmless, but I think it better safe than sorry.' He turned to face her, and cupped her wind-cold cheek with a shaking and gnarled hand. 'You've lost so much *cariad*. Keep them boys close, I couldn't bear it if–' He broke off. 'Ach, don't listen to the sentimental ramblings of an old man. G'on, get home.'

Ffion blinked back sudden tears, and leaned forward to press a kiss to Old Man Morgan's forehead. 'Thank you, Cynfor. I'm going to miss you.'

The old man smiled sadly, understanding in his eyes. 'Aye, I dare say I'll miss you too, *cariad*. And those little storms you call sons.' He winked as she smiled softly.

ABRAXUS ELIJAH HONEY

Sea Holly.
December, 1815.
Tias.

Tias' boots were still damp. He had grimaced with every step he'd taken on the way back to Roseate Cottage, the wool of his socks rubbing against the heel of his foot. Smythe had chivvied them out of The Five-Pointed Compass a little after the winter sun had risen, telling them to get home and get some thicker clothes on. 'And if I catch either of you out in so much of a brisk wind, I *will* lock you in the cellar.'

Abraxus either hadn't returned from *Tua'r Môr* Bay, or had sequestered himself back in his room. Wherever the man was, he certainly didn't put in an appearance for Tias and Eli's departure from the inn. Eli had pestered Smythe about it, clearly wanting to speak with Abraxus some more about everything that had happened the previous night. All he received in return was an earful from the innkeeper. Despite his more than confrontational attitude with Abraxus last night, Eli was clearly deeply intrigued by the man. He had muttered all the way home, much to Tias' begrudging amusement.

The fire was stone cold as they entered the cottage. The half-light made everything inside look dank and grey, and Tias found himself suddenly wishing for the polished wooden gleam of The Five-Pointed Compass' barroom. Eli kicked off his boots and trudged over to the hearth, stacking kindling up and searching for the strike light.

Meanwhile, Tias rummaged underneath the long workbench by the door, coming up with some stale bread and a few strips of dried fish left over from the autumn smokehouses. The crackle of an infant fire soon filled the cottage, the weak yellow light chasing away the clinging damp as best it could. Tias gathered up Eli's boots and set them next to his on the hearthstones. He nudged his brother, handing him a chunk of the bread and sitting down next to him, bare feet turned toward the fire. Eli chewed thoughtfully on his bread, staring absentmindedly into the flames. Neither of them spoke, but merely sat in companionable silence for a while. Tias was sure his brother was just as consumed with curiosity as he was; Tias' mind was alight with everything he had seen and heard last night. The strange eyes of Abraxus swam up into his thoughts from the depths.

There was a tap on the window. Tias turned, half expecting to see Smythe peering through the glass, making sure that both of them were still inside and not gallivanting over the seagrass meadows. He started when the pale, thin face of his mother looked back at him. A gentle half-smile on her lips, she tapped musically on the glass with long fingers.

'Mam!' Tias ran over to the door and flung it open. His mother pulled him into a tight hug, running her hands through his hair.

'Don't bother Eli, I've already seen.' Tias turned at his mother's amused tone in time to see Eli straightening up guiltily, having been trying to shove a pile of discarded cloaks, scarves and jumpers under the table. 'Come here.' Ffion held onto Tias with one arm, and wrapped the other around Eli's shoulders, kissing his temple. 'I've missed you.'

'Missed you too, Mam,' Eli muttered, ducking his head slightly. Ffion smiled that half-smile again, ruffled his hair and stepped into the cottage properly, dropping her bag by the door, Tias closing it behind her. The clouds had dissipated since they had returned to Roseate Cottage, the sky was now a fragile blue, the sun a white gem at its centre.

'Um... there's not much food,' Tias said sheepishly, looking at the half-eaten bread and strips of fish that now lay abandoned on the hearthstones.

'You could have at least eaten at the table,' Ffion said, picking up the food and shoving it back into Tias and Eli's hands. 'You may as well finish that now. I'll see what I can do.' She turned away to the workbench, pulling the large iron dish they used to cook over the fire. Tias and Eli looked at each other, and sat down at the table, watching their mother.

'How was *Dyffryn Cernunnos*?' Tias asked, stumbling a little over the name.

'Fine,' Ffion said. She reached up and pulled down a bundle of dried herbs from the rafters, pulling the leaves from them and adding it to the pot.

'Did you get that business sorted out?' Eli asked. 'To do with – with Da?' Ffion went very still, shoulders hunched. 'Mam?'

'I need to speak with you.' She addressed the little window that overlooked the hill and onto the sea.

'About what?' Tias asked slowly. He could feel the pressure increasing in the air, like smelling a summer storm about to descend upon the bay. The atmosphere crackled with things unsaid and about to be unleashed. Ffion sighed, and hefted the pot off the workbench, carrying it over to the fire and hooking it above the flames.

'*About what*, Mam?' Eli said, an edge to his voice.

Ffion pulled out a chair and sat down, looking between Tias and Eli.

Tias felt a cold wave wash over his neck, and watched Eli as he subtly gripped the table.

'I was not lying when I said I had affairs to deal with back in *Dyffryn Cernunnos*. However, I didn't tell you all my intentions for visiting.' She took a deep breath, and then plunged. 'Porth Tymestl can no longer be our home, be *my* home. It hasn't been home since your Da passed away. I've made arrangements with Tudwr, and my *Nain*'s house is to be cleared and made ready for our arrival. I don't know exactly when we'll be leaving, but I expect it will be soon.' Whilst Ffion had been speaking, she had determinedly stared each of her sons in the eye, but now she lowered her head, tracing patterns onto the tabletop with a finger.

There was silence in Roseate Cottage. Tias felt nothing but numb shock. A snide, more calculating part of his mind whispered that *you knew this was coming, you should have seen it when she told you she was leaving for the forest vale. Why didn't you notice?* He glanced at his brother, and all thoughts suddenly vanished.

Eli looked furious. His face white, jaw clenched and eyes blazing with light that Tias only saw when Eli was four punches deep into a fight.

'Eli...' Tias started, wanting to head off the storm before it landed.

'No.' His brother's voice was cold and clear. It rang through the cottage like a bell. Ffion winced, and looked up.

'Eli, listen. We can't stay—'

'*No.*' Eli cut her off. '*You* can't stay maybe, but I will not leave Porth Tymestl. You can't take me away.'

Ffion pursed her lips, anger making its way onto her face now too. 'Eli, you will not speak to me like that. I have made a decision, one that I think will benefit us all. Now, I don't expect you to be thrilled about the matter, but I also expect you to act with more decorum and grace than this.' She stood up, and Tias suddenly saw the strong, commanding woman that had dominated village meetings when he and Eli were younger.

Eli stood up too, chair screeching over the stone floor. 'Be *thrilled* about it? No, of course I'm not! You're taking us away from everything we've ever known, and expect us to follow you blindly into the forest without so much as a fight!' He was close to shouting now.

'Elias!' Ffion *did* shout, but Eli took no notice.

'This is all because you can't face what's out there anymore,' he gestured wildly to the window, to the seascape beyond.

Ffion's eyes hardened to flint.

'Eli, *enough.*' Tias hissed, standing up and grabbing his brother roughly by the shoulder.

'No, I'm right, aren't I?' Eli spat, staring at their mother dead in the eye.

'The sea took your father away! It took him away from you, your brother and from me! I can't *stand* to even look at it anymore!' Ffion roared. She slammed her hands onto the table.

Tias looked away, feeling tears prick his eyes. He understood his mother's anguish, her thoughts. Part of him even agreed with her, that getting away from the wild coast would do them all good. Put away the tragedy that haunted them, the spectre of their father and bury it in the moss. It had taken him a while after his Da's death to go down to *Angorfa* Beach, let alone the more secluded *Tua'r Môr* Bay. He'd caved under Eli's insistence, and found some solace in the lonely cry of the gull. But there was still a ragged tear inside him that not even the susurration of the tides could wipe away.

'Da loved the sea! He loved it, and it's my last piece of him to hold onto! You say that it took him away, but now you're doing the same thing, you're taking *me* away from him. The only things I have left from Da are his lantern and a splinter of his ship, and even those I've had to keep from you. You can't take this away from me too.' Eli's voice broke. 'You can't.'

Their mother's expression softened for a moment, tears rolling freely over her cheeks. She reached out across the table, and then stopped. Her hand swung back to her side, and she drew herself up to her full height. 'We are leaving. I will not change my mind on this.'

Eli had opened his mouth, starting to argue back again, when something snapped inside Tias. 'Enough!' He yelled.

Both Eli and Ffion stared at him. Tias rarely raised his voice in anger.

'Stop it, both of you! I don't want to listen to this anymore. Eli, I don't want to go either, do you think I would? But I also agree with what Mam is saying.' He took in a shuddering breath. 'Da's gone, and it's *awful* and I don't know what to do. I'm either trying to stop *you*,' he rounded on Eli, 'getting into every fight you can pick, or I'm trying to mediate between the pair of you. I'm not doing this anymore. Sort it out without me.' Tias pulled his cloak from under the table, and swung it over his shoulders. He strode over to the door, pulled it open and took off toward the cliff path. He neither stopped nor even turned when he heard Eli call his name from the doorway. His cloak still smelt of salty air and late-night adventure. Tias angrily dashed away tears and broke into a run.

The meadow hadn't been cut since summer. The tall fronds of seagrass rose above Tias' head. He was sitting at the very edge of the field, curled up, arms hugging his knees to his chest. The drystone wall had crumbled here, allowing him a vista of the village, and beyond that the sea. The good weather had allowed the fishing fleet to go out onto the waves today, the sails distant. A few had already made the journey out and were now heading back to *Angorfa* Harbour.

Tias was sure that he was completely hidden here. The meadows didn't really get much usage anyway; they were more for the spring, when the small flock of sheep and a few cattle Porth Tymestl had were allowed to roam freely through them. He was surprised, then, to be abruptly brought out of his thoughts by a kick to the back. He yelped, more out of a shock than pain, and scrambled around to see who had come across him. He had expected Eli.

'Why are you always showing up underfoot where I do not want you?' Abraxus said, eyes cast toward the sky as if looking for answers in the eggshell blue void. 'This time, almost quite literally.'

Tias felt a surge of annoyance. 'Well, you could have looked where you were going a little more carefully.' He yanked on the edge of his cloak, which was trapped under Abraxus boot. And then he added childishly, 'Anyway, I was here first.'

There was a moment of silence between the two, and Tias thought suddenly that Abraxus might shout at him. But then Abraxus smiled – albeit more exasperated than amused – and said, 'Aye, you were.' He flicked his long coat out behind him, and settled on the damp grass next to Tias.

Tias stared.

'Yes?' Abraxus said, not looking at him.

'...Nothing.' Tias said, a hint of resignation in his voice. He went back to staring through the gap in the wall. Abraxus reached out and began plucking several long strands of grass from the earth. Tias watched from the corner of his eye as Abraxus began to braid the strands together, fingers deft and flying.

'I have learnt,' Abraxus said a moment later, still focused on the grass, 'to tell the difference between when someone wants to truly be alone, and when someone is alone, and yet yearns for company. I am thinking that perhaps you might fall into the latter?' He looked at Tias levelly.

'Maybe,' Tias muttered.

'Hm. Well, company is here. It is up to you to decide what to do with it.'

Tias sat quietly for a while, not looking at Abraxus. There was a steady presence to him, fluid yet somehow solid. Dependable. Part of him wondered whether or not he should explain why he had secluded himself in a lonely meadow, but Abraxus probably didn't want to know about the turmoils of the Kincarran household, and anyway, Tias didn't want to particularly recount it all. He'd rather just sit and be for a while, listening to the distant waves and the rustle of the grass.

A far-off call had Tias straightening up, peering over the grass. He should have expected Eli to come looking for him eventually. Tias had just hoped Eli would find him a little later. 'Your brother?' Abraxus said, as Tias hunkered back down, hoping Eli wouldn't come any further into a field he thought empty.

'Yes,' Tias said. 'Usually, it's me trying to find Eli, so this makes a change.' He laughed, but there was little humour in it.

'Ah, so *you* are Tias.' Abraxus said.

Tias looked up at him, puzzled.

'Well, our first meeting was under the night sky, in a storm with naught but a small lantern for light, boy. Did you expect me to know you right then and there?'

'Well... no.' Tias conceded.

'Smythe had only ever described you as 'the taller one', and as you can see,' Abraxus gestured, taking in Tias' hunched sitting position, 'that descriptor does not really apply here.'

Tias felt a flicker of a true smile pull at the corners of his lips. 'Fair enough.' Eli's voice had grown a little less distant during the pair's conversation, and Tias sighed, making ready to pull himself up and let his brother find him.

'Why are you going?'

'I – what?'

Abraxus was still studying the braid of grass, now knotting it intricately at various intervals. 'You clearly do not want to be discovered yet. Nor, I suspect, go back to whatever conflict made you turn to this lonely meadow in the first place.'

'How did you–?' Tias began.

Abraxus cut him off with a look. 'It was not hard to guess, boy.' He shifted in the grass a moment, turning to look Tias head on. 'Stay a while longer. Listen to the sea and the wind and calm yourself. There is no need for you to go back now. Your brother will try somewhere else soon enough.'

'But he'll be worried...' Tias said half-heartedly.

Abraxus shrugged. 'Then let him be worried. You are not gone, you are simply... away.'

Tias stared into Abraxus' face, thinking for a moment. 'Alright,' he said and settled back into the grass more comfortably. Sure enough, Eli's voice began to drift further and further away until it was lost to the afternoon sky.

'Here,' Abraxus said after a moment, handing the now complete grass-braid to Tias. 'Tell me how I did this.' Tias started to study the intricate weaving and knots, following the strands of grass lightly with his fingertips. He had just started to explain how Abraxus had managed the original weave base of the strand, when he faltered. Abraxus quirked an eyebrow, and Tias carried on. But his mind wasn't on the grass braid anymore. It was on Abraxus' eyes. The left was a deep indigo blue, shot through with strands of deep green. The other was a light pastel blue, a haze of white running through the soft colour. They mirrored the sea below and the sky above Tias perfectly.

Honey.
December, 1815.
Eli.

The silence Tias left behind *ached*. He felt it as a physical thing, sharp and unpleasant, almost choking in how it crackled in the air. Eli had seen his brother upset and angry before, of course he had. In fact, on several occasions, it was probably his own fault that had driven Tias into such a state. But he had never just left before. Like Tias had said before the door slammed and Eli and Ffion were left alone in stunned silence, he was often the mediator between the two of them. If their mother was the sturdy, immovable forest, and Eli was the sea gale, then Tias was often the tide. Coming in and sweeping away any imperfections made in the shifting sands that constituted their lives.

Ffion sank back down into her chair at the table, staring into nothing. Eli didn't move. He continued to stare at the door, waiting for it to swing open again and reveal his brother, marching back inside and ready to give them both a talking to. He looked to his mother, but she gave no indication of what he should do next. Eli felt very lost all of a sudden, cast out into a churning current with no visible place to make land. He wanted to wrap his arms around his mother's shoulders, tell her he was sorry and that he would pack up and go quietly wherever she directed them. He wanted to shout some more, telling her she was being ridiculous, and *didn't you see, that if you left here you'd be leaving Da behind too*? He wanted his brother. That was a good starting place. Find Tias, calm the gale of his temper and find an anchor.

His boots were still slightly damp from the previous night's excursions. He pulled them on regardless, stooping beneath the table to find his jumper and cloak. 'I didn't stop by the market towns on my way ho – here.' Ffion's voice was low, and tear stained.

Eli resolutely ignored the spark of anger, still hot and smouldering, at her refusal to call Porth Tymestl home any longer.

She looked up at him, eyes hollow and face drawn. 'But I did bring back a few things from *Dyffryn Cernunnos*. For you and Tias.' She stood and drifted over to the pack still by the door jamb. Eli felt a pang of guilt as he watched her; Ffion moved now with the breakable quality of mist, one swipe and she'd be gone. From inside the well-worn canvas bag his mother pulled out a small jar and a thin rectangular package wrapped in two large leaves. She placed both down on the table, pushing the small jar toward Eli. It was filled with what looked like liquid sunshine, thick and warm. He reached for it, the guilt intensifying. Honey was not a commodity in Porth Tymestl, as no one in the village saw a reason to keep hives. It either had to be bought – usually for an extortionate price – from the market towns, or else bartered from *Dyffryn Cernunnos*. Eli had only ever tasted it three times in his life, and savoured every one of them.

'*Diolch*.' He said quietly. He stowed the jar inside a pocket, and then reached for the package. The leaves it was wrapped in were rough, small spiky fronds of hair making the surface of them look insubstantial as the light fell across the table.

'For Tias.' Ffion said. Eli picked up the package, and tucked it safely in an inside pocket sewn into his cloak.

'I'll give it to him when I find him.' Eli said. Their words were as fine as spider silk, a thin and brittle bridge between the two of them. Aware that there was still a connection, a broach to some form of peace, but that it was easily broken. Eli turned to the door, suddenly desperate to get out of Roseate Cottage and put his worries under the sky, where they might feel smaller. Just as he was about to let the door close, he looked back into the small cottage, at his mother sitting at the table, small and weary.

She turned to him, and for a moment, it seemed like they were both about to speak. The apology that had worked its way up Eli's throat and was on the tip of his tongue died. The sea glinted in his peripheral vision, the soft winter air sharp and crisp in his lungs. He turned away, and closed the door softly behind him.

Part of him wondered if he'd find Abraxus down on *Tua'r Môr* Bay as he scaled the cliffside path. Eli refused to look too hard along the stretch of beach as he descended toward it, not wanting to know until his feet hit sand if he was alone there, or if the tall figure of Abraxus would break up the vista of sand, sea and sky. He gave himself a little mental shake at that; he wasn't here to find out more about Abraxus, nor the bones that were now beginning to litter the far end of the bay. Tias came first. And to that end, Eli strode off down the beach in the direction of their cavern. It was the most likely place he could think of where Tias might have secluded himself, and he would be lying if he said a part of him selfishly wanted to be by the sea for a while.

Abraxus wasn't on the beach. It was just Eli, alone under the sky, making tracks in the sand. High tide clearly wasn't far away, the beach beginning to be reduced to a sliver of sand nestled close to the steep cliffs above. In the distance, only the tops of the bones were visible over the water. Eli shivered; like this, they seemed more like teeth than ribs. He rounded part of the headland and then stopped, realising that as the tide came in, the cavern would slowly be filling with water. Usually, at a calm high tide, it would only lap over the shelf where they made fires. But during a storm, the tide could rage its way inside and almost drown the entire place. Neither Eli nor Tias had ever been inside the cavern during a high tide storm, and neither of them wanted to be. The high-water mark that was just below their bundle of driftwood told them the depth.

Eli pulled off his boots, socks and rolled his breeches up as high as they would go. He set his cloak under his boots, to ensure it didn't fly away down the beach, carried by the sea breeze. With that, he took a steadying breath and carried on walking. Around this curve in the headland lay the cavern, and with it the height of the tides changed. Soon, Eli was wading knee deep through frigid waters, gritting his teeth as his toes slowly went numb. He was glad the tide wasn't fully in yet, as he didn't have to resort to swimming before he reached the cavern. Tias wasn't in there. Eli cursed, and briefly considered lifting himself out of the water and onto the shelf, which was still above the waves. In the end, he decided that it was better to get back to the beach – now essentially a sandbar running the length of the cliffside – and carry on searching. Not only was his worry over Tias' absence growing, he also reasoned that a brisk walk back up the cliff path would warm his feet nicely. The current pulled deceptively at his ankles as Eli made his way back out of the cavern, trying to trip him and send him under. He resolutely half buried his feet into the sand with each step, not wanting to be any wetter or colder than he already was.

Eli kept his head down as he made his way through the village, not wanting to be stopped by anyone or be drawn into a time-consuming conversation. Thankfully, the cobbled streets were mostly empty. Eli could smell the smoke rising from the smokehouses along *Angorfa* Beach, and if he turned to face the open sea behind him, he knew that the cluster of sails and masts housed within the harbour walls would be gone. He slipped through a gap between the bakery and a cottage, turning sideways so as not to get his cloak caught on the rough stone of either wall. Had it only been less than three weeks ago when Eli had pulled Tias through this very same gap running from Thomas Gillet and his cronies? To Eli, it felt like another lifetime; one where his future in Porth Tymestl was secure, where there wasn't an impassable gap between himself and his mother. Where there weren't bones on the beach, nor a man who had mystery wrapped around him like a fog. Eli resolutely pushed the thoughts away, and carried on.

The paths up to the meadows that formed the natural border inland around Porth Tymestl were slick and wet. No one had thought to cobble these, since they didn't get much foot traffic anyway. They were devoid of cattle, the long grass drifting hither and thither in the wind. The low rush of it through the strands mimicked the waves breaking against the shore, far below on the beaches. Eli jumped the gate and stood for a moment, peering over the grass. It had grown even longer since he and Tias had taken refuge here, and now brushed his waist.

'Tias?' The name ran over the meadow, disappearing into the green-grey-blue of the strands. There was no reply. Eli started to head further into the field, calling for his brother intermittently. He wondered if he should just start talking, say he was sorry for it all in the hopes that Tias might hear him and appear from within the tangle of plant life. He decided against it, not wanting to cast his worries out into the open air where anyone might hear them. He just called for Tias again.

After nothing but the harsh chitter of a shearwater answered him, Eli left the meadow with its raucous call ringing in his ears. The low winter sun was beginning to make its way steadily toward the horizon now, the wind nipping more viciously at his cheeks and fingers. The fishing fleet was coming to harbour, and Eli could hear distant chatter emanating from *Angorfa* Beach. He vaguely wondered if it had been a good catch today. No one took any notice of him as he slipped quietly through the darkening streets.

Almost everyone was heading home, their beds and loved ones calling them in from the elements with promises of warmth and comfort. Eli spotted Aron and Thomas Gillet heading into their little cottage, Thomas' mother waiting on the doorstep. He ducked into the shadow of The Five-Pointed Compass, hoping that he remained unseen.

Eli didn't know where else to check. Cold, numb anxiety had dulled his senses and he stared off over the bay and out toward the sea. His back met stone and he realised that he had sunk to sit against the wall of the inn. A perfect square of golden light illuminated the ground just in front of his feet, shining out through one of The Five's small windows.

Eli felt his stomach cramp slightly, hunger making itself known. Both he and Tias had turned down Smythe's offer of a breakfast when they'd woken that morning at the inn. Neither of them had wanted to take more than they had to from the innkeeper, already having spent the night there and not to mention the countless quarter pints of ale that appeared by their elbows whenever they were in The Five-Pointed Compass. A chunk of stale bread and some smoked fish, however, was not enough to last a day. Eli gazed at the patch of light, and wondered if he had anything on him that would buy a small bowl of stew or soup. He knew that he should go home, that his mother would now be worried on his account as well as Tias', but he found himself unable to fully entertain the idea. It seemed as if a chill wind crept around Roseate Cottage, sneaking in through cracks and slipping under the door, freezing all life inside. The thought of the hollowness waiting for him there sent an involuntary shudder through Eli. He decided, resolutely, that he would not return home until he had Tias by his side.

However, another pressing issue was rapidly making itself known. Eli's stomach cramped again, and a wave of light-headedness rolled over him. Despite knowing he didn't have anything, Eli rummaged through the pockets of his trousers and cloak, searching for anything that might be traded in exchange for some food. All he came up with was the sliver of bone broken off one of the ribs, long forgotten in his trousers' pocket, the jar of honey and Tias' gift from their mother. Eli stared at the honey, tilting the jar this way and that, watching it languidly roll from one side to the other. It would be sweet and warming, and part of him wanted nothing more than to pull the lid off and gulp down the contents. But he knew it wouldn't fill him, not properly. Eli looked at the jar again, resignation settling over him. Honey would certainly be a good trade for a simple inn meal.

Standing up proved more effort than Eli would have liked. Night was truly sweeping over the coast now, the distant pinpricks of stars beginning to glimmer into life alongside the brighter, more robust flames of lanterns and candles. He peered in through the window, and was glad to find that The Five was having a quiet night. From what he could see, there were barely more than four other patrons dotted throughout the barroom. A sudden thought had him hastily heading toward the door; *Tias might be in here.* Eli knew that his brother liked the ambience of the inn, and that it gave him a place to sit quietly and think for a while. Perhaps he'd taken refuge there? The door swung open and Eli hurried inside. His hope was immediately dispelled. None of the people settled around the tables or at the bar were his brother. They all looked up, and upon recognising the newcomer, went back to studying their mugs of ale or indistinct conversations.

'Eli?' Smythe was staring directly at him, cloth and glass in his hands forgotten. Eli cast about, looking for something to say. The jar of honey was still clutched in his hand. He opened his mouth, ready to ask if Smythe would accept a trade for some food – he could smell a rich fish soup permeating the air – but the words dried up before he could utter them. 'Are you alright?' Smythe seemed openly concerned now, lifting the hatch and walking over to Eli from behind the bar.

'I can't find Tias,' Eli said helplessly. He felt a prickle of embarrassment as tears stung his eyes. The lanterns hanging from the ceiling seemed very interesting all of a sudden.

A gentle hand landed on Eli's shoulder. 'Come on, lad, over 'ere.' Smythe led Eli over to the bar, and got him settled on one of the high stools. 'I was lyin' when I said I didn't have any more of this.' A small cup of amber liquid was pushed into Eli's free hand. He recognised it as the brandy he'd always been asking for after Smythe had slipped him some at a celebration a year ago. 'What have you got there?' Smythe asked, leaning his elbows on the counter and gesturing to the jar of honey, partially concealed by Eli's fingers.

'Gift from Mam... s'honey.' Eli dropped the jar onto the counter.

'Ah, Ffion's back?'

'Hm.'

Smythe raised an eyebrow, but didn't push for any more answers. 'What brings you in here then? I thought I made it clear to both you and your brother that I didn't want to see neither hide nor hair of you both until some sense had managed to find a way in through those heads o' yours.'

Just for something to do, Eli picked up the cup and sipped at the brandy. It burned his throat, leaving a rich heat behind. When it was clear he couldn't avoid Smythe's question any longer, he set the cup down and measured what he could say next. What he ended up saying, in a strangled voice was, 'M'sorry.'

Smythe clearly hadn't been expecting that, he leaned even further over the bar toward Eli. 'Eli, what's – ?' He started.

'*I can't find Tias!*' Eli burst out. He ignored the other patrons around him looking over their drinks curiously. 'I can't find him and it's my fault he's gone and Mam came back and said we're *leaving* and I said some horrible things and – and–' He broke off, angrily scrubbing at the tears he felt beginning to drip down his face.

'Alright, Elias. Alright.' Smythe gently reached out and pulled Eli's hands away from his face. His voice was calm and smooth. 'Drink that, I'll be right back.' He pushed the cup back into Eli's hands and came back around the bar, heading over to the hearth. Eli shakily drained the contents of the cup. A bowl of thick creamy soup was placed before him, alongside a slice of buttered bread. 'Eat, no one can think straight on an empty stomach.'

'I don't have anything to pay–'

'None of that. *Eat.*' Smythe said sternly. He watched as Eli dipped his spoon into the soup. It tasted heavenly, and it was all Eli could do not to lift the bowl and drink it down in one. He forced himself to tear a small chunk off the bread. Smythe didn't say anything until both bread and soup were gone. Eli let him clear away the bowl and then slumped forward onto the bar. Tiredness pulled at him suddenly, bone deep and weary.

'Tell me what happened.' Smythe said, bringing a glass of water over to Eli. 'From the beginning.'

Eli had been a deckhand on a fishing ship. He'd been in countless fights. He'd climbed part of the cliff-face once just to prove to Tias he could do it. He'd swum in the freezing waters of the Irish Sea, coming home dripping, shivering and grinning. But Eli didn't think he'd ever felt as tired as this. It wasn't the type of tired that he knew would be fixed by a good night's sleep, nor a day lounging in the sun by the water's edge. This was the kind of tiredness that resided *within*, not physical but in the very fabric of his being, and Eli didn't really know how to fix it. But talking to Smythe had helped.

'I should apologise, shouldn't I?' He said.

'Yes,' Smythe replied, 'I understand your hurt lad, but some things are better left unsaid, knowing that if they are voiced, it'll only cause pain.'

'I know.' Eli traced the grain of the wooden bar with a finger. 'I just wanted to... oh, I don't know.'

'You wanted to hurt her the way she hurt you,' Smythe said quietly.

'Aye.' Silence fell between them again. 'I think I'll go home now.' Eli said, a little listlessly. Part of him wanted Smythe to say he could stay the night at The Five again, so he wouldn't have to face home.

Smythe didn't, instead straightening himself up with a slight groan.

'I think that would be wise,' he said. 'I'll be back in a moment, it's getting rough out there again and I don't currently trust you to walk home alone without bein' swept off on some hairbrained adventure.'

Eli managed a wan smile at that, and watched as Smythe disappeared into the cellar.

The jar of honey still sat on the bar, Smythe having resolutely refused to accept it as payment in return for the drink and meal. Eli picked it up and weighed it in his hand. His eyes drifted to the staircase, slightly concealed by the shadows. After the briefest moment of indecision, Eli glanced over the bar toward the hatch, and, seeing that Smythe wasn't on his way back up, slipped off his seat and up the stairs.

It wasn't difficult to find which room belonged to Abraxus. All of them were locked, of course, but Eli knew exactly how to shove against the door and lift the latch at the same time to open it. He muttered a quick thanks to Smythe himself for showing him that trick all those years ago. Tias and Eli had been involved in a game of Seek, and Tias had managed to lock himself in one of the rooms. Eli had fetched the innkeeper when Tias' voice had become panicky, and Smythe had shown Eli how to get into the rooms without the aid of a key. He wondered slightly guiltily if Smythe had this in mind when he'd imparted that wisdom to Eli. Probably not.

Abraxus' room was the last one on the left, facing the coast. It looked like all the other rooms at The Five-Pointed Compass; a single cot, a small writing desk and rickety chair, and a chest for clothes. A small sprig of sea heather sat in a glass vase in the windowsill. Eli lit the taper on the desk and looked around. He knew he didn't have much time, but he could feel his curiosity getting the better of him.

The room was littered with strange items. The staff Abraxus had been carrying leant in a corner, the strings of sea glass and shells making a soft clinking noise as they were stirred by his presence. Up close, Eli could see carvings running along its smooth surface, curling down the staff. The indents were stained with a light blue dye, making the patterns and symbols stand out against the almost white wood. His fingers itched to pick it up, but something kept him away. He knew, instinctively, this wasn't his – wasn't *his place* – to touch.

Eli placed the jar atop the writing desk, next to the lit candle. Perhaps a peace offering, perhaps a jest, perhaps an attempt at some connection, Eli wasn't sure. He grinned in spite of himself when he remembered Abraxus' last name. Alright, perhaps more of a jest than anything else. Eli was heading for the door, when something copper glinted in his peripheral vision. Lying on the cot, half buried in a tangle of blankets, lay something that looked like a crown. Frozen for a moment in indecision, Eli listened at the door in case Smythe had returned from the cellar and was looking for him. Nothing. He crept over to the cot, and pulled away the blankets.

Up close, Eli could see that whatever it was, it wasn't ornate enough to be a crown, it was more like a circlet. Made of many strands of copper wire curled and spun together, it seemed to be meant for atop the head. What was strange, however, was that instead of a single closed loop of metal, it was an open horseshoe shape. One side was clearly meant to be hooked around and over the top of the ear, but the other protruded further. Eli turned it in his hands for a moment, and then slipped it over his head. Sure enough, one side settled over his ear, the metal biting slightly into the joint of his jaw. The other curling frond of copper, however, extended over his cheekbone and under his left eye. It followed the lower curve of his eye socket, the wire here split apart slightly leaving a gap, as if something was meant to be slotted into it over the eye. Eli wondered if it were for a type of eyeglass that Abraxus needed, although he couldn't see anything that resembled a crystal lens nor glass in the room.

The sound of the door to The Five opening and closing had him pulling off the circlet, cursing as it got momentarily stuck in his tangle of curls. Eli hastily tucked it back into its nest of blankets, snuffed the candle and left the room, pulling the door closed firmly behind him, hearing the lock click back into place.

Gifts.
December, 1815.
Abraxus.

The other boy – *Eli*, he reminded himself – was waiting at The Five-Pointed Compass, dithering beside the bar. There was a strangely furtive look about him, Abraxus thought mildly as he and Tias entered, but it vanished from his face the moment he saw his brother. Eli hurried over toward them, ignoring Abraxus entirely. 'Where have you *been*?' He said, relief in his face but hints of anxiety and anger in his voice.

Tias shrugged and pointed to Abraxus by way of answer. He clearly still wasn't ready to talk with his brother.

Abraxus moved away and toward the bar, where Smythe was just shutting the hatch down to the cellar, giving the boys some space. Smythe glanced over to the door. 'Ah, good. I was just about to put together a search party.' Abraxus couldn't tell if he were joking. 'Has he been with you all this time?'

'Aye.' Abraxus sat down at the bar, glad that it was mostly empty. Those who still lingered there stared at him unabashedly. Both he and Smythe watched from the corners of their eyes as Tias and Eli spoke. It seemed to be a heated conversation, albeit in hushed tones. Abraxus watched Tias gesture wildly, ending it with a firm prod to Eli's chest.

Smythe winced slightly, and then moved away to get Abraxus a drink. 'Anything to eat?' He called from the taps.

'No, thank you.' Abraxus turned his back fully to the brothers and turned his attention instead to the pint of mead Smythe had just pulled for him. 'In the cellar?' He asked, taking a sip.

'Fetching some more candles, I've run out up here.' Smythe

said evasively.

Abraxus raised an eyebrow questioningly, 'Down there with him in here?' He tilted his head in Eli's direction.

'He didn't follow, *peidiwch â phoeni.' Do not worry.* Smythe waved him off, changing the topic. 'Anyway, where have *you* been with Tias?'

Abraxus debated being annoyingly evasive just to give Smythe a taste of his own medicine but decided against it. 'Found him in the meadows. Practically tripped over the boy.' He went on to tell the innkeeper that after Eli had given up searching in the fields, he and the boy had gone on to walk around the inland edge of the village. Abraxus had found himself begrudgingly impressed with Tias' level of knowledge about the various flora and fauna of the area. He'd even asked the boy a few questions regarding tide times and how the weather generally was in the little fishing village. Naturally, Tias had seen right through the shoddy attempt at casual questions and had immediately asked if this was to do with the bones on the beach. Abraxus broke off at this point, catching Smythe's smirk. 'Boy is too clever for his own good,' he said gruffly, raising his mug to his lips again.

Tias and Eli seemed to have finished arguing. Abraxus could no longer hear the hiss of words behind him. His eyes flickered in the direction of the pair, and Smythe, noticing his interest, murmured, 'I think they've both said their piece.'

'Do they fight often like this?' Abraxus asked, and then cursed himself when Smythe looked sharply at him.

'Interested, are you?'

'No.'

Smythe had to obviously hold himself back from rolling his eyes, and instead answered, 'No, not like this. They bicker and rag each other, but so do all siblings. This... this is something new.' Smythe bit his lip, looking over Abraxus' shoulder at the boys. 'They'll be alright,' he said eventually, sounding as if he wanted to convince himself more than anyone.

Abraxus was finishing the last of his mead when he felt a

small tap on his shoulder. He turned in his seat and came face to face with Tias.

'Thanks,' he muttered, 'for keeping me company and all.' He reached inside his pocket and pulled out the grass braid Abraxus had made. 'You can have this back now.'

'Keep it.' Abraxus said, 'I have no use for it.'

Tias stowed it carefully away again. Abraxus spotted the edge of a small notebook in his other pocket, the binding a soft green with yellow marbling running through it. Tias absentmindedly touched the pages, then nodded at Abraxus and Smythe and headed over to the door where Eli was waiting for him. They left, the winter air fighting its way inside before it was cut off and once more banished into the night.

Silence lay gently against the timber and stone of The Five-Pointed Compass, broken only by the wind battering lightly against the windows. Once again, Abraxus found it was only himself and Smythe remaining in the barroom. He drained the rest of his mead, placing the mug down against the bar. He had intended to seek out the relative comfort of his room, perhaps try and get a full night's sleep. Since arriving on the shore, he had noticeably missed the creak and snap of his ship's canvas and rope, drawing him down into dreams each night. Instead, Abraxus found himself motioning toward Smythe, catching the innkeeper's attention. 'Those boys... they are the Kincarrans, yes?'

'Aye. The Kincarrans have always had their roots in Porth Tymestl. Roseate Cottage has been passed down father to son, mother to daughter for as long as the church books go back.' Smythe looked at Abraxus for a moment. 'Why d'you ask?'

'There is a new grave in the church yard. John Maredudd Kincarran.'

Smythe stilled for a moment.

Abraxus wondered if he should have bit his tongue and just gone to bed. 'A friend of yours?' He asked eventually.

'John was a friend to everyone in this village,' Smythe said, voice taut with emotion. 'Even to the really prickly men like Aron. It's odd, ain't it? How one person can feel so... *alive,* and the next moment, they're just gone. I always thought I'd see John live out the rest of his days, leavin' the fishing behind and pass the *Dawnsiwr y Wawr* onto Eli or Tias.' Smythe shrugged slightly, casting his eyes down to the bar.

'The *Dawnsiwr y Wawr*?' Abraxus asked.

'The Dawn Dancer. John's ship and his pride an' joy. After his boys, of course.' Smythe added. 'She was a beauty, red sails, two masts, Brixham trawler build. You'd have liked her.'

'Can I ask..?'

'What happened? Yes, I suppose you can. Not a happy ending sort of story though, I warn you.' Smythe took a breath and thought for a moment. 'The grave in the churchyard is empty, did you know that? There's a coffin under there, but all that's in it is John's coat and pair of boots. Never found any body, an' I think that's what made it so tough on all of them. No closure. Nothing *to* bury, save memories. John's ship was strong, and John was an even stronger captain at the helm. But even the best seaman can underestimate the water. John went out alone. His true reasonin' why I never knew, no-one does, but I guess it was to feel completely alone and liberated under that big sky. And I think he also liked the idea of a challenge. Ever since his mentor, Cynfor Morgan, sailed through Finfolk Point, he'd been desperate to try it 'imself. That was October fourth. Two days later, Eli comes across splinters of a wreck down the far end of *Tua'r Môr* Bay. Poor lad didn't even know it was his Da's ship 'til he finds a scrap of red sail and part of the ship's nameplate. Tias found him hours later, sittin' and shivering by the tidepools, clutching those bits of wreck.

Tias keeps himself together long enough to run back up 'ere, back to The Five, and say they've found John's ship. We'd all been wondering when he'd make port again, but none of us were too worried. Like I said, he was an able seaman. His crew head down to the Bay, Tias stayin' with me. One of them must have gone to get Ffion, she's down here sharp as you like. She leaves too, and that's when it must have all hit Tias; he sits down on the floor by the bar and cries. I just sit with him. There ain't no easy way to tell a boy his Da isn't coming home.

Eli is brought back up with Medwyn. The rest still combing the Bay for any sign of John. But I knew, and think so did those boys, that nothing would be found. Medwyn's wife, Efa, and Cynfor come back up the street leading Ffion. Efa takes her inside, and even through thick walls and across the street, I heard Ffion scream. Went right through me, like a wounded animal it was. The only other time I heard her make a sound like that was after the funeral, standing at the cliff's edge and callin' out onto the winds. Tias and Eli are just holding onto each other, Eli still staring at nothing and shaking. My inn has seen a lot of things, Abraxus. Fights, singing, celebrations, meetings. But never, not once, have I seen such sorrow within these walls. It was like tar, it clung to everything and dripped. Three days later, the surviving Kincarrans buried an almost empty coffin, and John was left to the sea. He loved it in life, but now it was to be his final bed. I hope the current treats him kindly. He deserves no less.'

Smythe's telling left him feeling cold. It was almost as if he were deep down below, alongside John Kincarran. The brine clung to his skin and forced its way down his throat. Abraxus knew that the sea was treacherous, he knew that people and ships upon it were merely the playthings of nature. But he also understood the marrow deep call of the waves, of the cormorant and the kittiwake's shriek. John might have been foolhardy to go out alone with naught between himself and the water but his ship, but Abraxus understood *why*.

The little hallway to his room was chilly, a draught blowing in from the small window at the end. It opened onto nothing but black. Distantly, Abraxus could hear the murmur of the sea as it shifted ceaselessly in its sleep. His door creaked slightly as he pushed it open and closed it again, shutting out the cold. Immediately, he knew something was out of place. Where before the room had only held marks of him and his passing, there was now the subtle presence of another. Abraxus recalled the furtive look on Eli's face before he'd caught sight of his brother at Abraxus' side, and shook his head. Of course. He'd have done better to ask about the boys, rather than raise old ghosts with Smythe that evening. Nothing seemed to be missing; his staff still stood sentinel in the corner, the circlet upon his bed. At first the only thing Abraxus could spot that had been changed was that the candle on the desk was a little shorter than it had been before he left. And then he saw the jar.

An incredulous laugh filled the little room for a moment, and in one swift movement he reached out and swept the jar into his hand. Abraxus turned it over in his fingers, admiring the way the candlelight reflected in the liquid gold held inside. Honey was something that he didn't tend to carry with him, only rarely picking some up if he was making a port stop. Abraxus pulled the lid off the jar and dipped two fingers into the honey, scooping some out. It was delightfully sweet and sticky, coating his tongue and lips in the taste of lush meadows and summer. He knew on some level that he should be annoyed, if not angry, that Eli had essentially broken into his room, but all Abraxus could summon up was begrudging amusement and exasperation. Eli Kincarran certainly knew how to not give up.

Realisation began to wash over Abraxus' thoughts. He went over to the little casement, opening the window and letting the sea night air drift in. The charms and talismans woven into the threads on his staff shifted, making a soft musical chime. Setting down the jar in the windowsill, Abraxus leaned against the wall, gazing out into the night. The image of the coastal path came unbidden into his mind, one path diverting into two. He felt as if he stood at that divide once more, weighing up his options, casting logic against emotion. Continue alone, walk the wild paths belonging to the cliffs with nothing but his thoughts for company? Or turn around, and head back towards the village and its people? Abraxus closed his eyes as his decision was made unconsciously for him. Part of Smythe's story drifted to the forefront of his mind. Abraxus fancied he could almost hear the grief-stricken cry, let loose to the wind and waves. Whether he liked it or not, the boys, *Eli and Tias*, were wrapped up in this now.

Glancing back over his room, Abraxus noticed what he had missed the first time. The circlet, whilst still here, had definitely been moved. Picking it up, he noticed that the metal that was shaped to slip neatly over his head had been ever so slightly bent, as if someone else had tried it on. He adjusted it unthinkingly, looking back out of the window again. He wondered if Eli had figured out what it was for. Unlikely, as the stone was still in his pocket. Abraxus brushed his fingers against the slightly raised edges of leather, feeling the familiar rounded shape. Perhaps that was where to start? Tias had proved himself to be quick witted, and Eli was more curious than a seal pup. Abraxus found a small smile playing at the edges of his lips. Yes, this way he could continue to work undistracted, whilst sating the boys' need for answers. And if they caught up and understood what he was doing here, well then... just because the wild coastal paths called him and him alone, it didn't mean that they couldn't be desolately lonely.

He had expected to feel more resistance to this. Smythe would call him 'set in his ways', and Abraxus couldn't really blame him. But there was something that felt undeniably right about this, some *pull* from within that he didn't fully understand, nor had much desire to examine closely. *At least it might get the damnable innkeeper off my back for a while*, he thought wryly. Moving with a new purpose, Abraxus hurried around the room collecting various things he might need for this impromptu nightly excursion. The circlet he clasped back onto his belt, making a mental note to not leave it lying around where curious fingers might bend it out of shape again. He stopped for a moment as he picked up his staff, feeling the weight of it and letting his fingers play gently against the hand-worn wood. Then Abraxus gripped it tightly, and slung it across his shoulders, hooking the 'C' curve around the back of his neck and draping his arms across the ends protruding over his shoulders. The candle flame guttered as he passed, and went out entirely as the door swung closed.

Smythe was nowhere to be seen in the barroom, either having retired to bed or sequestered himself once more in the cellar. The night outside was substantially less wild than the previous one, although the edges of the storm still hung in the sky's memory, threatening more rain. The way to *Tua'r Môr* Bay was becoming familiar to Abraxus, and he found that his feet took him most of the way whilst his eyes were trained on the skies above, hoping to catch a glimpse of the stars. Once he reached the sand, he kicked off his boots and stowed them by the path's end. He didn't have a lantern, nor a candle. Despite the inky black that swirled around him, Abraxus knew what he was looking for, and didn't rely on sight to find it. He strode off toward the breakwater, a true smile crossing his face as he felt the cold waters lap against his feet.

After taking a moment to let the water flow around him, Abraxus began to walk slowly through the surf, clenching his toes slightly with every step, in order to feel the sand and stones below him. He had unhooked his staff, and was probing the ground with it as he walked. It wasn't long before he found one. As the point of his staff touched the rock, he felt a soft thrill running through it and into his hand. With the precision of a spear fisher, he thrust the staff into the water, and guided the stone onto the point. Gently, as so not to lose his prize, Abraxus brought the staff up and out of the waves, tilting it horizontally. A stone with a hole smoothed through the middle of it hung, dripping. It was a dark slate grey that Abraxus knew would dry into a softer cloud colour. The hole was a near perfect circle, eroded and sculpted by time and tide. He flicked it from his staff and up, snatching it from the air and turning it over in his fingers. Abraxus grinned, it was perfect.

His bare feet made a slightly unpleasant, wet slapping sound as he crossed the barroom. It was past midnight now, and the edges of Abraxus' thoughts were muzzy and hard to catch. In one hand he held his boots, having not bothered to put them back on once he left the Bay, and in the other was his staff. The new stone clicked against his old one in his pocket. He had just reached the stairs when Smythe's voice stopped him. 'You had better be on your way for a cloth to clean that up.'

Abraxus turned sheepishly and looked at the prints of water and sand he'd left behind on the floor. Smythe was standing behind the bar; Abraxus could just see the top of the cellar hatch open over the counter. Dropping his boots and placing his staff down, Abraxus crossed over the bar and grabbed the rag that Smythe used to clean glasses. He dropped it onto the floor, and using his foot rather than bending down, ran it over the stone.

'For the love of–' Smythe snatched the cloth from Abraxus as he held it out to the innkeeper. 'I would hate to see what sort of state your ship is in.'

'She is in excellent condition, thank you,' Abraxus said a little haughtily. This was precisely the reason Abraxus *hadn't* invited Smythe down to his ship since he arrived. She was in excellent condition... if you were Abraxus.

'Where were you?'

'*Tua'r Môr* Bay. Collecting.' Abraxus reached into his pocket and pulled out the new grey stone and his ivory white one. Smythe looked up at him sharply.

'Are you–?'

'Aye.' Abraxus sighed, 'I really do not think they will leave me alone. This is, of course, entirely your fault. So, I would rather have them close by so they can stay *out* of trouble rather than just wandering blindly into it.' Abraxus scowled as Smythe broke into a broad smile. 'Oh, do not *gloat,* Stooger, it is most unbecoming of you.'

'I ain't gloating,' Smythe said, still smiling. 'When are you going to tell them everything?'

'I am not.' Smythe seemed confused at Abraxus' words. He elaborated. 'I am going to let them piece it together, and see how far they can get. With a little aid from myself, and yourself naturally. I imagine Tias would like the riddle.'

'Ah, there's that infuriatin' penchant for mystery,' Smythe said. 'But I understand you. How are you going to let them know that they are now a part of this though?'

Abraxus reached into his other pocket and pulled out the now empty jar of honey. He'd given into temptation and eaten the rest of it on the way back up from the Bay. 'Eli left me... a gift, I think. Or at least, I took it as such.'

'That wily little so'n'so! That's the last time I teach him how to open doors he has no business goin' through.'

Abraxus chuckled, 'I did say, did I not, that this is all your own fault?'

'Yes, yes. Now, what about it?' Smythe said, gesturing to the jar.

The next morning, as Smythe was unlocking the door to The Five, and Abraxus was swinging his legs out of bed and glancing to the window, two figures careened into the barroom. Abraxus couldn't help but smile a little at the barrage of questions Eli and Tias were firing at the innkeeper, words muffled through the floorboards. It seemed that the empty jar of honey, left alongside the slate grey stone on the doorstep of Roseate Cottage had done the trick. He got dressed quickly and headed downstairs, staff in hand. Eli and Tias fell silent as they saw him, faces eager and alight.

'Find your own path,' Abraxus said. 'But when you do, come and see.'

XIII
then.

Red Sails at Dawn.

'We can't wait much longer, the day's wasting!'

'They'll be here, don't worry.' John stared over the rail of the *Dawnsiwr y Wawr* toward the harbour wall. Already, it was lined with people, throwing provisions, nets, oars or just well-wishes down to the ships docked below. The tide glittered as it rolled onto the sands of *Angorfa* Beach, a crystal-clear azure today. Far out, beyond the shelter of the harbour, the blue deepened into turquoise and cobalt. Darker shades beneath the surface demarcated the shifting tangles of kelp, a forest beneath the waves. Although the sun had only just summited the cliffs, the day was already hot. Wisps of clouds hung in the sky, moving lazily at the whim of the breeze. The gathered red sails of *Dawnsiwr y Wawr* stirred and rippled, eager to take them over the sea and away. The crew were getting a little restless, albeit still in good spirits. They lounged against the masts, or else sat cheerfully on the rails, talking and letting their legs dangle over the edge. All was ready to make sail, and all members of the crew were accounted for, but two.

John supposed it was his own fault really; they had spent the night down on *Tua'r Môr* Bay, building a bonfire and letting its sparks join the riot of distant gems in the night sky. Much to his sons' delight, John had spent most of the evening telling tall tales of the sea and various half remembered myths stitched together roughly with boat twine and a leaping imagination.

Tias had kept trying to correct him, but Eli had helped further the patchwork of stories by bringing in his own ideas. Ffion had laid back on a blanket they'd brought down from the cottage, watching their antics with a smile and half lidded eyes. At one point, John had swept up Tias onto his shoulders, telling a mangled version of Icarus. Eli had broken in and said that after the winged boy fell into the sea, he had become a selkie. John had dropped Tias into the soft sand, and then threw his younger son over his shoulder and proceeded to wade into the sea. Eli alternated between laughing and thumping his father on the back to try and release him before the inevitable dunking.

The night had still been warm as the moon rode high overhead, Eli and Tias succumbing to sleep on the blanket; Tias curled up facing the fire and Eli flat on his back, head pillowed on his arms behind his neck. John and Ffion had sat quietly intertwined together and watched the fire burn low. With a soft kiss Ffion had murmured that they should probably get home and get some proper sleep before tomorrow. John had agreed, a little reluctant to leave the gentle night behind and put a door and walls between himself and it, but nonetheless had set about waking his sons. Eli and Tias were still half asleep as they made their way back up the cliff path, stumbling into one another and being steadied by their father's hand or mother's arm. They had both collapsed into bed, neither of them bothering to even change into their night clothes or wash the sand from their hair.

John had been up with the dawn, heading down with the rest of the fishers of Porth Tymestl to *Angorfa* Beach and the harbour. He had decided against waking his sons, as most of the preparation could be done more quickly without them. Eli and Tias had, of course, grown up with the sea as a constant companion, and both knew their way around the smaller skiffs that ranged the harbour. But this was something relatively new to them; the *Dawnsiwr y Wawr* was a much larger ship, and it needed a full complement of crew members to make her ready for the day. John had been ecstatic when Ffion had said that she thought the twins were ready to begin learning under their father, especially on the ship that he had hoped one of them or both might inherit. John and Ffion had decided to break the news to their sons on their eleventh birthday; Eli had taken off around the cottage in several excited laps, whilst Tias had bombarded his father with questions about what he might need, what conditions to look for, could he bring his notebook *ad infinitum*. And of course – and he really shouldn't have expected anything different – both of them were late. On their first day as ship's boys. John couldn't help quirk a fond smile at that.

Sunlight fell in shafts through Roseate Cottage, catching dust motes dancing in the air. The front door was flung open, letting the deep summer's breeze tumble through the cottage. The double bed near the hearthside was empty and neatly made up. Up on the balcony, Eli and Tias slept peacefully, letting the scents of grass and sea salt and earth pull them away into green tinged dreams. Eli snuffled slightly into his pillow and rolled over, pulling the blankets up and over his ears. Tias stirred, a beam of sunlight playing over his face, tugging at the edges of his consciousness. Cracking his eyes open, he stared contently at the beamed ceiling for a moment, listening to the birds call outside. Reaching up, he ruffled his hair, sending grains of sand flying from it and over his pillow. He chuckled slightly, brushing them away and onto the floor. Tias looked over at his brother, who's coppery hair was the only part of him visible, sticking up in curls and cowlicks all over his head. Rolling onto his back, Tias let himself drift for a moment on the cusp of sleep. There was something else though… not the annoying itch of sand in his sheets, but something he was forgetting.

'Eli, we're *late*!' Tias sat bolt upright in bed and flung the covers off.

'What?' Eli lifted himself up on an elbow, craning his neck to see Tias.

'We're late!' Tias repeated pulling on his shirt. 'For Da, remember?'

Eli's eyes widened and he also sprang out of bed, his foot tangling in the sheets as he did so and went down with a clatter. Tias momentarily forgot his rush in order to laugh at his brother, who was now trying to free his ankle.

'Are you two alright up there?' Ffion's voice drifted in from the open door. 'I heard a crash?'

'We're fine, Mam!' Eli called back, succeeding in disentangling himself. 'Tias, *shut up*.' Tias managed to pull himself together and threw Eli's boots at him.

'You're both late, you know,' Ffion said, as her sons came racing down the ladder, both jumping the last two rungs, and toward the table. 'Here, you'd better eat this as you go.' She handed them a thick slice of the morning's bread, jam spread liberally on top.

'Thanks Mam, come *on* Eli!' Tias grabbed Eli's wrist and all but dragged him to the door. Eli had been trying to pilfer another slice of bread off the table.

'Be careful, and listen to your father!' Ffion called after them, shaking her head as they rounded the bend and disappeared from view.

The streets were a hub of chatter; a bright haze of cheerfulness hanging over those who lingered there. Eli waved with jam-stained fingers to Stooger Smythe, who raised a hand back in answer. As they reached the main street, *Angorfa* Beach and the harbour came into view below them. The only sails remaining in the shelter of the wall were a bright, fiery red. 'Da's waited for us, see we didn't need to rush!' Eli said.

'But if he's the last one left, they might be going soon anyway,' Tias said worriedly.

Eli studied his brother's face for a moment. 'Alright, let's be quick then.' He crammed the rest of his bread and jam into his mouth, chewing thickly. 'C'mon.' And then Eli set off at a flat sprint down the cobbled streets. Tias stared after him for a moment, and then began to run too, grinning. He caught up, and together they hared down the street, leaping over the little rain gutters and once over a basket left in the road by its carrier. The harbour wall grew closer and closer, as did the red sails.

Eli could see the figures on the ship's deck heaving on rope and loosening the sails. He ran faster, reaching out and pulling Tias with him. 'Wait!' He yelled. Several good natured cheers went up at the sight of them, but then Eli noticed that with the sails down, the *Dawnsiwr y Wawr* had already begun its slow exit from calm waters into the wild open sea. He narrowed his eyes in determination, and bounded onto the harbour wall. Those who still lined jumped back and out of their way, reprimands mingling in with laughed encouragement.

'Eli, wait, what're you—' Tias started as the end of the harbour wall was rapidly coming closer. The *Dawnsiwr y Wawr* had just drawn level with the edge of the wall, and, not really thinking about what he was about to do, Eli leapt from the wall, dragging Tias with him. He heard Tias yell something, but it was lost to the few seconds of freefall and the exhilaration as the sea wind whipped through his shirt and hair. In reality, the jump wasn't all too far, the harbour walls being relatively low set into the water. But in that moment, Eli was convinced he was flying. Both of them hit the deck, scrabbling to stay on their feet. They were met with yells, whistles and a ripple of relieved laughter from the crew of their Da's ship.

'See, I told you all they'd be here!' John's voice roared from the rudder, eyes alight with amusement and pride. Eli and Tias ran up toward him, and he reached over and ruffled Tias' hair. 'Maybe don't tell your Mam about that, eh?' He said quietly to them, winking. He straightened then, and began to call orders down to the waiting crew. 'That means you two as well, off you go! And I want those knots tight, Eli!'

John tilted his head up and closed his eyes for a moment,

letting the sun warm his face. He felt the jolt in the ship's prow as they hit the open waters. He let his body roll with the motion of the waves, and tasted salt spray on his lips. 'Let's see what she can do!' He shouted, and was met with a roar of approval. John turned the sails toward the horizon and watched as Eli and Tias melded into the crew as if they'd always been there.

Red Sails in the Mist.

Everything was quiet, the world held still by the mist that pressed in from all sides. It was neither creeping nor insidious, but merely there. Hanging gently over the land and sea. Eli's lantern did little to penetrate its pearlescence. Despite it being early afternoon, his mother had insisted that he take one with him. As he peered through the mist, Porth Tymestl seemed to remake itself around him; once familiar shapes and outlines of buildings were brand new. He felt as if he were walking through a strange new land, made up of shades and spectres. His feet, however, never led him wrong and soon the slick cobbles gave way to rough path and, finally, to sand.

Tua'r Môr Bay was similarly shrouded. The mist blew in from the sea, the rolling foam bringing with it something more insubstantial. Eli shivered and huddled down into his cloak. His hair hung in limp curls against his face, the mist having soaked it through without him realising. Raising the lantern a little higher, as if that would help burn the mist away, Eli headed off down the beach listening to the unseen waves and cries of the seabirds. Even in the cavern the fog hung, curling into swirls and wisps in the point of the ceiling and drifting up from the sand, disturbed, as Eli entered. In movements that were more unconscious memory than active choice, Eli pulled down the driftwood net and built a fire. He wondered if the light from it might spill out from the slash-like entrance and shine out to sea. Perhaps his Da might see it and use it to guide him home?

For a while, Eli merely sat and stared out into the nothingness that billowed beyond the cavern. His wandering mind constructed a land far away and unknown to people, which he painted onto that stretching canvas before him. Unknown to him, the sun reached its zenith and moved on. The days were steadily shortening, late autumn beginning to shift almost unnoticeably but irrevocably into winter. It was the chill that finally got him to move. Flexing numb fingers and toes, Eli left the fire to burn out and walked out into the grey world. He'd forgotten the lantern.

At the farthest end of *Tua'r Môr* Bay, the sands ended and the rocks began. Chunks of the cliffside that had tumbled down and shattered created a series of connecting tidepools that flooded and dried with each high and low tide. They gradually ascended in steepness, until they reached the cliff face, which reared, black and impassable, bookending the bay. Eli clambered over the rocks, wincing slightly as the sharp limpets cut and grazed his hands. He had no particular destination in mind, but was just content to wander aimlessly for a while. Eventually he came to one of the larger tidepools – one that stayed filled with briny water even when the tide retreated. It was a good place to swim in the summer, the pool catching the sunlight and heating the water slightly warmer than the surrounding sea. Its emerald depths looked inviting even now, in the bleak fetches of October. For a moment, Eli was tempted to discard his clothes and dive, but shook the idea away. Sitting by its waters, it seemed to be the last true place of colour in the world. An oasis in the white that clung so persistently to the air.

Something bumped quietly against the rock. Eli looked down, and saw a length of wood rhythmically tapping against the edge of the pool, carried by the gentle lap of the tide. Sliding down the damp rock, Eli came to the edge of the pool and reached into its waters, scooping out the wood. At first, he was merely going to stow it somewhere higher up on the beach, let it dry out to add to their collection of driftwood in the cavern. But then he noticed that unlike most pieces of driftwood, this length wasn't bleached white by the salt, nor stripped of its bark in tatters. In fact, the wood was smooth and a deep brown that spoke of hands smoothing and treating the surface. Eli turned it over in his hands, noticing a slight curve to it. A shiver ran through him alongside the realisation. This was wreck-wood.

Eli stood and began to pick his way around the tidepool toward the muted sound of the waves. It was unlikely that a full wreck would have washed up on the shoreline, but it was the least he could do to check. One unspoken rule in Porth Tymestl, one Eli didn't even remember learning it was so ingrained into their community; if you find wreck-wood, search the shoreline, there may be people who need help. The sound of the sea became louder as he walked, until the breakwater lapped at the toes of his boots. The mist made it nearly impossible to see anything more than a few steps away, but Eli reasoned that if there was a wreck, it would loom darker and more solid through the shifting fog. He traced back to the cliff edge, intending to start from one end and do a full length of the bay. It turned out he didn't even have to make it all the way back to the cliff-face.

It wasn't a full wreck. The sea overwhelmed the boat, and it was merely splinters. Nothing remained but the skeleton of the ship, futtocks snapped, and a single mast sheared in half. Eli stopped, staring at it. He occasionally forgot how cruel the sea could be; *not a good way to think for a sailor* a voice whispered in his mind. He began to walk over to the wreck, cautiously. It was unlikely there were any survivors waiting for aid here. Eli tripped, and managed to catch himself, stumbling, before he could be sent down into the shallow water that now washed over his boots. Looking down, he saw that he'd tripped on a piece of wood protruding from the sand upwards. Like the rest, it was splintered and ragged. Eli reached down and pulled it from the sand, using the cuff of his shirt to wipe away the grains that still clung there. There was lettering on half of the length, the rest missing where the wood had snapped. *Dawn–*

There could be a number of ships with 'dawn' in their name. It meant nothing. Deep within his chest, Eli's heart began to pound. He looked up at the wreck, and began walking toward it again. His feet stumbled over the sand, although there was nothing catching underfoot. He reached one of the shattered futtocks, placing a hand against it. Something drifted in the water in his peripheral vision. Everything seemed very far away and quiet as he bent down and plucked it from the water. The canvas was waterlogged, the edges fraying. The red colour of a sunrise had darkened into a shade darker than wine. Eli clutched it in his fist, the water dripping in between his fingers and back into the sea.

The mist pressed in from all sides. He couldn't see. Everything was white; the sound of the waves transformed into a dull roaring in his head. The world blurred, refracted, broke apart and cleared. Again and again. Eli didn't know if it was salt water on his face or tears. This wasn't right. It *wasn't*. This wouldn't happen to him, to his family. Blank refusal numbed his mind and it seemed as if the mist swirling about his head had suddenly whited out his thoughts. Eli found himself sitting. Still clutching the fragmented name of his Da's ship and the piece of torn sail to him. The chill water washed over him, but Eli didn't notice where he stopped and the cold began. Overhead, a single call of a gull, pinwheeling through a sky he could not see.

part two

the open seas

I

now.

Steam.
December, 1815.
Tias.

The door opened and closed quietly before Tias had even got his shirt on. He looked over at his brother's bed, unmade and probably still holding some heat within the blankets. He sighed, and pulled another jumper on, trying to eliminate some of the chill that pervaded the cottage. Eli had been out every day since Abraxus' words a few weeks ago. Tias had kept his distance for a while, the gentle simmerings of anger and hurt still raw from their argument. He had mainly stayed inside, sitting hunched over their battered little writing desk and feverishly filling the pages of the new notebook his mother had brought back from the forest vale with her.

The weather had deteriorated again, wind lashed at the windows, and Porth Tymestl had woken one morning after a particularly violent night to several inches of snow blanketing the ground. Boats still made valiant efforts to reach open waters, but it was becoming more and more difficult to do so without unnecessary exposure to the dangers of storm-tossed seas. There had been mutterings of rationing; insidious anxiety that the food stores would run out before the weather broke. The roads inland had become nearly impassable, slick with ice or else churned into a muddy mess by those who had tried to traverse the coastal moorland with wagons.

Despite how foul it was outside, Eli was still out there, coming back each evening when the early winter dark lowered the temperature further and let the elements prowl freely. He often came back shivering, pale and huddled down in his cloak and scarf. Their mother would look up from whatever work she had laid out on the table or over the workbench, sigh, and fetch him something hot to drink. Eli would be in bed soon after, burying himself under the blankets and asleep before Tias could even ask him where he'd been. Once the residual hurt had dissipated, Tias found himself feeling lonely, slightly abandoned by Eli. Part of him had wondered whether he should try and make the first move back into some form of normalcy, ask his brother where he was going, if he could come along. But each time Tias opened his mouth to ask, or held Eli's gaze for a moment longer than necessary, he would find that all he could see were the tears dripping down his mother's face, and the cold fire of Eli's anger. And the words would die, and Eli would leave.

Tias climbed the ladder down into the main room of Roseate Cottage, heading over to the fire. He shivered slightly, sticking his hands out in front of him as if he could leech the warmth of the flames into his palms and through his body. Ffion was bent over the table, paper scattered haphazardly around its scarred surface. The intermittent scratch of a quill and the crackle of the fire mingled seamlessly into the muted roar of the gale outside. Tias looked toward the window, watching eddies and swirls of snow dance chaotically beyond. 'What are you doing?' He asked, moving away from the fire and toward the table.

His mother looked up from the paper she was currently examining. 'Nothing that'll interest you, *cariad*.' She smiled a little wanly, and sat back in the chair, the wood creaking slightly. 'Are you cold?'

'A little.' Tias shrugged. Roseate Cottage didn't have the shelter of nearby buildings to help insulate it against the winter's cold. It sat alone higher up the hills, partially overlooking *Angorfa* Harbour.

'I'll make something.' Ffion stood, and moved to the workbench, pulling down two thick clay mugs from hooks nailed into the wall. The kettle was placed over the fire, and Tias watched as his mother put a mixture of dried leaves and flowers into the mugs. He knew it was an old recipe, one she had brought with her from *Dyffryn Cernunnos*. Tias remembered her joy when his father had managed to procure several small bunches of the same herbs to plant in their garden.

A soft aroma rose from the mugs as Ffion poured the hot water in, curling gently in the steam. 'Let it sit for a minute,' she said, slapping Tias' hands away as he reached for his drink. He sat down heavily at the table, slumping and folding his arms. His mother rolled her eyes fondly, and turned to tend to the fire.

Tias let his attention wander, eventually alighting on the pages spread over the table. He picked one up at random, and then blinked. He had thought for a moment that he'd somehow forgotten how to read – before he realised that the page was covered in vertical lines, cross-hatched with smaller, diagonal ones. He made out his mother's name at the top, and there was another name signing the bottom, "Tudwr". A letter then.

'What's this?' He asked, holding the letter up.

Ffion turned to look. 'Just a letter, *cariad*.'

'I can see that. I mean what's it say?'

'Did anyone ever teach you not to pry?' His mother came over, carrying the mugs and set one down beside Tias before plucking the letter neatly from his hand. 'It's between myself and a very old friend.' She sat down opposite him, biting her lip.

'About – about leaving?' Tias said, uncertainly.

'Aye.' Nothing more was said; they both sat in silence just a little outside of comfortable, occasionally sipping the flowery tea. Tias let himself revel in the warmth it left him with, feeling it trace lines of heat through him as he drank. Finishing it, Tias put aside the mug and glanced over the table again. Nothing had been discussed since that day, everyone working on their own assumptions of what was to come. Eli resolutely refusing to believe they were leaving, their mother resolutely refusing to stay. Tias, caught in the middle, dithering and tired of it.

Droplets of water clung to the windows, rolling down the glass and making tracks in the steam that had fogged the panes. Tias looked up toward the balcony, the candle he had left burning there lighting the space and making shadows dance in the recesses of the ceiling beams. He thought of the desk there, and his notebook open and waiting for him, of the cramp that would make his shoulders ache and fingers spasm. Suddenly the cottage felt too small, the walls too thick and unyielding. Tias stood and wordlessly began to pull on his boots, gloves and cloak.

'Where are you going?' His mother's voice cut through his thoughts.

Tias headed for the door, setting his hand on the handle. Making his choice an irrefutable action. 'I'm going to find Eli.' And with that he opened the door and stepped out into the chill.

The third time Tias slipped on the icy cobbles, he considered turning around and going home. He wasn't even sure if Eli would want to talk to him, let alone discuss what Tias found himself so desperate to say. But turning around now felt like giving up, so Tias gritted his teeth, and carried on walking, one hand trailing the sides of the buildings for a quick handhold should his feet slide out from under him again. Most of the cottages he passed were lit up from within, golden patches of firelight flickering over the white coated ground. The day was deceptively dark already, despite it only being midmorning. Heavy, slate grey clouds blocked out the sun, and snow continued to fall in thick flakes. His scarf snapped behind him, caught in the wind.

The long steep path down to *Tua'r Môr* Bay was inaccessible. Tias stood at the top for a while, gauging whether or not he could make it down to the beach in one piece, and then had decided against it. He could only hope that Eli hadn't been foolhardy enough to try and make it down. There was little shelter around the village in the meadows, so Tias had ruled those out almost immediately. As he had turned into the street that led him directly through Porth Tymestl, there was a strange sense of role reversal from the weeks prior. Only this time, Tias was hoping Eli would want to be found, even if it was only on a subconscious level.

It seemed to be one of those rare occasions where, despite the bad weather, The Five-Pointed Compass was empty. Apparently, the conditions outside were *too* horrendous for anyone to even entertain the idea of leaving their own hearthsides for the inn's. Tias kicked the toes of his boots against the door jamb, dislodging the snow that had stuck to them, and pulled his scarf away from his face.

As he stepped into the barroom properly, Tias saw that it was completely empty; Stooger Smythe wasn't behind the bar. 'Anyone here?' He called tentatively into the quiet. A muffled response came from overhead, soon accompanied by footsteps.

'*Bore da*, lad!' Smythe jumped the last step leading down from the rooms and strode over. 'I thought it was you.' He appraised Tias for a moment, eyebrows together in a slight frown. Before he could say anything more, however, Tias noticed Abraxus standing in the shadows of the staircase.

'Tias,' Abraxus said, voice gruff. Tias nodded his head slightly in a return greeting.

'Can I get you anythin', Tias?' Smythe asked, a warm hand on his shoulder.

'No, thank you, Smythe. I'm actually looking for Eli, have you seen him?'

There was a soft huff from the direction of the stairs. It could have been an exasperated sigh or a quickly stifled laugh. 'You two seem to run parallel to one another,' Abraxus said, coming closer. Tias noticed that he looked a little tired, eyes hazy. Both were a dark, uninviting grey today, the left shot through with tiny flecks of white.

'I just need to talk to him. I think he's been avoiding me.' Tias thought for a moment, 'And I him. And it needs to stop.' He took a breath, and looked up into Smythe's face. The innkeeper was smiling slightly, and Tias could see the relief there. 'So, have you seen him?'

'No.' Abraxus said shortly. He reached over the bar and produced a bottle, bringing the label up to eye level.

'Very helpful. And get your hands off that, it's for paying customers only,' Smythe said. He turned his attention back to Tias. 'He's been in and out of here over the past few days. Askin' questions.' Smythe leaned closer conspiratorially, 'To tell the truth, I think he's been drivin' Abraxus mad.'

'That sounds like Eli,' Tias said. 'Did he find out anything interesting?'

'Ah, no, that was not part of the agreement,' Abraxus said, now behind the bar and perusing the drinks Smythe had stacked there. 'You two are to leave me alone and see what you can find for yourselves. *Then* you come to me.'

Tias scowled and Smythe laughed, 'Nice try, lad.' He sobered a bit, saying, 'You can stay here 'til the weather drives young Elias to us, if you'd like?'

'I think I'll keep looking. Thanks though.' Tias turned to go, drawing his scarf up again.

'If he turns up here, I'll send Abraxus out after you,' Smythe called as Tias opened the door. The sounds of Abraxus' indignant voice was cut off abruptly as the winter wind whipped it away.

Once outside, Tias was left feeling a little stuck. 'Not the beach, not the harbour, not The Five... then where?' He muttered to himself. It was a habit that he sometimes slipped into, one that drove his brother insane; particularly if Tias had lost track of the time and was working late into the night on a spread in his notebook. He started walking again, mainly to stay warm. Tias wasn't really aware of the route he was taking, concentrating on his feet to make sure he didn't slip on a patch of black ice. He only glanced up to make sure he wasn't unconsciously heading back to the cliff paths.

In front of him were two figures, heading away from where he stood. One was taller, and thickset across the shoulders and chest. The other, further away still, Tias recognised as Eli. He hurried after them, not caring too much about the person behind Eli. It was only when he was nearly level with them did Tias realise it was Thomas Gillet, and that his voice was calling to Eli. Eli still hadn't turned, confusing Tias completely, as Thomas' words would be carried loud and clear to him on the wind. He thought that given the current circumstances, Eli would be spoiling for a fight.

'What're you doin' being seen with him anyway, Eli?' Thomas called, trying to catch up with his quarry. 'He's a demon, everyone says so.'

'Leave him alone, Thomas.' Tias reached out and grabbed Thomas' shoulder, pulling him around.

Thomas stumbled a little over the slick ground. Shock warred slightly with anger as Thomas looked at Tias. Anger won. 'Don't shove me, *Matthias*.'

'I didn't. You slipped.' Tias snapped back. He glanced past Thomas', and saw that Eli had finally stopped walking. He was turned toward the pair, half of his face hidden by the hood of his cloak. 'What are you doing anyway, following him?'

'Saw him come out of the church yard,' Thomas said defiantly. 'Da had told me about him an' you talking with that strange man at Stooger's inn. He saw you. I wanted to see if they were doing anything unnatural like.' Thomas lifted his chin, staring down Tias.

Tias cursed himself for not noticing that Aron Gillet had been one of the few men left in The Five when Abraxus had returned him from their wanderings over the village boundaries together. 'What of it?' He said. 'I don't think it's really any of your business.'

'It's for the *common good*.' Thomas said the last two words with such an inflection that Tias immediately knew that he was parroting what Aron had said after seeing them with Abraxus.

'Tias, leave it.' Eli's voice was barely audible, his approach masked by the gale.

Thomas whirled around, a delighted expression making its way onto his face. 'So, what were you doin', Eli? I didn't see *him* with you.'

'Go away,' Eli said. Tias cast him a look. Eli's voice was flat and disinterested. Thomas clearly noticed too, and bristled slightly, annoyed he wasn't getting a rise.

'Saw you by the graves,' he said. 'Did that *abnormal* show you how to talk to the dead?' Thomas goaded, all his attention focused on Eli. He should have been looking at Tias. At Thomas' words, Tias had a sudden moment of realisation of what Eli had been doing. Both Tias and his brother had found a small measure of comfort in visiting their father's grave, and whispering to it as if they could still converse as father and son.

The realisation was quickly wiped away, however, by a bright and fierce anger. After all the stress and pressure of the previous weeks, Tias had just simply had enough. He reached out, once again grabbing Thomas' shoulder, and spun the other boy back to face him. But instead of stopping there, Tias drew back his arm and punched Thomas across the jaw. Clearly not expecting it, Thomas reeled backwards, falling to land heavily on his backside.

Tias stalked forward. 'Don't you *dare*,' he spat, looking down at Thomas.

The other boy scrabbled to his feet, shock replaced by ugly rage. He lunged for Tias, but Tias, using the ice to his advantage, merely stuck out a foot, causing Thomas to trip and fall back onto the cobbles.

'Leave us *alone* Thomas. It is absolutely none of your concern, or your father's for that matter, what Eli and I choose to do or who we associate with.' Tias' voice was colder than the ice beneath their feet.

Thomas hadn't tried to get up this time, but was staring up at Tias wide-eyed, a drop of blood snaking its way down his chin from where Tias had split his lip.

'Am I understood?' Tias asked. Thomas nodded. 'Good. Now, *cadw di i ffwrdd.' Stay away.*

Thomas didn't need telling twice. Both Tias and Eli watched him go, almost running down the street, heading for home. It was only when he was completely out of view did Tias shake his hand out. 'Ow.' He inspected his sore knuckles. 'You never said it *hurt you* to punch someone else.' He looked up.

Eli was staring at him, mouth open slightly.

'What?' Tias said warily.

'That – Tias, you... *what?*' Eli seemed incapable of normal speech at the moment.

'Can you try that again, but more coherently please?'

'*That was amazing!*' Eli all but yelled it, throwing his arms up. 'The look on his face, you just knocked him flat!' Eli continued to rant, pacing erratically along the street. Tias chuckled slightly, still flexing his fingers. Eli managed to come to a standstill, grinning at his brother. His expression dulled a little, as he said, 'Thank you.'

Tias shrugged. 'You've done the same for me. I thought I should return the favour.'

'What are you doing out here?' Eli asked, grimacing slightly as a particularly vicious gust of wind blew down the street. His hood was flung back, and he fumbled with it, gripping the edge to keep it up.

'Looking for you. And a fight apparently.' Tias said. 'Eli I–'

'I'm–' Eli started saying at the same time. 'Oh. You first.'

Tias thought for a moment and, taking a breath, said, 'You've been avoiding me. And Mam too.' He said it as a statement, not a question, leaving no room for Eli to deny it.

Eli shuffled slightly, looking to his feet.

'And I understand *why*, Eli, I do. But it can't carry on. I miss you.' Tias said truthfully.

Eli looked up sharply at that, biting his lip.

'I'm not sorry for leaving this between you and Mam to sort out, because I shouldn't have to. But I am sorry that I avoided you too.'

'No, don't. You don't have to apologise. I was being difficult, and it wasn't fair. *I'm* the one saying sorry, Tias. I just–' Eli broke off, his voice wavering a little at the edges. 'You remember how it felt? When Da... well, leavin' here feels a bit like that. Like – like a big hole right through you. And I didn't want anyone to see that. Again.' Eli took a steadying breath, and looked Tias right in the eye. 'I'm sorry.'

Tias was quiet for a moment, and then he reached out and pulled Eli into a hug.

Eli immediately began to thrash, but after a second, relaxed. 'Alright, get off.'

Tias smiled sheepishly and disentangled himself. 'Good?'

'Aye.' Eli said solemnly. 'We are.' Then he shivered. 'It's freezing out here, can we go somewhere slightly less arctic?'

'That is an excellent idea. C'mon, The Five is empty.' Tias didn't miss the way Eli relaxed subtly when he suggested the inn rather than home. There was still a rift between Eli and their mother, and whilst Tias hoped they'd closed the one between them, he knew that the other distance would take longer to cross.

Together, they set off back up the street, occasionally grabbing onto one another's arm to steady themselves. Reaching the door to the inn, Tias once again knocked the snow off his boots. He was starting to feel hungry, it was surely past midday now. Despite the rumour of the impending food shortages, Ffion had made sure that there was always some form of meal on the table at least twice a day. Tias hurried inside the inn, not waiting for Eli.

'Ah, found 'im then?' Smythe called, looking up from the ledger he was scribbling in. Abraxus sat by the fire, staring broodily into the flames.

'Yes, finally. Can we take you up on that offer to stay here 'til the weather's fit?'

'Of course, lad. Come in, get warm.' Smythe finished whatever he was writing with a flourish and slammed the ledger shut, glancing up. 'You both look half frozen.' Smythe opened the hatchway and came around to them, ushering them closer to the fire. 'Give me those, I'll hang them up to dry.' Tias dutifully pulled his cloak off, snow still glinting silvery white over the wool. Eli fumbled slightly with the clasp on his, and Tias noticed for the first time that Eli wasn't wearing any gloves. His fingers looked stiff and pale. Eventually, the cloak was handed off to Smythe, and Tias nudged his brother over to the fireside.

As Eli went over, Tias appraised him for a moment. Eli seemed thinner, and now that he was out of the cold, there was a definite stumble to his steps. In fact, just before he reached the hearthside, Eli tripped on the uneven stone floor.

Abraxus was up and at his side in an instant. 'Careful, boy.' He said, setting Eli straight.

'*Diolch*,' Eli muttered, face flushing slightly. Tias came over and sat next to his brother on the hearthstones, warming his back. Abraxus had settled himself back into his chair, looking out through the window, a slight crease in between his eyes.

'Are you alright?' Tias asked quietly.

'I'm fine.' Eli said, waving his brother away. Tias studied him, Eli's words at odds with his appearance. He looked pale, the beginnings of dark smudges under his eyes. Tias was about to press the matter further, but was interrupted when Smythe came bustling over, two plates up one arm and two mugs in his other hand.

'Here y'are.' Smythe handed the plates over. 'Nothing hot today, unfortunately. But perhaps the fire can make up for that.' The mugs he set down on the floor by their feet. Tias picked up the chunk of cheese and bit into it. By the time he'd finished with it, Eli's plate was empty.

'Hungry?' Abraxus asked, looking vaguely amused.

'Hmm.' Eli reached for his mug, and drained it in one. Wiping his mouth with his sleeve, he murmured, 'Didn't have breakfast.'

Tias was about to refute that, saying that Ffion had left out bread stuck on the end of toasting forks for them, but then he remembered how one sat untouched as Tias had held his over the flames. In fact, now that he thought about it, Eli had left nearly every day before having anything to eat, only reappearing for tea in the evenings. Tias felt a small swoop of worry; had Eli really not been eating anything more than perhaps a single meal a day? Tias bit into the thick slice of bread coated liberally in butter, thinking. After a second of consideration, he pulled half off the slice, offering it to his brother.

'Oh no, it's fine,' Eli said, pushing Tias' hand away. Tias saw the want in his brother's eyes.

'I had something before I left,' Tias insisted, dropping the bread onto Eli's empty plate. 'Go on.'

Eli didn't need any more convincing; the bread was gone in seconds.

Ribbon.
December, 1815.
Eli.

'Eli. Come on.' Someone was shaking him. He shifted and tried to bat them away. '*Eli.*'

'No.' He moaned, burying his face deeper into whatever it was underneath him. He distantly heard a laugh and a sigh. He felt so comfortably warm and heavy, soft burnished light playing behind closed eyelids.

'Sleeps like the dead, this one.' A voice like the rolling of the ocean.

'You have no idea.' That was his brother. 'He once managed to sleep for a full day after deciding it was a good plan to try tagging along on one of the night catches our Da sometimes did.'

'Well, you're either going to have to hit him, or take him upstairs, it's getting on.' Lantern light and ale. Eli indistinctly heard people moving around him, and then the annoying hand was back on his shoulder.

'*Get up.*' Tias tried again. 'I'll shove snow down your shirt.'

'You wouldn't.' Eli shot up, a wave of light-headedness washing over him with the sudden change in elevation.

'I would.' Tias looked stern, and Eli knew that he meant to make good on his threat.

'Fine.' Eli rubbed the sleep from his eyes, looking around. Apparently, he'd been left on the hearthstones, curled up, with Tias' cloak over him for a blanket and his own wadded up as a makeshift pillow. "Time is it?' He muttered, stretching.

'Sun is down.' Abraxus said. How he knew when the sky was still clouded, Eli couldn't tell.

'We've got to get home, Mam will start to worry.' Tias said as he pulled on his boots. Eli grumbled something that hopefully sounded close to an agreement, and stood up to fetch his own boots from the door. After a few minutes, which they both spent layering up their various items of clothing, both Eli and Tias were ready to face the elements again. Neither of them were particularly looking forward to the slog home, but they both knew it would be unfair to take any more from Smythe without at least some form of payment in return.

Smythe was busy flitting about them, making sure cloaks and scarves were pulled tight and snug. Abraxus didn't move, merely raising a hand in a lazy wave as a form of farewell.

'Straight home, the both of you.' Smythe said at last, turning to open the door.

Tias nodded and strode out into the night, Eli following close behind. He cast one last look behind him at the rectangle of warm light before Smythe closed the door and they were left in the cold.

Neither of them spoke much on the walk home, finding a solace in the quiet that lay between them, now cleared of any awkwardness. Their mother was waiting on the doorstep, skirts swirling about her in the gale. She hurried them both inside, wrapping Tias into a hug and pressing a swift kiss to Eli's temple.

'I was worried you wouldn't come back,' she said lightly, but Eli heard the deep current of true fear underneath. He knew that after he had made things right with his brother, that he should try and bridge the gap between himself and Ffion. But all he could think about right now was his bed. Exhaustion pulled heavily on his mind, clouding his thoughts and making him feel slow. The impromptu nap at The Five-Pointed Compass had taken the edge off it slightly, but now he was back in the warm, it all rushed back with a creeping vengeance. His mother came over to him, cupping his face with her hands. She looked long into his eyes. Eli held her gaze for a moment, and then looked away. Ffion's hands dropped down, lingering for a moment on his shoulders. 'I think,' she began, 'a little something to eat, and then bed. For both of you.'

After a quick supper, Eli and Tias said their goodnights and slipped up the ladder to their balcony. Just before Tias pulled on his nightshirt, Eli silently gestured to the roll of fabric that hung from one of the ceiling beams. Tias reappeared from inside his nightshirt, sandy brown hair tousled, and nodded. Reaching over the banister that protected the edge of the balcony from the drop into the main room below, Eli undid the ties at either end of the roll, letting the fabric drop down to create a curtained wall. It had been a joint invention between Eli and Tias once they had reached thirteen. Not only did it afford them some privacy from their parents, it also acted as an excellent screen for shadow puppets, of which their mother was a master. Tonight, it was down because Eli wanted to talk.

He jumped into bed, rubbing his feet together in a bid to warm the blankets quicker. Tias reached over and snuffed the candle that sat on the chest that separated their beds. The smoke curled through the half-darkness, the wick reduced to a single red point. Below them, Eli could just make out the sounds of their mother closing the shutters for the night.

'Eli?'

'Mm.' Eli rolled onto his side toward the sound of his

brother's voice. 'You know,' he began slowly, 'I think I'll cherish that image forever.'

'What image?'

'You standing over Thomas Gillet looking like you were about to murder him.' Eli grinned into the darkness.

'I did not!' Tias sounded indignant.

'You did, he was *terrified*.' Eli didn't mention how he'd been a little more than shaken at that too. He was suddenly quite glad that he and Tias had never really had a proper physical fight before.

'Well... he had it coming.' The blankets rustled slightly as Tias shifted. 'And my hand still hurts. Anyway, what did you want to tell me?'

'Oh right. So, when I was out–'

'Avoiding me.'

'Yes, alright, we've established that. *Anyway*, I was in The Five for a bit, just seein' if I could learn anything by listening.'

'Eavesdropping, you mean?'

'Look, d'you want me to tell you or are you just going to keep interrupting?'

'No, carry on.'

'Hm.' Eli glared in the direction of his brother, despite knowing Tias couldn't see him. 'I didn't get anything. And then Abraxus caught me.' He snorted, 'Apparently I wasn't being subtle.'

'Well now there's a surprise.'

'What did I *just say*? But before Abraxus kicked me out, Smythe called over to me and told me to 'ask the obvious question', and that if I did, then the answer would help us figure out what's going on.'

'"The obvious question'?'

'Yeah, that's not particularly helpful, is it?'

'No.' Tias was silent for a bit, clearly thinking, like Eli, what the innkeeper could have meant. 'No, I can't think of anything.'

'Me neither,' Eli said through a yawn. '"But at least it's

somethin''.' He felt sleep reach out its fingers to pull him down. He lifted the blankets a little, letting them settle around his ears. Tias had started to say something, but the meaning of it became jumbled and thick at the edges. Outside, the wind tumbled and tried to seek entry through any crevice it could find.

What felt like only seconds later, Eli was jolted from sleep by the sounds of the church bells ringing out for Christmas morning.

They didn't join the congregation that morning. In fact, most Sundays passed without the Kincarrans leaving for the draughty chapel; they had never been the most pious family. Ffion had grown up with not one omnipotent God, but rather a pantheon, each deity presiding over a section of her little world. Their Da had made it clear that the only true power he believed in was the sea. Eli had once asked about his father's beliefs, and all John had said in response was, 'I have everything I need right here. What more do I have to see or believe in to be happy?' He had looked between his family and the harbour as he spoke, eyes lit up from within.

Eli woke up late, Tias already downstairs at the hearthside with their mother. They were roasting nuts over the flames, the woody, rich smell filling up the cottage. Climbing down the ladder and reaching the bottom, Eli stopped and studied them for a moment. Despite Tias and his mother sitting so close together, there was such an obvious gap made by the absence of their father. He had to physically steady himself, catching a hand out onto one of the rungs of the ladder. Tias turned, and held out a toasting fork, two nuts browned to perfection on the prongs. He tried to say something, probably to wish Eli a happy Christmas, but all he managed to get out was something unintelligible.

Eli grinned and settled himself on the warm hearthstones. 'That's a good impression of a squirrel if ever I saw one.' He leaned to one side as his brother made to swipe at him.

'Tias, swallow that before you choke.' Ffion said, exasperation warring slightly with amusement in her voice. '*Nadolig Llawen, cariad.*'

'*Nadolig Llawen*, Mam.' Eli returned quietly. They sat for a while in peace, the silence broken only by the sounds of the winter wind outside and the distinct crackling pop of roasted nuts.

Once the little wicker basket was empty, and the toasting forks had been hung back over the mantlepiece, their mother stood and walked over to the bed beneath the balcony, kneeling and reaching under it. She came back to the fireside with two small packages in her arms, wrapped in brown paper and tied off with ribbon in yellow and green. Eli and Tias looked at one another; they hadn't been expecting anything this year. In fact, all thoughts about the festive season had been eclipsed by the passing of their Da and then the subsequent upheaval Porth Tymestl had been facing. Eli felt the sickening churn of guilt rear up again as his mother placed the package down into his lap. He looked up, and saw nothing but open kindness in Ffion's face. Blinking a little rapidly to try and clear his stinging eyes, Eli traced the soft silky ribbon with the tip of a finger. Their mother sat back down, watching them closely. Tias had already pulled the ribbon loose and had wound it around his wrist, tying it neatly back into a bow. A crackle of paper, and Eli saw from the corner of his eye Tias lift from the shreds a small shoulder bag, dark brown leather, with a single brass clasp in the centre. The strap was long and thin, but with a wider section where it was meant to sit on the shoulder. It was the perfect size for the notebooks Tias was so fond of.

'I worry about you not having hands free to catch yourself with,' Ffion said, throwing the paper into the fire, making it flare momentarily. 'Hands out of your pockets, *cariad*, and books in this.' She tapped the leather bag twice, smiling.

'I love it,' Tias breathed, still looking at the bag, eyes wide. He ran his hands over the strap, and slipped it over his head, adjusting the length with the buckle there. '*Diolch*, Mam.'

'Eli?' Ffion said. Eli started slightly, and turned his attention back to his own gift. It was smaller, and a perfect rectangle. Undoing the ribbon, and, like Tias, tying it around his wrist, he pulled off the paper. Inside was a small wooden box, simple, the grain still a little rough. Eli lifted the lid.

'What is it?'

'Do you like it?'

Nestled on a bed of dried moss was a folding knife. The blade was tucked away inside an ivory white handle, a small ridge of silver metal just visible to lift it out of its setting. Eli plucked it from the box, turning it over and over in his hands. The grip was as long as his palm, and shaped to fit nicely there. He studied it a little closer, and realised that it wasn't constructed from wood. The blade lifted smoothly from its casing, glinting red in the firelight. It looked wickedly sharp.

'The grip is made from a stag's antler.' Ffion said as Eli balanced it on the tip of a finger. It was weighted perfectly. 'I got both from *Dyffryn Cernunnos*. I'm surprised I managed to keep them secret, you two are like gannets when it comes to presents.'

'It's... *diolch*.' He tried to put everything he could into the single word, looking his mother straight in the eye. Perhaps it worked; Ffion looked away into the fire for a moment and seemed to sniffle slightly.

'That's quite alright. I'm glad you like them.' They spent the rest of the morning with quiet festivities. Their mother had instructed Eli and Tias to head outside and find some nice winter plants to weave into the wreath they were making at the table. Normally, one would adorn the door all the way through December, but with everything that had happened, Ffion hadn't found time. The slow fire kept the cottage warm, the cold that pressed in from outside not touching them here. They hung the wreath on the old and rusty nail that had been driven into the wood of the front door many years ago, hanging the circlet of seasonal plants and flowers with the ribbon their mother had used to tie up their gifts.

Eli and Tias were now engaged in an increasingly ridiculous game that Tias had invented when they were young; a page was torn from one of his notebooks, and then was passed between them, each writing two words. The result was often a nonsensical story alternatingly written in Tias' cramped handwriting, and Eli's taller lettering. Eli always knew exactly what kind of narrative Tias had constructed in his head, and always did his best to take it in a completely opposite direction. He suspected that Tias knew that he did this, but had never yet been called out for it. The words *rotten jam* had just been scribbled down, following Tias' *fell into*, when there was a soft knock at the door. Ffion looked up from where she sat by the fireside, knitting in her hands. Putting down her needles, she stood, stretched for a moment, and then walked cautiously over to the door. Eli and Tias watched openly, paper forgotten between them.

The wind swirled into Roseate Cottage gleefully as the door was pulled open a crack. Tias lunged forward to slam his hand down on the little pieces of paper that littered the table from previous games, stopping them from parodying the snow now falling outside.

Their mother looked through the gap for a second, and then stiffened slightly in surprise. 'Medwyn, Efa.'

The door was opened all the way, and Ffion quickly stepped aside to allow them entry. Medwyn stamped his boots on the doorstep before stepping in.

'*Nadolig Llawen!*' Efa said cheerfully as she followed her husband in. Her apple cheeks were bright red from the cold. She bustled over to the table, catching both Eli and Tias in a hug. Eli had always liked Efa; her easy and kindly disposition had often felt like a balm after a particularly long day of serving as an extra pair of hands on his Da's ship. She had often waited for the *Dawnsiwr y Wawr* on the harbour walls, when she wasn't needed in the salt or smokehouses, greeting her husband with a smile and usually a slice of *bara brith* or a bakestone. Efa often 'accidentally' brought too much, making sure she had enough to give to Eli and Tias as they stepped from sea to stone.

'Tias, fetch the kettle, *cariad*,' Ffion instructed as Efa released her hold on them both. Tias stood, but Medwyn held up a hand to stay him.

'We aren't planning on staying long,' he said. Eli forced himself to stay in the present; Medwyn's voice reminded him of spray and sky and red sails. 'In fact, we were rather hoping you might leave with us.'

'I'm sorry, I don't quite–' Their mother looked between Medwyn and Efa, the latter's face full of excitable cheer.

'That's because he's doing a terrible job at explaining,' Efa said, smiling exasperatedly at her husband. She turned to Ffion, taking pale hands in her own reddened ones. 'There's a gathering at The Five, most of the village is there. Celebrate the festive period, forget our troubles for a while, that sort of thing. I hear that Stooger's put on quite the spread.' At that she looked toward Eli and Tias, winking. 'We thought we should come and invite you, since you weren't there last Sunday when Stooger announced it at the end of the sermon.'

Eli looked to Tias, seeing his own longing reflected there. For once, he wasn't thinking about going to the inn merely to get some cryptic half-answers, but rather for the *life* that was surely teeming there. A person now gone walked disquietly through the cottage, and Eli could feel his Da's unseen eyes on them.

'Can we, Mam?' He asked, voice coming a little softer than he had intended.

'Tias?' Ffion asked, looking over Efa's shoulder.

'I – I think it might be nice,' Tias said, catching his mother's eye for a moment and then looking back to the table again. Their mother seemed to think about it, eyes cast down at her hand still intertwined with Efa's.

'You deserve some joy too, *cariad*.' Medwyn broke the silence.

Ffion shifted slightly. Eventually, she said, 'Thank you. Give us a moment to wrap up and we'll walk with you.'

Eli grinned and hit Tias in the chest with the back of his hand, taking off toward the ladder. His brother followed close behind, the tips of his fingers occasionally catching Eli's heels as they climbed up. 'Do you think Smythe will have done that fruit cake again?' Eli asked, trying to pull on two jumpers at once. He got stuck, wrestling with the thick wool.

'Hopefully,' Tias said. Eli heard his brother walk closer, and then Tias yanked the collars of the jumpers down, where they came to a stop on Eli's forehead. 'Dress like a normal person, can't you?'

'No.' Eli emerged from the clothes, blowing a strand of hair from his face.

'Ready?' Their mother called from below.

'Nearly!' Both Eli and Tias called back. Eli heard Medwyn chuckle lightly.

A few minutes later, the group were out in the cold, with Ffion latching the door behind her. They hurried down the path toward the village, not talking much so as not to linger in the sharp air. The Five was alight with laughter, the sound of clinking crockery and mugs and the odd burst of a carol. The barroom was completely packed, even more so than on the night when Smythe had revealed Abraxus' name to them. The innkeeper himself was bobbing and weaving through the crowd, handing out plates and bowls and a seemingly never-ending supply of drink. With a slight thrill of vindication, Eli saw Thomas Gillet shift slightly behind his father as they entered, eyes firmly fixed on Tias. Eli wasn't sure if Tias noticed or not, and decided not to say anything and just enjoy the apprehensive expression on Thomas' face.

'I reckon Abraxus is probably hiding in his room,' Tias muttered, leaning over to Eli.

Eli looked up to the ceiling, imagining Abraxus sitting on his cot with a dour expression. 'Probably. He's missing out though.' He added, spotting the food laid out along the bar.

Smythe had clearly reached back into his reserves to provide, and it was likely that some people had brought whatever food they could spare along too. Eli made a beeline for the bar, dragging Tias with him. Ffion had disappeared into the crowd a few moments after they had arrived, chivvied away by Efa.

As the winter night rolled in over Porth Tymestl, the noise rose and fell within The Five-Pointed Compass. There had been a particularly raucous round of carol singing at one point, which Eli had joined in with enthusiastically. For a while, it felt like everyone had forgotten the looming worries of the past few weeks, and were merely content to be together and enjoy the vitality that seemed to soak into and seep from the timbers and stone of the inn. The lanterns blazed in multicoloured spots of light, keeping the dark away. The hour latened, and still no one made a move to leave for their own homes. A cosy contentment had now settled over the people of Porth Tymestl, families and friends splintering off and finding places to perch and recline around the barroom. Eli and Tias found themselves once again underneath the hatchway to the bar. Eli was watching his mother from the corner of his eye, as she conversed animatedly with Alys and Catrin's parents. He found himself smiling; it was one of the first times he could remember over the past few months when Ffion had seemed truly content and at ease with those around her. *Why couldn't she see that she'd be giving all this up when we leave.* The voice was insidious; Eli resolutely pushed it away. This was not the time. He turned to Tias and started up another game of two-word stories.

Shortly after, Eli and Tias were ambushed by a few of their peers. Marcus Selwin peered into the hatchway and asked what they were doing. Alys and Catrin stood behind him, watching. Eli stiffened slightly, waiting for a potential fight, but Tias had clambered out from underneath the hatchway and showed them, sitting cross-legged on the floor. Eli approached warily; he and Tias had never really been all that friendly with other children their age, preferring the easier and closer company of each other. Marcus, Alys and Catrin seemed intrigued by the game and asked to join in. Tias waved Eli over, and, as he settled next to Tias, wrote the first two words on the paper, passing it to Marcus. Eli felt himself relax into the company, not even feeling uncomfortable when more joined the circle. Thomas hovered on the edges of the group, clearly unsure if he could participate. After three pages had been filled on both sides with a multitude of handwriting, Smythe approached the group, snatched the papers from Tias' hand and started to read them aloud to the rest of the inn. The innkeeper had darted and danced out of Eli's grasp as he'd tried to wrest them back, much to the amusement of the gathered crowd.

'I think it's time to head home.' Their mother's voice was smoothed out at the edges from several glasses of mulled wine. Both Eli and Tias put up the token protestations, despite the fact that Eli was getting ready to head to bed and Tias seemed halfway into a doze already. The Five had begun to empty as the moon reached its zenith, those with younger children leaving first, followed soon after by the sailors that hoped to be out upon the waters tomorrow.

Eli stood, groaning as he stretched and hearing his back crack quietly. Ffion was helping a slightly uncoordinated Tias into his jumper and cloak; Tias still not entirely present and a muzzy tiredness in his eyes. 'Alright, ready?' Their mother asked.

Eli was just about to nod, when he noticed something missing. The little leather bag that Tias had received that morning wasn't strung over his brother's shoulder. Eli definitely knew Tias had brought it with him, as Tias had dithered for a full minute about bringing it outside into the snow where the leather could be marked.

'Wait a moment,' Eli said, spotting the bag still underneath the hatchway, where it lay forgotten. He hurried over and scooped it up. It felt a little heavier than he remembered. Tias slipped the strap over his shoulder, nodding his thanks to Eli, and together they waved their goodbyes and called thanks to Smythe, stepping out into the night.

The next morning dawned pale and white and no less cold than the one before. Eli was surprisingly first up, Tias still huddled under blankets. They discovered two things that morning.

The first was that their mother was gone, a note on the table left for them. She had left for *Dyffryn Cernunnos* early, and the note said she was sorry, but she had thought it easiest this way. Eli was still clutching the note, white knuckled, when Tias woke up and came down to meet him.

In his hand was a stone, with a hole eroded through the top right corner, and another note. *I do not celebrate Yuletide,* it read in a thin, scratchy script, *but I understand it is customary to give gifts. Keep it safe.* Tias exchanged the stone for the note their mother had left behind. It fit perfectly into the palm of Eli's hand, and sat there, collecting warmth that he no longer felt.

II
then.

A gilt edged adventure.

Despite the lit hearth, framed either side with impressive scrollwork, the heads of lions and griffins rearing up from within tangles of ivy, the room was cold. Dank moorland fog pressed in against the small windows, seeping in and rolling down the stone from the arrow slits. Torches flickered spasmodically in their wall sconces, casting sickening orange-black shadows deep into the hollows of the vaulted ceiling. The rushes cast upon the well-worn floor did nothing to disguise the passing of many pairs of boots; they were trampled and crushed, and would soon need replacing.

Sebastian kept close to the walls as he entered the hall. Slipping from shadow to shadow, making sure not to step on any of the rushes still fresh enough to snap beneath his weight. The hall was empty, but that didn't mean it would remain so for long. Despite its chill atmosphere, this was the heart of the castle. For now, the tables had been pushed away, the chairs cleared. Only the decorated seat of dark oak and red velvet remained, sitting open and silent. Even without its occupant, Sebastian found himself looking subserviently to the floor as he passed it. It wouldn't be long until his absence was marked, the castle's record keeper alerted to his solitude when he next called for his apprentice. All Sebastian wanted to do was look. One more quick look, and then, surely, he'd be content. This is what he had told himself all the previous times he'd snuck into the hall. Studiously, he kept his eyes trained on the floor before him, not wanting to glance up too soon and ruin the moment of reveal. He'd seen it dozens of times before, but each somehow felt like the first.

Reaching the hearth, Sebastian took a moment to warm his cold fingers against the bubble of warmth that emanated from it. They were pale and stiff, the roughly knitted gloves doing nothing to keep warmth in, cut off as they were at the knuckles. Sebastian had wanted proper gloves, like the sort the record keeper often wore to handle the older books, but he had been denied. In part, because he was too young yet to be permitted to touch the ancient texts, and in part because an apprentice scribe could not wield a quill as accurately between wool-encased fingers. The hearth before him was nearly double his height, the fire within a living, roaring thing. Even if he stood on the raised hearthstones, Sebastian wouldn't have been able to reach the mantlepiece. He had tried to clamber up to it once, when it had been summer and the fire was merely cold ash. He hadn't managed it, and instead had fallen on the flat of his back against the stone below. Something had cracked in Sebastian's shoulder then, and had never quite healed properly. Despite being only around eleven or twelve winters old, Sebastian now walked with a perpetual stoop to one side of his back.

Finally, after several minutes of excruciating, careful self-restraint, Sebastian looked up. There it was, in all its glory above the hearth. He felt the breath rush from him, the impact of the painting washing over him all over again. It was truly the only thing of beauty in the cold, grey castle. The castle stood, squat and hunkered down into the moorland, battered by the wind and hail and fog, but here, in this painting Sebastian found himself to a world transported. His eyes ran the familiar contours and curves of the waves contained within the frame, drinking in the blue, white, green and hints of ochre yellow that blended together into a dance of colour. Sebastian always worked upwards looking at the painting, starting with the waves and then rising through the depths to the shallows above. Atop the waves sat a ship, resplendent and proud. Sails full with a wind he could not feel, prow cleaving the waves in a frozen moment in time. It was always at this point that Sebastian closed his eyes, and imagined himself on the deck of that ship. But no matter how much he willed it, wished it, he never could escape that static moment. Sebastian had never seen the sea, let alone stood tall and mighty on the deck of a ship. And yet, he felt homesick for a thing he'd never had.

Sebastian lost track of the time then, drifting as surely as the tide captured within a gilded edge. He found himself sitting on the hearthstones, gazing upward, a crick in his neck and shooting down his crooked shoulder. Stories told at banquets he'd been forced to serve for echoed distantly in his mind, tales of the sea and the horrors within. Of the sailors lost there, how desolate and lonely it was. Sebastian had drunk them all in like a man dying of thirst. He had heard one visiting King say that the water out there was salty. After the feast was over, Sebastian had snuck into the kitchens, careful not to wake the dog there, and shook some flakes of salt into his palm. Knowing that if he were caught, he'd likely be severely punished – salt was a rarity for the higher born only – Sebastian looked around cautiously, and then licked the flakes from his hand. He might not have ever seen the sea, but he knew now how it tasted.

'Boy!' The voice cut through the dripping quiet of the hall, and Sebastian startled, jumping to his feet and turning. It was a miracle he didn't trip. The record keeper was standing in the entranceway, framed by the arch there. 'I have been looking all over for you, *why* in the name of the gods are you in here?' He swept into the room, long robe shifting the rushes in a miniscule wind as he passed. Despite the record keeper's age and thin frame, he was a man of imposing stature. His hooked nose cast clever brown eyes into partial shadow, and Sebastian was always forcibly reminded of the hunting birds the King kept in the aviary tower.

'I – I merely wanted to warm up a little,' Sebastian lied. 'The archives are so cold, and I was struggling to hold my quill for the shivering.'

'Do not lie to me, boy.' The record keeper's voice was soft, and Sebastian risked a look directly into his master's eyes. He had expected anger there, or at the very least annoyance. Instead, all he saw was the deepest flicker of understanding, tinted gently with something akin to sadness. He drew level with Sebastian, looking up at the painting. 'You are in here quite a lot.'

Sebastian said nothing.

'I think,' the record keeper carried on, 'that there is something that draws you here, time and time again.' His gaze didn't break from the painting. 'Am I correct?'

'Yes,' Sebastian said quietly. He had turned to look at his master, half seeing the painting from the corner of his eye. 'I will endeavour to do better.'

The record keeper's stare came sharply down upon him. 'I did not hear myself say that this was a fault. Did you?'

'N-no.'

'Quite.' The record keeper set a hand on Sebastian's shoulder, turning them both away from the hearth and out into the creeping cold of the hall. 'I understand the pull, boy.' The record keeper said as they walked through the deserted passages of the castle. 'I came from a family by the sea. I miss it.'

Sebastian watched his master's face as he hurried to keep up; he'd never heard the older man say anything about his past before. 'Is it like it is in the painting?' He asked.

'No,' the record keeper said bluntly. Sebastian felt something fall within him. The record keeper looked at him, hand resting on the iron handle to the archives. 'It is *more*.' And with that he opened the door and ushered his apprentice inside.

III
now.

Carvings.
January, 1816.
Smythe.

Tua'r Môr Bay had always been a long stretch of empty sand, cliffs rearing up on three sides, with the ocean casting away on the one remaining. Smythe used to frequent it more in his younger years, finding peace in the quiet there. It made a contrasting change to the low-ceilinged woody darkness of The Five. But now as he stood at the surf's edge, looking out over the shoreline, his view was no longer that remembered stretch of beautiful desolation. Ahead of him, Abraxus' coat and long hair whipped and tangled in the wind, casting his silhouette as blurred and mirroring the constant motion of the tides to his left. Further on still, the bones reared up; harsh lines of blackish brown against the grey sky. There were more now, countless more sets had washed up against the sands in the past few days alone.

Smythe pulled his coat around him, turning up the collar against the fresh morning wind that tangled his hair and made his eyes water. Shoving his hands deep into the recesses of his pockets, he hurried after Abraxus, following the pair of boot prints in the sand, punctuated occasionally by a nearly perfect circular hole from where the point of Abraxus' staff had fallen. Smythe eventually caught up, watching Abraxus as he weaved through the newest set of bones, looking up at their points and lips moving in a silent count. Tiredness itched at Smythe's eyes, a result of the late-night conversation they'd shared over soup and through storm. By the time Smythe had stumbled into bed, the sun was not far from rising, lightening the sky in the smallest increments as he forced his mind to be still and quiet, desperate for some rest. Both he and Abraxus had agreed that it was time to try and send the bones – or at least, some of them – back to the water. Partially, Smythe reflected, to rid the beach of their eerie presence, and restore it to the bay he loved.

'I will start with this one,' Abraxus broke through Smythe's hazy thoughts. He was standing beside one of the bones closest to the current tideline, hand pressed against its slick surface. 'It is closer to the water, and one of the newest.' He was silent for a moment, and then in a very gentle motion, Abraxus leaned his forehead against the rib. He muttered a few words Smythe didn't catch over the sounds of the waves.

'Do you think it'll help?' Smythe asked as Abraxus pulled away.

'No,' Abraxus said levelly. 'But it will send a message. I am here, and I am at work.' With that, Abraxus strode off toward the sea, not slowing his pace even as he waded thigh deep into cold water. Smythe watched from the shoreline, unsure as to how to help. The new year's sun shone weakly through the cloud cover, reduced to a hazy white-grey glow. Smythe had deliberately closed The Five-Pointed Compass for the day, needing a break from the steady flow of patrons who came to drink away their sorrows and cares in his ale and wine. The silence that came with the closure was uncanny; the barroom echoed with quiet, rather than the sounds of life with which he had come to associate the space.

Smythe took a tentative step toward the breakwater, intending to join Abraxus and lend assistance in whichever way he could. But as the leather of his boots met the water's edge, Abraxus turned. 'Not out here, Stooger.' He said. His voice should have been indiscernible from the noise that overlaid it, but Smythe heard the ocean currents take the words and carry them to him on the shoreline. He felt no pang of hurt or resentment at being turned away; the sea was wholly for Abraxus, not him. He understood that the only reason Abraxus had waited for him by the door that morning was so he could act as a deterrent for any that might wander onto the beach.

Smythe cast one last look at the bones that littered the end of *Tua'r Môr* Bay, and set off back down the length of sand. As he meandered along, the wind changed direction sharply. Now, his coat and hair tangled about him, rather than away. The scent of woodsmoke from last night still pervaded the wool. It was one of Porth Tymestl's more unique celebrations. At the turn of the year, a bonfire would be built on *Angorfa* Beach, and kept burning all through the night. Most of the village came out for the burning, sitting around the fire huddled under blankets and swapping stories. This year had been no different, but an undercurrent of melancholic hope had run beneath the surface chatter this time. Silent wishes that this new year would bring something more hopeful, something better for the village and its occupants. Smythe had attended only for a while, heading back to The Five before midnight, where he had come across Abraxus standing in the shadows of the staircase.

Smythe was suddenly aware that the gales around him had suddenly abated. He started, looking up, wondering if this was somehow Abraxus' doing, despite the skies not belonging to him. It was not the work of Abraxus, but rather the unconscious journey Smythe had made as he had walked. The cavern walls deadened the sounds from beyond the slit-like opening. They reverberated dully around the ceiling; punctuated with the slight creak from the ropes that held the pile of driftwood. Smythe smiled, walking further into the Kincarran boys' den. He'd been here only a handful of times; once before the boys had even been born. The rough surface of the walls were covered in smudges of chalk, as if something had been drawn over them, and since been washed away by the tide. His suspicions were confirmed as Smythe spotted several large chunks of chalk sitting on the ledge at the back of the cavern.

Hoisting himself up onto the ledge took a little more effort than Smythe would care to admit to. Eventually, he got himself settled, ankles and feet hanging off the edge, his back to the wall. Someone – probably Tias he thought – had layered sacking on the ledge to provide some form of rustic insulation or cushioning. He hadn't seen either Eli or Tias down at *Angorfa* Beach last night. Smythe had heard from the bakery line chatter that Ffion was gone again, apparently, she had left the day after Christmas. Smythe had winced when he had heard that, suspecting how her sons would feel about that, Eli in particular. Somewhat worryingly, he hadn't seen nor heard from either of them since the passing of the festive period. Smythe resolved then to head up to Roseate Cottage after he and Abraxus were finished with whatever business Abraxus was doing. For now, however, all he could do was wait and keep an eye out for anyone traversing the bay from his hidden vantage point.

'Smythe?' The voice was rough with cold air and salty spray. Smythe jerked upright, cricking his neck and yelping slightly at the sudden lance of pain. He glared at Abraxus as he straightened fully, rubbing his knuckles into the base of his neck.

'There are other ways to wake a man than causin' him to jump a foot in the air,' he said irritably.

Abraxus shrugged, the smallest hint of a smile on his face.

'Are you finished?' Smythe asked, shifting to alleviate the numbness that had settled in his thighs and lower back.

'Yes,' Abraxus said, leaning his staff against the ledge, and fluidly climbing up to sit beside Smythe. 'I have done all I can for now. The sea will reclaim some of the remains tonight.' Abraxus rested his head back against the wall, eyes unfixed and drifting.

'It's a start,' Smythe said softly.

'It is. But it will not be enough. I need to find the *cause*, Smythe.' Abraxus lowered his gaze to the vista before them. He sighed, and then rubbed his eyes with pinched fingers.

'Here. A little pick-me-up.' Smythe reached for an inside pocket, pulling out a medium sized flask. He was just unscrewing the cap when a sudden thought occurred to him. Roughly shoving the flask into Abraxus' hands with a short command of, 'Don't drink it yet!', Smythe jumped off the ledge, and walked stiff-legged to the pulley system. He figured it out with relative ease and lowered the netting down, plucking some choice pieces of wood from within its confines.

'What are you doing?' Abraxus asked. 'Somehow I do not think that the boys would like you interfering with their... stash.'

'Can't have cold wine on a day like today,' Smythe said, grunting as he clambered back onto the ledge, wood stacked precariously in his arms. In a matter of minutes, he had a small fire lit and crackling merrily. Briskly rubbing his hands together by the heat for a moment, Smythe then plucked the flask from Abraxus' hands and set it against one of the stones that hemmed the blaze in. 'Give it a few moments.'

'Hm.' Abraxus had gone back to staring distractedly to the sea beyond.

Smythe measured his next words carefully, starting slowly, 'It's fixable. You've done it before, I've *seen* you do it before.' He nudged Abraxus with his elbow. 'This time it's just takin' a little longer than you're used to.'

Abraxus said nothing, but Smythe saw the gentle crease between his eyes fade a little. Smythe was reaching for the flask, nicely warmed through now, when a new voice broke through the stillness that had descended between the pair.

'We don't invade your rooms, Smythe.' Tias was standing in the opening, looking a little annoyed at the unexpected company he'd found.

'Tell that to your brother, Matthias,' Smythe said with a raised eyebrow. Tias looked confused.

'What?'

'Never mind. You're just in time for somethin' hot. You interested?' Smythe held up the flask, and then promptly dropped it, hissing between his teeth as the heated metal bit into his numb fingers.

Abraxus deftly caught it, and then began to toss it between his hands. 'Smythe, you said you were *heating* this, not boiling it.' Abraxus glared at Smythe, still passing the flask from hand to hand.

A low laugh brought both Smythe and Abraxus away from the petty argument that had no doubt been about to break. 'I'll have some boiling drink,' Tias said, coming over to the ledge. Smythe watched as his eyes flicked to the staff, and then determinedly away again. Abraxus opened the cap, and took a long pull, wiping the mouthpiece off with part of his scarf. He leaned forward and handed it to Tias. '*Diolch*.'

'Where is your brother?' Abraxus asked as Tias stood on tiptoe to pass the flask back to Smythe. A shadow crossed Tias' face for a moment.

'He carried on further down the beach. I think he just wanted to walk for a bit.' Tias bit his lip. 'Alone.'

'Everythin' alright, lad?' Smythe asked gently. He shifted toward the side wall, opening a gap up for Tias to fill. Tias looked between Smythe and Abraxus, and then joined them on the ledge. Smythe had to sit with his legs to his chest to avoid setting fire to his trousers, but he didn't particularly mind. He also noted that Abraxus didn't make a fuss about having another person he was somewhat unfamiliar with in quite close quarters.

'Tias?' Smythe prompted when it became apparent that the boy wasn't going to start talking.

'Mam's gone again, did you know that?' Tias said.

'Aye, I did.' Smythe confirmed.

'She didn't even say goodbye.' Tias' voice quivered over the last word. 'She left a note saying she thought it was easier this way. Maybe she was right.' What Tias left unsaid spoke volumes.

'How have you an' Eli been managing?' Smythe said, thinking about the food shortages that were becoming a desperately increasing issue.

'She left what coin she could again, and we've got Efa and Medwyn looking out for us.' Tias said. Smythe studied him a moment.

'And I'll ask again, but with a different intention. How have you an' Eli been *managing*.'

Tias let out a half-hearted laugh at that, and then lapsed into silence once more, clearly thinking. 'Not great.' He said eventually. 'I'm... I'm upset that she felt she couldn't tell us she was leaving again. And I'm angry?' Tias phrased it as a question, looking to Smythe as if he had the answers.

'Why?' Smythe asked, knowing it was better to let Tias voice whatever he needed to.

'Because she's left us in this awful position. Again. But then I feel cross with myself for being cross with *her*, because I also understand why.' Tias broke off with a long groan and rested his head against his knees, which, like Smythe, he had brought up to his chest. 'It's all just really confusing.' He said eventually, words muffled.

Smythe was about to reach out and lay a comforting hand on the boy's shoulder, but he was beaten to it. Abraxus looked down at Tias, waiting for him to meet his mismatched gaze. 'I would advise you,' Abraxus began levelly, 'to ride this as best you can. There is no point in fighting a storm, stop trying to wrest control and just see where you end up.' Abraxus held Tias' eyes for a moment longer, and then broke the contact, his hand slipping off the boy's shoulder and reaching out for the flask again.

Smythe passed it over. 'Sound advice. As difficult as it may seem, I'd try and heed his words lad.' Tias looked from Smythe to Abraxus, considering.

'I'll try.' He came to eventually.

'Can't ask for more than that.' Smythe pinched the flask back from Abraxus, saying as he did so, 'Leave some for the rest of us, can't you?' He looked toward the cavern opening, 'Eli better get here sharpish if he wants anythin' to warm himself with.'

They sat in companionable quiet, each wrapped in their own thoughts. Tias had picked up one of the chunks of chalk and was doodling small pictures by his feet, having rucked up the canvas to expose the stone.

After an indeterminable amount of time, smoothed slightly by the consumption of wine, a voice broke their reverie. 'What are you doing here?' Eli was standing perfectly framed by the slitted entrance.

Tias looked up immediately, fumbling with the chalk. Smythe watched the corner of it shatter as it hit the stone below, leaving behind a starburst of white.

'We were–' Smythe started, but was then broken off by Tias.

'Actually, yes, what *are* you doing here?' Tias looked vaguely disgruntled, clearly wondering why he hadn't asked that sooner.

'Nothing of your concern,' Abraxus said. Eli and Tias looked to him; Tias' face full of curiosity, and Eli's filled with sharp irritation. Smythe closed his eyes, cursing Abraxus mentally.

'Well, if it's none of *our* concern,' Eli started, voice low, 'then maybe you'd like to leave?' He had come further into the cavern now, and Smythe finally got a good look at the boy. Eli looked unwell; pale and tired and somehow more angular. Some of this was reflected in his brother's face, but to a less extreme degree. Even Abraxus seemed to notice, as he sat a little straighter, frowning again.

'Eli, don't,' Tias said quietly. He looked at his brother, and the air between them seemed to tense and tauten with a conversation unspoken. Tias seemed to win, as Eli's shoulders slumped infinitesimally.

'C'mere,' Smythe said, holding out the flask. 'Get some o' that in you.'

Eli took it gratefully and drank. He came over to the ledge, resting his arms on it and looking up into the faces above him. Silence lay rockily between them, seemingly impassable. And then it was broken by Abraxus, 'I was sending some of the bones back to the seabed.'

'How?'

'What do you mean?'

'Abraxus, you just said it was none of their concern!' Smythe's exasperated words cut over Eli and Tias' immediate questions. Abraxus looked to him and, infuriatingly, merely shrugged.

'It is not. But would I be correct in saying that you have hit something of a... block in trying to find out my purpose here?' Abraxus said, looking somewhat sternly between the boys.

'No!' Eli said indignantly.

'So yes, then,' Smythe said, feeling the quirk of a smile beginning. Eli shot him a dark look, which made him smile even more.

'A little bit.' Tias admitted. 'To be fair, you didn't exactly make it easy!'

'I never intended to.' Abraxus said. 'But perhaps you needed a little more direction here.'

'What are the stones for?' Eli said abruptly, rummaging in his pocket, pulling out a tangled mess of items before loosening a stone from the middle of a clump of string. Abraxus just looked at him. Eli growled and shoved all the detritus away. 'You are really irritating, you know that?'

'Yes.' Abraxus spoke plainly, but Smythe could see the glint in his friend's eye that meant he was enjoying himself. Tias snorted at the single word, amusement creeping into his expression. Eli tried his best to continue to frown, but failed as his lips kept wobbling upward into a half smile.

Not long afterward, the group left the cavern, with Eli and

Tias still heckling Abraxus with questions or half guesses and theories. Abraxus stolidly ignored them and kept walking, reaching the path back up the cliff face first. As gravel path and sea grass gave way to cobbles and stone, Smythe noticed that both boys became a little more subdued, a little less inclined to smile or talk. He was just about to invite them back to The Five – for something to eat more than anything else, he wasn't at all convinced that either of them were getting enough – when a commotion caught his attention. People were hurrying down to *Angorfa* Harbour and Beach, anxiety swirling off them as mist off the moorland. 'What's happened?' Smythe said, catching the arm of Owen as he passed.

'Wreck-wood came up onto the beach.' Owen said shortly.

Smythe looked to Eli and Tias, noting how still they had both become. 'Abraxus, take them back to The Five,' he said, leaving no room for argument. Abraxus nodded and pulled both boys away by the edges of their cloaks. Smythe himself turned away from the street that would lead to his inn and followed the crowd down toward the sea.

He didn't linger long. There was no doubt that it was one of their ships that had been pulled asunder. Smythe, alongside everyone gathered at the harbour, recognised the scrollwork that Gethin had spent his summer evenings carving along the rails of his ship, *Niwl y Môr*. Someone started to sob, loud harsh noises that could never fully encompass the true depth of grief. Smythe closed his eyes, lips moving silently in an ancient prayer, and then turned away. There was nothing more he could do here, and there were people waiting for him at The Five-Pointed Compass who needed him more.

ELLA RUBY SELF

Meetings.
January, 1816.
Abraxus.

This wasn't his grief to share in. This wasn't his cloak of sorrow to pull around his shoulders, letting it shroud him. He shouldn't go. It had been three days since the wreck-wood had come ashore at *Angorfa* Beach. The man, Gethin Roberts, and his crew of two had all been lost to the depths. Abraxus had made sure that they were at peace below. Smythe had returned quickly from the beach, face grim and set. Without a word, he had walked behind the bar and pulled himself a drink. Abraxus had watched as the innkeeper drained the mug in one, wiping away the foam that clung to his top lip and in his beard with a sleeve. Still, he said nothing. Smythe hadn't asked where Eli and Tias had gone – Abraxus had sent them home, his tone brooking no argument – but rather he'd opened the hatchway to the cellar and disappeared down the short ladder. The snap of the trapdoor closing behind him told Abraxus everything he needed to know. The inside of his little room seemed dull and oppressive as the door swung open. He'd snuffed the candle before coming out, and now the shadows hung long and thin from the rafters and in the recesses of the window casement.

Abraxus had remained in his rooms since the event. For three days he had paced, confined, but not willing to free himself from his cage. The writing desk was littered with parchment, several sheets cascading onto the floor. Spots of ink decorated the soles of his bare feet, from where he had paced over the parchment unthinkingly. Now taking up his usual spot leaning against the wall and looking down through the window, Abraxus lapsed into black thoughts. A curling, cold voice had whispered in his ear that *this is your fault, you could have prevented this if only you had worked a little harder.* Abraxus knew he shouldn't listen to it. He did anyway, letting the sick spike of guilt solidify and sharpen into resolution. Icy determination.

Porth Tymestl had been quiet that night, the lanterns hooded, and doors locked tightly. Grief buried the village, as surely as the splinters of the *Niwl y Môr* would be buried in the church yard. John Maredudd Kincarran's grave would no longer be the only empty one deep within the earth.

Distantly, he heard the sounds of the barroom filling below him, noise seeping through the floorboards. A meeting had been called, the village vicar, whom Smythe referred to as 'Crow', announcing it as necessary after the ceremony for the three lives lost. Smythe, still mostly uncommunicative, had slipped a note under his door that morning, saying that if Abraxus wanted to join the gathering, he could. Abraxus knew he shouldn't go, he had little *right* to go. The thought still played in his mind as he pulled on his boots and stepped into the little corridor. The seaweed laces were brittle and close to snapping. He'd need to submerge them in water soon, or else have to begin the arduous task of gathering more from the rockpools to cut thinly and plait.

Abraxus found that he was, thankfully, still early to the meeting. As he slipped down the staircase and into the barroom properly, he felt the weight of unsolicited and curious stares land heavy on his shoulders. Crossing the room in several long strides, Abraxus raised two fingers in a half wave, half salute to Smythe, behind the bar. Smythe nodded his head in response. There was an alcove that sat at the far end of the inn, furthest from the fireplace. A single lantern of pewter, set with panels of blue and yellow glass hung over the small round table. Abraxus slid into the nook, settling himself on the bench that Smythe had built into the wall around three sides. The early twilight was already filling the barroom with a damp grey half-light; the multitudes of lanterns beginning to glow a little brighter. Abraxus leaned back against the wall, feeling the chilled stone press against his back. He wished for a moment that he had brought his coat, if not to provide a little more warmth in his chosen spot, but also to use it as a shield of some sort. Hide within its salt-stained leather, wrap the smells of home around him.

Over the next half an hour, The Five-Pointed Compass filled with the inhabitants of Porth Tymestl. They all spoke in hushed tones to one another, an unsaid agreement to not raise the noise above what would be deemed suitable for a wake. Which, Abraxus thought idly, in some ways this was. Smythe remained behind the bar, nodding to those who greeted him, speaking a few words to the few that approached the counter. Much to his relief, Abraxus seemed to have become partially invisible. Eyes slid over the alcove, and him, searching for friends and family members to convene with. Some did notice him, but his presence went uncommented upon. He was an oddity, yes, but right now, he was an oddity that could be reasonably ignored. The barroom seemed to have reached its capacity; people were sitting on the floor, on the hearthstones, or standing in the spaces in between. Abraxus noticed that some had perched on the stairs leading up to the rooms. He felt a singular note of panic; his potential escape route was blocked. Pushing the anxiety forcefully away, Abraxus' attention was caught by the door opening and closing once more. There were murmurs of mild annoyance as those closest to the entrance were doused in deep winter cold; its bite felt more deeply as the warmth of the inn wrapped them close. Through the assembled crowd, Abraxus caught a glimpse of a dark blue cloak and a flash of coppery hair. Eli and Tias stood shoulder to shoulder as well as they could in the throng and despite their differences in height. As soon as Abraxus had spotted them, they disappeared once more, threading their way further into the barroom.

An uncanny moment of total silence fell through The Five-Pointed Compass. No one had signalled that the meeting had begun, but Abraxus felt the shift in the atmosphere from a tense waiting to a taut attention. He leaned forward unconsciously, resting his elbows on the scarred wooden table. The vicar spoke first. As he stood from his seat near the centre of the room, Abraxus saw why Smythe called him Crow. The man was tall and thin with a beady look about his eyes; a shrewd sense of intelligence hung about him as surely as the black cloak. 'Thank you for gathering here today,' he began.

Abraxus immediately pitied the Porth Tymestl congregation; the man's voice was soporific.

'I would like to suggest that we first have a moment's silence for those who cannot be with us, and for their loved ones.' Crow bowed his head, and many of those gathered did the same.

Abraxus sent out his own prayer, glad that no one else could hear it.

'Thank you. Now, to business.' Crow straightened. 'This is not the first time we've had to have meetings like this, as some of you older here may remember. However, I think we can all agree that our situation is markedly more immediate and dire than previously.' Murmurs of agreement met Crow's words, and Abraxus found himself for the first time getting a true insight into how difficult life must be here, eked out of salt and sand and graft. 'We have two major things to discuss, and I'm sure there will be dissent on either side. The first, then, is what we intend on doing about the food shortages we face. This winter has been harsh, and the weather shows no sign yet of breaking.' Crow spread his hands wide, opening the discussion. Abraxus had to give him credit where it was due; the man knew how to command a room.

'Can't we go inland?' A woman called from the bar.

'Roads are nearly impassable, Bronwyn, we can't get the carts down 'em, let alone back up full o' food.' A thick set man answered, rubbing his hands together in a seemingly unconscious movement.

'By foot then?' Said another.

'What, you want to brave this weather to only bring 'ome enough for a few weeks?' And so the conversation went on, a dizzying back and forth, solution, problem, rebuttal, and eventually discarded. Abraxus listened to every word, his attention remaining sharp, even when the meeting grew from one hour to two. Several of the younger generations had lost interest by the time the idea for calling along the coast to other port towns had been battered down.

As people's postures slumped, or more found themselves sitting on the floor, Abraxus got a clear view of the Kincarran twins for the first time since they arrived. They had managed to sequester themselves underneath the hatchway to the bar, faces peering out into the sea of bodies that rolled beyond their den. Neither of them had contributed anything, but Abraxus noticed that Tias was determinedly scribbling in a new notebook. The boy kept glancing up, eyes fixing on whoever was speaking at the time. Abraxus felt a small smile quirk his lips. No one had officially been given the role of taking the minutes of the gathering, but naturally Tias had taken it upon himself to have a record. Eli sat behind his brother, watching. Abraxus caught a glimpse of white-ish grey between the boy's fingers, and with a slight shock realised it was the most recent stone he'd given to them, left in Tias' bag as Abraxus had come up from the cellar, spotting it forgotten underneath the hatchway.

The discussion was quickly now degenerating into what seemed to be an argument, with less suggestions being bandied around, and more snide jibes or frustrated exclamations. Crow, sensing the slip into disorderly, stood once more calling over the steadily rising tumult for peace. He went unheeded. A particularly large man with a thick beard was engaged with another fisherman, scarring decorating his knuckles and forearms from several unfortunate incidents with hooks. Their words became more heated, sharper, until a high whistle broke through them. Everyone stopped, and turned to look at Smythe.

The innkeeper lowered his fingers from his mouth and glared around the room. 'I'll have none of that in here. This is not settling *anythin'*, we're all just getting het up and frustrated. Take a minute, calm down and we'll resume in a moment.' Smythe shot a glare at the bearded man and his scarred combatant. 'That goes for you too, Aron, Medwyn.' The fishermen sat down, looking thoroughly chastised.

Abraxus let out a slow breath he hadn't realised he'd been holding, some of the tension in his shoulders lessening as the mood in the barroom sank back down into quiet discontent. Crow nodded his thanks to Smythe, sitting back down and playing absentmindedly with the cuff of his robe's sleeve. Abraxus caught the innkeeper's eye for a second, inclining his head slightly at Smythe's unspoken question. No one had made a fuss at his being present – yet. Smythe then sank down behind the bar, crouching beside Eli and Tias, conversing with them softly. Tias held up his notebook, flicking through the pages quickly. Smythe grinned as Eli visibly rolled his eyes, albeit fondly.

'If we could..?' Crow had taken control once more. All eyes snapped to him, Smythe rising to lean over the bar. Once Crow had commandeered everyone's attention, he cleared his throat, shifting. Abraxus realised that he was nervous. This was the crux of the meeting, he could feel it. The current had pulled everyone in; it was time to see if they would swim, or if they would drown.

'The second item we need to discuss,' Crow began, clearly choosing his words carefully, 'is whether we continue to send fishing vessels out onto a sea that has become increasingly more hostile. Or,' he continued as chatter began to swell, 'if we ground all boats for the safety of our fishermen.'

The talk died immediately. Outside, Abraxus could hear

the increasing howl of the wind as the daylight died around them. He studied the faces of Porth Tymestl, seeing a range of emotions cast out upon them. Some looked at Crow with open annoyance or anger. Others seemed to be torn between the need to agree but the *want* to oppose. He glanced toward the bar, but Smythe had kept his expressions carefully neutral. Underneath the hatchway, Tias had stopped writing, the point of his pencil still resting on the page in a manner that suggested he had forgotten it was there. Eli had leaned forward, jaw clenched slightly. Abraxus himself understood the turmoil that Crow had just unwittingly thrown upon the residents of the village. The sea was not only their means of survival, but their way of life. Everything in these hardened, salt-soaked people belonged to the sea, was shaped by it. But now their numbers were being slowly picked off a fishing vessel at a time; their oldest ally had turned against them.

'No, obviously not.' It was the scarred man who spoke, Medwyn. 'If we ground the boats then we will surely starve!'

'But we might lose more men,' a woman said from the fireplace. 'We lose those able to fish, we forsake the future of Porth Tymestl entirely.' Her words were met with murmurs, the noise level once again growing.

'Edwina, we have to think about *now*, not the future.' Abraxus watched as another fisherman stood up, his face closed and set. 'I for one will not abandon my profession. I know the risks, we all do.' His words were met with a low cheer from other men around the room.

'Aye,' the big man, Aron, stood, 'we've lost people, good people. But if we do *nothin'* we'll lose a lot more.'

'Ground the boats.' The voice was quiet, but carried through the barroom as if the speaker had been shouting. All turned to look, Abraxus leaning forwards slightly against the table to get a good view of the owner of the new voice. A stocky man with a shock of hay-blonde hair stood by the door, arms folded.

'Ground 'em.'

'Owen...' Crow started, raising a hand placatingly to the man.

'No. We shouldn't even be havin' this discussion. Out there,' he jabbed a finger toward one of the windows and the rolling seascape beyond, 'is far too treacherous for anyone, able or not, to even try and brave. We'll find other ways, but *no one* should lose anyone else to the waves.' Tears glinted in his eyes as he spoke, and he looked up toward the lanterns, blinking rapidly.

'Owen, we hear you,' someone from the crowd spoke up. 'And we're sorry about Gethin, but...' The voice tailed off, letting the distraught man pull meaning from things left unsaid.

'No, Hywel, don't you *dare*.' Owen had straightened now, glaring. 'He wasn't *your* blood. You cannot possibly comprehend what this feels like. Imagine Marcus never comin' back to you.' The other man, Hywel, looked like he'd been struck. 'Exactly. Losin' someone to something you love, that we all love, is not anything I'd wish even upon my greatest enemy. Ground the boats, we find other ways to survive.'

'We don't survive without the sea!' Aron shot back.

Owen lost his temper then. 'And we'll lose our families, our *lives*, to it! You've seen what that does to people, Aron. Look at the Kincarrans!' Deathly silence fell through The Five-Pointed Compass, only broken by the sounds of the fire and Owen's heavy breathing. Eyes drifted toward the bar's hatchway, and then looked away again quickly. Eli and Tias seemed to have frozen entirely, pale and staring out into the crowd, eyes unseeing. Abraxus closed his own eyes for a moment, feeling a sudden wash of pain pour down upon him.

'That was uncalled for,' Smythe said into the thick silence. His face was stony, hands curled into fists resting on the bar.

'*Mae'n ddrwg gen i.*' *I'm sorry.* Owen said, seeming to break free of his anger. 'I didn't think – I just wanted to...' He trailed off, looking directly at Eli and Tias.

'I think we should suspend this for now,' Crow said slowly,

looking around the barroom. 'We can come back to the matter in hand when–'

'Don't do it.'

Crow's head snapped over toward the bar. There was a shuffling sound, and Eli appeared from underneath the hatchway. Tias still sat partially obscured; Abraxus could see him looking up at his brother warily.

'Elias?' Crow said, voice a little softer.

'Don't ground the boats.' His words were met with surprised, and then hastily muffled, exclamations. People glanced around to their family and friends, as if having silent conversations. 'Owen, I understand it. I really do.' Eli's voice wavered horribly on the last word. He cleared his throat, and continued, 'But we *can't*. Medwyn, Aron, Hywel, they're all right, it would kill the village. It's dangerous, and I suppose we have to face the very real possibility that we will lose more of our people. But we will lose *them all* if we pull the ships aground.' Eli seemed to think for a moment, 'And I don't just mean losing lives either.' The implications of his words hung in the air, flickering in the lantern light. Eli then seemed to become aware that he was the focus of attention, and looked hastily down at his boots. Abraxus noticed Tias reach up and tug gently on the cuff of Eli's shirt, and Eli sank back down into the relative concealment of the hatchway gap.

No one seemed to know what to say in response to that. Ripples of chatter rose, fell, dissipated. Abraxus looked around the room, at the people who were desperately torn, and felt the uncertainty pervade the air. It was true night now outside, and the colours from the lanterns sang out into the barroom, painting those beneath in strange light.

'I would agree,' Abraxus said. He didn't stand, nor did he speak loudly. But everyone's gaze was on him in a second. Abraxus leaned back against the wall in a feigned show of casualness. 'One amongst you has angered the waters. But this is not a reason for you to abandon it so hastily. Have strength, be patient. Anger is but a passing thing; it will dissipate.' Abraxus' words left a stillness in their wake that ached. He regarded the room, wondering who would be first to break it. It was his first address to anyone inside the village who wasn't infuriatingly stubborn or infuriatingly curious.

'Angered the waters?' It was Aron who spoke first. Incredulity warred with annoyance over his features. 'What in the name of God d'you mean?' The wave broke, and the tide came down upon Abraxus. Jeers, disparaging mutters and even some outright laughter filled The Five-Pointed Compass.

Abraxus fought the urge to roll his eyes. Or lose his temper. He stood, saying, 'I see you do not have the ability, yet, to comprehend the truth. Perhaps in time.' He rounded the table in the little nook, stepping out properly into the barroom.

The people closest to him shrank away.

'I think,' Crow began icily, 'that you should leave village affairs to those who live here.'

'Very well.' Abraxus inclined his head, and started for the door. As he passed Owen, he said quietly, 'Your brother is at peace. The waves will not roll his bones over the rocks.'

As the door closed behind him, Abraxus heard the explosion of talk break out. It was abruptly cut off by the night as Abraxus strode into it. He knew, a moment later, that he had a shadow. One that was not caused by the dying candlelight expelled from the cottage windows

IV
then.

Fish skin.

It was nearing the witching hour when they brought the stranger in. Sebastian was not sleeping; he was sitting up in bed with a thick book perched on his knees, arms aching from the strain of keeping it upright. There was a headache beginning to blossom behind his eyes, from tiredness or from too long studying the too small text, he didn't know. A knock at the door brought Sebastian out of his reverie. Closing the book gently, not wanting to damage the age-spotted vellum, he pulled back the blankets and walked toward the door. The cold of the stone bit into his bare feet. Sebastian was no stranger to late night calls; it was his job to provide information and answers, after all, and some questions were so pressing that they could not wait until the light of day. 'Yes?' He said, opening the door.

'Your presence is requested.' Of all the people he'd been expecting, it had not been one of the castle guards. Dark shadows upon sallow skin told of too many night watches. Sebastian appraised the guard for a moment, wondering what he could be needed for in person when the night pressed so closely around them. The guard gave him no chance to ask, but rather turned back down the hall, the torches flickering as he passed.

'Will I need anythin'?' Sebastian called after him. The guard didn't stop, but rather raised a hand and beckoned. Sebastian growled softly, and stepped out into the hallway. By the time he'd caught up to his quarry, his toes ached viciously. He'd had no opportunity to pull on his boots, nor change from his night things. As the pair silently walked through the sleeping castle, Sebastian had a moment of sudden panic. What if he had done something wrong, something to offend the king? It was a logical reason for being called out of bed at this hour; the king was a fickle man, and his black moods could take over his mind at any time. Sebastian had almost managed to convince himself of his own imagined treason, when the guard turned abruptly left instead of right, away from the main hall and toward the more domestic side of the castle. Sebastian let himself relax, this wasn't the place to sentence someone to a grisly execution. He had always preferred the left wing of the castle, the stone floors became smoother and more cheerily polished, well-worn underneath the staff and servant's feet. Chatter became more pronounced, and laughter rang occasionally from the many antechambers. Sebastian saw people shaking off the imposed facade of servitude, replacing it with wholly themselves.

The guard stopped outside a wide wooden door, studded with iron. Sebastian looked at him quizzically. This was certainly not the place he had been expecting. The guard indicated for him to step inside. Sebastian did, letting the herby aroma of the healing hall wash over him. It could never quite disguise the sharp smell of illness, and Sebastian found himself wrinkling his nose. All the cots lined out neatly on the floor were empty, save for one at the end.

The healer, a stout woman with an expression like a hunting dog, looked up as the door closed behind him. 'Ah good. Here.' She pointed to the spot beside her imperiously. Sebastian fought the urge to roll his eyes as he walked over. The healer had the mannerisms of the nobility, and the temper to match.

'What is...' Sebastian trailed off as he looked down to the occupant of the cot. He'd never seen a man like this one before. His skin was ebony dark, the cut of his clothes and hair unfamiliar. He appeared to be unconscious, but there was a slight furrow between his eyebrows, as if in thought. 'Who is he?' Sebastian asked, voice hushed.

'Not sure. The night watchman on the eastern fortification saw him reach the gate and just collapse. They brought him to me.' The healer looked down at the stranger, and Sebastian noticed she hadn't even laid out any of her usual supplies.

'Why did you call for me?' Sebastian said, kneeling down on the opposite side of the cot.

The healer worried a piece of dry skin on her lip for a moment. 'I don't know *what* he is,' she said eventually.

'He's a man,' Sebastian said, confused. The healer looked at him, and then reached over to pull the stranger's shoulder toward her, exposing the man's back to Sebastian.

'Lift his shirt.'

'What?'

'Lift his shirt. You'll understand.' The healer's grip stood out starkly against the man's dark skin; her knuckles were bone white.

Sebastian reached out and tentatively hooked a finger underneath the hem of the man's shirt, revelling for a second at the softness of the fabric. He dragged it up to the stranger's shoulder blades and gasped.

'Do you see now why I called for you?' The healer said, easing the man back down.

'I'll fetch some books.' Sebastian said, standing and hurriedly heading for the door. As he walked, he made a mental list of everything he might need from the archives, left to his care now for nearly a decade. Sebastian wasn't sure if he had the right sort of information. After all, how was he supposed to find a way to treat a man with iridescent scales on his back, in place of skin?

Chimes.
January, 1816.
Eli.

His heart was still beating loud in his chest as he left the inn. Eli took a deep breath, letting the cold air clear his head and soothe the hammering of his heart. He'd never been one for speaking in public, let alone something akin to an impassioned speech about the wellbeing of his home. But the words had reared up inside his head, and the next thing he knew, he was staring out into a sea of faces, Tias' hand gripping his sleeve gently. Owen's words had stung, but Eli couldn't deny that there was a grain of truth in them. All the rest of the village's population had to do to see a family torn apart by the waves was look at them. But that shouldn't mean that their oldest provider, their oldest *ally,* should be so readily abandoned.

Eli had been just as surprised as everyone else when Abraxus spoke up. He initially hadn't even spotted the man, shadowed as he was in an alcove. Tias hadn't let go of his sleeve when Eli had re-joined him underneath the hatchway, and his grip had tightened somewhat painfully around Eli's wrist as Abraxus spoke. Together, they had watched as the man was spurned, and then strode away into the night, murmuring something to Owen as he left. Whatever he had said had left a visible effect on the baker; he was pale with his eyes glinting overbright in the lanterns' glow.

It hadn't been the sickening beat of his heart, nor Abraxus' leaving that forced Eli out into the deep winter's embrace, but rather the noise. In the wake of Abraxus leaving, The Five-Pointed Compass had burst into conversation, layer upon layer of different voices calling to one another, speaking over their friends and family. It had become cacophonous, and Eli felt that it was a sudden weight, pressing down and suffocating him.

'Need some air,' he had mumbled to Tias, gently prising his brother's grip off his sleeve. Tias had started to say something, but Eli had already pushed past him and elbowed his way through the crowd. No one remarked at his passing.

He took in another breath, feeling momentarily dizzy. With all the sound cut off from inside, the quiet was almost disorientating. A particularly vicious gust of wind came up the street, blowing off the sea, which was crashing, unseen, further down towards the south-west. Eli realised he'd forgotten his cloak, and shivered. He weighed up his options, and decided that he'd rather be cold than face the oppressive heat and noise of the inn again.

'Alright?' Eli started slightly, whipping around and nearly losing his footing on the frost-bitten cobbles. Tias offered him a wan smile, his hand halfway to Eli's arm to steady him. 'Sorry.'

'It's fine.' Eli turned away from the porch again, staring off down the street, watching it fade into black as the light from lanterns and candles became more sporadic. 'It got a bit too loud.'

'They're all still talking about it,' Tias said dryly, wrapping his arms around himself. He too seemed to have left his cloak in The Five. 'A few of them actually called for Smythe to remove him from the guest quarters.'

'I bet he didn't take too kindly to that,' Eli said.

'No.' Some soft mirth had entered Tias' tone, 'He used some *very* choice words. You should have stayed, there were a few even I didn't know.' Tias nudged Eli gently with his elbow. Eli shot him a half smile, attention turning back to the night beyond. 'So... shall we head back in?' Tias shuffled, clearly wanting to be in the warm.

'You get in, I think I'll stay here for a bit longer.' Eli didn't have to look this time to know what sort of look he was getting from his brother. 'Tias, really, go on.' He sighed, gesturing back toward the door.

Tias turned away half-heartedly. Eli heard the slight metallic creak of the handle being turned, and then his brother said, 'Just don't do anything... unwise, alright?'

'When have I ever?' Eli said, looking back and winking. Tias rolled his eyes, looked one last time meaningfully at Eli, and then slipped back into The Five-Pointed Compass. 'When have I ever,' Eli said again, barely whispering. His voice was lost immediately to the wind and the night sky, the stars above intermittently veiled as wisps of cloud passed overhead.

He knew which direction Abraxus had walked off in; he'd been quick enough out of the inn to see the beads and metal in the man's hair glint a sudden golden in the light cast by a lantern left burning on a doorstep. What was strange, however, was the fact that Abraxus didn't seem to be heading to either *Tua'r Môr* Bay or *Angorfa* Beach. He'd taken the less well traversed route toward the cliff paths, cutting through the graveyard.

Eli took an unconscious step forward, his feet seeming to know his true intentions before his mind fully caught up. And before he had time to truly think it through, he was briskly walking through the darkened streets. As he passed unlit cottage and closed up shop, Eli wondered vaguely about all the times he had acted before he had thought, and then more wryly, how many of those times had led to a thorough berating from his Mam or Da. Or even Tias. He reached the graveyard, passing through the crumbling and cracked stone archway that demarcated the beginnings of holy ground. Studiously, he kept his gaze down, ignoring the rows of stones. To distract himself as he passed the patch of ground that held the memories of his father in an earthy embrace, Eli thought about what his finest example of acting before thinking would be. Eventually, he settled on the time that he had climbed part of the cliffs at *Tua'r Môr* Bay. Eli felt himself grin slightly at the memory. It had been a matter of pride – no matter how many times Tias had said it was sheer bloody mindedness and idiocy. Tias had said he couldn't. So, Eli had taken off for the cliff-face and was his own height up the rocky surface before Tias could even get out of the cavern.

The cliff paths were harder to traverse in the dark, and Eli found himself wishing for a lantern, or even just a stub of candle. He knew that as long as he could feel the crunch of the gravel beneath his well-worn boot soles, he was safe. The cold bit through his shirt, making him shiver forcefully. Once again, he found himself acting before thought, and started to run. Keeping one ear out for the tell-tale sound of loose stones underneath his pounding feet, Eli reasoned that not only would running warm him up, he would also catch up with Abraxus faster before he lost him to the swirling blackness. Eli let all thoughts then disappear from his mind, and lost himself to the rhythm of movement, how solid the earth felt beneath him, the harsh kiss of the wind against his cheeks, tangling his hair. Eli pushed himself harder, stones flying out from behind his heels as he kicked them up. For a moment, everything else in the world, on his mind, shrank into insignificance.

Eli was broken from his reverie when he saw the pale glow of light in front of him. He skidded to a halt, nearly overbalancing. Abraxus had clearly taken one of the night lanterns left out on someone's porch to guide his way. Eli bit back a laugh; as if the man wasn't already unpopular. Abraxus didn't seem to notice Eli's approach, and suddenly Eli found himself wanting to remain hidden. To silently observe the man who so clearly secretly observed them. He hung back, slowing his pace to stay outside of Abraxus' lantern light glow should he turn around. The crash of the waves masked Eli's footsteps as he followed. They came to the fork, and without hesitation Abraxus took the one that would lead him further along the coastal paths, rather than looping back around to Porth Tymestl. Eli followed, wondering if Abraxus, like him, had just wanted to get some air and clear away the clutter of thoughts.

Abraxus stopped, and lifted the lantern higher. He seemed to be looking for something, although what, Eli couldn't guess. There was nothing out on these long stretches of cliff path, aside from the sea to the west and stretches of moorland and vale to the east. Abraxus turned toward the sea, stepping off the path and toward the crumbling dry stone wall that ran the length of the cliffside. Eli hung back, eyes narrowed in an effort to see what Abraxus was looking for. After a moment of the man studying the wall, Abraxus nodded to himself, and stepped through a small gap. A cold wash of panic came over Eli as he vanished; he was sure that Abraxus had fallen over the cliff. Forgetting his desire to remain hidden, Eli ran to the spot where Abraxus had stood not a moment before, and peered cautiously through the gap.

The lantern light was still burning a gentle gold against the night, and was moving steadily downward. Eli breathed out a sigh of relief; the lantern was bobbing up and down in tandem with the motion of walking, rather than the straight plummet down he'd been expecting. The dizzying relief was then overlaid by confusion. Eli couldn't recall a cliff path heading down to the sea here. *In fairness*, he thought, *this part of the coastline isn't one he traversed very often*. Both he and his brother preferred being close to the water, rather than tossed out under the vast skies above.

Kneeling, he ran his hands over the wall. The wet seagrass immediately soaked through the knees of his trousers. There was nothing he could find that would act as a marker for the path, no raised pole nor a smear of colour. Eli had just begun to stand, running his fingers absentmindedly over the rough surface of the stones, when he felt something carved into a flat expanse. His eyes had become accustomed to the dark by then, enough to pick out the paler path against the dark earth, and to see the denser dark where the cliffs fell to the sea. But the carving was so fine, and so small that Eli knew he'd have to rely on touch alone to tell him what it depicted. Tracing the indents, he found a circle, with four points protruding from it at quarter intervals. A compass, then. Eli frowned; the compass seemed to have another ring running *through* the points, creating two concentric circles. There were several lines etched along the top of the outer circle, although what it was Eli couldn't tell. He made a mental note to come back during the day, armed with paper and pencil, to try and decipher the symbol. He stood fully, remembering his quarry. The lantern light was now nothing but a speck, a fallen star dancing so far below. Eli felt for the edge of the path with his foot, not wanting to miss it and plummet to the rocks and water below.

It was much steeper and narrower than the path down to *Tua'r Môr* Bay. Eli stayed close to the rocky wall, fingers aching from the cold, feeling moss and mud underneath his nails. Reckless ambition mixed with fear to make a heady concoction. Part of him wanted to race down the path, see how fast he could go. The other part – the part that sounded suspiciously like Tias – told him to cling to the cliff-face and think about his every step. The path curved to the right sharply about three quarters of the way down. Eli swore as his foot skidded over the edge, not anticipating the sudden change of direction. He flung himself backward, pressing his back firmly against the damp rock, catching his breath. After a moment, he let out a shaky laugh and felt for the corner, traversing around it carefully. The wind had dropped this far down, the sea calling out louder now. The breakwater sounded fierce tonight, crashing and cracking against the land. Again, Eli wished for some light, to be able to see the black expanse of water, endlessly deep, crested with white foam. He kept walking.

The bridge was only discernible by the change of tension underneath his boots. One moment the ground was solid beneath him, the next it was slick and rocked sickeningly up and down. Eli reached out, catching himself on the thick strands of rope that had been strung up at waist height. The bridge seemed to span an inlet, one of the many jagged cuts into the land that ranged the coastline. Bites of the earth taken away by the hungry sea. Eli felt little droplets of icy cold water hit his cheeks, and wondered how far above the sea he actually was. The sounds seemed redoubled, and echoed horribly around the inlet. Gritting his teeth, Eli pressed on, hating the sway of the bridge as he walked.

Just as Eli was beginning to think that he was wasting his time, and the warmth and crowds of The Five-Pointed Compass seemed more appealing, light blazed into his vision. He instinctively threw a hand up over his eyes, blinking to clear the spots of bruise-green and purple that danced before them. The bridge had given way to a steeper path, and then to the shingle of a beach. Atop the waves, drifting slightly with the motion of the current, was a ship. It was sheltered in a natural harbour, tall spires of rock jutting out from the cliff-face and out into the ocean in a horseshoe shape. The shingle beach Eli now stood on was just inside one of the walls; he had unknowingly passed through an archway eroded through the black rock. Eli stared at the ship. For one heart stopping moment, he had thought it was the *Dawnsiwr y Wawr*.

The frame was undeniably a Brixham trawler, but the more he studied it, the more he saw it differed. For a start, it had a raised quarter deck, companionway, and a spoked wheel. It was longer too. And, Eli realised, the sails were green and blue. The light that came from the ship emanated from several lanterns strung up in the rigging and one at the bowsprit, casting the canvas in a fiery wash over the top of the vibrant colours. The wood was golden, and seemed to gleam. His father's ship, whilst well cared for, had taken on the grey-red colour that told of many days and nights at sea. It was a thing of beauty, and Eli felt an ache in his chest. It was the sort of ship he would have loved to command, to run away over the horizon on. The shingle scattered noisily beneath his feet as he walked toward the water's edge. A broken and distorted reflection of the ship played in the mirror-like water, the image seeming ghostly.

The ship was docked close to the opposite wall; the flatness atop the rock telling Eli that someone had carved a path there. Sure enough, he found narrow stairs cut into the rock, and climbed them. There was a plank laid out from the ship to the path, and Eli stopped by it, dithering. This was undoubtedly Abraxus' ship, and he was most likely not welcome aboard. But something called to him, like a voice speaking when he hung just on the edges of sleep. As Eli took in the deck, the quarter deck and the bowsprit, he spotted letters painted near to the prow. They were in the same seaweed green as the mainsail. *Asherah.*

The plank bowed a little as Eli stepped onto it. He closed his eyes as his feet hit the deck, feeling the familiar sway beneath him. Becoming wholly a part of the sea and the tides. It felt like coming home. His mother had forbidden both himself and Tias from stepping foot on any vessel, terrified that the sea might claim more if they were cast out upon it. Eli took in a deep breath, relishing the snap of the canvas, the soft creaking of the ropes and wood as they shifted.

His Da had once told him that ships, just like those that work on them, are alive. They breathed and moved, needed care and love. 'A ship is not just a tool', he had said, 'it is family.'

The door to the little stateroom underneath the quarter deck opened, and Eli scrambled away, finding a haphazard stack of boxes and a coil of rope to hide behind. It was a relatively abysmal hiding space, and he waited for Abraxus to call him out. Eli held his breath, and listened as Abraxus' footsteps moved over the deck, and then up the little staircase to the top of the quarter deck.

Risking a glance, Eli straightened, looking over one of the boxes. Abraxus was barefoot, his steps light. As he passed the wheel, ornate and well-polished, Abraxus ran a hand over one of the spokes almost lovingly. The merest hint of a breeze rippled through the canvas as his fingers swept off the edge. Eli looked up, noticing that the flag at the very top of the mainmast hadn't moved at all. Curling his fingers over the edge of the box for better balance, Eli watched as Abraxus reached inside his pocket, and pulled out a mess of twine. With a cat-like grace, he hopped up onto the rail that ran along the edge of the ship, settling himself to sit with his back against a taller piece of wood that protruded upward from the rail.

Abraxus seemed to lose himself in knotting and threading the twine into a pattern, stringing alternating lengths off small pieces of driftwood. Eli watched, just as enthralled. He wanted to get closer, but there wasn't much else on the deck to give him sufficient cover. After a while, Abraxus held up his creation by a loop at the top. It was the beginnings of a chime, the pieces of wood twirling slowly as Abraxus inspected it. He seemed happy with it, and reached into his other pocket, bringing out a handful of white and grey stones. He started tying the stones onto the string through holes carved through them. Reaching into his own pocket, Eli brought out the stone that had been left for them on Christmas day, turning it over in his fingers. He knew it had a purpose. It was just a question of what?

Quilts.
January, 1816.
Abraxus.

The boy needed to learn how to hide better. Abraxus could see the glint of his hair in the lantern light, the white curl of his fingers over the top of one of boxes he hadn't yet cleared away. He added that to the list of things he had to do. Abraxus had settled himself at one of his many perches around the deck of his ship, the *Asherah*. This one was his favourite when out on the open waters. He'd even added the backrest to make it more comfortable. From here, he could watch the white trail of the *Asherah*'s passing, cut cleanly into the waters as surely as a road. Abraxus might not be on the open sea now, but the illusion was as good as any whilst sitting here. The chime was nearly finished, he was tying on the last stone. Shards of sea glass clinked softly against one another, woven through the twine itself.

Internally, Abraxus was having an argument with himself. He had known Eli was following him, and yet, he hadn't tried to apprehend the boy. Instead, Abraxus had made it easy for Eli to stay on his trail. And now, here he was, making a chime with the stones that both boys knew to be important somehow. *Too many clues*, he thought to himself, *you* want *them to find out.* Abraxus growled lowly and tied off the last knot. *No, I do not. Be quiet.* Holding up the chime, he watched it twist and spiral in front of him. Satisfied, Abraxus swung himself off the rail, and walked quietly down the stairs, letting his fingers trace the carvings there, and onto the main deck. He chose a spot of rigging at random, and began to tie the chime to it. One of the stones, now raised to eye level, spun slowly around and for a moment, Abraxus looked straight through the hole eroded there. The sea remained dark, and although that was firmly a good sign, he couldn't help but feel a little disappointed. Abraxus heard a soft creak behind him, and smiled despite himself.

'I wonder,' he said aloud, not turning, 'if being in places you are *not* supposed to be is a special talent.' Reaching up, he set the chime spinning.

There was no reply.

Sighing, Abraxus turned around in time to see a shadowed figure take off down the thin path atop the harbour wall. He found himself vaguely worrying that Eli had nothing to light his way back home. Shaking off the worry, after all, he'd made it down here, Abraxus turned back towards the stateroom beneath the quarter deck. He had no desire to return to The Five-Pointed Compass that night. Smythe would understand. Opening the door, Abraxus slipped inside and let himself breath in the familiar smells of wood and paper and salt.

This was his haven: the room was mostly taken up by a large desk at the centre, its surface covered in scrolls and maps and half-finished projects that Abraxus vowed to finish *at some point*. Along the starboard side of the cabin ran a bookshelf. Smythe would probably describe it as eclectic, the actual horizontal shelves were intermittently spaced with diamond shaped recesses for scrolls, and the books themselves were stacked haphazardly. Abraxus knew his collection would put the library of Alexandria to shame. In fact, some of the older, more sun-bleached scrolls had come from that erudite store.

His bed called to him. It was set into the port wall, canopied with bolts of fabric he'd picked up from markets across the world. The nook was lit by a single candle, and in its flickering light the quilts and blankets looked heavenly. Pulling off his clothes down to his undergarments and leaving them strewn on the floor, Abraxus sank back into the bed and pulled the heaviest blanket over him. He didn't snuff the candle, letting it keep the shadows away. The gentle rolling motion of the tide beneath the *Asherah*'s hull had sleep beckoning at his mind before Abraxus had even fully closed his eyes. Despite wanting to savour his first night back on his ship since arriving in Porth Tymestl, he found himself sinking, held close and warm. Around him, the *Asherah* settled quietly, the snap of the canvas fading away.

VI
then.

Beyond the door.

The man with the fish skin back was awake. Sebastian watched him sit up, pass a hand over his eyes and look around the healing hall. Confusion warred with tiredness, and Sebastian leaned forwards unconsciously as the man tried to push himself up to kneeling, but swayed heavily. The door creaked slightly as Sebastian pressed against it, watching through the gap. He cursed himself silently as the stranger's head snapped around, eyes fixing on the door. Sighing, Sebastian slipped into the hall, shutting the treacherous door behind him.

The man looked at him quizzically for a moment, head canted to one side. He spoke, but it wasn't a language Sebastian recognised. At the no doubt blank look he was receiving, the stranger spoke again. This time, Sebastian knew the shapes of the words, but not the meaning. It sounded like Latin, but the cadence was rougher, earthier. He shook his head, and the stranger frowned. He tried again, and again, eventually letting out a low growl as Sebastian kept shaking his head. Inside, he was amazed; *how many languages did this man know?*

'How about now? Do you understand this one?'

'Ah!' Sebastian smiled, coming over finally to the man's cot and settling himself down beside it. 'Yes. Glad to see you awake,' he said, juggling the books and scrolls in his arms.

The stranger seemed a little perturbed. 'This was not... where am I?'

'The kingdom of Mercia, my friend. In the halls of the king, no less,' Sebastian said, a little proudly. The king might be a vile tempered man, more predisposed to wage war first and ask questions never, but nonetheless, he was powerful. And Sebastian was that powerful man's archivist.

'How far from the coastline are we?'

That caught Sebastian off guard. 'A few days' walks,' he said, not truly able to quantify the length since he had never undertaken it himself. 'Why?' His question went unheeded, as the stranger cursed – in yet another language Sebastian didn't know, but he understood the inflection *perfectly* – and tried once more to get to his feet. 'No, no, stay down.' Sebastian reached out and pushed the man firmly down by his shoulders. 'You were cold and exhausted when they brought you in, take time to rest and recover. What's your name?'

'No, I have to go, you do not understand.' The man said insistently, 'I am supposed to be meeting someone.' He closed his eyes suddenly, clearly trying to fight over a wave of dizziness.

'Well, I'm sure they can wait for you.' Sebastian levelled him with a stern look. He took his hands off the man's shoulders, and held one out. 'Sebastian.'

After a second of indecision, the man clasped Sebastian's forearm with his own rough, long-fingered hand. 'Abraxus.' The man – Abraxus – then raised an eyebrow at Sebastian's surprised expression, one that he quickly tried to smother. 'Not a common name, perhaps?' There was a lightness in his tone that told Sebastian he was jesting.

'Quite.' They dropped the grip simultaneously, Sebastian settling back down now it was clear Abraxus wasn't about to try and do something stupid again. He set about arranging his books and scrolls around him, ordering them by what he thought might be most useful.

'A good collection,' Abraxus said.

'Thank you,' Sebastian shuffled one scroll on Pict mythlore next to a series of children's fables. 'I am the archivist, it's my job to have expansive knowledge.' He looked up, tipping a wink, 'And some superfluous facts too.'

Abraxus smiled slightly. Quiet descended between them, only the slight call of the wind punctuated by the crackle of the long fire in the hearth. 'So, archivist, why am I being seen to by the book-keeper, not a healer?' The question was asked lightly, but Sebastian's fingers stilled on the spine of a book he was examining. There was an undercurrent of something darker in Abraxus' words. Not quite malice, nor a threat, but something that sent a shiver down Sebastian's neck.

'They deemed me the most suitable to attend to you,' Sebastian said, a little stiltedly. He kept his eyes trained down, fiddling with the edge of a scroll on kelpies.

'Is it because I have been deemed *inhuman*?' Abraxus' tone was scathing. He didn't wait for an answer. 'Because I can assure you, they are wrong. Mostly.'

'Something like that, yes.' Sebastian, for reasons unfathomable even to himself, found himself relaxing. At least this strange man was honest. 'Can I... no, never mind. Are you feeling anythin' adverse at the moment?'

Abraxus appraised Sebastian, a knowing look in his eyes. They were two different colours, but this didn't bother the archivist too much. One of the kitchen girls had the same condition. 'You may ask,' he said softly.

'I really should be getting on with an examination–'

'You *can* ask,' Abraxus said, this time with more inflection.

'Your back... it's unlike anything I've ever seen before.' Sebastian shuffled forward a little, the points of his knees bumping against the cot. Abraxus mirrored his position, sitting cross-legged and hunching over.

'It was a – a *gift*, I suppose. Something to remind me of my purpose.' He reached up and slipped a hand beneath his shirt, tracing the scales Sebastian had seen last night.

'Purpose?' Sebastian asked.

'I am from the sea,' Abraxus said cryptically. 'From it, and of it and wholly belonging to it.'

Sebastian knew he wasn't going to get any more from the man after that, so instead he asked, 'Can I see them?' He felt himself flush slightly at the question, immediately anxiety-ridden that it was too personal.

Abraxus grabbed the hem of his shirt, and pulled it over his head. He turned his back to Sebastian, rolling his shoulders forward to better expose the scales there.

Sebastian stared.

They were even more spectacular in the soft morning light. Starting at the nape of Abraxus' neck, they flowed down his spine and along the back of his ribs, fanning out delicately over his shoulder blades. They shifted as he breathed, interlocking in a beautiful pattern of blues, silvers, greens and a few very deep purples. Sebastian instinctively reached out a finger, desperate to trace the line down Abraxus' spine, but he stilled himself before he made contact. Seeing was one thing. Touching was another.

'I am surprised,' Abraxus said, rucking his shirt back over him. Sebastian felt a twinge of loss as the scales disappeared beneath the fabric. 'Usually, I would have been denounced as the product of black magicks, and cast out.'

'There are many things in this world we don't yet understand, and to call them all evil would be a hideous misunderstandin',' Sebastian said passionately.

'Hm.' Abraxus had turned his attention to the slitted window. He seemed to be far away for a moment, and then abruptly snapped back to the present. 'Well, is your curiosity satiated?'

'Very.'

'Good. Now, a favour deserves a favour.' Abraxus uncrossed his legs, and gingerly placed his feet on the floor. Before Sebastian could protest, he had lifted himself off the cot and stood. He barely swayed, but did press the heel of his hand to his forehead. 'I need directions.' He then muttered something under his breath that sounded distinctly like, 'Because *someone* does not believe in signposts.'

'Where were you tryin' to get to?' Sebastian asked, also standing, books forgotten at his feet.

'A drinking hall. I was told to take the western road from the coast and keep travelling until I passed a king's lonely castle. I can only assume she meant here.'

'Plenty of alehouses around here, do you have the name?' Sebastian asked, already making a mental map of his favourite haunts when he managed to escape the dusty presence of the archives.

'The Heathered Antler.'

'Hm.' Sebastian couldn't recall that one. 'Come with me, I have maps in the archives.'

'Are you sure you don't want to wait for better weather?' Sebastian said, not turning from the window slit.

'I am already three days late, I would do better not to delay this any further.' Abraxus was pursuing the stacks in the archive, occasionally pulling a book or a scroll down and thumbing through it. Sebastian had caught him the day before trying to sneak a small roll of parchment into his pocket.

'Not that one,' he had said, reaching over and plucking the scroll from inside the man's jacket. 'That one stays here.' He gestured to the western wall of the shelves and cubbies. 'Anythin' else over there though, you can take.'

The pack Abraxus was borrowing sat by the doorway to the archival rooms, filled with provisions for a journey and several pilfered texts. Sebastian had slipped a few medicinal herbs in there too, should the man come across trouble again. The Heathered Antler, it turned out, was not too far from the castle, perhaps two days' hard walk. Sebastian had tried to offer his company to Abraxus, partly because he was still a little concerned for the man's health, and partly because he was the most interesting thing to have happened to Sebastian in over a decade. His offer had been flatly refused, however, and now Sebastian was beginning to contemplate how dull life might look now. He wanted it to shimmer like the scales that hid beneath layers of rough clothing.

Outside, the rain fell in lines and the cloud cover was low. A few moments out there, and one would be thoroughly soaked. And yet, Abraxus had insisted on leaving today. What business he had at the alehouse, he hadn't disclosed to Sebastian either. A rustle behind him told him Abraxus had shouldered the pack. He turned, watching the man settle the folds of his coat comfortably underneath the shoulder straps. 'All in readiness?' Sebastian asked, coming over to open the door out onto the corridors.

'Yes,' Abraxus said, stepping out. 'I find myself in your debt.' He looked seriously at Sebastian with his two-toned eyes, and Sebastian felt something weighty drop into the air between them. 'I shall find a way to repay it.' With that, he strode away, forcing Sebastian to hurry in order to catch up.

As he walked, he had a sudden thought. They were heading for the staff's entrance, as was suitable for men of their social positioning. But there was something Sebastian had been intending to show Abraxus from the moment he learned he was of the sea.

'No, this way,' Sebastian said as casually as he could manage, his heart beating oddly fast against his chest. He steered Abraxus toward the main hall, knowing that it would most likely be empty at this time of day; the king and his entourage would have taken up residence in the private rooms after a decadent lunch. Feeling all of eleven or twelve winters old again, Sebastian pushed open the grand double doors and slipped inside.

'Why have we come this–' Abraxus started as he entered behind Sebastian. He faltered, eyes fixed on the painting over the mantlepiece. 'Ah.' He studied it for a while, eyes tracing the lines of pearlescent white spray, the tiny curve of a gull's wing.

'This is the only thing of the sea I have,' Sebastian said softly, walking toward the hearthside. 'I used to come 'ere as a child, stare at it for hours until I was caught.' He turned to look at Abraxus, who was now standing side by side with him. 'My mentor, he came from by the sea too. I once asked him if it was like that.'

'And what did he say?' Abraxus asked quietly.

'He said it was *more*.'

'A wise man. No oil daubed on cloth can hope to capture the... *magnitude* of the open waves, nor the depths of the water. No canvas is big enough to hold a horizon.' Abraxus stepped lightly up onto the hearthstones, reaching up as if to try and touch the painting. 'Why did you bring me here?'

'I just thought... perhaps you could tell me more?' Sebastian said hopefully. 'More than what the old archivist told me,' he clarified, 'he said nothing after that one instance, and I was always so desperate for – for *more*.'

'I cannot stay.' Abraxus actually seemed disappointed, looking at him with an honesty Sebastian hadn't yet fully seen.

'Not now, then, but perhaps that could be how you repay your debt? Come back, and tell me tales. I could even write them down.' Sebastian tried, and probably failed, to keep the excitement from his voice. He looked to Abraxus imploringly.

'I think that can be arranged,' Abraxus said with a small smile. 'The business I have at The Heathered Antler should not take me more than three or four days.' He looked back to the painting, and then gripped the straps of the pack. 'For now, however, the road calls me onward.'

'Yes, of course.' Sebastian led Abraxus through a side door and into a draughty antechamber off the main hall. A narrow and tight set of spiral stairs sat above and below them, and Sebastian began to descend. There was a little used service door set into the mulchy earth of the surrounding moorland. The bolt that kept it locked from the outside was rusty, and flakes of reddish-brown metal came away under Sebastian's hand as he pulled it. 'I'll leave this unlocked. Come this way when you return.' He held out his hand, and Abraxus clasped it the same way he had done when they'd first met.

'Thank you.' He stepped out into the rain, his figure immediately becoming blurred and insubstantial at the edges. Sebastian raised a hand in farewell. Over the drive of the rain, he heard Abraxus call to him. 'The ship in the painting. She has a name. The *Asherah*.'

'How do you know?' Sebastian called back. He had never seen a name inscribed on the prow of the ship.

'Because she is mine!' Abraxus' voice was distant, its owner all but vanished into the swirling grey of the low sky. Sebastian stood very still, framed by the doorway. Blue water and green sails danced in his mind.

Somewhere above him, there was a creaking of hinges. He hastily slammed the door shut and turned in time to see a steward standing on the stairs, ducking his head to better see Sebastian.

'What're you doing down 'ere?' The steward didn't wait for an answer. 'The falconer is looking for you. Needs some text or other.'

'I'll be there in a moment.' Sebastian inclined his head, and the steward left, footsteps echoing around the spiral staircase. Sebastian forcefully pushed Abraxus, the sea, and the man's parting words from his mind. Four days. He could wait that long. After all, he'd waited his entire life for something like an adventure.

'Close the hall doors up as you leave, Smythe!' Sebastian rolled his eyes as he entered the main hall once more. No one ever called him by his first name anymore.

VII
now

Memory.
January, 1816.
Tias.

'Like this?' Tias held up the stick, letting the rest of the twine knotted underneath drop down, hanging over the ledge. The two stones gifted to them spun gently, spiralling the rope this way and that.

'Aye,' Eli said, hoisting the pulley system back up. He turned his attention back to the knots, making sure that the driftwood supply was secure, before jumping up to join his brother on the ledge. The day outside was fair, icy blue sky just visible through white cloud. The shadows on the beach slid by quickly, the wind was up and in the perfect direction to catch sails and send them out over the waves. Angorfa Harbour had been a hive of activity that morning as Tias and Eli had made their way to Tua'r Môr Bay, although the usual excitement at the prospect of a day at sea was tinted slightly with a taut desperation. If the catch failed again today, or worse, if a ship was lost to the depths, then the mostly collective decision to keep the fleet running would become unfounded. Porth Tymestl was only a few bad days from becoming grounded.

Tias had suggested the trip down to the cavern, since they really had little else to do. Eli's discovery of Abraxus' ship had kept them both up for most of the night talking, and as such they both felt tired and a little listless. Tias had asked his brother to describe the ship, and had done his best to recreate it on paper. Eli had gently pulled the notebook from Tias, studied the drawing and then silently held out a hand for the pencil. When the book had been passed back to him, Tias noticed that Eli had written in miniscule lettering over the prow the word Asherah. 'The name?' He said, trying not to show his annoyance that Eli's handwriting was substantially messier than his would have been.

'Mm. It could be just a name, I don't know the word,' Eli said. 'Do you?'

'No.' Tias had held up the page to the candlelight then, watching the paper blaze a sudden golden-brown. Eli had also described the symbol he'd felt carved into the rock, demarcating the start of the hidden coastal path. What Tias had scribbled into his book apparently had been similar, but Eli was still at a loss as to what the lines running around the outside ring were. Possibly letters, possibly decoration. They'd have to go back at some point to see it properly. Silence had fallen between them, Tias closing his book and placing it on the bedside table. Sleep came on swift wings, pulling him down into dreams of salt and canvas.

Now, Eli took the chime from Tias, holding it up toward the entrance of the cavern, letting a sudden patch of sun play through the holes eroded in the stones. 'I'm not really sure what it was for, but–' He started.

'If Abraxus is doing it, then we probably should too,' Tias finished. 'Did he seem to hang it anywhere specific?' Tias idly reached out and flicked a length of twine, making the stone at the end of it jump wildly for a moment.

'His was on the rigging. So maybe facing the sea?' Eli suggested, voice hesitant.

'Seems reasonable to me,' Tias said, reaching for the chime. It was a lot simpler than the one Eli had described, made with only one length of driftwood from which three pieces of twine were knotted – two hanging down to hold the stones, and one in the middle of the wood, tied into a loop from which to hang the chime up. Tias slipped off the ledge, shivering slightly as the wet sand forced itself between his toes. He'd left his boots on the ledge by the fire in order to dry them out a little, the tide still somewhat high as they made their way to the cavern. 'Catch.' Tias plucked a weathered stump of a candle off a small shelf by the entrance to the cavern and tossed it back to Eli. Either his aim was abysmal, or Eli hadn't really been paying attention: his brother had to lunge backwards and to the side to catch it.

Easing the loop open a little wider, Tias hung the chime from the outcrop of rock, adjusting it slightly as it balanced itself. He stood back to admire it. The wind picked up a little, gusting through the cavern and making their little fire spit. Eli fed the end of the candle to it, the smell of melting wax permeating the chilly saline tinted air. 'Throw the chalk,' Tias called to his brother, standing by the wall and looking over its uneven surface. The chalk hit him squarely in the ear, and he glared at Eli as he stooped to pick it up. Eli was sniggering, determinedly not looking at Tias as he made a show of stoking the fire.

'Very amusing,' Tias said dryly, reaching into his pocket. Flipping his notebook open to the drawing of the Asherah, Tias began to copy it out onto the wall, cross-hatching neatly within the outlines of the sails to show colour. He was vaguely aware of Eli watching him as he drew, but soon lost all self-consciousness in the scratch of the chalk over stone, the lines meeting neatly to form a whole.

'We should try again.' Eli's voice broke him out from his reverie. Tias fumbled with the chalk, nearly dropping it. His feet were completely numb with cold now.

'What?' He asked, nonplussed.

'We should try and come down here again. At night,' Eli said, looking over Tias' head toward the sea. It was retreating now, opening up the beach a little more.

'Abraxus said–' Tias started.

'I know. But after that,' Eli gestured to the chime, 'do we really have anywhere else to go?' He looked to Tias, who shifted under his gaze. 'We still can't figure out what Smythe meant by 'the obvious question', no matter how many times we sit down an' write in your book.' It was true, several pages of Tias' notebook were now filled with lines upon lines of questions, both in his small writing, and Eli's taller lettering. 'The bones keep turning up, but we haven't seen where or what they're coming from. We should try again.'

Tias couldn't help but want to agree. It was getting... frustrating to say the least. The answers felt like fog, there and hanging before him, but untouchable. Dissipating whenever he tried to get a grip on them. 'We might even see how he was sending them back...' Tias muttered to himself.

'Exactly!' Eli said eagerly. 'We've done it before, it really shouldn't be all too hard.'

'In the summer, Eli,' Tias pointed out. His brother waved him away.

'We'll bring more blankets.' He looked Tias directly in the eye. 'What d'you say?' There was a liveliness in his expression that Tias had come to see less and less of late. He fiddled with the chalk, staining the tips of his fingers.

'If we were prepared...' He started, thinking through the logistics of it all. He turned to look at the drawing of the Asherah on the wall. Its sails were stretched out, an invisible wind drawing it along. 'Yes. Let's do it.'

Eli whooped, grinning broadly. 'Tonight?'

'No, wait a moment, we need to plan this properly, not dive headlong into it.'

'Diving headlong into things is what I do best.'

'Evidently.' Tias dropped the chalk onto the outcrop and came back over to the ledge, clambering up to sit by the fire. 'Not tonight.' He said it decisively, knowing that Eli would try and argue his point.

Sure enough, Eli prodded the fire a little too harshly and said, 'We need to do it soon, though. We don't know when Mam will be back, and that'll make it a lot harder.'

Their mother had yet to return to Porth Tymestl, staying away longer than the first time she had departed. It would be a month in two days. The Griffiths had been keeping an eye on them, Efa making sure that both of them had enough to eat. Smythe had insisted on seeing Tias and Eli at least once a week for an evening meal at The Five-Pointed Compass. Tias always felt a little uncomfortable when he first arrived at the inn, or at Efa and Medwyn's house, Heather's End. It was a debt he wasn't sure how he could begin to repay.

'Soon.' Tias conceded, not wanting to rehash all the things unspoken surrounding their eventual departure from the village. 'But not tonight, alright?' Tias made sure Eli was looking at him as he said this. Eli might be headstrong and infuriatingly stubborn, but Tias had broken out his best defence against his brother's nature. Their father had once called it 'the elder stare', and it had stuck. Tias was never quite fully aware if he was doing it or not, but the result was always the same. Eli would grumble, complain, and then back down and concede. It was times like this that Tias was never so glad that he had an extra ten minutes over Eli.

'Fine,' Eli said moodily. They stayed at the beach for the rest of the day; Tias making an effort to ignore the hunger that crept up on him as they passed into the late afternoon. It had been a conscious decision to not bring lunch down to the seafront with them; if they wanted to eat tonight, they would have to forego a midday meal. Tias noticed with a slight pang of worry that Eli didn't seem to share his discomfort, but rather just carried on doing whatever it was they'd found to occupy themselves with for the time being. He knew that Eli still wasn't eating properly, but then again, was anyone in the village at the moment?

'Ship?' Eli asked, bringing Tias out from his thoughts.

'Now?'

'Do we have anything else to do?' Eli said, a slight challenge in his voice. Tias sighed; he should have known Eli wouldn't truly leave it be.

'No, I suppose not.' He headed back toward the cavern, the pair having left it a while ago to look in the tidepools. Eli fell into step beside him, holding his boots in one hand. The bottom of his trousers were soaked through, the cuffs matted with wet sand. They'd dry later into salty stiffness, and remain that way until one of them decided to do some laundry. Which wouldn't be for the foreseeable future, most likely. 'Do we have any rope?' Tias asked.

'Not in the cavern, no. But I think there were some old net-edges by the cliffs that washed up a while ago.' They'd come to where the long sets of bones started in earnest. Tias walked carefully around them, not wanting to disturb them. Eli stayed by his side, looking up at the sharp black line against the white-blue sky. Strings of seaweed hung down, slapping wetly against the sides. The effect was uncanny: it was like someone had just ripped up a burnt forest and thrown it haphazardly onto a beach. Tias shivered, keeping his hands firmly in his pockets to resist the urge to reach out and touch.

'Soon.' Eli's voice was so quiet Tias could have reasonably ignored it. 'We'll know soon.'

Tias couldn't think of anything to say to that, and just nodded. They split up, Eli heading off to find the washed-up lengths of rope, Tias back to the cavern. The chime spun lazily as he passed it, clicking against the rock wall. He untied the knots of the pulley, lowering the net down and picked out several of the longest and flattest pieces of driftwood, stacking them neatly on the sand at his feet. Hoisting the pulley back up, he then started on the fairly laborious task of dragging the wood onto the beach, and lining them up in a rough rectangle. As Tias worked, he felt a soft thrill of nostalgia. It had been a while since he and Eli had done this.

It was a game invented by their mother, to occupy them as children when Da was out on the waters for a day, perhaps even two. Both Tias and Eli had been frustrated that they couldn't join their father on the open seas, and so Ffion had brought them down to Tua'r Môr Bay and set them collecting strips of wood. Together, they had built a 'ship', one long stick for a mast, and an old blanket as the sail. Tias had sat at the 'prow' and called directions to Eli, who had insisted he was the Captain – although after ten minutes Eli had evidently felt bad and dubbed them both co-Captains. Their mother had taken the opportunity to sit down further along the beach and read, or else stare absentmindedly for hours out over the water. As they'd grown, the ships they had built on the shore had become more elaborate, Eli writing their names in the sand.

Once, Tias had tried to construct one that would float, lashing together the wood of the base to form a raft. He'd ended up very wet, very cold and then thoroughly chastised by his mother. When their father had come home that night, he'd only laughed and pulled Tias onto his lap. That had been only a few days before their eleventh birthday, after which they had finally joined John on the Dawnsiwr y Wawr.

Now, having passed their sixteenth birthday and forced to shake off childhood, Tias had forgotten about the game. He was surprised, but glad, Eli hadn't. His brother was coming back over the beach now, neck and shoulders draped in rope. He held it up as he got closer for inspection, tossing strands of it into the air. 'Enough?' He called.

'More than.' Tias had finished the base, and was waiting for Eli to pull the mast up. Another thing forgotten and then recalled: the mast was never pulled up alone. They worked in companionable quiet, securing lines of 'rigging' and forfeiting Eli's cloak for the sail. Tias stepped back, looking at what they'd built. He had had a moment of worry, that he would look at the ship and see nothing but a childish game that should be left for the current to take. But instead, he saw what he had always seen; a ship, waiting for the waves and for them to board. He smiled a little sadly to himself. Some things never really changed.

'Have you got a name?' Eli asked, kneeling in the sand by the stern. His eyes were bright with something young, his expression open.

Tias thought. 'How about… The Memoria?'

'I like it,' Eli said, writing it out in the sand. 'Is that with an e-r?'

'I-a,' Tias replied. He didn't comment on the thickness in his brother's voice. Nor did Tias draw attention to his quick swipe at his eyes.

The Memoria, officially named, set sail as the early darkness swept over the village. The clouds were finally brushed aside, and Tias lay back against the splintery wood, Eli next to him, to watch the stars spring into life.

Storm.
January, 1816.
Eli.

The shiver that ran down Eli's neck had nothing to do with the biting cold. The thrum of his heart in his chest beat in time with the waves he could hear distantly crashing against the beaches below. In only a few hours' time, he and Tias would be scaling the cliff path down to Tua'r Môr Bay, laden with provisions for the night.

They had spent the day packing up whatever they thought they would need for the night into the two small sea chests their Da had commissioned for them on their thirteenth birthday.

'No sailor should head for open waters without one of these to keep memories of home anchored.' He had said, gesturing to the boxes that sat neatly on the kitchen table. They had been gleaming in the morning sunlight then; wood highly polished, their initials carved above the lock and highlighted in a soft blue for Eli, and a deep green for Tias.

Now, they were battered, and their lustre had faded with use. Eli's had chips taken out of the corners, the dark wood splintered to reveal the lighter colouration inside. He had taken a moment to look at the contents of the chest when he'd pulled it out from underneath his bed. Tias referred to it as his treasure chest, and if Eli was honest with himself, he couldn't fault the description.

To anyone else, it would look like the chest was filled with the same random detritus that lined Eli's pockets. But to him, it was pure memory. He had taken what his father had said on that sun-soaked birthday to heart. Except, this chest would never see the open waters, and all the items within pertained to one person only. The length of wood Eli had found that day took up most of the space inside; it was too long, and so it had to be propped diagonally from one corner to the other. There was the stub of candle from his Da's bowsprit lantern, a scrap of red canvas, and a few letters he'd written to Eli when he'd been away on longer trips. The letters of course couldn't be delivered from the sea, but his Da had slipped them under his and Tias' pillows late at night, or else propped them in the hearth, claiming that they must have blown there on the prevailing winds. Eli traced the rise and fall of his Da's handwriting, barely touching the paper in case the long-dried ink smudged. And then with a wrench, he scooped out the contents and transferred them into a spare pillowcase. That went back under the bed, away from prying eyes.

Looking over to his brother, he saw that Tias was trying to shove another blanket into the chest. Eli grinned slightly; he knew that there were already two in there. 'If you wanted to bring all of Mam's fabric, you should have picked the wheelbarrow,' he said.

Tias shot him a look. 'Very funny. I think – we just need one – more, come on!' His words were punctuated with Tias forcing the length of wool down, only for it to spring back up.

'Tias, we'll have a fire,' Eli pointed out.

'Yes, but who's going to stay up all night to make sure we continue to have a fire?' Tias said, raising an eyebrow.

'Alright, fair enough. Look, pass it here, I've still got space.' Tias threw him the blanket, which Eli didn't catch so much with his hands but his face, and crumpled it into his chest. 'What else?' He asked.

'I've got some bread, and some of the last salted fish.'

Eli groaned at that.

'I know,' Tias said sympathetically, 'a little past its best but it'll have to do. What have you got?'

Eli rummaged for a moment through the contents. 'That blanket, a strike light, some dubious looking cheese, and another pair of socks.'

'Socks! I knew I was forgetting something.' Tias stood and crossed to the chest of drawers they shared, riffling through it until he came up with a lumpy woollen ball. 'That's everything right?' He asked. There was a tinge of nervousness in his voice.

'Yes,' Eli said. He shuffled for a moment, thinking. 'Tias...' He began slowly.

'Mm?'

'If you want to... wait a little longer we can.' Eli fiddled with the lock on his chest as he felt Tias' eyes fix sharply on him.

'Why? I thought you were desperate to do this?'

'I am, but...' You're not, he finished in his head.

Tias seemed to have heard him nonetheless. He turned to face Eli head on, sitting with his back resting against his bed frame. 'I admit, I am nervous. Yes, we've done this before, but never this early in the year, and never when the weather was this changeable. But,' he stressed the word, 'I also acknowledge we have no other leads to follow. And, I think we're due another adventure.' As his brother had spoken, Tias' voice had become stronger, until the undercurrent of nervous energy had been swept away. There was now a light in Tias eye that Eli knew all too well. He'd seen it many times he stained hand mirror they owned.

'Are you sure?' Eli asked, still wanting to offer Tias a way out if he truly didn't want to do this.

'Definitely.' And then, 'We're packed, aren't we? No going back now.'

Eli smiled properly then. 'No going back now.' He said.

The cloud cover was rolling in thick and fast as Eli stood by the window. Cold seeped in around the leading, pin pricking his skin. He shifted slightly, trying to get an unobstructed view of the sea. It was a churning mass of grey, peaked with froth and foam. It looked exceptionally uninviting. The day had begun to die now, the meagre light from behind the clouds dwindling until all colour seemed to leak from the world, taken away by the rolling sea and sky. The chests sat on the table, and the fire was banked low.

'We should go soon,' Eli said, not looking away from the window. 'It looks like there's a storm rolling in.'

'A storm?' Tias said. He came over to Eli, peering over his brother's shoulder. 'Oh.'

'Best not to get caught in that as we go down.' Eli could feel the anxiety beginning to roll off Tias in waves. He turned, forcing Tias to back away a few steps so they didn't end up nose to nose. 'We'll be fine,' he said encouragingly. 'The cavern will give us shelter, and if need be we can rig up some sort of wind-break.'

'Aye,' Tias sounded only a little convinced. Eli watched closely as his brother looked to the sky again, and then resolutely set his shoulders. 'Aye. Let's get going.' He moved over to the table, shouldering his chest in a practised motion. Eli felt that thrill again, and hurried to do the same.

Together, they stepped out into the evening air, both immediately huddling down into their cloaks and jumpers as the wind tried to bite through the layers of cloth. Tias locked the door, stringing the key around his neck on a piece of twine. Wordlessly, they moved down the short garden path and toward the village. The streets were mostly deserted. The fleet hadn't gone out today, instead Porth Tymestl's workforce had been gathered in the smoke and salt houses, trying to preserve what meagre food they had. Light shone out from the windows of The Five-Pointed Compass, a beacon in the dark. They hurried past it, keeping to the long shadows and hoping Smythe wouldn't spot them.

Through the church yard, along the cliff path and down the narrow track they went, occasionally shifting the chests on their shoulders into a more comfortable position. Around them, the clouds grew thicker, the wind more ferocious. As they reached the beach, thick spots of rain began to fall. Eli pulled his hood up and kept walking. They had decided to forego a lantern: it would be an obvious marker to their location, and besides, he doubted that even in a covered lantern a flame would be maintained in this wind. Tias was slightly ahead of him, and Eli was brought to a sudden stop by a shout.

'What's wrong?' He called over the tumult around them.

'Tide's coming up!' Tias called back, coming toward Eli. 'It's up to my ankles already.'

Eli cursed silently. In all their planning, they'd forgotten to ask about tide times. 'We can still make it to the cavern,' he said. 'We'll just have to stay there 'til low tide.'

'Eli...' Tias started.

'No going back now, remember? We can get across at the moment, and it probably won't come higher than the ledge.' He didn't wait for a response, and carried on forward. The water lapped over his boots, finding the small stress-cracks in the leather to seep through. Eli gritted his teeth, and kept walking.

They reached the cavern a little while later, having to take it slowly through the shifting waters. The tide hadn't quite reached the entrance yet, leaving the inside dry. Eli shook out his hair after pulling down his hood. It was a welcome relief to be out of the wind. Although the temperature wasn't much warmer in the cavern, the wind-chill was now factored out. Eli deposited his chest on the ledge, took Tias' from him and then clambered up whilst his brother fumbled with the pulley for firewood. Eli set about making something that resembled more of a nest than a bed with the blankets they'd brought with them, lining the rocky floor with their cloaks. They'd need them later, when they decided to venture out onto the beach, but for now they became a thin mattress to rest on.

Tias shoved the wood toward him, and then came up onto the ledge and settled in next to Eli. He didn't speak until the crackle of the fire joined the rush of the wind outside. It painted Tias' face in a golden glow, and Eli could see it catching in the copper of his own hair where it fell damply over his face. 'I didn't think about the tide being up,' Tias said.

'Me neither,' Eli admitted. 'But it's just a little unforeseen event.' He knocked Tias' shoulder with his own. 'We're here! We might get some answers!' Tias looked at him and managed a wan smile. Eli felt his own excitement curl up a little. 'Tias–' He stopped abruptly. The ripple of thunder outside would have drowned out his words anyway. Eli laughed, a little nervously. 'Well, we were right about the storm.'

Tias was looking out to the dark beach beyond. His lips moved in a silent count. Another crack of thunder. And no lightning. 'It's like before,' he said quietly.

'Before?'

'Remember? When Abraxus caught us here last time. The thunder and lightning didn't come in pairs. It was random.' A flash of brightest white outside. Tias gestured toward it. 'Like now.'

'This is perfect!' Eli said, not even trying to curb his enthusiasm now. 'Abraxus might come down here again, we can see how he's sending the bones back.' More thunderless lightning lit the inside of the cavern. 'We should go and see.' He burrowed around in the blanket nest, eventually coming up with the hood of his cloak. 'Tias move, you're sitting on it.'

'Eli, wait a minute.' Tias said, putting a hand firmly down onto the edge of the cloak Eli was trying to yank up. 'I think we should go back.'

'What?'

'Listen to me. These are not good conditions at all. The tide is coming in, there's an almighty storm raging by the sounds of it, and we're both already cold.' That last part was undeniably true. Eli had been trying to suppress the shivers he felt coursing through him since they had stopped moving. 'I know what we said earlier, but this could be really dangerous.' Tias' voice was imploring, and Eli looked resolutely away. He didn't want to have this conversation, he just wanted to lose himself and all the worries crowding in his head for at least one night. He wanted one last proper adventure before their mother returned and took him away from everything he'd ever known.

'I'm staying,' Eli said flatly.

'Eli.' There was anger creeping into Tias' voice now, and Eli could feel his own rising to match it. 'For once in your life will you just use your common sense?' Tias pulled on Eli's shoulder, forcing him to look at his brother.

'I'm staying,' Eli repeated, shrugging Tias' hand off. 'You go.'

'I'm not going to leave you here.' Tias said, ice in his voice.

'Especially with it like that outside.' The storm had grown worse since they had started arguing. Eli could barely hear the roar of the sea over the wind and sporadic thunder and lightning now. They were wasting time, anything could be happening out there and they were missing it. He said as much to Tias.

'Eli, right now the entirety of the Roman army could be marching along the beach and I wouldn't care! This was such a stupid idea, we didn't plan enough, we should have–'

'Stupid idea?' Eli scoffed. 'You agreed to it, in fact you made me wait! If we had just gone last night, none of this would have been a problem!'

'Oh, so it's my fault now?' His brother rounded on him, 'Of course it is, you suggest something idiotic and when the consequences catch up it's my fault.'

'That's not fair,' Eli said coldly.

'Well, you aren't being fair.' Tias snapped back. He looked properly angry now, the fire casting shadows into the harsh lines of his expression. 'Get up, we're going.'

'No.'

'*Dyro nerth!* Look down there!' *Give me strength!* Tias pointed over the ledge.

Eli lent over the gap, peering into the semi-darkness that lay below. It wasn't so much seeing than hearing that got Tias' point across to him. The water had risen, now carpeting the cavern's sandy floor in about an inch of water. 'You know how a storm can affect the tide, especially down here.' Tias gestured to the high-water mark neither of them could see in the flickering half-light.

'I can swim.' Eli knew he was being facetious now. But he wasn't going to let the opportunity go. He didn't know if he'd get another. Glancing at Tias, Eli recoiled ever so slightly. Tias honestly looked like he might hit him. The sudden image of Thomas Gillet laid out over the cobbles with Tias standing over him flashed through Eli's mind. The look on his brother's face then had been something of a novelty, something Eli didn't get to see. Now, with it being directed at him, he had to admit: Tias was scary when he wanted to be.

'What's so important about this anyway?' Tias said. The ice still lined his voice, cracking through the words.

'I see you've changed your mind! Weren't you the one always wanting answers? Solve the riddle at last? We are so close, Tias, and now you're running!'

'I'm running because it is the sensible thing to do! I don't want to drown, or die from the cold.' Tias was standing now, cramming things back into his chest. Eli refused to move. 'You didn't answer my question.'

'What?' Eli snapped.

'Why is this so important to you?' Eli shivered as Tias ripped away the blankets, blindly bundling them up.

'I want to know what's happening—'

'Yes, we've established that. I mean now, Eli.' Tias looked down at him, eyes flinty.

And then Eli was on his feet, and it all came tumbling out. 'Because we're leaving and this is our last chance at a proper adventure, just us two before Mam takes us away from all of this! And now you're doing the same thing, you're taking me away from here because it's bad weather out!' Eli knew it wasn't merely 'bad weather', but he had to make his point. 'Why is everyone so determined to keep me away from things?' His knees felt weak all of a sudden, and he reached out to steady himself against the wall.

'Are you—?' Tias started, and Eli hated the note of worry underneath Tias' still cross tone.

'Fine.' Eli said shortly. 'Leave, if you're leaving.' He sat back down, staring dejectedly into the fire.

'You are the most—' Tias started, but then broke off with a short exhale. 'Alright. Fine, I'm going. Stay here and freeze.' He jumped off the ledge and landed with a splash. 'I'm sick of fixing your mistakes. I'll see you in the morning.' And with that, Tias waded out of the cavern and into the night. Eli watched him go, and felt a twinge of regret. He stamped it down and huddled closer to the fire. At least Tias had left him a blanket.

The tide was rising. The tide was rising, and the storm hadn't abated and Eli was cold. He had tried to keep the fire in, but the wind had changed direction and was now lashing through the cavern's entrance. It was now reduced to the smallest of embers, low and a dark red in a pile of half-charred sticks and ash. The water had come in faster than he had anticipated. Faster, and also higher. It was already three-quarters of the way up the ledge. If he left now, he could still make it onto the beach and away. It would be unpleasant, but manageable. But there was that spark of defiance he kept burning where he could not with the fire. It was hot in his thoughts, spitting out you go now, and you give up. He would not give up.

The fire died completely a little while later. Eli had lost all sense of time. The world was reduced to dark water and cracking thunder. Something clicked against the side of the ledge. Eli glanced over it, not really seeing anything there aside from the void of the water below. A flash of grey-white caught his attention, and he plunged his hand into the frigid waters. Immediately his fingers went numb. Fumbling for a moment, Eli then grasped something and pulled it from the water. It was the chime they'd made yesterday. It must have come loose from the shelf where Tias had hung it, and floated over, buoyed by the driftwood from which the stones hung. Eli clasped it to him.

He wasn't sure if he'd somehow managed to fall asleep, or if the cold was sapping his energy more than he realised, but Eli came back to his senses with a yell. The water was lapping over the ledge now. If he were to stand on the floor of the cavern, it would be nearly shoulder high. Eli stood quickly, but it was too late to save the blanket. Already, it was sopping. He didn't know what to do. Tias had been right, of course he'd been right, he was Tias. And, once again, Eli hadn't listened. Panic was beginning to claw its way up through his chest and into his throat. What could he do? Try and swim for it? The currents when the tide was up were unpredictable at best, treacherous at worst. He could be swept away into the open sea. But staying here seemed like another bad option.

The water was around Eli's knees now, and still quickly rising. The waves were pouring in, and he had a sudden, slightly nonsensical image of an hourglass. Water in place of sand cascading in and pulling him under. Staying here was not viable, Eli knew. Exposure would surely kill him. He'd have to swim. Pulling off his cloak and letting it drop into the water, Eli flexed his fingers nervously. He still had the chime in one hand. Reaching down, he unfastened his boots. They were extra weight he couldn't afford to be carrying. The water hit his hips in a high wave and he let out a gasp. It was achingly cold.

The thought of submerging himself entirely in it was terrifying. Especially in the darkness.

Scaring himself like this wouldn't get him to the cliff path any faster.

Eli took a deep, steadying breath, and then another. And dived.

ELLA RUBY SELF

Prayers.
January, 1816.
Tias.

The anger had died, and panic had replaced it. What on earth had he been thinking? He had just left his brother down on an exposed beach in the middle of a horrific storm. Tias had been so furious that it had seemed like a completely reasonable thing to do. But now he was standing in the middle of Porth Tymestl village, rain soaking his hair and running down the back of his collar and he had left Eli.

Tias dithered in the streets, wondering which way to go. Back to Roseate Cottage? No, the empty bed beside his would no doubt haunt him. Tua'r Môr Bay? By now it would be mostly submerged by the encroaching tide. Tias tried to tamp down on the fresh wave of panic that hit him after that thought. Even if he tried to get back to Eli, he was sure Eli would refuse to come with him. Again. Tias cursed himself mentally; he should have forced his brother, grabbed his arm and not let go until they were both clear of the coastline. The lightning arced overhead, and Tias flinched. He needed to get help.

But who would answer him? Everyone knew that the sea was no longer an ally to them. If Tias told any of the fishermen his predicament, they would sympathise surely, but would they risk their own lives to save Eli's? Especially when Eli had put himself into said predicament. Tias started walking, unsure of his destination, but the motion gave him something else to focus on other than the crushing, breath-stealing panic. He passed Heather's End, its windows shuttered. The bakery, the Gillet's, Crow's cottage. A glimpse of golden light from the corner of his eye, and suddenly Tias knew who to get. He wanted to kick himself for not thinking of them sooner, but instead of berating himself and wasting precious time, he hurried toward The Five-Pointed Compass.

Bursting through the door, Tias wasted no time and breathlessly yelled, 'Abraxus!' Thankfully, the inn was empty, which gave Tias some indication of the time. Smythe started and dropped the glass he was replacing on a shelf overhead. It hit the floor and shattered out of sight.

'Matthias! What are you doing?' He sounded a little annoyed, and Tias couldn't blame him. But he didn't have time to be sorry for causing the innkeeper alarm.

'I need Abraxus, now.' He came over to the bar, looking into Smythe's blue grey eyes. 'Please, Smythe.'

'What's happened?' Smythe asked, picking up on the sheer terror in Tias' voice.

'We were on the beach, and I said we should go but he didn't listen and now—' Tias' words were broken off by an almighty crack of thunder. He jumped, glancing to the windows. 'I need Abraxus.'

Smythe's eyes had widened, 'You were on the beach?' He said.

'Yes,' Tias' voice was tiny, breakable. 'And Eli's still there.'

Smythe swore loudly, hurried around the bar and disappeared up the stairs. Tias was left alone in the barroom, with nothing but the steady lashing of rain for company.

'Where?' Abraxus appeared, closely followed by Smythe.

'The cavern, we wanted to see... but the tide was coming in so quick, and we argued and – and I left.' The dam broke and Tias bowed his head and started to cry in earnest. An arm looped around his shoulders, and he caught the smell of ale and rich stew and wood.

'Abraxus, how long 'til you can get there?' Smythe's voice rumbled in his chest, Tias pressed in close.

'I can go now,' Abraxus said. 'I will need a skiff, something light.'

'Take the Esgyll Gwerin, she'll manage the waves.'

'I will need to take the boy, too.' Tias looked up at that. Abraxus' gaze was on him, and it was steady. 'He knows the bay better than most, and in a storm like this, I will need someone navigating.'

Tias was already nodding, ignoring Smythe's protestations. 'I'll go.'

'We do not have time to waste,' Abraxus said, holding up a hand to stop whatever Smythe had been about to say. 'You know as well as I where the high-water mark comes to in that cavern.' Abraxus had opened the door, and was waiting for Tias to step out first.

'I'll be alright,' he said to the innkeeper, trying for a brave smile. He could tell by Smythe's expression that it had fallen flat.

'Bring them both back safe, y'hear?' Smythe said to Abraxus. His tone brooked no argument. Abraxus nodded, and followed Tias as he left The Five. The door swung shut behind them, closing off the light from within.

It didn't take them long to reach Angorfa Harbour. The boats there were pitching and yawing wildly with the surge of the waves, even behind the thick walls. Tias ran along the lengths, mindful of any coils of ropes that might have been left out by accident, looking for Old Man Morgan's little vessel. The Esgyll Gwerin was barely more than a skiff, but she was sturdy and acrobatic on the waters. It had been a good suggestion from Smythe.

He found it on the far side of the harbour, docked between two larger fishing boats. 'Here!' He called over the sounds of the sea to Abraxus. The man emerged from the darkness, coat swirling around him and hair tangled. He glanced at the Esgyll Gwerin and nodded once. Tias traversed the rungs set into the harbour, slippery with saltwater and seaweed, feeling with his feet until they touched slick wood. He almost overbalanced, and probably would have toppled into the churning water inches below him, but a strong hand caught the back of his collar and pulled him straight. 'Diolch.'

Abraxus nodded stiffly and turned to the mast, setting the sail loose. 'Can you sail, boy?' He called.

'Well enough on calm waters,' Tias responded, 'but never in something like this.' He came over to where Abraxus was working, and a length of rope was shoved into his hands.

'Tie that off,' Abraxus ordered, 'and then get to the prow. You will need to keep a sharp eye.'

They were out of the harbour quickly, Tias lurching forward as the small boat crested out into wilder waters. He clung to the railing, the meagre light of the bowsprit lantern barely illuminating the water below him. Abraxus had tossed him a compass, produced from one of his many pockets, and Tias had to keep wiping away the beads of rain that clung to the glass casing. It was a heavy weight in his hand, and he took comfort in it. It was a means to get back to Eli. He called back directions, and Abraxus steered the Esgyll Gwerin accordingly. Soon, the tall, denser blocks of the cliffs came into view, and Tias knew they were now sailing along the length of Tua'r Môr Bay. This part of their voyage was imperative: if Tias over or under shot the distance to the cavern, Eli didn't have much hope.

If he had any hope to begin with. The voice in Tias' mind was insidious and he recoiled from it. There was just enough of a grain of truth within it, and that scared him more than anything else. The storm was brutal, and Tias knew how long someone could survive in winter waters. Porth Tymestl hadn't lost a man to that end in a while, but as the world tore itself apart under the wrath from both sea and sky, Tias knew anything was possible.

'Where, Tias?' Abraxus shouted from the helm.

'A little further!' Tias called back, the wind stealing his voice away. He clutched the railing as the Esgyll Gwerin bucked wildly. The sea seemed to be trying to dislodge them from its back. A wall of water reared to their left, and Abraxus swore, grappling with the rudder so the wave didn't hit them portside. Tias was already drenched, but the icy shock of the water crashing down on them scattered all his thoughts. The wave had carried them closer to the cliff-face, and Tias could tell Abraxus was now grappling not only with the storm, but with the currents as well. They seemed to have no direction, pulling them out one moment, and towards the land the next. For the first time since his father's funeral, Tias closed his eyes and started to mumble an old prayer. It wasn't one Crow had hammered into them, but rather one he'd heard his mother recite before, translating it from her mother-tongue into theirs.

He wasn't alone. Behind him, Abraxus started to speak, the words flowing into a chant. It was in no language Tias recognised, the rise and fall of it entirely unfamiliar, but beautiful. There were harsh consonants, rolling 'r's and a rhythm to it that would have lulled Tias into sleep at any other time. He wondered distantly what it meant. The chanting grew louder, and for a split second, Tias swore he felt the current's pull on the Esgyll Gwerin give a little. As if Abraxus had momentarily wrested control over the water. Tias turned to look at him, and Abraxus, not breaking his chant, gestured toward the cliffs. Where?

Scanning the cliff-face for a darker slit in a world that seemed to have been dipped in ink was near impossible, particularly from a boat. Instead, Tias looked at the jagged line that marked the top of the cliffs against the sky. Closing his eyes, he pictured it in daylight, where the path down to the beach was in proximity to the cavern. He looked back to the monochromatic vista before him. There was a slight dip in the land where the path started. He called back to Abraxus, telling him to get closer. The tide was fully in now, so they ran no risk of grounding themselves. And besides, the Esgyll Gwerin had such a shallow hull, she could navigate any depth of water with little difficulty.

They came up alongside the cliffs, waves buffeting the portside of the skiff as Abraxus took them down the edge. And there, in the dark, was a deeper slash of black. Tias felt his heart leap sickeningly; less than a quarter of the cavern's entrance was visible above the roiling sea. He pointed, his voice failing him. Abraxus understood nonetheless, and threw the anchor over the side. After a second of consideration, he tossed the spare over the starboard side too, as an extra precaution against the everchanging currents. Tias looked to the cavern, and realised what he was going to have to do. Standing up on trembling legs, he started to pull off his soaked cloak. A hand on his shoulder stopped him.

'No, lad.' Abraxus had something over part of his face. It looked like an unfinished crown in burnished copper wire. His left eye, the one with the colouring of the ocean, was obscured by a flat bone-white stone. The hole eroded through it lined up perfectly with Abraxus' iris. He handed Tias his coat, with a gruff, 'Put it on.' And then leapt with a cat-like grace onto the railing.

Tias knew what Abraxus was about to do a second before he did, and reached out a hand, grasping for the man's shirt. A cry died on his lips, and his hand closed too late. His fingers brushed the fabric of Abraxus' shirt as the man dived in an arc into the water below, and disappeared.

Tias sat alone in a boat that suddenly felt too flimsy against the power of the sea, and pulled Abraxus' coat around him. *'Wyt ti dal yn fyw?' Are you still alive?*

Cold.
January, 1816.
Eli.

All he knew was cold. He was so bone-shakingly cold. It seeped into his bones, into the very fibre of his soul. Thought had fled him, and Eli did all that he knew how to. He clung to the rocky wall and waited for the sea to swallow him. The way it had swallowed his Da.

Diving hadn't worked. The current had battered him back, and he'd surfaced, head tight and pounding from the chill, gasping. He hadn't even made it out of the cavern. That didn't stop him from trying again and again. Each time, he managed less under the water, quicker to come up for a chest full of searing air.

Eventually, Elias Kincarran did something he never did. He gave up.

The tide was in fully now, but the cavern was periodically filling a little higher and then emptying with the motion of the waves. It was all he could do to keep his chin above the water. Particularly powerful waves forced him under completely, and Eli tried to fight the panic as all sense and direction was lost to him.

In one numb hand, he still clutched the chime. He wasn't sure why he hadn't just discarded it. It was useless to him, but for some reason he wanted it near. Maybe it was because it was the only thing that wasn't water and rough rock cutting into his hands. Maybe it was because Tias had tied the knots. He didn't know. He was just so cold.

Time became lucid, and Eli felt the chill change into something sweeter. Gone was the shivering, and now all he felt was a pleasant weightlessness accompanied with a weariness the likes of which he had never felt. Perhaps this wouldn't be such a bad place to sleep? The water would hold him in its embrace, and he would just sink away into dreams. Eli felt his grip loosen on the crags in the wall, and just as his fingers were about to slip out of contact, he remembered something Old Man Morgan had once said. 'A man who falls asleep in the arms of the waves is as good as lost.'

Eli wrenched his drooping eyelids back open, and slammed himself against the wall. His legs had stopped cramping from continually treading water a while ago, and now they felt like lead weights, dragging him down.

'Hold on, Eli,' he whispered to himself. It gave him a little courage to hear a voice, even if it was his own. 'Don't sleep.' He repeated the words over and over to himself, creating a strange, slightly garbled mantra. It helped, for a little time. And then his focus drifted away again and the cold clung to him and he was so tired. A wave knocked his precarious grip on the wall away, and Eli was tumbled over and hit the back wall hard. Air bubbles burst from his mouth and the taste of salt overwhelmed his senses. Scrabbling desperately, Eli found another nook to cram his fingers into, kicking with legs that no longer seemed to work properly. He gasped, and spat mouthfuls of water. Bringing up his other hand for more purchase, Eli accidentally hit himself across the cheek with the chime. One of the stones passed over his eye as it happened, and, just for a split second, the sea lit up. Great undulating shapes came into focus and then were ripped away again. Eli blinked, and the water was back to a void.

Another wave came crashing into the cavern, and once more Eli was plunged down. But this time he couldn't find the wall. There was nothing; he was suspended in endless black. If he had had the air to, Eli would have screamed. His back collided with something solid, but it didn't feel like the wall. It was far too smooth. His chest ached for air, but Eli had no idea which way was up. He guessed, and seemed to have luck on his side, just for a second. Breaking the surface, Eli gasped in sweet air. And then luck abandoned him again. He simply had nothing left to give. The sea had taken it all. It now may as well finish the job and take him as well. He barely noticed when his head slipped back under the water. *I'm sorry Mam, Tias.* And then, comfortingly, *Wait for me Da. I'm coming.*

The dark water pulled him under, and Eli was drifting further and further into its hold. He didn't even feel the strong arms wrap around his waist.

VIII
then.

From soil to sea.

The seed had no concept of what was to become of it. It was nothing particularly remarkable, merely one seed cast out onto the winds with hundreds, if not thousands of its kin. The wind took it, showed the seed the sky, the boundless depths of the blue, and then hurled it to earth. Perhaps it was this first contact with something akin to freedom that made the seed become what it was.

It grew, pushing green fronds up through the hard dirt and into the light once more. From bud, to sprout, to sapling; it reached unendingly for the sky and the blue it contained. After many days and nights, countless and ceaseless, the seed had become a tree. It ate the light, drank what water it could find in the harsh soil and stood tall against the storms that threatened to uproot it.

Men came with metal that bit and scraped and tore, and suddenly the tree was no longer tall. It fell with a creaking groan that, if men had been able to understand, would have been a cry of pain.

The tree was taken from its forest into a building devised by the hands of men, away from the sunlight and the rains. It was stripped of its bark, the armour pulled away to reveal the soft insides. Branches were cut, and the needles of the tree littered the floor; a windfall not of its own choosing. And then the tree was no longer recognisable as what it had once been. Smooth and straightened, it was propped in a corner of the house man had built, and for a time forgotten.

And then, the light returned. The tree now became part of something larger than itself, made and crafted by the hands of man once more, but this thing danced and roamed and was made *of* nature. Crafted from the raw materials the earth gave man, and then cast back into it, reshaped and new. Heavy bolts of canvas were hung from the tree, lines of rope attached and knotted intricately. The colour of the canvas was the same, distant, long-ago memory of the sky, alongside the greens that reminded the tree of its beginning.

The water came back with the light, but it was drying, rather than for drinking. Harsher than the rain, but so alive. The tree shook off the memories of the forest, the moss sleep and the lichen dreams, and embraced the blue of the sky and the wild of the sea. After a while, it forgot that it had ever been a tall, breathing stone pine. What it recalled now was only the hush of the waves and current, the whispers of the man that commanded the helm. The mast held up high the colours of the world, and sailed onwards

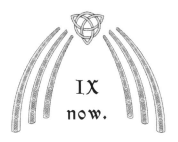

IX
now.

Anchor.
January, 1816.
Tias.

The storm overhead had quietened. The occasional rumble of distant thunder played far away over the black water, and the lightning seemed to have all but dissipated. The only light Tias had was the bowsprit lantern, swinging to and fro from the motion of the waves. He clung to the glow it gave him: all around him was nothing but swirling black, and it was all he could do to try and stop the darkness from pulling him under into unknowable fear. The wind and rain were still up, and Tias found himself grateful for the second anchor Abraxus had thrown over the side. If the *Esgyll Gwerin* drifted, then Abraxus might not be able to find his way back.

Tias considered himself to be patient. He had to be, with Eli as his brother. But now, he found himself tapping out random patterns on his thigh, standing up as much as he dared with the roll of the boat, peering over the rail into the water below. The seconds seemed to drag into hours, incomprehensibly slow and agonising. He found himself counting, breathing the numbers aloud as if he could make time work again by doing so. He lost the thread of numbers again and again. Now, instead of seconds, Tias focused on counting the beat of his heart, trying desperately to slow it in his chest. It barely worked; but it did give him something more substantial to focus on.

A movement in the water. The barest hint of white as something broke the surface for a moment. Tias forgot everything else and rushed to the rail, leaning precariously over the drop. Whatever it had been – *please let it be them* – had vanished again from sight. Tias was about to try and uncurl his fingers from the rail, his knuckles white and cramping slightly, when they surfaced right alongside the *Esgyll Gwerin*.

The next few minutes were a blur to Tias. He reached over the side, hands grasping desperately for the still and pale form of his brother. Abraxus was keeping them both afloat, treading water and somehow maintaining his position next to the boat in the churning sea. Eli's head rolled against Abraxus' shoulder. Tias braced his knees against the side, and leaned further, hooking his arms around Eli's chest as Abraxus thrust him forward and upwards. With an almighty pull, the ocean's grip finally loosened around Eli. He was so still and cold. Where before Tias had tried to slow the beating of his heart, he now was waiting for it to restart. He barely noticed when Abraxus hauled himself up onto the *Esgyll Gwerin*, swinging his legs over the rail.

Sinking to the floor of the ship, Tias held Eli close to him, tucking his brother's head beneath his chin. With numb fingers, he wrapped Abraxus' coat around both of them as best as he could. A moment later, his attempt at covering Eli up was stripped away, Abraxus throwing the coat aside and roughly pulling Eli out of Tias' embrace. Tias fought back, desperately trying to keep hold, beating uselessly on Abraxus' strong shoulders and back. And then he realised what the man was doing. He had laid Eli out, his head to one side, and was repeatedly pressing down hard on his chest. Tias had seen this before, only once, when a small child had wandered down the beach and out of their depth. He hadn't seen what had happened in the end, their Da hurrying them away. Tias knelt by Eli, his hands fluttering over him until they came to rest, feather-light, on his brother's shoulder. Abraxus was muttering under his breath, the words too fast and low for Tias to catch. He was still wearing that strange circlet, the white stone shimmering as water clung to its surface.

Eli convulsed once against the wood of the deck, and started to cough. Sea water dripped from his mouth, and the coughing turned to horrible hacking and gasps. Abraxus sat back on his haunches, relief flickering over his face. He reached out and gently pushed Eli onto his side, running a comforting hand down the length of Eli's back. 'Steady, lad. Deep breaths.'

'Eli?' Tias said, his voice sounding panicky and high pitched to his ears. Eli had stopped coughing, and was taking in long, shuddering breaths. Tias felt shivers rip through his frame. He peered over Eli's shoulder, looking at his face. Eli's eyes were at half mast, flickering. Eventually, they settled hazily on Tias. The ghost of a smile quirked his lips.

'Came back.' His voice sounded horrible, rough and water-logged.

"Course I did,' Tias said with a shaky laugh. And then Eli's eyes closed completely, and he became boneless under Tias' hands. 'Eli? *Eli*!' Tias shook him, and then looked wildly to Abraxus. The man had one hand pressed against Eli's chest. There was a second of absolute dread; it seemed to stretch and distort until Tias thought he would drown too.

'He still lives,' Abraxus said lowly. The *for now* was unspoken. He pulled away, making for the anchor rope. 'Keep him warm. Try and wake him if you can.' He pulled one out from the depths, seemingly with little effort. The other anchor followed, and Tias felt the *Esgyll Gwerin* immediately move to the whims of the current and waves. Abraxus grasped the rudder, and wrested control back from the waters. The dark line of *Tua'r Môr* Bay began to disappear into the night. Tias turned his back to it, focusing instead on his brother.

Once more, Tias pulled Eli to him, his own shirt now thoroughly wet from Eli's sodden one. Twitching Abraxus' coat over them, Tias leaned back against the side of the ship. He took Eli's hands in his, and started to absentmindedly rub the frozen fingers. Tias found himself shaking; whether from the raw terror that was still coursing through him, or due in part to the force of Eli's shivering, he didn't know.

'Do you remember when we saw whales with Da?' He said quietly. 'They came right next to the ship, and I thought we were done for.' It had been a moment so otherworldly that it played out in vibrant colour through Tias' memory. Huge tail fins had reared suddenly from the still water, coming back down with a force that rocked the boat. Eli had been perched in the rigging, leaning out to get a better view. Tias had called to him to come down, worried that he might fall and be swallowed whole by the leviathans below. Eli had scrambled down the rigging, grabbed Tias' hand and pulled him over to it. Tias had fought him, frightened.

'It's alright, Tias, promise,' Eli had said solemnly. 'You don't have to go high, but you *have* to come and see.' And Tias had, climbing only a little lower than Eli had. All fear had been forgotten the minute another tail had breached the surface. Tias could still remember the white speckles of limpets embedded into the blue-black skin.

'We watched them for an hour, following them. Da didn't know the name for a group of whales, so we made them up.' Tias thought for a moment. 'I don't remember them now.' Eli was quiet against him, still shivering. Still breathing. 'Mam was furious, we stayed out much longer than she thought we were going to. Da followed them for a few miles. I think he would have taken us over the edge of the world if it had been just us and Mam with him, not his crew.' Tias felt a sting in his eyes, and closed them, momentarily dropping his head against Eli's. He felt the wet strands of hair sticking to his own cheeks. 'I'm sorry,' he breathed. 'Please stay.' It might have been a trick of his own imagination, desperate for some form of response. But Tias was sure he felt Eli's fingers tighten over his own hand for a moment.

Tias kept up a steady stream of half-remembered stories

from their childhood. He was relatively sure most of it was nonsensical, but it served to fill the silence that was left between them. And if Eli found his way back to consciousness by Tias rambling, then Tias would keep talking until his voice gave out. Abraxus seemed statuesque, solid and unmoving aside from the slight readjustment of the rudder. Their flight out onto the water had felt so quick, so sudden compared to this trudge back toward the flickering lights of Porth Tymestl. The rain was beginning to let up ever so slightly, but the wind was still high. No more thunder and lightning chased them from the skies above. Eventually, just as Tias had started what felt like his sixth story, the thick silhouette of the *Angorfa* Harbour walls came into view. Sitting a little straighter, Tias looked over the rail, watching them approach.

'We're nearly home,' he murmured to Eli. Eli didn't move, save for the shivering that had seemed to become a little more sporadic in force over the last couple of minutes.

Abraxus guided them into the harbour skilfully, the *Esgyll Gwerin* gliding smoothly from open sea into the more sheltered waters of the harbour. They docked in the same place they had cast off from, Abraxus leaping from the rail to the rungs in the wall. He had looped a length of mooring rope over one shoulder to save Tias having to move to toss it up to him. Once the boat was secured, Abraxus came back down, hurrying toward Tias. He reached out, most likely to take Eli, but Tias found himself shrinking away, pulling Eli minutely closer toward his chest. 'We have to get him inside, Tias.' Abraxus' voice was gentle in a way Tias had never heard before. 'I swear to you, I would not take him if I thought you could carry him.'

'I can–'

'Matthias, you are shaking nearly as much as he is. I cannot help both of you to Smythe.' He levelled Tias with a look. 'I do not think Eli has the time for that.' Abraxus reached out once more, and this time Tias did not flinch away.

'Smythe?' Tias asked as Abraxus pulled Eli into his arms, one underneath his knees, the other around his shoulders.

'Closer than that cottage of yours.' Abraxus lifted Eli up onto the wall of the harbour, and then quickly scaled the ladder himself, bending once more to scoop Eli up. Tias scrambled up the rungs, hands numb and slipping over the metal. 'And he will know what to do.' There was worry in Abraxus' voice, and Tias felt fear break over him again. Already, the man was striding away from him, and Tias hurried to catch up, drawing level with him and looking at Eli. Abraxus had shifted his grip on Eli so that his head was tucked into the crook of Abraxus' arm. As they passed by the night lanterns left on doorsteps, Tias caught a glimpse of Eli's face washed in the golden glow they emitted. Under the rose flare, his brother seemed to have passed pale and ventured into realms of grey. There was the merest hint of blue in his lips, and Tias had to suppress a shudder.

They were passing the shut-up bakery when Tias noticed that Eli's eyes were open. It was clear that he was only semi-conscious, not really taking in his surroundings. Nonetheless, Tias came closer and put himself directly into Eli's line of sight. 'Eli?' He said hesitantly. Abraxus looked down sharply, and then lengthened his stride. Eli mumbled something incomprehensible, rolling his head so one half of his face was pressed firmly against Abraxus. Tias watched as, in the light of a candle left in a windowsill, Eli blinked once, twice, and then slipped back down into unconsciousness.

The Five-Pointed Compass was ablaze with light as they approached. Tias stepped forward, pushing the door open. He was immediately set upon by Smythe, who pulled him into the barroom, fussing with his wet clothes and slinging copious amounts of blankets around his shoulders. The fire was roaring in the hearth; the flames licking the blackened back-stone. Tias was barely listening to Smythe as he flitted about him, looking dazedly around the barroom. It was as if he were floating, his sight tethered very loosely just outside of his body. He felt dizzy with it.

'–wet through, and by the gods, freezin' cold! Get by the fire, I'll go fetch something–' Smythe broke off, hands frozen in mid-air over Tias' shoulders. 'Eli,' he whispered. Tias looked to where Abraxus stood by the door, Eli still nestled in his arms. He looked lost. 'Is he..?' Smythe started, voice constricted.

Abraxus shook his head, and all the tension seemed to flood from Smythe's hunched posture. 'I can take him upstairs to–'

'No, there's nowhere for a fire upstairs. Leave him on the hearthside, Tias, can you sit with him?' Smythe seemed to have realised that someone needed to take control of the situation, unspooling as it rapidly was in the safe warmth of The Five-Pointed Compass. 'Tias?' Smythe prompted.

Tias snapped back to awareness. 'Yes, I can.' He turned and walked toward the hearthside, where Abraxus had already laid Eli out, covering him with his battered coat. Reaching out, he gently lifted a strand of damp hair from over Eli's right eye. His skin was still cold to the touch, but it seemed as if a little of the blue tint to Eli's lips had faded.

Smythe and Abraxus must have left the barroom at some point, unnoticed by Tias. They came back down the stairs, holding one of the cots from a room above between them. Smythe piled blankets and quilts onto it, padding the thin mattress with what seemed to be all the pillows he possessed.

'We'll need to get 'im out of his wet things.' Smythe said, coming over to Tias. Tias nodded numbly, and started to fiddle with the collar strings of Eli's shirt.

'Where are his boots?' Abraxus asked. Tias looked, and sure enough, Eli was barefooted. Smythe shrugged helplessly and turned back to stoking the already roaring fire. Realisation came down hard and fast on Tias, and he felt his finger slip away from the hem of Eli's shirt.

'Tias? You alright, lad?' Smythe asked gently.

'They would have been too heavy.'

'What would?'

'His boots,' Tias said, staring at nothing. 'He would have taken them off so he could swim better.' After everything that had happened that night, Tias found out that this was what broke him. The image of Eli shucking off his boots in a cavern slowly filling with water played over and over again in his mind. Distantly, he was aware of someone pulling him close. Distantly, he was aware there were tears slipping down his cheeks. Tias kept his eyes open, looking at his brother.

Fever.
January, 1816.
Abraxus.

His hands were shaking. Abraxus stared down at them, as if in wonderment. Fine tremors ran through his fingers, making them twitch. Clenching them into fists, he tried to stop the movement, only to find that it wasn't just his hands that shook. No, he seemed to be shivering all over; although whether it was from shock or the cold that still clung to him he didn't know.

Tias had curled up on the cot next to his brother, pulling Eli close to him as he'd done on the little boat. His eyes were closed, but Abraxus was sure he wasn't sleeping. He knew that *he* probably wouldn't find rest tonight, and consigned himself to hazy thoughts and a vigil over the Kincarran boys.

'You'd better get those off too,' Smythe's voice broke through the fugue that was steadily descending on him. Abraxus looked at the innkeeper in confusion, and Smythe gestured to Abraxus' dripping clothes. A little puddle had formed around him, beads of water hanging momentarily suspended from the hem of his shirt. He nodded numbly, and began to pull his wet things off, leaving them unceremoniously on the floor.

'I will be back,' Abraxus said, heading for the stairs. He hadn't thought to quickly duck into his own room to collect a spare change of clothes when he and Smythe had gone to fetch a cot. And, besides, he needed a moment alone, in which he could hopefully stop this damnable shaking.

His room was chilly, the lantern and candles unlit. Nothing seemed disturbed, and for a moment that completely threw him. Everything was still in its place – papers over the floor and desk, his staff leaning in the corner, blankets rucked up and tangled into a mess. It all looked as it had done from before Tias had burst into The Five-Pointed Compass, calling for him and near out of his mind with panic. He dressed quickly, and fastening a loose belt around his waist, made for the door again. It was only as he reached for the handle did he notice the slight pressure around his ear and over his left eye. The circlet. He'd forgotten entirely about it.

Reaching up, Abraxus loosened the wire around his right ear slightly and pulled it off. Slipping the stone from its holder, Abraxus held it in one hand and regarded the circlet in the other.

When he'd dived into the cavern, under the crushing blackness of the waves, he'd found Eli near the back wall, drifting steadily downward, his hair swirling around him, and eyes closed. In one hand, Eli had been holding what had originally looked like a bundle of sticks and string. It was only as Abraxus had caught the boy around the waist and hauled them both up to the surface that he realised it was a rudimentary version of a chime. Abraxus had only had the time to acknowledge that, before it slipped from Eli's loose grip and sank. After that, all thoughts of the little chime had been thoroughly forgotten, lost in the tempest of panic and fear that had raged through him as he struck back towards the boat.

Now, however... Abraxus cast the circlet onto his bed, not caring where it landed and opened the door. As he walked down the short corridor toward the stairs, he wondered if Eli had finally figured out what the stones were for. Or, if in what he thought to be his last moments, he had reached out for something, *anything*, that hadn't been churning water or icy rock. Abraxus had seen many people drown. It never got easier, but he had never quite felt as helpless as he did watching Eli shiver uncontrollably in the arms of his brother.

The barroom was deadly silent as he slipped back down the stairs. Smythe was sitting on the floor next to the head of the cot, idly carding a hand through Tias' messy sandy-brown hair. Four empty clay mugs had been set out on the hearthside, a large black kettle suspended over the flames. Abraxus came over and sank down beside Smythe, watching the occupants of the cot. 'Is he..?' He asked, tailing off and gesturing to Tias.

'No,' Smythe responded, 'I don't think he quite dares.' The innkeeper kept up the soothing motion, brushing away the curls that fell into Tias' face.

'And Eli?' Abraxus made himself ask.

'Not woken up,' Smythe said, worry colouring his words. 'But he's less cold now, I think.'

Abraxus reached over and gently set the back of his hand to Eli's forehead – the only place he could touch since Eli was practically buried in blankets. 'Hm.'

'How bad–?' Smythe started, but Abraxus cut him off by raising a hand.

'Do not ask,' he said. Smythe seemed about to argue, but Abraxus cut in, 'I do not think I can go over it again tonight, Stooger.' He looked Smythe full in the face, and Smythe seemed to read the slight desperation there.

'Alright.' Nothing more passed between them until the shrill call of the kettle broke the silence. Smythe visibly jumped, and hurried over to the fireplace, using the poker to lift the kettle from the hook. The mugs were filled, and a sweet scent filled the air, borne aloft by the steam curling gently from the top.

'Tias? Tias, m'boy, can you sit up and drink this?' Smythe had bent over, and was shaking Tias' shoulder. Abraxus watched over the rim of his own mug as Tias shook his head minutely and buried his face deeper into the pillow and Eli's back. He was curled around his brother now, his arms wrapped securely about Eli's chest. 'Tias, you need to get somethin' warm in you,' Smythe said, voice stronger now.

'He is right, Matthias.' Abraxus added, seeing that Tias still wasn't about to give up his grip on Eli. After a moment, Tias rolled over slightly so he could look at Abraxus and Smythe seated on the hearthstones behind him. There were the beginnings of dark circles under his eyes, made even more prominent by how pale his complexion was.

'You can let go for a bit,' Smythe said gently. He offered the mug. Slowly, Tias disentangled himself, sitting up. He took the mug and brought it shakily to his lips, sipping the sweet concoction. Outside, the wind seemed to have died down finally. Abraxus had lost all sense of time; the night seemed never ending, just perpetual black swirling around them with the faintest hint of light from a weak moon high above the earth.

A soft clink from beside him brought his attention back to Smythe, who had exchanged his empty cup for the fourth one. The innkeeper pulled himself up from the hearthside and came around to Eli, kneeling down with a low groan. 'These old bones aren't meant for bedside tendin',' he said, seemingly to Eli. 'Eli? Can you come on back to us for a moment, lad?' Smythe set down the mug and patted Eli's cheek softly. Tias was watching sharply, hands still gripping his drink. Eli twitched, the barest movement, but it was enough to light a tiny spark of hope in Abraxus. Smythe carried on talking quietly to the boy, drawing him out of unconsciousness with his smooth voice.

'Smythe..?' Eli's voice was cracked, and Abraxus had to listen closely for it again over the spit of the fire. He leaned forward, watching as one of Eli's eyes opened. He seemed to take in the barroom, Smythe and then his eyelashes fluttered.

'No, come on,' Smythe said, tapping Eli's cheek again, this time a little more forcefully. 'We all know how you can sleep, lad, but right now you need to wake up a bit.'

Eli shifted under the covers, turning onto his back and pulling the quilt up a little closer around his neck. 'Tired.' he mumbled. And then after a pause, 'Warm.'

Smythe looked up and caught Abraxus' eye. The relief was evident on his face, and Abraxus allowed himself to share in it. 'I promise you can get cosy again in a minute Eli,' Smythe said, 'but this first.' He lifted the cup and let some of the scented steam drift over Eli's face.

'What issit?' There was still a slur to his voice, but Abraxus reasoned that was more to do with the fact that the boy was still only semi-conscious rather than in immediate danger.

'Drink it and find out,' Tias said, a small smile pulling at the corners of his lips. Where Smythe's voice seemed to have failed to rouse Eli fully, Tias', it seemed, did the trick. Eli shifted toward the sound of his brother's voice, before opening his eyes again.

'Tias?'

'Hey.'

'Why're you in m'bed?' Eli asked, looking confused. Smythe let out a huff of laughter, looking down at the pair fondly. Abraxus was torn between similar amusement and exasperation. Not even fully awake yet and *already* the boy was asking questions.

Tias just looked at his brother, and then laughed. 'You *twpsyn*.' The laughter died and Tias reached out and squeezed Eli's shoulder. 'Don't do that again.'

"M sorry.' Eli shifted again, this time turning onto his other side facing Tias. He sighed slightly and seemed to relax. Abraxus saw that he was about to fall asleep again, and leaned over Tias to prod Eli's shoulder.

'No. Sit up.'

Eli let out a whine that was more befitting of a five-year-old, but did as he was told. His arm shook as he pushed himself up, threatening to give way entirely. Tias and Smythe were there immediately, placing steadying hands against his back. Eli ducked his head, but not before Abraxus saw a flush creeping up his neck and cheeks. Once he was upright, Smythe pushed the mug into his hands, Eli fumbling with it for a moment. He drained it quickly, wiping his mouth with the back of his hand. Looking to Smythe, Eli said plaintively, 'Can I go back t'sleep now?'

'Aye,' Smythe said, ruffling Eli's hair as Tias plucked the empty cup from his brother's hand.

'Will he be alright?' Tias asked, biting his lip.

'I think so,' Smythe said.

'We cannot make promises though,' Abraxus said, quirking an eyebrow at Smythe. 'Tis better to err on the side of caution.' He ignored Smythe's exasperated look, watching for Tias' reaction. He seemed to think for a second, and then nodded once.

'I understand.' He then yawned, and brought up a hand to rub at his face.

'Get some rest,' Abraxus said, pushing Tias down by his shoulder. 'We will be here.' Tias followed his brother into sleep, no longer holding onto him, but leaving no space between them either. Stretching out, Abraxus propped himself on his elbows, tipping his head back. The warmth of the fire was seeping into his bones now, shaking out the salty chill left there by the sea.

'You should do the same.'

'What about you?' Abraxus countered. He could feel sleep edging into his mind, but he resolutely ignored its call.

'I wasn't the one who dived into the sea,' Smythe said. 'You still need rest as much as 'e does.' He nodded his head in the direction of Eli.

'Wake me before dawn then,' Abraxus relented, letting himself drop to lie on the pleasantly hot stones. Just before sleep claimed him as its own, Abraxus thought about the cavern. Eli hadn't been alone in there. He found himself hoping that on some level, Eli had realised that.

Dreamless sleep was no longer a luxury that came to Abraxus. He'd always remembered his dreams *before* and now it was no different. Except now, his dreams were always full of dark blue water, shifting tangles of seaweed, of waves crashing endlessly against cliffs destined to crumble at some point under the force of the ocean. Tonight, his dreams were a knotted mess, images that melted into one another and blurred at the edges.

It was the coughing that finally brought Abraxus back to the waking world. Weak sunlight was filtering through the little windows of the inn, falling in beams of pale light over the floor and bar. Dust motes danced there, and Abraxus had the strangest thought that it was snowing *inside*. He shook it off, and rubbed his eyes with the heel of his palm. Abraxus rolled his shoulders, and grimaced at the loud series of cracks that ran down his back with the motion.

'–wrong with him?' Abraxus only caught the tail end of Tias' question, his thoughts still slow.

'This sometimes happens.' Smythe was kneeling on the floor by Eli's side of the cot once more. He had his hand laid against Eli's forehead, and was frowning.

Tias was hugging his knees to his chest, wrapped up in blankets. His hair stuck every which way, and he still looked tired. Abraxus was about to ask what was happening, when Eli shifted restlessly and started to cough. It sounded painful, rasping and wet. Smythe removed his hand, and looked up. Abraxus saw the tension in his face. 'When you got 'im back onto the *Esgyll Gwerin*, did he get up any water?' Smythe asked.

Abraxus came over to kneel beside Smythe. 'Yes.' He glanced

at Tias, and then sighed. Despite the fact that the boy had been on the skiff with him, Abraxus wanted to keep certain details to himself. Tias would probably be having nightmares about this for a while yet, without Abraxus adding to it. But Smythe was looking at him expectantly, so Abraxus forced himself to speak. 'There was a moment where... where Eli was not breathing.' Abraxus found himself unable to meet anyone's gaze, instead turning his attention to his hands. His stone was nestled in the palm of his hand.

'I thought so,' Tias said very quietly. 'I didn't want to believe it, but...' He took a steadying breath, and Abraxus finally managed to tear his gaze from the stone. Tias was looking directly at him. 'You brought him back.' There was something steely in Tias' eyes, a determination that Abraxus did not currently have the capacity to puzzle out.

'I – I did,' Abraxus said. The stone was once again very interesting.

'That explains this, then.' Smythe spoke up, attention still fixed on Eli. The boy seemed to have settled again, but there was a tightness around his eyes that spoke of disturbed sleep. 'Fever.'

Abraxus sat back on his haunches, staring out of the window. It was nearly daybreak now, the sky outside painted in a wash of pinks and lightest blue. Inky black still hung on the periphery of the sky's edge. The storm seemed to have blown itself out as Abraxus had slept, or else shifted further inland.

'What can I do?' He asked Smythe, who was now rearranging the tangle of blankets on the cot. He listened as the innkeeper reeled off a list of herbs and where Abraxus could find them around The Five's barroom and storeroom, and nodded.

The rest of the day passed slowly. Several knocks sounded on the door from would-be patrons of the inn; Smythe turned them away, saying that the roof of the building had been damaged in last night's storm and rain had leaked through. They made the decision to move Eli upstairs into one of the empty lodging rooms, adjacent to Abraxus', where hopefully he would be less disturbed.

In the growing light, Abraxus could see from the box window many small white specks dancing away to the horizon. No doubt the fishermen of Porth Tymestl were uplifted by the break in the weather. Even from this distance, Abraxus could tell that the sailing conditions would be near perfect; the sea still and reflecting the late winter sky above.

Tias spent his time either curled up at the foot of Eli's bed, or by the window, staring in the direction of *Tua'r Môr* Bay. Both he and Smythe were insistent on Tias getting some more sleep; the boy looked exhausted, and, Abraxus thought with a pang, a little haunted. But Tias seemed to have taken a leaf from his brother's book and was resolutely refusing to lay down and sleep. After the fourth time Smythe asked, nearly imploringly now, Tias had snapped at him and said that the innkeeper might as well just drop the issue, and was there anything he could do to help, since sleeping wasn't an option. Smythe had pursed his lips at that, but to his credit didn't try again. He knew when he was beaten.

Smythe had left a concoction with Abraxus as he went to fetch some lunch. Abraxus eyed the contents of the cup suspiciously. Tias had asked what it was for, and Smythe had explained that it was to try and bring Eli's fever down, and also worked as an expectorant. The effects were yet to be fully seen, but Smythe had certainly been right about the expectorant part. It had been unpleasant to watch.

As the sun was beginning to touch the horizon, and the fleet of boats were returning one by one to *Angorfa* Harbour, a soft thud broke the relative stillness of the room. As one, Abraxus and Smythe looked up to see Tias resting against the wall, sitting on the foot of his brother's bed. A notebook lay on the floor from where he'd dropped it.

'Finally,' Smythe whispered, reaching over to pick up the book. Tias' eyes were closed, his head rolled slightly to one side to rest on his shoulder.

'He was worried,' Abraxus said, wringing out the cloth they'd taken to using as well as Smythe's herbal concoctions. He gently shifted back the wild tangles of Eli's hair and placed the damp cloth against his forehead.

'I know,' Smythe sighed, running a hand through his hair. 'I think we all are.'

Abraxus said nothing to that. Eli twitched on the cot, muttering something incomprehensible. Over the past hour, he'd gotten more restive, although not properly waking once. Abraxus had caught snippets of words, or half a garbled sentence here and there. He'd mostly not paid attention to Eli's fevered ramblings, until one partial sentence had caught him. Eli had said something about the sea *glowing*, and movement in the water that wasn't only from the waves. Smythe had looked sharply at Abraxus, an eyebrow quirked in a silent question. Tias hadn't been paying much attention, sitting again by the window, clearly far away in thought.

Smythe was making sure that Tias was as comfortable as he could be in his slightly collapsed position. Eli seemed to have returned to making no sense. Abraxus murmured to him softly in his own tongue. The words were nothing of consequence, just a very old story. But he hoped the shape and cadence of the words would help lull Eli into a more peaceful sleep.

Night fell through the inn, and Smythe stood to light the candles. Both he and Smythe left the room to fetch another cot. Once it was in place, Smythe all but collapsed onto it and was snoring within the minute. Abraxus chuckled in spite of himself, and turned his attention back to Eli.

'– fins an' scales below...' Eli muttered, before twisting away to face the wall. Abraxus slipped a hand into his pocket, and brought out his stone. After a second of consideration, he tucked it into Eli's hand, watching as the boy's fingers curled around it slightly.

'Do not worry. They will not harm you,' he whispered.

X
then.

Singing colours.

Everyone that walked the planks described her as "she". Why she was given this title, she didn't know, but so many used it that in the end she assumed it must be correct. After a time, she came to make it her own. The issue was that no one wanted to *own her*.

Too wilful, they said, *too quick and light for true waters*. Her temperament made her undesirable, but she had no inclination to change it. Why should she apologise for something that made her *herself*? The bright colours she was draped with made for drawing attention, attraction, but once they saw beneath the surface, not even the colour could keep them close.

In the end, she sat in the still and calm waters. Deep within her forest-bound bones, she felt the longing for the expanse of water that lay just behind the stout walls. Every renewed interest in her brought with it some time upon those waters, and she revealed in the salt smell, how the water-stained dark patches on her colours. But it was not enough, and she wanted more. But, as time went on, it seemed no one was willing to give her more.

And then *he* walked the planks that led out over the waters. He came when the night was old, the sun beginning its hike toward the horizon, and the water below glittered with the stars overhead. He was alone, and his footfall was light, measured. As he walked past her, she felt the sea-mist that clung to him, coiled about his thoughts and embraced him in salt. More than anything, she wanted to call out to him, invite him to her. Surely this was a man who was worthy of her prowess? Perhaps he heard her, as he stopped by the gangplank. She could feel his indecision, and if she had a voice to do so, she would have cried out when he walked away from her. A moment of silence, and then a distant ripple reached her hull. The man had shed his human cares and given himself to the waters, slipping under with grace she could only hope to emulate *upon*, instead of in.

The man returned the next night, and the night after that. Each time he paused at the invitation she gave to him, and she could sense his resolve waning. Four nights after the first, she felt the movement of him under the water by her prow. The water around him seemed to hold him closely, and she wondered why. He swam the length of her hull submerged, running his fingers over the sea-slicked wood. She knew, from that lightest touch, that he was meant for her. She longed to show him the world, to feel his awe as she danced over the waves. And then he was gone, and she had to endure another day closeted behind sea walls, freedom so close and yet unreachable without a hand to guide her to it.

Something changed the next day. There was chatter on the walkways, many people crowding around where she was docked. Something new came to her on the air, and it tasted sweet. The flock of people parted as the man walked toward her. She could sense the incredulity rising from them. He was alone, young. How did he expect to handle a ship like her without a crew of great numbers, without experience? She had no such doubts. Finally, he walked the gangplank and stepped onto the wood of the deck. It might have been the muted motion of the waves seeping in from behind the seawall, but as he climbed to the wheel, she felt something *twitch*. It was as if his touch painted her afresh with colour, made them sing.

Together, they took to the sea. Despite his work as a fisherman, she was never bored nor restless. He delighted in her speed, in her wilfulness, and she knew that he would not let her go. He would take her over the horizon, far away from any walls that would cage her. Soaking his hand in saltwater, he pressed his palm flat against the mainmast and murmured his name. Later, she would get a name of her own, painted by his hand on her prow. He told her that it meant "she who dances on waves".

Together, they grew and changed and were stained. Memory stains wood as much as saltwater does, and she could feel the bounds of herself, her knowledge expanding as he taught her and was taught by her. But she did not understand the whispers from below that grew stronger every day. She did not comprehend what lay beneath, and how it pulled on his mind. And on the day when he came out onto the blue expanse alone, and sank them both, all she could do was feel how his life slipped away, and then was snatched back by something old and *roaring*.

Asherah lay at the bottom of the seabed, refusing to rot, and waited for the time when he would call her back to him.

XI
now.

Herbs.
January, 1816.
Smythe.

Smythe opened his eyes, and then wished he hadn't. It was undoubtedly past midday, the sun streaming in through the half-shuttered window. It fell in patches over the floorboards, the light rippling slightly as someone stirred in the room, or else a cloud passed over the sun. He rolled over, seeking out the cooler side of the cot, thinking that if he lay still enough, perhaps he'd fall back into sleep.

'Smythe.' Abraxus' voice was rough with worry and exhaustion. Sighing, he sat up, yawned and scrubbed a hand down his face.

'M'up,' he muttered, stretching and listening to his shoulders crack in protest. 'Everythin' alright?' He looked over to the cot opposite his.

'For now, yes,' Abraxus said, pinching the bridge of his nose.

'Then why did you wake me?' Smythe tried to keep the irritation out of his voice, and apparently did a poor job as Abraxus levelled him with a look.

'Because you either need to move over, or get out of the cot,' he said flatly. It was testament to how slowly Smythe was waking up that it took him a full minute to understand what Abraxus was saying. Once it had fallen into place, he stretched again, and threw back the covers.

'Could've just asked,' Smythe muttered as he got to his feet. Abraxus didn't respond, already lying down and pulling the blankets up almost over his head. Smythe shook his head, smiling a little. 'Sleep well.' He turned to Tias. 'How're you feelin'?'

Tias shrugged noncommittally. He looked out the window and then back to Eli.

When it became apparent Smythe wasn't going to get a verbal answer, he settled himself next to Tias, reaching over to check Eli's temperature. 'Did you get much rest?' He asked Tias as he reached for the bowl of now lukewarm water.

'Some,' Tias said quietly.

'Hm. I would say try and get some more, but I don't think you'd take all too kindly to that suggestion.'

Tias smiled a little sheepishly. 'Sorry, I was just–'

'You don't have to apologise lad. I understand,' Smythe cut in, 'but I want you to remember that it's not just this one I need to care for right now.' He looked at Tias, who was very interested all of a sudden in his hands. He was fiddling with something flat and white, turning it over and over in his fingers.

'I know,' he said eventually, voice small.

Silence came down between them, broken only by the rhythmic deep breathing from Abraxus and the occasional distant call of a gull. 'What have you got there?' Smythe asked eventually.

'It was in Eli's hand,' Tias said, holding the object up. Smythe recognised it immediately. He looked to Abraxus, feeling a soft smile work its way onto his lips. 'He dropped it.'

'It's Abraxus',' Smythe said, beginning to push himself to stand. 'Keep it safe for him.'

Tias studied the flat stone, turning it slightly so that the afternoon sun bounced off the pearlescent surface. And then he reached up, and brought the stone to his eye, looking at Smythe through the hole. 'This is what they're for, isn't it?' He asked.

'You know very well that I cannot give you any answers,' Smythe said primly, turning for the door. As he reached it, he looked back and winked, putting a finger to his lips. Tias' pale face split into a smile, and he held up the seeing stone again.

'But what do you *see*?' He muttered to himself as Smythe slipped into the corridor.

The Five was disconcertingly quiet, the only sounds the creak of the stairs as he descended them and the distant pounding of the sea. Apparently, the rumour Smythe had started had spread sufficiently enough, as no one else had knocked on the inn's door looking for comfort in the bottom of a mug.

The empty barroom felt like a balm against the swirl of his thoughts. The sounds of the sea were louder here, the little windows rattling slightly in their casements. A draft came in from under the door, causing the little bunches of herbs to sway from where they were suspended in the rafters. Slipping behind the bar, Smythe eyed the bottles of amber liquid lined up neatly beneath the counter. It took him perhaps a little too long to decide that it was *too* early for a drink, even a small one. And anyway, he'd need his wits about him.

Instead, he pulled a heavy iron pot from the bottom shelf and heaved it onto the bar. His mind wandered for a while, before settling on the image of Abraxus' stone in Tias' hand. At this point, Smythe knew he would be willing to tell the boys all. Especially, he reflected grimly, the obsession for answers had nearly driven Eli to the seabed. He knew that if he broached this with Abraxus, however, he'd be met with flat refusal. The man was stubborn to a fault, and would only give Eli and Tias the answers they wanted when all his minute criteria had been met. Smythe ran through the list, absentmindedly ticking them off on his fingers. The bones, the circlet and now the seeing stone. The only one that had gone unanswered, or perhaps unexplored, was the obvious question. Smythe couldn't help but feel a little surprised at that. He had thought that, with Tias' love of riddles and word games, and Eli's ability to get anything out of anyone, that that particular clue would have been solved first. Clearly, he'd been wrong.

The hammering on the door almost caused Smythe to topple off the slight ledge of the hearthside as he reached for the now cooked soup. It sounded like whoever it was on the other side was pounding on the wood with both fists. Standing, and ignoring the protest of his joints, Smythe walked over to the door, calling, 'We're shut! Leak in the roof!'

'Smythe? Smythe, open the damn door this instant!'

Smythe went cold. He'd forgotten. Without bothering to respond, he lunged for the door, fingers fumbling with the latch for a moment in his haste. He yanked it open, and came face to face with Ffion Kincarran. She looked torn between utter terror and cold fury. 'Ffion, I can expla-' he started.

'Stop.' She held up a hand, abruptly cutting him off. 'Where are they?' Her voice was steely, but there was a tremor underneath that spoke of tears not far below the surface.

'Come in,' Smythe said, standing aside and ushering her through. He latched the door again, turned, and found Ffion glaring up at him. Instinctively, he took a step backward.

'Where are *my sons*?'

'Upstairs,' Smythe said tiredly, running a hand through his hair.

'Why, in the name of the gods, are they here and not at home?' She didn't let him answer, her voice growing louder. 'And *why* does it look like they've not *been home* for at least a night, and that all their blankets from their beds are missing?' She was shouting now, and Smythe saw the barely restrained wave of emotion that threatened to crash down upon them both.

Smythe opened his mouth to speak, and then closed it again. What could he possibly say that would soothe her? He was still processing it all himself. In the end, Smythe gently took Ffion's shoulder and guided her to the stairs. 'They're up here. I swear, we've taken good care of him... of them both.'

Ffion took the stairs two at a time, the hem of her travelling cloak heavy with mud. Smythe noticed belatedly that she still carried a small pack on her back. They reached the landing, Ffion looking around slightly lost. Smythe pointed wordlessly to their room, and let her push the door open. He followed.

Tias had sat up straight on the bed, the stone clattering dully to the floor. He stared at his mother, seeming to drink in her image. Ffion looked back, and the pair seemed caught in time, if only for a second. And then the second rolled into the next and Tias was throwing himself from the bed and into Ffion's arms. He clung to her back like a child would, and Ffion reached up and pulled his head closer to her chest, whispering words Smythe could not catch into his ear.

Ffion had released Tias and was holding him at arm's length, firing questions at him. Tias couldn't manage more than stammered answers. Her eyes, looking over Tias' head, were fixed on Eli. The boy had stirred, it seemed, since Smythe had left the room. There was still a pinch to his brow that spoke of restless sleep. Smythe stepped around Ffion and Tias, kneeling beside Eli's cot and pressed his hand to the boy's forehead. Still warm to the touch.

'Please.' Ffion's voice was raw, as if she'd been screaming for hours. 'What happened?'

'The sea seems drawn to your kin.' Abraxus had sat up properly, sitting cross legged on the cot. 'They – it tried to take Eli.'

Ffion muffled a sob, a hand over her mouth. The knuckles were white. Tias gently took her other hand, and pulled her over to the bed. Smythe stood and got out of their way, coming to lean against the windowsill. She turned and looked directly at Abraxus. 'You're the one they've been so interested by, aren't you?' Her voice, whilst thick at the edges, was forged in ice and iron.

'I am.' Abraxus regarded her levelly. 'I am also the one who, over the course of time, has tried my absolute best to rebut your sons' intrigue, tried to keep my business to myself, and, eventually when I saw that was not an option, tried my best to keep them at arm's length, and therefore, safe.' Abraxus looked away, through the window toward the sea. He added quietly, 'Or at least, so I thought and intended to.'

There was remorse in his words that sent a pang through Smythe. Abraxus was, for the most part, sure of himself and his actions. This particular work, however, had seemed to shake him to his core. Something had shifted irrevocably inside him, and, if Smythe had been blessed with such gifts, he was sure that he would see lines of bright red fate strung between the man who walked the waves, and the boys who lived by them.

Lullabies.
January, 1816.
Ffion.

If icy panic hadn't been tearing through her very soul, Ffion would have found herself somewhat fascinated by the man that had inserted himself into her sons' lives. His appearance was odd – *his eyes* – but there was beauty in it; Ffion had never seen someone with such dark skin before. She got the impression that if the man wasn't sleep-mussed, nor sitting like a child on a cot, he would an imposing figure. As it was, she couldn't find it in herself to be intrigued, or even to speculate about him. She had eyes only for Eli and Tias.

Her eldest seemed to be alright in health, although he was pale in a way that spoke of restless nights and fear. The dark smudges under his eyes looked nearly as black as the ink that so often flecked his wrists and cuffs. She always noticed, no matter how many times Tias tried to roll them up. Ffion reached over, and tucked a strand of loose hair behind Tias ear. It was getting long. '*Cwsg, fy machgen.*' *Sleep, my boy*

Tias shifted slightly, bringing long legs as close to his chest as he could manage. Ffion kept up running her fingers through his hair. Eventually, Tias' blinking became slower until his eyelashes fluttered and he seemed to relax completely into the cot.

'I've been trying to get 'im to do that for nearly two days now.' Smythe muttered behind her. Ffion turned to look at him, and the innkeeper flushed. Ffion felt a tiny spark of victory when Smythe actually shuffled his feet like a schoolboy caught in the act of writing a rude word on a slate. 'I'll – er... I'll go fetch some food.' And with that Smythe turned and all but ran for the door. As it closed, she heard a soft chuckle from the other cot. For now, she ignored the stranger.

Eli looked ill. Ffion knew he was feverish, but it almost went further than that. He was pinched and pale, and there was a set to his mouth and brow that she had not really seen before. She took one of his hands in hers, clasped it to her. It felt *breakable*, thin and light and cold. *Eli's hands were not that*, she thought distantly. It had been a constant in their lives that if anyone in their family was afflicted with cold hands, they would go to Eli and demand he hold them and warm them up. They were hands meant for climbing, knotting endless bits of string pulled from pockets, prodding Tias and stealing things from Ffion's workbasket. Hauling on canvas and rope out at sea. Now, they felt like twine and dry sticks.

Ffion knew that she hadn't been as attentive as she should have been. It wasn't that she didn't love them, she did. So much so that it hurt, it eclipsed everything else. But there were days now, after John, where she felt like she didn't know how to be a mother, how to *cope*. And now, here both of her sons lay, bearing the marks that her unwitting carelessness had wrought. Too thin, too quiet. Ffion took a breath, and vowed to make it better. She would fix this.

It was clear that the stranger wanted to talk to her. He kept shuffling on the cot, or else standing up and walking aimlessly around the little room. Every time he came close to Eli or Tias, Ffion would level him with her frostiest look, and he'd look down and turn away. Smythe was watching from a corner, a slim book forgotten in his lap. She could tell he was doing his best to not look amused, and she got the sense that the stranger was a man who was used to being listened to, doing as he pleased and not cowed by a mother. No matter how protective he'd seem to have become over her boys, no one could rival Ffion.

The afternoon sank into evening, and with the changing of the light came a changing of the weather. Fog poured inland off the sea, wreathing the cottages and creeping through the streets. Eventually it crested up the side of The Five-Pointed Compass, and when Ffion looked out of the window, all she saw was a blank white wall. It quickly darkened as night flew over the coastline, leaving them seemingly in a void. She found herself longing for the susurrations of the leaves, the stars that littered the night sky, unknowable and distant.

Ffion didn't realise she had been humming until a soft voice asked, 'An old song?' It was the stranger. He was sitting kitty-corner to Smythe, who appeared to have drifted off. The book in his lap had been dog-eared to mark his place, and Ffion was glad Tias wasn't awake to see.

'One from my home,' she said shortly, turning her attention to Eli. He seemed no better to her eyes.

'Where is home?' The man was clearly not going to be deterred now that he had finally gotten her to converse with him.

'Inland.' After a moment, she relented and said, 'A wooded vale north-east of here. Four days of travel by foot. *Dyffryn Cernunnos*.'

'The first word I know,' he said musingly. 'The second I do not.'

'It is the name of one of the old gods,' Ffion explained. 'Back home we don't have a deity, singular, but many.'

He seemed to consider this for a moment, and then said thoughtfully, 'It seems that is two of us beholden to the old gods.' A smile quirked his lips. 'Plural.'

Of all the things she might have considered speaking about with this man, Ffion hadn't expected it to be her dormant faith. To her surprise, she found herself breaking the silence. 'I don't know your name.'

'Abraxus.' The man's response was quiet, and Ffion turned to look directly at him. He was staring at her with an intensity that made the back of her neck prickle, but she stood her ground.

'Ffion.' After a moment of consideration, she stretched out her hand. Abraxus leaned forward, causing Smythe to mumble something and turn away. The book slid to the floor. Instead of grasping her hand, Abraxus curled his fingers just beneath her elbow, their forearms pressed together.

'I really did try to keep them safe. Away.' He sounded so small, so *contrite* that Ffion blinked.

Looking at her sons, she sighed and knew that her worry, twisting into anger, shouldn't really be directed at Abraxus. 'I think,' she began carefully, 'that they don't really know when to leave well enough alone.' Looking at Abraxus, she allowed herself a rare smile. 'That would have been John's doing.' The smile slipped, and for a moment she faced that howling black ocean once more.

'I like them.'

'Oh?'

It looked like it had cost Abraxus rather a lot of effort to speak those three words. He was staring determinedly at the floor now, the braid of his belt being twisted and looped over his fingers. Ffion had the sudden thought that the man before her was a lonely one. She didn't have time to fully inspect that idea, as Smythe suddenly awoke with a yelp. He looked between Ffion and Abraxus, sleep clinging to his features but already a sharpness in his blue-grey eyes.

'We've been properly introduced,' Ffion said.

'Good...' Smythe said slowly, as if waiting for more. Ffion glanced sideways at Abraxus and saw the man's mismatched eyes alight with mischief. She could suddenly see why Eli was drawn to him.

'Do not worry, she has made no threats to my life. As of yet.'

'Good to hear. I'll bring up some food,' Smythe said, and then hesitated in the doorway. In the end, he merely nodded, and left, closing the door quietly behind him.

'*Will you teach me the song?*' There was something strangely familiar in Abraxus' words, a subtle change in his cadence. Ffion brushed the notion aside.

'*It's more of a poem really, put to music for late nights.*' She spoke the old words slowly, letting the green sound unfurl into the room. When she was finished, she realised her eyes had closed.

'*I should like to learn it,*' Abraxus said, voice low. '*Would you write it down?*'

Ffion nodded. This seemed to demarcate the end of the conversation for Abraxus, as he stood, rolled his shoulders and moved to the little casement window. With a deft flick of his fingers, he unlatched it. Fog curled gently over the ledge, dissipating as it hit the warmer air inside. Standing almost in a sentinel position by the window, Abraxus gazed out into the night. There was an expression of deep thought written over his face, but over what Ffion couldn't tell. On the cot, Tias stirred, yawned and brought a hand up to rub his eyes. He kept his eyes closed but muttered, 'Time is it?'

'After sundown,' Ffion murmured.

'What were you saying?'

The question didn't make sense to Ffion, and she put it down to Tias only just having woken up. Smythe opened the door with a kick to the bottom, walking in backwards with five bowls expertly balanced up his arms. He handed one to Ffion and she all but fell upon it. The stew was more broth than anything else, and that told her all she needed to know about the state of Porth Tymestl's food shortages. The one person anyone could count on for getting a sturdy, hot meal from was Stooger Smythe.

Eli stirred, brow furrowing. Ffion reached over and ran her thumb over the pinch, hoping to get him to settle. Instead, Eli moaned softly and, after what seemed like a moment of effort, opened his eyes. They were glassy, and it was clear that he wasn't completely with them.

'Mam..?'

'Right here, *cariad*.' She cupped Eli's face and gently bent over to rest her forehead against his.

'Where are we?' Eli was close to falling back into sleep, she could tell.

'The Five-Pointed Compass, lad.' Abraxus said softly.

'Compass only has four points,' Eli pointed out matter-of-factly. 'Why s'one got five?' And with that, his eyelashes fluttered, and he relaxed back into the pillows.

Tias had made a small noise at Eli's question, somewhere between an exhalation and a quiet 'Oh.' But Ffion wasn't focused on that, instead she was looking at Abraxus. She replayed their conversation, her recital of the old vale lullaby. The change in cadence suddenly made sense to her. Abraxus hadn't changed his voice, he'd changed his *language*. She stared at the man who had addressed her in her mother-tongue, and not for the first time that night, wondered who he really was.

XII
then.

The roaring god.

It was cruel, she thought. She had had only a taste of what she had longed for, of the open waves and the billowing wind in her colours. Salt spray had stained her decks, weathered her into something not quite new but wholly unique. And now, she was submerged. Deep below, the light was only a distant glint. It played through the surface waters, but the shafts of sapphire light never reached her. It was dark, and cold, and quiet. Such a far cry from the freedom he had given her. But he had forsaken them both, taken them out into the middle of seas, to a place not charted on any map, and sank them.

The sea had taken his life quickly, hungrily. She should have noticed, should have known from the start. The sea fret that surrounded his mind had only grown stronger each day, wrapping him up and numbing him to the pleasures in which others around him indulged. It was only a matter of time before the sea claimed what it had marked as its own.

There had been no fear from him. No sense of urgency. He had merely dropped her colours, leaving what was once a sturdy tree bare again. No anchor had been dropped, and for a time they had drifted together aimlessly, at the whim of the currents. And then, with the same ease he had when walking the deck, he leapt onto the rail, balancing lightly. She waited, feeling an eerie calmness rolling from him. And then, with no warning, he'd fallen. Simply leaned forward and disappeared into the waters below. If she had a voice, she would have screamed.

Instead, *Asherah* had drifted atop the waves for a while, until the storm came and bowed her down. She went gladly, unwilling to be locked in the harbour again, looked at covetously and then dismissed. But as she sank, she sensed him near. He hung in the water, peacefully. His hair and coat drifting around him. There was no breath in his body, no twitching of his hands. But she heard his mind singing. *Asherah* wanted to sing back, to call him out of the dark place he'd slipped into.

Something else was listening. Something old, something deep and *roaring*. It held him close, and over time she realised that whatever it was surrounded them on all sides. The years passed, the light coming and going above her. The roaring thing still clung to him, whispering briny secrets into his ear, pulling out the things that she understood as *human*. Her colours faded, but the fabric did not tear or wither. *Asherah* felt herself begin to float further and further away, until the wind and the kiss of the sun was but a fleeting memory. During one of these lucid moments, *Asherah* finally comprehended what it was that kept him from her, that held so tightly to him. For the first time, she knew fear. Because in comparison to a god, she was but a plaything.

When the time came for them to be returned, she went willingly. She understood that hers was a greater role to play than merely a fishing vessel. *Asherah* surfaced first, lifted from the seabed and coral by an unseen hand. A moment later, he was released from the watery hold. Breath filled his chest once more, and he cast about, searching. He knew she would be there, waiting for him. As he clambered up onto her deck once more, *Asherah* felt something shift. Something fell back into place, and she knew she was whole once more. The sunlight and water-glare caught her colours, which he quickly unfurled. Life bled back into them, and *Asherah* knew that this was a beginning. He walked the deck, and where before he had needed a crew of others to help, everything he desired was done quickly. The roaring god had given her more than a second lease of life.

He was changed, that much she knew. She heard the roaring god deep below, murmuring kelp secrets and scaled promises. His servants swam lazily in the water around them continually now. Just as her colours were renewed, *Asherah* saw his were too. He held the sky and sea in his eyes, and together, they set off toward the horizon.

XIII
now.

Repairs.
January, 1816.
Tias.

Once, when Tias had been out with his Da on the *Dawnsiwr y Wawr*, a wave had hit the ship's starboard side. The conditions had been less than ideal for a day's fishing, but John Kincarran was not to be cowed by such trivialities. The wave had caught them all by surprise, and Tias had been slammed backwards across the deck, hitting the opposite rail. His back and side had been black and blue for nearly a week afterwards. He didn't think he'd ever quite forget the sensation of gallons of cold saltwater being all but thrown at him, how it stole his breath and made him ache like he'd been punched. Whilst nowhere near as drenched as that particular time, Tias felt like he'd been hit by that wave all over again. Eli's question, although spoken through a fevered haze, had been the piece they'd been missing. *The obvious question.*

Tias wanted to hit himself, it had been *so* obvious now that he stopped and thought about it. Although, he mused, that was often the way with riddles. Confounding, until the answer was revealed.

'Tias.'

'Hm?'

'You alright there, lad?' Smythe asked. 'Seemed far away.'

There was a glint deep in Smythe's eye that told Tias he didn't need to answer that.

'I think,' Tias said in a low voice, causing Smythe to lean toward him a little, 'you made that as infuriating as possible.' He grinned as Smythe made to swat him, a motion made difficult as the innkeeper was currently balancing five bowls in one hand.

'What are you conspiring about?' His mother asked, not looking up from her tending to Eli. Her voice was light, but Tias could still hear an undercurrent of deep worry in it.

'Nothin', *cariad*.' Smythe said, straightening. 'Tias just got the answer to a question that's been botherin' him a while.'

'Tias?'

'It's...' He glanced to Abraxus, hoping for some indication as to what to say. Abraxus just looked steadily back at him, his expression unreadable. 'It's nothing, Mam. Don't worry about it.'

'Hm.' It was clear Ffion wasn't going to forget about it, but right now Tias knew she'd put it to one side. She turned to Abraxus and gestured to the now vacant cot. 'Are you..?'

'No. I need to talk with Smythe.' Abraxus pushed himself off the wall, pulled open the door and left abruptly. His mother blinked.

'Is he always like that?'

'Like what?' Tias said absentmindedly, fiddling with the frayed hem of the blanket.

'Stop that. Terse.'

'I suppose.' Tias thought back, and then smiled in spite of himself. 'He reminds me a little bit of Eli on a bad day to be honest.'

His mother huffed a laugh, picking up one of the discarded mugs on the floor beside Eli's cot. 'I can see that, yes. Tias, *cariad*, what happened?' Ffion turned to him, her eyes pleading for answers. 'I came back and you were both gone, beds not slept in, the spare key missing. I thought... I thought for a moment that you'd both left.' Her voice became thick and wavered over the last words.

Tias closed his eyes briefly, as if trying to ward off pain. Of course, that's how it would appear to her. 'We made a stupid plan.' Tias muttered, picking up the blanket's edge again. 'We wanted to go down to *Tua'r Môr* Bay and – and spend the night in the cavern.'

'What on earth for?' Ffion looked confused, fear warring on her expression with something close to disgust at the mention of the long stretch of sand.

This was the crux of it: Tias had to decide whether or not to impart the truth – or at least, what he knew of the truth – to his mother. He looked at her for a moment, taking in her tired face, the fierce light in her eyes. Ffion had shaken off the salt of the sea, and was now sinking into the comfort and bracken of her home. The thought scared Tias, as if his mother was slipping out of his grasp. In that second, he made his choice.

'Eli and I – mostly Eli – wanted one last adventure.'

Ffion raised an eyebrow at that but didn't interrupt.

'It seems pretty set that we're leaving,' Tias continued, 'and we just thought we'd make the most of it before we have to go. I know you don't like the beach, and I know you've told us to stay away, but...' He took a deep breath, and went for the plunge. 'We love it, Mam. Down there. Eli more so than me, but still.'

'Matthias.' Ffion waited until he looked up at her. 'I know. I know that you love it. And it breaks me to take you both away, but I *cannot* be here any longer. I think you understand this, yes?'

Tias nodded.

'I also think that there is more you are not telling me.'

Tias started to respond, but his mother held up a hand to cut him off.

'But I recognise that whilst you are both my sons, you are also growing up. There are things you won't want to tell me anymore.' She smiled a little sadly, and laced her fingers in with his. 'That's alright, but I would say that if there is ever anything you feel unsure about, or perhaps think is a little foolhardy—' and at that she looked down at Eli in equal parts love and exasperation, '— you can *always* come to me.'

'I know, Mam.' Tias said quietly. 'We argued.'

'What was that?'

'Eli and I. We argued, in the cavern. I left.' Guilt clawed up Tias' throat, threatening to choke him. 'That's why he's...' He looked over Ffion's shoulder to his brother, still asleep.

'What did you fight about?' His mother asked gently. There was no blame in her voice, and Tias took comfort from it.

'He wanted to stay, I wanted to leave. The weather closed in so fast, and we just didn't think about the tide times.' It all felt like a blur now to Tias, brightly coloured but with the same hazy quality as a half-recalled dream.

'Did you know,' Ffion began slowly, now sitting beside him and starting to card her hand through Tias' hair, 'that I sometimes thanked the gods that you are more level-headed than your brother?'

'No, I didn't.' Tias broke the embrace and looked at his mother as she continued to speak.

'Whenever Eli would get into a scrap, or fall off something or run off, you were always there to talk him down, bring him home and patch him up. I realise now that perhaps that wasn't always your responsibility. But you did it nonetheless. Your father used to say that you were the shoreline to Eli's tide.' Ffion swiped away with the pad of her thumb the tears that were slowly trickling down Tias' cheeks. 'I understand if you argued. I understand he's the most stubborn boy this side of the valley – that's most likely from me. Tias, it's not your fault. Because you brought him home, again.'

If earlier he'd been hit again by a cold wave of understanding, he was now embraced in a summer sun heated tidepool. 'Well technically,' he said, sniffing, 'Abraxus steered the ship.'

His mother looked at him incredulously for a second, and then broke into laughter. 'You know what I mean.' She cupped the back of his neck and pulled him down, kissing his forehead. 'Go on. Get some sleep, *cariad*.'

Despite having slept not too long ago, he was still bone tired. 'Wake me up later on so we can swap.' His mother looked like she was about to argue, but Tias cut her off. 'I can sleep perfectly well sharing, you've been travelling. Wake me up.' Ffion sighed, but nodded nonetheless.

The cot held residual heat from whoever had slept here last. Nestling down into the blankets, Tias looked around the room through heavy-lidded eyes. 'Why does *this* compass have five points?' He whispered to himself. Before he could start to think of an answer, a soft wave of darkness pulled him under.

Connections.
January, 1816.
Abraxus.

When Abraxus had headed downstairs to talk with Smythe, it had been more of an excuse to leave the room than an actual need to speak with the innkeeper. It was clear even to him, as unversed in social interaction as he was, that the Kincarrans needed some time alone to be a family again. As it was, he had padded into the barroom feeling a little lost, a little tired but more at ease now than he had felt in the previous few days. They all seemed to blur together now, so much so that Abraxus thought that if the inn hadn't had windows, he'd have no sense of the passage of time at all.

'Here, make yourself useful.' Smythe was standing by the bar, a basin of gently steaming water on it. The empty bowls and cooking pot stood ready beside it. Before Abraxus could even open his mouth to respond, a ragged cloth hit him squarely in the face. He fumbled with it for a moment, before shooting a glare toward the innkeeper, who was smiling openly. Abraxus stumped over to the bar, not really begrudging Smythe his moment of playfulness. It had been a long few days. As Smythe plunged the first bowl into the water and began to scrub it, Abraxus glanced out of the window. The fog that had rolled into the cobbled streets of Porth Tymestl was now lost under the quilt of night. Before the night was over, Abraxus knew he had things to do.

'Doin' some mighty contemplation. there,' Smythe said matter-of-factly, breaking Abraxus' reverie. He started slightly as Smythe nudged a bowl into his hands. Distractedly, he started to dry it on the rag he'd been tossed.

'Just thinking about the next course of action.'

'And that would be?' Smythe's voice was light, but Abraxus heard the curiosity there.

'I need to go out tonight.' Smythe started to protest, but Abraxus cut him off. 'It is important, Stooger. I promise it has nothing to do with the bones.' He looked down at the bowl, and finding it suitably dried, set it to one side. Smythe handed him the next. He could feel the innkeeper's unasked question in the air between them. 'I want to try and retrieve what the boys left in the cavern.' Abraxus said quietly.

'Oh.' Smythe fell silent, opened his mouth to say something, and then apparently thought better of it. He nodded once. 'Alright.'

'I would also like your assistance with something,' Abraxus said, a half plan already forming in his mind.

'Certainly.' Smythe started on the pot, swilling it out. 'What can I do?'

'I think it might be... helpful for them to spend some time away from Porth Tymestl.'

'Who, Eli and Tias?' Smythe lifted the pot off the bar and carried it to the door, opening it and flinging the water out over the cobbles.

'Yes. Just for a while. They need to recover, Eli in body and Tias in mind.' Abraxus thought for a moment. 'And, I confess, I would feel better if they were away from here.'

'It weren't anyone's fault, you know.' Smythe's words caught him off guard.

'I know, but I cannot help but feel–'

'Responsible?'

'Aye,' Abraxus said shortly. 'I need to work now with no distractions. And whilst I admit I did like leaving the boys clues and having them somewhat *involved*, this has gone on long enough.' Abraxus knew he'd wasted precious time indulging Smythe's desire to include the Kincarran boys. The weather continued to batter the coastline. The catch was now near non-existent. It was only a matter of time before another ship was lost below. But now, armed with some beginning of answers from his conversation with Ffion, it was time to work. He'd been given a purpose, and it was his sole duty to fulfil it. Smythe was staring at him, face filled with glee.

'What?' Abraxus said wearily.

'You just said you liked 'em. Having 'em around.'

Abraxus sighed, wiping out the inside of the cooking pot. 'Yes, fine, Stooger. I like them, I liked having the company. I admitted nearly as much to their mother.'

'Well, you know what I might suggest now. What I *tried* to suggest the first night they asked about you.'

'I know,' Abraxus said slightly hopelessly. 'But after what happened... Smythe, I do not want to put them in unnecessary danger.' He looked meaningfully at Smythe, the innkeeper seemingly understanding him.

'I will say this on the matter, and then nothin' more. You know my mind. But I didn't agree to be your Wayfinder because I thought it would be safe. Those boys need a direction, Abraxus. You can give 'em one.'

'I will think on it, whilst they are away,' Abraxus conceded.

'You seem mighty sure that they'll go,' Smythe said doubtfully, his voice somewhat muffled from his crouched position.

'Well,' Abraxus said, coming over to the bar and leaning over it. His hair hung down, the beads and metal clinking softly. 'You are a *very* persuasive person, Smythe.'

The lantern light barely seemed to pierce the night and fog. Four panels of light shone out around him, illuminating the next four paces, but little else. He'd taken his favourite lantern that hung from the rafters; the little pewter one with blue and yellow glass. Cottages reared up out of the mist, and the now familiar pathways through Porth Tymestl felt like a maze of slicked cobble and alleyways.

Abraxus huddled down in his coat, wrapping his scarf closely around his lower face. Declining the offer of Smythe's company, he'd set out as soon as he'd collected warmer clothes from his chest and his staff, and had a peek into the Kincarrans' room. They were all fast asleep. Just as Abraxus turned to leave, there was a shifting of fabric. Glancing back, he saw the soft hazel eyes of Eli peering back at him blearily.

'Rax?'

'Go back to sleep, Elias,' Abraxus whispered. He did his best to not twitch at the nickname he'd always hated.

'Where you goin'?'

It was all he could do to not roll his eyes. 'Down to the beach, Eli. You left everything behind, and I think you might be needing your boots back.'

'Oh.' Eli contemplated him for a moment, and Abraxus saw a little more recognition in his eyes. '*Diolch.*'

'It is no problem,' Abraxus said. 'Now, get some rest.'

Now, as he traversed the streets toward the path down to *Tua'r*

Môr Bay, a darker part of his thoughts wondered what he would have done if Eli hadn't made it back to the inn. Would he have abandoned these people to their plight, running out of shame? Or would he have stayed, feeling indebted to these people who had lost another of their own? Shaking his head as if to clear these less than welcome *what-ifs*, Abraxus turned toward the cliff path.

Instead, he turned his thoughts to what Smythe had said. It was not common for people like him to take apprentices. But he had to admit, in this case it made sense. For some reason, the Kincarran boys had been tangled up with him since he arrived. He now had more of an understanding about why he'd been drawn so closely to the family, but that was pertaining more to Ffion than Eli and Tias. Perhaps because she'd been away so much, Eli and Tias had filled in the gap left by her absence. Whatever the case may be, he could not deny the lines of fate that now drew them all together.

So lost in his own hazed thoughts, Abraxus nearly overshot the cliff path down to *Tua'r Môr* Bay, and was forced to backtrack. The storm had made the narrow path treacherous, loose shingle and slick mud forced his mind to focus solely on his next step. The strings and beads tied to his staff swung wildly, clicking against the wood and his thigh. Eventually, Abraxus reached the sand without incident and lightly jumped the last few feet down to the beach. For a moment, he debated stowing his boots in the long grass by the path, but the thought of having numb toes for what was likely to be a long job was too unappealing.

A little way before him, Abraxus could hear the gentle ripple of water, the shushing noise each wave spoke before dissipating on the shoreline. Closing his eyes, he let that sound fill him and felt the last edges of worry and tiredness melt away. The ocean sound continued to soothe his thoughts as Abraxus walked out to meet the surf, and continued along the bay.

ABRAXUS ELIJAH HONEY

Dreams.
February, 1816.
Eli.

His memory of the past few days was hazy at best. The last thing Eli could recall was the cold grip of the water as it dragged him down to the sand. After that, it was all mixed up, as if he'd been drifting through dreams. There was the vague sensation of being at sea with his brother's voice in his ear. Eli tried to not examine that particular memory in too much detail.

The rest were similarly just feelings; the odd bit of snatched conversation, the impression of someone's hand on his cheek. One he couldn't place, however, was the cold, smooth feeling of what seemed to be a stone tucked into his hand. Eli wasn't even sure if that had been real, it could easily have been part of the strange and twisted dreams that had plagued him. They had been filled with twisting shapes just below the water line, things impossibly long with too many teeth. Sometimes they'd been beautiful, glowing and spiralling in the water that stretched as far as he could see.

But Eli mostly remembered feeling afraid. Of them, of the endless ocean that played as backdrop for those missing days. He felt as if he were standing atop the sea cliffs, some great precipice that the edge of his feet teetered on. He had tried diving before, but now the drop seemed to yawn deeper, the fall greater.

Eli had woken up properly to weak sunlight streaming in through the little gaps in the shutters. The shafts of light had fascinated him for a time, and it wasn't until Tias near kicked him in the back that he realised he wasn't alone. He was sleeping parallel to him, top-and-tail style.

The door creaked open, and Abraxus slipped into the room. Eli almost laughed, the man's actions were precise and delicate, clearly not wanting to wake anyone. He was carrying what appeared to be his coat that had been tied in some way to make a bag, which was then flung over one shoulder. Intrigued, Eli managed to prop himself up on an elbow and watch Abraxus' furtive movements around the room. It took the man nearly two full minutes to realise he was being observed.

'Eli!' He dropped the bag, all carefulness forgotten. It landed with a damp sounding *thud*.

Ffion and Tias both jolted awake, Tias spitting out a strand of his hair that had fallen over his face and mouth.

Abraxus was at the cot's side quicker than Eli's still lethargic mind could comprehend. 'Are you... awake?' Eli could not recall Abraxus ever sounding so *unsure* before.

'Well, my eyes are open,' he said flatly.

'He's fine,' Tias said, groaning and throwing himself back down. He landed on one of Eli's feet and they both yelped in pain.

'I meant,' Abraxus said patiently as Tias shoved Eli's feet away from his face, 'are you *with* us?'

It took Eli a minute to parse that out. 'I assume,' he began slowly, 'that I've been awake but not... here?'

'Something like that, yes.' Abraxus said.

'If he's complainin', or making a fuss, he's better.' Smythe had stuck his head around the door. 'I thought I heard voices. You get what you wanted from the beach, Abraxus?'

'Aye,' Abraxus said shortly.

'The beach?' Tias asked, sitting up again and scrubbing a hand down his face.

'Oh, so you *did* leave,' Eli said. Everyone looked at him sharply. 'I thought I had dreamt it. Was – was that last night?' He suddenly felt unsure, his sense of time had slipped.

'It was,' Abraxus confirmed. 'I went to see if I could salvage anything you had left behind in the cavern.'

Smythe seemed to be setting up an impromptu picnic on the floor. Eli watched languidly as his brother pulled something from his pocket and held it out to Abraxus. There was a flash of white, and whatever it was vanished into one of Abraxus' pockets. Tias looked over at him and mouthed, '*I'll tell you later.*'

After the breakfast Smythe had laid out for them had been devoured, Abraxus pulled the forgotten bundle toward him and untied the sleeves of the coat. Inside were several long shards of wood, Eli's boots and half of the chime they'd hung by the entrance.

Aside from being thoroughly damp, his boots seemed to have fared better than his other belongings. He knew though, from his Da's many pairs of boots, that the leather would crack as soon as it had dried. Vaguely, he wondered if he'd be forced to go barefoot for the rest of the winter. He usually went without his boots during the late spring and summer, but the cobbles outside still looked somewhat icy. Eli shivered lightly and pulled the blanket closer around his shoulders. The other items, the broken slats of wood, he didn't even touch. He knew it to be the sea chest his Da had given him. That was certainly broken beyond repair.

Not long after that, Eli felt his eyelids begin to droop. The conversation felt muted and far away, the candlelight dancing pleasantly through his lashes. 'Back to bed for this one.' Smythe's voice had the edges of a laugh in it, rolled out into fondness.

'Mm.' Was all Eli could manage. Abraxus hooked him up under the arm and propelled him toward the cot.

'Sleep well,' he muttered. After a moment, he looked directly at Eli. In his gaze was something inscrutable. 'If you dream of them again, know that they are not the stuff of nightmares.' A cold, smooth weight was tucked into his hand, and Abraxus withdrew.

It was not even midday yet, but to Eli it felt like he'd been awake all night. Heavy drowsiness fell over him, and he curled up under the blankets, instinctively drawing his hands to his chest. A soft smile curled the edges of his lips. The stone had been real too.

Two days later, they left The Five. Smythe had been forced to open up the barroom again the day after Eli had woken up, although not for the money. The bar was the centre of life for many of the residents of Porth Tymestl, a place to kick up feet and talk with friends without having salt spray coat their lips. He tried not to duck his head as they descended the stairs into the main barroom, aware that many of the patrons were looking at them curiously. Despite it only being a little past midday, there was quite a crowd; the weather was beginning to close in again, and although the day's conditions might have permitted a few short fishing trips, many of the sailors now seemed loath to cast themselves out onto the water. Too much had already been lost to risk another journey when the tides were so clearly against them.

Abraxus lurked in the shadow of the stairs, not stepping into the brightly lit room. Eli found himself wishing for the comfort of the man's hand, heavy and rough on his shoulder as he, Tias and their mother traversed past the tables and toward the door. Smythe saw them out, exchanging a few quick words with Ffion. Eli wasn't really paying attention to them, craning his neck to get a glimpse of Abraxus. He was merely a shadow on the staircase, the metal and beads in his hair the only indication that there was something more substantial there. In the crowd, Eli spotted Medwyn looking curiously toward the stairs and then glancing toward them still huddled in the little porch space. The silhouetted figure of Abraxus turned slightly, raising a hand in his direction. Eli returned it with a short nod. And then he was gone, slipping above like he'd never even been there at all.

The walk back to Roseate Cottage seemed to have grown several miles in the few days since Eli had last done it. By the time they reached the door, his legs felt shaky, and it seemed that someone had wrapped Tias' scarf around his ears and eyes. He stumbled over the threshold, distantly felt a hand wrap around his elbow to hold him steady. 'Bed.' His mother's voice, despite being oddly muted to him, was resolute. For once, Eli found himself agreeing wholeheartedly with her command.

A rare burst of winter sunshine painted golden squares on the floor. For the first time in a while, Eli did not dream.

XIV
then.

The Horned One.

It began with a willow tree. It stood within a forest of many of its kin, and when the wind ran through the boughs, the leaves whispered deep sky-secrets to one another. The willow was the keeper of many messages, both from the sky and the dark earth below. Within its hanging fronds, it held and sent alike words out into the quiet green of the world. How far the whispers went was unknown; the basin of the valley kept the forest hidden.

It began with a willow tree, but it also began with a man who was not a man. He walked through the wild places of the earth, passing mostly unseen into rocks, rivers and bark. Those that saw him, or perhaps those that *he* chose to see him all returned to their people with stories of a tall man, draped in moss and lichen with antlers that curled to sharp points around his face. Any other detail they could not recall. The people called him the Lord of Wildthings, and were not afraid by his walking.

On a morning that was covered by mist, the Lord of Wildthings met the willow that held the forest's secrets. The dappled sunlight fell onto the mist curling through the waving tendrils of leaves, and sparkled. Everything was ghostly quiet, and the Lord of Wildthings could feel the willow seeking him out, questioning what he was. With one hand that was coated in the raised edges of wood-ear mushrooms, the Lord of Wildthings sent his thoughts and intent to the willow. The valley was full of life, humming through the roots in the earth and dancing within the streams that fed them. But he wanted *more*. The willow, having heard all the whisperings of the wood and having kept them close in its bark and leaves, agreed.

And so, the Lord of Wildthings raised another, a sibling to the willow. It sprang from the earth as nothing more than a slender sapling, already reaching for the sun. With a word of caution to look after the young tree, the Lord of Wildthings walked away and disappeared into the crystalline mist.

The sun and the moon wheeled over the valley, and with each sunset and moonrise, the sibling willow grew. It had been many years since the Lord of Wildthings had visited the first willow, but it still remembered its promise, and sheltered the sapling, protecting it from the icy winters and the curious young deer that would find nourishment in its supple bark. The valley around the willows changed in imperceptible ways; the felling of old companion trees, the planting of new ones. It wasn't until the first willow, the willow that held secrets, had grown thin beards of lichen upon its bark, that its sibling had fully grown.

They stood, sentinel of the wooded secrets and held each other close in a gentle embrace. Over time, the fronds of the two willows began to weave themselves together, and eventually it seemed that they had become one tree, cleft in two at the trunk. The thick mat of green dappled the ground around them, and shafts of golden light danced over the moss and mulch.

The Lord of Wildthings returned that summer, on the day before the sun would stay in the sky until near middle-night. He looked at the willows, and was pleased with the seeds he had planted, and how they had grown. His work began in the afternoon, and did not cease until past the witching hour the next night. The process had already started, but the Lord of Wildthings had lent a hand to finish it. In the end, he stood back and, with his fingers coated in sap and stained green from the leaves, looked at his creation.

An arch of willow boughs hung over his head, creating a near perfect circular opening out into a place where the trees did not grow as dense. The leaves, in full summer bloom, hid the intricacies of the weave, but he knew that come winter, when all was stripped bare, the arch would still be as wondrous. Within the design, the Lord of Wildthings had hidden patterns; a running stag, a hare, the sinuous twist of an adder.

Satisfied, the Lord of Wildthings began to turn from the willow archway. But within the soft dark of his soul, he felt *something* missing. Casting a look back over to the arch, a flutter of red caught his eye. It was a torn and tattered piece of fabric, a trifle he had tied to one of his antlers during the riotous golden months of autumn. It would do perfectly. Untying the strip, the Lord of Wildthings approached the willow arch, and fastened the fabric into the hidden curve of the running stag's antler. He nodded, and walked away.

Something would grow there, he was sure. And whatever did spring up deep in the forest vale would be under his eye, like so many alive and wild things.

XV
now.

Charcoal.
February, 1816.
Tias.

The issue with needing to recover from any form of illness or injury was that the victim often had to remain still and quiet in bed for a few days, if not a week. The issue with *Eli* recovering from being unwell was that he could not sit still for longer than an hour at a time. Over the past two days, both Tias and their mother, with increasing exasperation, had threatened Eli with strips of fabric to tie him to the bed with.

The fourth time they caught Eli anywhere else that wasn't the loft space, he'd been by one of the kitchen benches, looking out of the window toward the sea. Both Tias and Ffion had been down into Porth Tymestl proper that morning, leaving Eli fast asleep in bed, needing to stock up on whatever food and supplies were available. It was precious little, Tias had thought, looking around the nearly empty smokehouses. Owen's bakery had been shut up for a little while now, as not enough grain or flour was making it to them from further inland. The baker himself had also scarcely been seen since his brother's ship went down. With the little basket not much fuller than when they had set out, they returned to Roseate Cottage.

Apparently, Eli had been far away in thoughts, as he started slightly when the door opened, banging into the edge of the workbench as the wind tugged the handle out of their mother's grip. 'Eli...' She started resignedly, setting the basket down and letting Tias shut the door behind her.

'I know,' Eli said vaguely, not turning away from the window.

'Have something to eat, *cariad*, and then maybe you can sit down here with us by the fire.'

Eli's eyes lit up at the offer, and he nodded. Tias smiled to himself as he began to put away what little food they had brought back with them – the atmosphere had warmed considerably between Eli and their mother since returning home. The content feeling faded slightly as an unbidden voice in Tias' head told him that *it had only taken nearly losing Eli to do it*. As if trying to loosen the grip of the thought, Tias shook his head and stowed the basket by the door.

Once they'd eaten and made a small nest of blankets by the hearth, Tias leaned over to his brother. Eli's eyes were set back to the window facing *Angorfa* Harbour. 'Please tell me you aren't wanting to go back out onto the beach.' Tias kept his voice pitched low, so that his mother wouldn't hear over the crackle of the fire and the steadily increasing pitch of the wind outside.

'No, it's just...' Eli's voice trailed off, and Tias knew that he was lying.

'Eli, even if you could get down there, why would you want to?' Tias hadn't been anywhere near *Tua'r Môr* Bay since they'd arrived at The Five-Pointed Compass. His attention had been focused on things, or *people*, closer to home.

Shifting slightly to meet his brother's gaze, Eli said with a bleak honesty Tias had rarely heard from him before, 'I don't know.' He seemed to cast about for the words for a moment. 'I just do.' He finished somewhat lamely.

They sat quietly together for a while, content to listen to the fire. Tias felt his mind drifting away, loosely tethered to his body as he watched the flames. He started to see shapes and patterns in them; a tree blooming from the earth only to fall a moment later, a phoenix rise from the white-hot bed of ashes, wings spread wide. It was when he started reaching for his notebook to start writing down some of the shapes, that Eli spoke again.

'Tias...'

'Hm?' Already, the book that his mother had brought back for him from *Dyffryn Cernunnos* was nearly full. He'd have to go back to the one currently abandoned on the desk upstairs.

'I'm not allowed to go out?' Eli made it sound like a question, and Tias sighed, shoved the notebook back into his pocket and once more turned to face his brother.

'No,' he said with the patience of a thoroughly tested parent. 'You are not.'

Eli nodded thoughtfully. 'But you are.' He said after a moment. '*No.*'

'Oh, come *on*, you don't even know what I'm going to say!'

'It'll probably be something ridiculous that I categorically do not want to do.' Tias sighed and scrubbed a hand down his face. A second passed, then another. 'Fine, what?'

Eli grinned and tried not to look too smug. 'So apparently I worked out the obvious question.'

'You were half out of your mind with a fever, but yes, continue.' Tias lunged to one side as Eli made to whack him on the shoulder. He needn't have bothered, Eli missed anyway.

'I've been thinking about it, 'why does this compass have five points?', and I remembered.' Eli shifted a little underneath the blanket that had been tucked over his shoulders. It was one of their many spares, since several had been washed out to sea from the cavern.

'What?'

'That night, when there was the meeting at The Five, about whether or not to ground the boats?'

'Aye...' Tias wasn't entirely sure where this was going, nor what it had to do with the obvious question.

'Remember I left? I followed Abraxus down to that hidden

inlet where his ship was.' Eli was still looking earnestly at Tias, but every so often his eyes would flicker back to the window over his head. 'There was that symbol I found, carved into a bit of broken wall.'

Understanding flooded Tias' mind, and he dived for his notebook once more. Eli leaned a little closer as Tias riffled through the pages, hissing slightly as the edge caught the pad of his finger, leaving a thin line of red behind. Sticking the cut into his mouth, he balanced the book on his knee, turning the pages one-handed before finding the spread he was looking for. One side had a rough drawing of the ship, the *Asherah*. The other had several iterations of the symbol Eli had described, each slightly different depending on the interpretation. 'A compass.' Tias breathed, running his hand over the page.

'Makes a little more sense now, doesn't it?' Eli said. 'Everywhere Smythe seems to go, or anything that seems linked to his business with Abraxus, there's a compass. Or more, specifically, one with too many points.' Eli reached out and traced the outer ring which encircled the classic compass shape within. 'But it was these that I couldn't work out.' He pointed to the lines, haphazardly cross-hatched through the ring. 'I didn't think they were just a pattern, they felt too random.'

Tias studied the drawings for a moment, thinking. Eventually, he sighed and looked into the fire. 'No, I can't think of anything either. Which is why I suppose you're asking if you can go out? Or rather, if *I* can go out?'

'Well, I mean–' Eli waved vaguely in the direction of the window. 'It's not raining.'

It might not have been raining, but the wind was blowing fiercely, Tias grumbled to himself as he pulled the collar of his cloak closer around his neck, balling his hands into fists in a vain attempt to keep already numb fingers a little warmer. Naturally, there was no one out on the cliff paths today; no one else in the village had an idiot brother, or, Tias reflected with a little amusement, no sense of self-control. Despite everything, he still found himself damnably curious.

Their mother had watched him go with barely concealed anxiety in her face, but when he'd turned back to her, she had merely nodded and turned her attention back to the papers spread over the table. There were more letters from whoever Tudwr was.

Porth Tymestl had been almost deserted that morning, but now Tias saw the stirrings of life on the cobbled streets. A few of the people that were out were fishermen, looking grim and stern-faced. Looking toward the grey-blue sea, peaked with wind tossed foam, Tias had shuddered and silently wished them all well. A macabre part of him wondered if he'd come back to the village later to hear about another set of splinters washing up on the beaches.

It didn't take him too long to find the hidden path that Eli had followed Abraxus down. In the dim light of the afternoon it still wasn't obvious, but it was certainly more discernible than it would have been in the middle of the night. Tias peered through the gap, eyes picking out the thin, winding path that curved down and out of sight. Apparently, if Eli was to be completely believed, there was a bridge that spanned an inlet and then an archway to the natural harbour's beach. Tias didn't have a particular wish to find out. Not with the wind howling around him as it was.

Instead, he turned his attention to the crumbled wall. There, etched into the stone was the symbol that was crudely drawn in his notebook. They'd got some parts of it wrong, especially, as Tias looked closer, the lines that ran through the second circle. Pulling out a stick of charcoal and a loose sheet of paper he'd snaffled from the kitchen table, he pressed the paper flush against the stone and ran the charcoal over it. The relief imprint of the symbol began to form on the paper. Once the rubbing was finished, he stood and was forced to take a step backward from the blast of wind that hit him now he wasn't hunkered down with some cover. The paper snapped in the wind, and he quickly folded it and shoved it into a pocket.

As he walked back to the village, Tias' mind was alight with possibilities and ideas. For some reason, the placement of the lines seemed familiar to him, although he couldn't figure out why. The streets were once again empty as he crossed through the churchyard arch. Out on the sea, three sails of white danced on the waves. Tias watched them for a minute, took a shuddering breath, and hurried toward the path that would take him home.

They had visitors. Tias was just crossing the threshold, calling out, 'It's *freezing* out there, Eli!' when he stopped short. Stooger Smythe and Abraxus were sitting at the table, steaming mugs in front of them. 'Oh. *Prynhawn*.' Tias looked to Eli, who was sitting cross legged on their mother's bed, glancing between the innkeeper, Abraxus, and their mother. He seemed caught between awkwardness and utter amusement.

'Ah, Matthias, perfect timing,' Smythe said, tipping a wink to Tias as he pulled off his cloak. His eyes never left the occupants of the table. Ffion was sitting rather still, hands wrapped around her own mug. At first, Tias thought she was on the edge of anger, but then he realised it was something much deeper than that. It was sadness, tinged with a longing Tias didn't see often. 'We've just been discussing with your mother here that–'

He was broken off by Eli, who sat a little straighter and stretched. 'They're sending us away.'

'*What?*' Tias came over to the table, cursing Eli and his badly timed requests.

'Nicely put, Eli,' Abraxus said archly. He was running a stone over the backs of his fingers, the movement slightly hypnotic.

'Well, we were thinkin'–' Smythe was cut off yet again, but by

Abraxus this time, who cleared his throat pointedly. 'Fine! *I* was thinkin' that some time away from the village might do you all the world o' good.' He glanced at Eli, who glared back.

'Why – but what... where would we *go*?' Tias stuttered, his mind, still full of half-formed theories, trying to catch up.

'The forest.' His mother spoke up. She looked Tias straight in the eye. '*Dyffryn Cernunnos.*'

'Oh.' Tias sank down into an empty seat, running a finger along the grain of the wood. 'So soon?' For reasons he couldn't quite fathom out right now, he felt oddly hurt that Smythe and Abraxus were suggesting they leave. He looked to Eli, who seemed to be taking it all with more decorum than Tias had expected.

'Not permanently.' Abraxus said. 'A month, maybe.' He cast his mismatched gaze toward the ceiling and then muttered very quietly, 'It would be rather dull here if it were permanent.'

Ffion glanced at Abraxus, but didn't say anything. Her fingers were bone white against the mug as she raised it to her lips. Tias swore he saw Smythe's mouth twitch with a barely suppressed smile. 'Yes, not forever. Not yet. Just perhaps a... a holiday.'

'Never been on a holiday before.' Eli spoke up from the bed. His brother seemed to have settled on 'flippant' for his current mood. He was now lying on his back, with his head and shoulders hanging off the end. Hazel eyes, still adorned with deep circles underneath, stared at them from Eli's upside-down position.

'That might be nice...' Tias said slowly. 'But only for a month?'

'Aye, you could get to know the forest valley a little better, since that seems to be featurin' in your future, and then come back here when the weather is a little more fit.' Tias nearly missed it, but he was sure that Smythe and Abraxus shared a knowing look at those words, which ended in a singular glance toward Ffion.

'I would like you to see it.' His mother spoke quietly, rotating the mug on the tabletop slowly.

Tias looked to Eli, who shrugged noncommittally, which looked odd inverted. His brother was, as he usually was, living in the moment. This was nothing more than a visit to their mother's home, and they would be coming back to Porth Tymestl soon enough. Tias thought about the roaring grey sea battering the sea cliffs, about the specks of sails tossed precariously on it. And then he overlaid that with a deep green velvet, and he felt his shoulders loosen a little. 'Alright,' he said, nodding.

Smythe sat back in his chair. 'Excellent. I can ask Medwyn or Aron if they'd be willing to help get luggage through the worst bits of the road.'

'I have a condition,' Tias said suddenly. Everyone looked at him, and he felt the back of his neck grow hot. Eli raised an eyebrow, a grin curling the corner of his mouth. 'When we get back, you have to tell us *everything*.' He put considerable meaning into the last word.

Abraxus looked sharply at him, and then toward Ffion. His mother was once again resolutely looking at her mug. 'Everything?'

'Yes.' Tias rummaged in his pocket, and brought out the now slightly crumpled rubbing and spread it on the table. 'Starting with this.'

Smythe had to run a hand over his face to hide the broad smile that was now solidly in place. He didn't quite manage it, and something like hope flared in Tias' chest. 'I think that is a very well-thought-out condition,' he said, mirth tingeing his words. 'And this,' he tapped the rubbing with a finger, 'is an excellent place to start.'

Tias and Eli exchanged a look, and Tias suddenly knew that Eli would be itching to go, only so they could get back quicker. He held out his hand. Smythe looked to Abraxus, who was watching with a look of resigned detachment.

The man leaned forward with a soft exhale, and gripped Tias' forearm with his dark, calloused hand. 'Deal. Everything.'

Looking into one blue-grey eye and one solidly slate eye, Tias felt a shiver run down his spine. A month, and the answers would finally be theirs.

XVI
then.

Ashes and antlers.

The first person to step foot in the valley was lost. Very lost, very cold; the spark of hope that most carried with them throughout their lives beginning to dim. She cradled it to her, as if it was a child of her own blood. She stumbled over an unseen root, and fell to her knees. The spark flickered dully as she clambered to her feet yet again. Her leggings were torn, the hem of her cloak filthy with mud, water saturating it. But she knew that to dispose of it would be folly.

Instead, Angharad picked herself up and kept walking. The evening pressed in around her, and she knew that night was swift behind. Claws of black already had latched onto the sky, tearing away the light from her. Back home, the night had been her favourite time. A time when the aches and cares of the day could be shrugged off and Angharad could lie out in the dew-soaked grass and stare up at the stars. She missed those times, when the sweet scent of the summer's harvest chased them through the day, staining the sky a wheat gold at dusk. But that was all behind her now. So far away that home now may as well be the stars. Beautiful and untouchable. The smell of smoke still permeated her hair, her clothes. She knew that it would never truly come out.

The earthy ground suddenly disappeared beneath her feet. Angharad let out a cry as she pitched forward, desperately trying to cling onto branches that stubbornly refused her help. Sky and earth and tree and rock all became one whirlwind of indiscernible colour, smashing into one another and then ripped apart just as quickly. Bright points of pain blossomed across her entire body as she fell. It seemed to last for an eternity, until Angharad was sure that she had somehow stumbled upon the opening to *Dubnos*. And then, quite abruptly, she stopped. She lay flat on her back across a smooth stone. It jutted out from the valley's side, offering a miniature plateau. The roots of a tree – it was too dark for her to make out which family it belonged to – grew over it in spidery tangles. Everything *hurt*.

Arms spread out lengthways, Angharad stared blankly up into the sky. True night had begun to fall now, chasing away the last of the sun. All she could do in that moment was gaze upward. The spark in her chest, the one she had been so careful to protect and nurture all her life, sputtered and died. It had burnt through the burning of her home, it had glowed dimly as she watched her father cut down by the blade of a gilded axe. But this had doused it. Alone, and under an incomprehensibly huge sky, Angharad lay and waited for the claws of darkness to pull her away.

Dawn came on swift, pearlescent wings. Staining the sky from the east, it spread over the sleeping figure on the rock, casting half of her face into shadow. A cut image from the stone that cradled her, all harsh angles and sharp lines. A bird flitted overhead, a black blur against the sky, there and then gone. The only traces of its passing was the song it left in its wake. Dew glistened on the branches, and warmed by the return of the sun, began to drip.

Angharad twitched as something cold hit her cheek. It was icy and at first, she thought, with her mind still in the fugue of sleep, that she was crying. But then another hit her chin, and she remembered it all. Jolting upright, Angharad looked around her, at the dawn and the birds and the dew. Without the veil of night, her surroundings seemed less threatening, less unknowable. It was a valley, that much she knew, courtesy of the bruises she could feel already beginning to mar her skin. The bottom flattened out below her, a carpet of lush green racing up the steep sides. A wind picked up, and Angharad sat for a moment and watched the valley breathe.

There was nowhere else for her to go. Home was an ashen husk by now, the strangers who arrived from the coast having delighted in taking a torch to it all. Angharad got to her feet, took a step forward, and faltered. Below, the valley beckoned her, a shifting sea of moss and pine. Behind her was a path she knew well, a tether to who she was before. But she could feel that tether thinning, the leather of it wearing away until it was threadbare and weak. The spark she had carried within her was now tangled in something leafy and green. Angharad took another step forward, and then another. The plateau of rock she had unwittingly made her bed was soon left behind, and she picked her way down the slope, walking on the sides of her feet as her Pa had shown her during her childhood.

Birds sprang to life around her, their songs adding to the colour of the air. Angharad found herself drawn ever deeper into the forest, tugged by the new thread and the harmonies of the birds. Her reverie was only broken when she found the arch. As Angharad passed through it, something moved in the treeline behind her. She whipped around, heart fast in her ears. For a moment, she thought she caught a glimpse of antlers, but they stood taller than they should on a stag. But then she blinked, and they were gone. Angharad walked on.

Days in the forest vale began to drip into weeks, which then began to cascade into months, until Angharad had lived a tide of years down amongst the verdant tangle of life that she had found shelter in. Her home was complete, and she slept each night knowing that the boughs of the tree she had built it around would keep her safe. More people arrived one by one in the valley, some by accident, some, like her, running for some unknown safety. With each new arrival, Angharad welcomed them, offered them sanctuary. Invariably, they all stayed.

Occasionally, as settlement grew around her, Angharad thought she saw glimpses of antlers too tall and too large to belong to any stag. But she felt no fear now. She knew who was peering over the valley sides, who tugged at the budding tangles of green thread around people's souls to bring them to her. Angharad named the valley for him, and spent the remainder of her days looking for stags in the shadowy corners of the forest.

XVII
now.

Mud.
February, 1816.
Eli.

'Wait a moment!'

His brother watched with detached amusement as Eli gripped the top of his boot and yanked. There was a fairly disgusting sucking sound as the sole and heel lifted from the thick mud. Quickly doing the same with his other, similarly held in place only a pace ahead, Eli shifted the pack across his shoulders and hurried to catch up.

The road out of Porth Tymestl was still impassable for a cart, but it had become somewhat traversable by foot. Smythe had managed to gall Medwyn, Aron and even coax Owen out of his self-imposed hiding to help carry some of the heavier packs through the worst of the road. Aside from curious glances, none of the three men had asked or made any comment about where they were going, and why so abruptly. The closest they got to it was Medwyn reaching out a hand to ruffle Eli's hair and muttering a gruff, 'Get well again, lad,' before they turned and trudged back toward the village. Each man had mud and clay spattered to the backs of their knees.

After that, the road was a little smoother, although Eli and Tias had both noted that the bad weather seemed to have come further inland than they had expected. It typically took their mother four days by foot to the forest vale, if the weather was fair and there were no unforeseen issues. Whilst the clouds never truly abated, remaining heavy and thick with the potential of rain, the conditions did seem more settled than anything they had experienced in the past few months.

It took them just under six days to reach *Dyffryn Cernunnos*. Eli knew that the slower pace was to accommodate him, and the fact that he needed to sit and rest for a while every other hour or so. Their nights were either spent at the infrequent inn off the main road, or under the stars. Eli, whilst not refusing a warm meal and bed, cherished the nights outdoors more. If he closed his eyes and listened to the crackle of the campfire, he could imagine himself back on *Tua'r Môr* Bay, his father beside him, thinking up another half-remembered story based on the constellations Tias picked out for them.

The journey became greener, the foliage that limbed the road thicker and more verdant. Every so often, Tias would dart off to the side and pick up a handful of leaves, still a fiery orange from last year's autumn. At a call from their mother, he'd return to walking, but as he did so, he would hold up each individual leaf to the sun and lightly trace the unfamiliar edges of it with a fingertip. He discarded a few, but most were carefully placed in between the pages of his notebook. They passed through a gorge that was, according to their mother, the half-way mark between Porth Tymestl and *Dyffryn Cernunnos*. Eli couldn't help but feel a little claustrophobic as the steep walls climbed around him, narrowing the grey skies above them to a slit. He'd tried to engage Tias in conversation to take his mind off it, but he was quickly hushed by Ffion. The walls, she had explained later, were made from soft clay with jagged pieces of rock interspersed throughout it, and it was prone to slipping at any slight provocation. Eli remembered the slick surface of the clay, the jut of the rock encased within, and silently thanked whoever might be watching that they'd made it through without incident.

On the sixth day, after a climb that left everyone winded, they crested the valley ridge. Tias came over to where Eli was perched on a flat slab of rock, his head hanging low. He could feel the slightly disconcerting thrum of his heartbeat in his ears. 'Here.' Tias pressed a battered metal water canteen into his hands.

'Thanks.' Eli took a few sips and then poured a little out onto his palm, splashing it against the back of his neck.

'How're you feeling?'

He made a noncommittal noise at that. It seemed to be a favourite line of questioning for both his mother and Tias at the moment, and Eli found himself steadily becoming sick of it.

'Well, it's all downhill from here,' Tias said, looking out over the valley.

Eli glanced at him, a smile fighting its way onto his face.

'What?' Tias then realised what he had said and rolled his eyes. 'You know what I meant.'

'I did.' They sat shoulder to shoulder for a while, catching their breath. The vista before them was spectacular. Eli had never seen a place so obviously *alive* before. Amidst the trees, the chatter of birds coalesced into a chorus he couldn't quite understand, but knew the tune of instinctively. It was a riot of colour: the evergreen pines still lush and glossy, nestled between the fires and sunlights of the not quite fallen leaves of autumn. And then there was the skeletal splinters of the winter trees running like cracks through it all. But even these radiated a life; quiet and asleep. As the wind rippled low over the crest of the valley, Eli watched it all sway, and then settle. Above was a delicate eggshell of sky, and below was a patchwork. Thin lines of smoke punctuated the air, rising in wisps to become false clouds. No clearing was visible, but Eli knew that was where they were headed.

Despite himself, despite everything that had been said and felt, Eli wanted to run off into the green and not come back until called for. Here was something new, and the newness called to him in a swirl of leaves and birdsong.

'Ready?' His mother had come over, shouldering her pack again. There was a light in her eyes as she looked past her sons and into the forest vale.

'I think so.' Tias said, capping the flask and stowing it back into his own pack. He looked to Eli, who nodded and pushed himself up to stand. As they began to descend into the valley, the wind picked up and clouds began to roll over the pale sky. Fingers of mist felt their way down the sides of the slope to coil gently against their ankles. The deeper they went, the thicker the fog became. Trees now seemed to rear out of the blank nothingness that pressed around them, spectral. The evergreens became a darker green, now almost black as the thick of trees grew alongside the mist. There didn't seem to be a discernible path, but their mother picked her way down the valley as surely as young deer.

She stopped quite suddenly, looking through the fog. Eli and Tias drew level with her, glancing at each other.

'Mam?' Tias said softly, nudging Ffion's side.

'We're here.' Their mother didn't look at them when she spoke, but rather kept her eyes fixed on some distant point neither of them had discerned yet. Listening, Eli could, only for a moment, pick up the sounds of quiet chatter. The wind blew again, and it was lost in a susurration of leaves. Without really meaning to, he started to walk forward, his feet lost in drifts of deadfall. And then he saw it.

Ahead, weaving itself together through the fog, was an archway. It seemed to be made of two trees entwined with one another. It arced into the canopy and its crest was lost to a veil of white. Small glimmers of colour in muted, earthy tones punctuated the mist as surely as a shout punctuates the silence. Eli kept walking. The scraps of fabric fluttered with the wind, reaching for him and then away again. As he drew level with the archway, he thought he saw the twisting shapes make outlines of animals for a moment. But then he was in the middle of the opening, and the shapes lost all meaning once more. Eli turned around to see Tias following him slowly, reaching out and letting the tips of his fingers catch the end of a faded and ragged burgundy piece of cloth. He joined Eli in the opening, looking up at the thin, twisting branches above them.

'This has been here a long time,' he said very quietly.

Eli couldn't bring himself to respond aloud, something about this place he felt deserved the soft introspective silence of Crow's church.

'I thought I saw... in the branches...' Tias' voice trailed off, and Eli saw his eyes flicker to where the burgundy cloth was tied, and then to a strip of seal-skin grey knotted intricately to their left.

'Me too.' Eli whispered. 'Out of the corner of my eye.' Something seemed to twitch at the back of his mind, something that he felt he was missing. Before he could put his finger on it, their mother had joined them in the opening. Her pack was resting against her front, hanging off one shoulder. She rummaged through it for a moment, before bringing out a handful of fabric.

'It is customary for newcomers to tie something onto the Siblings.' She offered the fabric, and Eli saw that they had been cut from the hems of blankets that were now too moth-eaten and ragged to be used as anything but scraps. Tias reached out and picked a dark lichen green, looking around for a place to tie it to.

'Siblings?' He asked absentmindedly. His voice was still low, dampened by the mist.

'Sibling willow trees,' Ffion said, her head tilting to take in the curve of the arch. 'It's what my *Nain* always called this. The Siblings. Go on.' The last was directed to Eli, who still hadn't picked a scrap.

'Oh.' In the end, he picked a deep blue, the stitching of the hem still visible in a white line along one edge. Tias had tied his up high, standing on the balls of his feet and stretching to catch at the lowest branch of the opening. He looped his, tying it at either end to make a crescent shape.

Eli looked to either side, and then walked over toward the right edge of the archway. A spindly trunk framed this side of the structure, and looking up Eli saw that its branches stretched and met others. One of the Siblings. He pressed his palm flat against the trunk for a moment, and then knotted his strip to a younger branch that had yet to catch onto another. Unthinkingly, he found himself tying it into a knot his Da had taught them. It was one to tie off sails.

Blossom.
March, 1816.
Tias.

One thing that had always fascinated Tias was the transition between night and day and the time lost between it in sleep. The evening swept over them, darkness rolled down like a blanket of cold velvet, and soon enough the aches of the day were made known, and eyes grew heavy. Then came that nebulous time of sleep; half-remembered snatches of dreams, awareness filtering back in only to be abandoned again. And before the mind could comprehend it, it was morning again. The velvet was peeled back, replaced by the satin of the dawn sky. It was an unbroken cycle, and one that most people accepted with the sure knowledge that this was merely part of life. However, Tias had dedicated several pages of one of his books to it – without really finding much success. Most of it was half-incomprehensible scribblings and rough sketches of the phases of the moon.

This was how the month in the valley had passed, as best as he could put it into words. They had arrived on a misty morning in early February, and from there everything was a blur of colour and seemingly half-remembered moments of awareness. Tomorrow was the day they were heading back to Porth Tymestl. Beside the doorway to the little hut they'd been staying were his and Eli's packs, stacked haphazardly and covered in decidedly more mud than they had been when they'd left home. Tias' was particularly grubby, moss and leaves and bits of branches sticking out from any pocket or place he could shove them.

He and Eli had spent the month in *Dyffryn Cernunnos* exploring the woods and the valley, following little streams as they wound their silver ribbon through the trees. At first, their mother was not keen to let them out of her sight, or stray too far from the village boundaries. But after Tudwr had taken her aside at an evening meal and spoken to her earnestly, she seemed to relax. Tudwr had even given them a map of the valley, drawn on supple vellum. It was a thing of beauty, and Tias had spent many nights beside the central fire scanning the contents, learning every brushstroke and highlight.

Tudwr had been the first to greet them in the village, pulling Ffion into a fierce hug. As he'd released her, he caught sight of Tias and Eli. It was hard to not be intimidated by Tudwr at first; he loomed tall and thick as an oak, with a face that seemed to be carved from the forest floor's clay. But then he approached, knelt down and offered his hand in turn to each of them. Even kneeling, Tudwr still came to Eli's shoulder.

'I see your ancestors in you,' he had said quietly, just out of earshot of their mother. He inclined his head to Tias, 'You are of the ash and elder,' and then to Eli, 'and you are of the sea and salt.'

With Tudwr walking strong at their side, Tias felt a little more comforted as they entered the settlement properly. The trees hadn't been cleared, aside from a central circle where a blackened pit was already stacked with kindling and dried moss. Beside it stood a wood store, the inside of the split logs a deep honeyed gold. People stopped to stare as they passed. Ffion occasionally raised her hand in greeting, something which, Tias noticed, often went unacknowledged. Deeper and deeper into the trees they went, and the houses became more sporadic. Only when Tias thought that Tudwr was going to lead them straight back out of the other side of the valley, did they come to a stop. He gestured towards a house. 'Welcome home.'

'You lived *here*?' Eli's voice was split between incredulousness and amazement. Tias couldn't help but agree with the sentiment. The house – if it could be called that, it was more of a hut – was perfectly round, with the walls built in the same style as a dry-stone wall. Moss and lichen tumbled from cracks that hadn't been patched with mud and clay. But the thing that had captivated both Tias and Eli was the tree that grew up through the dwelling itself. The roof was made of wooden shingles, and they had been cleverly arranged so that they seemed to join seamlessly to the trunk of the tree. Tias bent down and picked up a leaf that must have fallen from it in autumn. It was nearly as large as his hand.

'Sycamore,' their mother said. 'Our family has always lived underneath its boughs.'

Eli cast a look at Tias, and then before anyone could say anything else, had shouldered his pack a little higher and bounded toward the hut. Tias quickly followed. Over the sound of wind rushing through the foliage, he heard Tudwr and his mother laugh.

The Sycamore Hut had turned out to be surprisingly comfortable. Tias was used to living in close quarters with his family, so the small space didn't bother him at all. The people of *Dyffryn Cernunnos* took their evening meals together, settled around the fire pit, but after everyone had dispersed in search of their own bed, Tias took to sitting in the branches still in the living space, staring up through one particular crack in the shingles, watching the vast night sky pinwheel overhead. Lanterns hung from boughs that doubled as rafters, and some candles were set actually onto knots of the tree: wax having melted around them to mould into a strange candelabra.

As time dripped languidly around Tias, one moment remained sharp and clear within his mind. It had happened on a bright day, one of the first he could remember in a while. The sun actually had some warmth in it, and as Tias stepped outside, he lifted his face toward it and closed his eyes. A light breeze gently ruffled his hair and all he could smell was *green*. The morning had progressed as usual, and then in the afternoon Tias and Eli were released from their small menial tasks and given free roam of the forest.

Tudwr's map had nearly been fully explored by now, as it only spanned the confines of the valley bottom. Paths that were otherwise invisible were beginning to root themselves into his memory, and so Tias led the way with little preamble out into the woods. Winter was slowly being thawed by milder air, and the first signs of spring were starting to show themselves, shaking off the frost and deep-earth sleep. Tias was careful to not step on any of the new shoots and buds pushing their way upward, Eli following just as cautiously behind him.

'Tias?'

'Hm?' Tias was studying the map again, rotating it now and again to try and figure out which way the river was curving. There was one little section of its serpentine body they had yet to see...

'This is what these are for, aren't they?' Eli's words made no sense to Tias until he turned around. Eli was holding a flat and thin white stone to his eye, the hole near the top in line with his pupil. 'For seeing things that you only see out of the corner of your eye?'

'I didn't realise you still had that,' Tias said, remembering a low-lit inn room and the crushing weight of uncertainty.

'Abraxus never asked for it back.' Eli shrugged. 'So, I kept it.' He shot Tias a slightly wolfish grin, and lowered the stone. His grin faded a little as he turned it over and over in his hands. 'I don't really understand what you're meant to *see*, though.'

'Me neither,' Tias admitted. 'I suppose that's something we'll find out when we go home.'

'I've been trying it all around the forest, just in case.' Eli looked vaguely embarrassed as he spoke, and Tias couldn't help but pass up the opportunity to rib him.

'Looking for faeries, were you?'

'No!' Eli started to walk again, heading past Tias. The tips of his ears were pink.

'Wait, you're going the wrong way.' Tias hurried to catch up, and fell into step with his brother. 'It's over there.'

They walked on in silence for a while, and then, as they were picking their way over some weed-slicked steppingstones, Tias asked, 'What made you realise that?' He felt a little bad about the fact he'd completely forgotten to tell Eli what the stones were for. But Eli knew now and, in his defence, Tias thought, he'd had a lot to think about when the subject had come up with Smythe all those weeks ago.

'It was the Siblings.'

'Come again?'

'When we first got here, remember? I said I thought I saw things woven into the branches. And then as we passed through it today, I *know* I saw a stag in there, its antlers were all picked out in buds. But then I looked again, and it was gone.'

Tias knew what Eli was talking about. The Siblings had fascinated him ever since they had arrived, and he'd spent several full afternoons tracing branches with his fingertips, hoping to find the hidden pictures or even words that sometimes seem to be glimpsed when he wasn't looking for them. 'Did you try and look at the Siblings *through* the stone?' Tias asked, intrigued.

'Aye, but it was all the same.' There was a little note of defeat in Eli's voice. 'But it did give me the idea about looking through it for things that aren't really there.' He reached up and rubbed his palm against his forehead. 'This is confusing.'

'I know,' Tias said simply. He could only hope that Abraxus and Smythe would keep their promise and explain everything.

He was getting a little bored of living in a riddle. 'Keep that safe,' he said, pointing to the stone Eli was now running over his knuckles. 'I don't think Abraxus would be best pleased if you lost it in a corner of some woods.'

Eli nodded and pocketed it. They carried on through the soft green, listening to the deep quiet that held the forest together. Eventually, they found the place they had been looking for. It was a natural pool where the river widened out and slowed down to a lazy swirl. The valley side reared up unexpectedly here, rock face exposed and spotted with age. Standing toward the valley side in the water was a tall stack of rock. It had clearly been attached at one point as an arch, but the top had caved in over time. A tree was perched precariously at the peak, its roots sunk deep into cracks. Like everything else in the valley, it was beginning to bloom.

It took Eli all of three minutes to strip down to his undergarments and run for the water, and then another five of Tias nearly physically restraining him before he gave up and joined his brother. Over the time they had spent in *Dyffryn Cernunnos*, Tias had seen a remarkable improvement in Eli. There was colour in his face, and his vitality seemed to have been restored. Even so, Tias *knew* it probably wasn't a good idea to go for a quick swim after everything that had happened. He was also still a little surprised that Eli hadn't been entirely put off water since that night on *Tua'r Môr* Bay.

But the river was a cool green colour and the light fell in dapples over its surface. It was cold, he knew it would be, but once they had both gotten over the initial shock – with the usual shouts and a few curses – it was no different to the tidepool they swum in at home.

Tias let the current pull him gently around, floating on his back. All he heard was the rush of the water and his own blood in his ears, intertwined until they all became one. Above, the sun shifted across the sky. As the wind picked up a little, the branches of the tree on the stack stirred slightly. It shook loose a few of the new buds and early blossoms, sending them into the air where they danced seemingly in a pattern of the wind's own design. Tias watched them tumble and eventually come to settle with the barest touch upon the surface of the water. For a moment, for one perfect moment, it seemed as if it were raining petals.

'You aren't coming with us, are you?'

'No.' Their mother's voice was tiny inside the Sycamore Hut.

'I thought so,' Tias said, picking at the hem of his shirt. 'Our things...' He gestured half-heartedly toward the little pile of luggage by the door. Eli stood by it, and if Tias hadn't been so focused on his mother at that moment, he might have taken a closer look at his brother's face and marked it as "resigned".

'Tudwr has agreed to take you as far as the ravine,' Ffion said. 'After that the road home is clear. You remember it, don't you, *cariad*?'

'I do.' Tias said quietly.

'Why?' Eli's voice was soft, not at all what Tias had been expecting. Their mother turned to face him, and, once more, Tias found himself surprised. There was an open honesty in her features he had not seen for a while.

'Because I am not ready to go back yet, and I want to spend my time here making this place our home.' Ffion did not break eye contact with Eli, and continued, 'A home that I hope you will love as much as I did, and as much as the last.'

Eli nodded, biting his lip. There was a soft shine to his eyes. 'I... alright.' It was another thing to have grown out of the green of the valley. Eli had stopped challenging their mother so much. The delicate seeds that had been planted that night in The

Five-Pointed Compass had come up through the earth with the spring, and had the promise to grow into something strong and tall. 'Just, don't be away too long? *Os gwelwch yn dda.*' *Please.*

Ffion didn't respond. Instead, she crossed the space between her and Eli and pulled him into a hug, extending one arm out for Tias to join them. He went quickly, trying to make sense of the mess of feelings in his chest. Predictably, Eli started to struggle out of the embrace after a few moments. Their mother laughed wetly and released them. 'Be safe, be careful. I love you both.'

She stood in the doorway to the Sycamore Hut, raising a hand in farewell as they shouldered their packs and started to head toward the sloping valley side. Tudwr walked with them, silent but steady. When they reached the crest of the hill, both Tias and Eli stopped and turned to look back over the vale. The sky was slightly overcast, the sun fighting its way through the clouds; a pale stone suspended in a slate sky. 'Ready?' Tias asked his brother after the seconds stretched.

'Aye, I think so. Let's go home.' He said the last word with such longing that Tias' heart ached. He had tried to quell the feeling, but try as he might, the *need* to see the ocean again had grown stronger by the day. Tias found himself almost surprised by how intense the desire had become. The last night they had spent together in *Dyffryn Cernunnos*, he had dreamt of waves crashing against black rock and sand, and of a single seabird high in the sky. Its lonely cry had haunted him when he'd woken.

Tudwr gestured toward a path that led steadily south-west. 'To home I take you.' He said, his voice deep in the quiet. They walked on.

ABRAXUS ELIJAH HONEY

Compass.
March, 1816.
Abraxus.

He stood knee deep in the surf when the news arrived. Boots discarded on the sand behind him, the light of the dawn painting everything in watery hues of purple, pink and deepest blue at the horizon. The breakwater lapped gently at his calves, his feet pleasantly numb. Abraxus dug his toes deeper into the sand, sighed and cast his head back. He breathed in the salt on the air, and listened to the world at a standstill. There was something happening around him, a collectively held breath before the plunge. The air crackled with it.

Tua'r Môr Bay was a beautiful place to be alone. There were times when Abraxus sought out nothing more than that. A place under the sky to be utterly alone. The last man to walk on the earth, to sail its seas. The sensation of being so incomprehensibly small against something so vast was a feeling unparalleled in his mind. But, he knew deep down that he would be lying if he didn't admit that he had missed them.

The month had passed in a haze of lightningless thunder, late nights that clung to the shadows under his eyes and work. Seemingly unending work. Abraxus could feel the weariness settling in his bones. He had, of course, felt this before. But now it somehow felt harder to bear. The bones that had littered the beach had dwindled in numbers significantly, but that had not been because of any placation Abraxus could offer. Each night he sent them back to the seabed, and each night more replaced them. 'What do you *want?*' He whispered, looking back over the sea. 'What more could you possibly want?'

The stirrings of an answer began to filter into his mind, hissed through the waves folding over themselves. But before he could bring himself to listen, another, more welcome voice caught his attention.

'Abraxus! Abraxus, they're back!' Smythe was standing on the ledge where the path down the cliff face ended, waving.

Abraxus ignored the tug of the sea as he waded his way back to the shoreline. 'Later.' He said gruffly. He knew it was disrespectful, but at that moment, he couldn't bring himself to care.

'They're back.' Smythe was smiling widely. He leaned down to offer Abraxus a hand as he clambered his way back up onto the path. 'We should really put some steps there...' He muttered to himself as Abraxus cleaned off his feet with his socks.

'How do you know?' The question came out a little sharper than Abraxus had intended, but he had to be completely sure.

'Smoke from the chimney stack. They must 'ave arrived last night. I was up with the birds and didn't see them pass.'

Together, they started walking up the path. Hope had kindled in Abraxus' chest: he felt buoyed.

'D'you think that they'll–'

'Absolutely,' Abraxus said, cutting Smythe off. 'Be ready to answer a lot of questions, Stooger. Particularly because I am going to give them a prompt.'

'They won't *need* promptin', you know what they're both like.' Smythe rolled his eyes. He stopped suddenly, causing Abraxus to almost walk into him. 'What are you going to do?'

'Leave them something that needs its associations changing.'

'Sometimes I don't even know why I ask.' Smythe carried on walking, but not before Abraxus had seen the light glint deeply with the innkeeper's eyes. Abraxus couldn't help but find himself smiling. Alone under a vast sky was something he'd never give up, but just occasionally, and more so now, he'd found himself wanting to share that vastness.

It wasn't until the afternoon that the Kincarran boys made an appearance. Abraxus was shocked, he thought they'd be in The Five before Smythe could even open the shutters. But as they walked back through Porth Tymestl, he gleaned that they had arrived at Roseate Cottage very late last night.

The residents of the village were already up and bustling, the shouts of fishermen and their crews ringing down the cobbled streets and towards the harbour. The bad weather hadn't necessarily abated, but there had been more days where the sea seemed less treacherous. No one was beckoned by blue waters, but the slate grey and white tipped waves didn't send them under or away either.

Abraxus had made a quick trip to his room to gather some supplies, and then slipped back out onto the streets. People still avoided his gaze, but he noticed, with some dark humour, that some didn't move to the other side of the street when they saw him coming. He was becoming a part of the scenery, becoming as unchangeable as the harbour walls or cliff edges.

Roseate Cottage was quiet and dark when he arrived. The gate to the little walled garden creaked slightly as he pushed it open. Abraxus eased it back into place and found himself treading carefully up the path. Smoke was indeed rising from the chimney stack, but it was thin and almost colourless. An old fire, embers most likely at this point.

He set down the things he'd brought with him on the front step, making sure they were arranged in a way so that they'd be obvious to the boys, but near invisible to anyone passing by. Satisfied, he turned and headed back to The Five-Pointed Compass.

The hours until lunch time dragged. Time seemed to drip like tar, and it was all Abraxus could do to not go back to the little cottage and hammer on the door. He didn't let himself examine this feeling too much. After all, there was no reason to put that smug look back on Smythe's face.

The innkeeper had kept The Five open in the morning, despite the near non-existent patrons coming in. Those who did come in mostly seemed to be looking for some breakfast before heading out onto the sea. It was something Smythe struggled to provide; food was still in high demand, with not much more coming in. Abraxus had helped out where he could, taking *Asherah* out and casting his old nets over the side. Smythe never said a word as he took Abraxus' catches off him, merely nodded. To Abraxus, that meant more than any verbal thanks.

The sun had passed its zenith, and Abraxus was now deeply involved in a game of knucklebones with Smythe, who had resorted to the old game just to keep Abraxus in his seat and not, in the innkeeper's words, 'Pacing holes in my floor.'

The soft click of the bones against the wood of the bar were the only sounds permeating the stillness inside. Until the door was opened with so much force that it bounced off the wall and began to close again. Smythe jumped so violently that the knucklebones went flying across the bar, some dropping out of sight on the other side.

'Maybe try that again Eli, you didn't manage to get it off its hinges.'

'Oh, *shut up* Tias.'

'I think they're here,' Smythe said dryly.

Abraxus turned on the stool to face the door. This time it opened at a much more sensible pace, revealing Eli and Tias Kincarran. It had only been a month, but as was the way with boys just reaching the end of their childhood years, both of them had changed. Tias seemed to stand a little straighter, emphasising his tall stature. He had gone from thin to lean, a certain wiriness to him.

The change in Eli was a marked improvement. His complexion was back into the realms of healthy, and there was a gleam in his eyes that Abraxus remembered seeing in his earlier days in Porth Tymestl. He, like his brother, stood a little stronger, a little firmer on the earth. For just a moment, Abraxus knew what John Kincarran had looked like in life.

'I trust you got my message.' He said levelly.

'It was hard to miss, I nearly tripped over it.' Tias said, reaching into his pockets. He pulled out a flat shard of sea slate and read the words scratched onto it. "Come and see.' And then the Roman numerals for "five".' He flipped it over. "Return what is mine."

'I kept it safe,' Eli said, stepping forward. Tias closed the door behind them and came over to the bar.

'My thanks.' Abraxus reached out and took his seeing stone from Eli's proffered hand. 'It has not seen the woods in some time.'

'I don't suppose we'll need that one now,' Eli continued, reaching inside his cloak, 'now that we have our own.' And he pulled out the chime Abraxus had repaired and left for them. It now had two tiers to it, and was fastened together by a complex weave of fishing net and line. Three stones hung at intervals from the smoothed driftwood, alongside sprigs of heather and dried seaweed.

'Indeed.' Abraxus said, amusement fighting its way out into his voice. A moment of silence fell between them all. Eli and Tias regarded Smythe and himself levelly, their eyes roaming over their faces and then around the bar. And then Smythe let out a laugh, rounded the bar and came over to the brothers.

'It's good to see you again,' he said gently, a hand on one of their shoulders.

'You too, Smythe,' Tias said, and he pulled the innkeeper in for a brief embrace. '*Diolch*.' He added quietly.

Smythe cleared his throat, looking down at the floor as if it was an interesting puzzle. 'And Ffion? How's she?' He said after a moment, his voice a little rough.

'She stayed,' Eli said with a shrug.

'In the vale?' Abraxus asked, leaning forward.

'Aye. Said she wasn't ready to come back yet, and that she'd come to us when she felt she could.' Tias' expression gave nothing away, and after a second of scrutiny, Abraxus realised it was because there *was* nothing to give away. Both boys seemed genuinely at ease with the decision Ffion had made.

'Interesting...' Abraxus breathed. Eli looked sharply at him, and Abraxus cursed his lax tongue. He cleared his throat and stood. 'Well. I imagine you are not here to merely greet each other after time apart.'

'No,' Eli said. He looked Abraxus directly in the eyes. 'We're here for answers.'

'And we want them all,' Tias added, fixing his gaze on Smythe. He pulled out his notebook, and flicked through the pages. Eventually he found a loose sheet and pulled it out. Smythe took it delicately from him, and turned toward the bar, unfolding it.

'Ah, I remember.' Abraxus leaned over the man's shoulder. There was a rough charcoal imprint of the sigil Smythe used to mark the path down to the hidden harbour. He felt a presence beside him and turned to see Eli and Tias flank either side.

'What does it mean? Why is it always a compass?' Eli asked.

'And what's this bit mean?' Tias said, tapping the outer ring with the markings etched through it.

Smythe looked at Abraxus, and then turned to face the boys, forcing them both to back up a few steps. 'Well, all interesting questions, wouldn't you agree?'

'I would.'

'But perhaps not the right one.' Mischievousness was playing in Smythe's blue-grey eyes.

Eli let out a low growl of frustration. 'You said—' He stopped short when Tias tugged his arm.

'Eli, wait.' He looked up. 'Why does this compass have five points?'

ABRAXUS ELIJAH HONEY

Gorwelion.
March, 1816.
Eli.

He felt like his chest was too fragile to contain the beating of his heart. It was the same sensation that came in the seconds just before a cliff dive, or when a wave pulled him under unexpectedly and he rolled in blue and white, before emerging, wet and grinning.

Abraxus' eyes were alight, the colours contained in them vibrant and alive. He looked to Smythe, who was smiling. 'An excellent question, Tias. Would you like to know the answer?'

'Yes.' Eli and Tias spoke at the same time. Smythe turned back to the paper, and picked it up. He ran his finger along the outer circle.

'*Gorwelion.*' Horizon. 'Written in an old language, now mostly forgotten to time.' Smythe turned, opened the hatch to the bar and walked over to the cellar trapdoor. 'The fifth and truest point of a compass.' Abraxus followed him. 'Are you coming?'

Eli looked to Tias, and knew that his brother was feeling the same beat of excitement against his ribs. Tias nodded almost imperceptibly, and together they followed behind the bar. The trapdoor opened onto a short ladder, the rungs worn to a smoothness in the middle that spoke of many feet passing this way. Smythe gestured, and Eli stepped forward, clambering over the edge and down. Tias quickly came after and was passed a lit candle down by Abraxus. At first, Eli thought it was an ordinary inn's cellar; barrels and casks lining the walls. But then, he caught sight of a shadowy expanse in the corner. He wandered a little way out of the globe of light from the candle and put out his hand. It met nothing, the air taking on a slightly deeper chill. It was a passageway. 'Tias,' he called softly, 'I think it's this way.'

Tias brought the candle over and peered into the passage. The light caught momentarily against one of the walls, and Eli saw something on there, something undulating and serpentine. He looked back toward Smythe and Abraxus. 'Go on.' Smythe said. 'Go and look.' It was all the encouragement they needed. Together, they plunged into the darkness.

The passageway was narrow, the floor, ceiling and walls all carved from the same rock. It twisted downwards in slightly claustrophobic spirals, the rough stone of the ceiling uneven and jagged. As they walked, Eli kept one hand on the wall, feeling the carvings that were traced there. They moved up and down in waves, the texture like scales. Since Tias was behind him, he could only make out glimpses of what they were, the light creating a relief effect. Down and down they went, deeper into the earth. Just as Eli was half convinced they'd end up at the sea level, a soft glimmer of light caught his attention. There was something beyond the next turn of the stairs. Taking a breath, he rounded the corner. And stepped into a place that he was sure was not of this world.

It was almost like a natural cave, the walls and ceiling rough with unhewn rock. But the floor was smooth and covered in a variety of rugs, all in an eclectic hue of colours and patterns. It seemed that Smythe had transposed his lantern collection from above. A fireplace set deep into the right-hand wall was blazing, the heat from it eating the shadows that lurked in the corners. Several thickly cushioned chairs stood around it, alongside one armchair with its mismatched footstool. On the opposite wall were shelves upon shelves of books, scrolls and what seemed to be even a few clay slabs, stacked upright. The shelves themselves seemed to be made from the planking of old ships, worn and salt stained. They bowed slightly in the middle.

Above all, the one thing that caught Eli's attention was the rowboat suspended from the ceiling by thick rope and sturdy hooks. The seats inside the boat had been removed, and instead, it held blankets and cushions. It swayed gently as he approached it. Some hand long ago had carved the word *Morpheus* into its prow, alongside an ornate looking eye, mirrored on the parallel side.

He seemed to have forgotten how to breathe. Everything about this place was bathed in a magic that seemed to cling to the rock, permeating the very air. This was a place that was not seen by people, it was secret and silent deep within the earth. It was tangible, but something unseen had settled over them all, holding them and promising things unreal. Promising a life outside of what they knew.

The fifth point of the compass called.

Turning away from the suspended boat-turned-bed, Eli moved over to the shelves. He found himself moving carefully, as if one misstep would shatter this dream. At random, he pulled one book off the shelf and opened it. He was delighted to find he couldn't read a word of the tangle of sigils and runes that crossed the page seemingly at random. A drawing of a massive stag stood sentinel in the centre of the spread, its antlers covered in ivy and moss. The book was solid and heavy in his hand. So very real.

'This is them, isn't it?' Tias' voice seemed far away. A jolt of the known in a space made of liminality. Eli turned, placing the book back, to see his brother by the fireplace. Framing it were two arches. The colouration was not that of the ones on *Tua'r Môr* Bay. Where they were stained a wooden brown, these were polished and ivory. They were unequivocally bone. Tias reached out and placed his hand against one. 'This is all real.' He whispered.

Smythe came over and set his hand on Tias' back. "*There are more things in heaven and earth...*"

"*Than are dreamt of in your philosophy.*" Eli finished the quote as he drew level with his brother. 'Will you tell us what these come from?' He asked, looking to Abraxus.

'Soon. And I will not tell you. I will show you.' He came over to the hearthside, and gently rested his forehead against the other rib bone. After a second of deep silence, Abraxus pulled away and said, 'But first there is one more thing to see.'

The wall opposite the passageway was not made of the same dark grey rock. Instead, it seemed to have been built up from slate, pieces of rockfall from the cliffs. In the gaps left by the haphazard stacking, moss and seagrass had grown. A soft breeze emanated from it, a briny tang clinging to it. There was a heavy tapestry in the middle, the bottom of which shifted almost imperceptibly against the floor. Eli realised that it was made from sail canvas, and that someone had painted and stitched countless scenes across it. Before he could make out even one full picture, Abraxus reached out and pulled the tapestry back. Beyond it was the ocean.

A natural outcropping of rock created a balcony of sorts that looked out over the waters. As Eli and Tias stepped out onto it, the warmth of the room behind them faded. Abraxus turned sharply and started to pick his way down a very narrow and very precarious looking set of stairs carved into the rock, rather a set of handholds than an actual staircase. Tias followed, Smythe behind him. Before Eli started to descend himself, he spotted a stack of flat stones by the edge of the outcropping. A small crystal stylus was next to them, as if they were for writing on.

The stairs were slippery and took every ounce of Eli's concentration. So much so that he didn't realise that he'd been here before. His feet met shingle, and he looked up to see the golden wood and blue-green sails of the *Asherah*.

'The way *you* came down is over there,' Abraxus said in Eli's ear. Sure enough, there was the natural arch he had passed through that night.

He looked up at Abraxus and grinned sheepishly. 'I'm not particularly sorry that I followed you.'

'I know. Come.' He set off toward the harbour wall.

'She's beautiful.' Tias murmured as Eli fell into step with him.

His brother's eyes had never left the *Asherah*, taking in the point of the bowsprit, the curve of the stairs, the rich colour of her sails.

'I thought so too.' Eli whispered back. The sun was beginning to set now, the clouds finally breaking up a little toward the horizon. The water seemed to become liquid gold, molten and rippling. It was mirrored in the polished gleam of the *Asherah*'s planking. Abraxus had reached the deck, and was busy lighting the lamps that hung from the rigging and rails, Smythe having perched himself on one of the boxes that still sat haphazardly across the deck.

Tias halted at the walkway, looking from it to Abraxus. 'Can I..?'

Abraxus looked up and nodded. 'We invite you in, Tias.' There was a soft smile playing at the corners of his lips. 'Come on.'

Tias nodded once, and walked onto the deck. Eli watched as his brother's shoulders straightened, how he drew himself up and accommodated the slight roll of the deck in his pace. Eli looked to Abraxus, and no words passed between them. None needed to. Eli, for the first time invited, stepped aboard the *Asherah*.

The lanterns strung in the rigging stirred as a wind picked up, the light flickering. Ropes creaked and the sails filled momentarily. The sea beneath them rippled in the new breeze, the deck shivering with the motion.

Eli barely noticed. He turned and headed straight for the upper deck, where the wheel was. As he ran his fingers over the grip-worn wood, he didn't see the look that crossed Abraxus' face, nor the knowing glance that Smythe tossed his way.

Eli saw none of these things. Instead, he was far away, across the sea, feeling the waves against the prow of the *Asherah* as she danced toward the unknown. Toward the *gorwelion*.

part three
the deep

I
then.

Voices and eyes below.

Deep below, in the cold and salt-soaked places of the world, there was darkness and weight and a pure emptiness untainted by anything as imaginative and ephemeral as life. It was a desert of the deep. Something did reside in the silt and sand that lay on the bottom, curled in on itself, either sleeping or dead. They were unconscious of their own waiting, but wait they did. Reawakening or resurrection was coming.

Through the silence, the currents stirred, changed direction and just for a moment, the debris of the bed was disturbed. It plumed upwards, an explosion captured not in a second, but several slow-moving minutes. And as it finally returned down to the unseen floor, something changed. The currents rioted on, now perhaps with more passion than they had before, and the deep below knew now that something different was possible. The reawakening or resurrection had begun, layers of mist and salt peeled back from eyes that would wake to a new and endlessly possible world.

First, came the listening. It was not a conscious listening, more an understanding and a placid perceptiveness. The listening heard the ceaseless beat of the waves, the dance of the seasonal current, the moon-pull of the tides. It heard the unbreakable patterns of a thing so vast, it could be deemed entirely incomprehensible by a mind smaller than the one that was waking.

After the listening, a voice came into being. The voice spoke no words in any recognisable language; letters and sounds with no form, no shape. A rule of speech was made unto itself. It was a roaring whisper in the depths, grinding and hideous. As the moon above grew and diminished, the voice added intricacies to their un-language. It still roared and moaned and scraped along the fabric of existence, but now there was a rhythm to it, a song beneath the grit.

There exists on this earth a mere handful of people that are imbibed with the power to hear the words and songs and incantations of things greener, bluer and more eternal than they. If one of these people had stood at the seas' floor, amidst the sand and shipwreck coral, they might have heard the endless chant, a spell reverberating through the brine.

Hold Me In The Salt And Pour Sand Through The Hourglass Of My Fingers. Paint The Horizon In Blue Across The Space Of The Mind, Too Infinite To Hold Fully. No Canvas Can Hold Forever. Down In The Deep, The Selkie Slips Through Strings Of Kelp. Hidden Siren Song Crashed Against The Rocks, Dashing The Love Of Temptation Into Dust. Drown Out Those Not At Quiet With The World. Call Me Out. Call Me Down. Hold Me Gentle Amongst The Waves. Be Careful With My Bones. I Am Fragile And Salt Shaken.

After the voice came the perfect and instant realisation that it desired to *play*. On and on the voice spoke, calling things unreal out of the dark that surrounded them on all sides. Scales and skin and bone and muscle were pulled apart, resewn with kelp and shells, broken against the sharp rocks. Forged in the heat of the underwater fire vents. Set into shape by the crushing deep and cold. They had no desire to see the sun, content with the hazy refractions that played on the surface so far above. With these too, they played. The waters changed colours, shifting imperceptibly from a sapphire, cobalt, indigo, aventurine, jade and deepest inky black. Each wave was crested with a crushed pearl dusting of foam. And from the voice, sprung sight.

With sight, came the understanding that they did not have to be confined to the depths. It was home, it was where they began, but suddenly a longing to be at the whim of the current stole over them. From down below, something vast stirred, reared up and detached. They had no form, save for the ones that they desired to borrow and play with once again. As a school of swirling fish, they rose up and up, watching as the hadal dropped away. So much space, so much potential. The hugeness of what was truly theirs threatened to overwhelm them. Within the core of them, something came together and broke apart all at once.

The oldest story men of the sea tell each other began then. Born from things new and broken and *loved*, they tumbled out from inside and rioted in their newfound forms. Scales and teeth and horns, ribs of shipwreck wood exposed and spines of sediment rock. The serpents were thrown to every corner of the world, taking on the colouring of their own little piece of it. They were a gift, benevolent creatures given freely and out of love to guide those less understanding, less sure of the waters. The voice spoke out again, the words reverberating through the centuries and dripping through the ink of a storyteller.

Do Not Be Afraid. Here There Be Monsters.

Content with listening, sight, voice and play, the entity now knew themselves. They understood what they were and how they fitted into a world amongst their distant kin. They were the blue, salt places of the earth. And when man began to venture out truly into their domain, they accepted them with curious understanding. It was true that their temper flared as quickly as a lightning flash, tossing those who did not show the proper respect into the depths. Bones of a traitor sink easily.

Distant kin of sky and forest and mountains and beyond called to souls who seemed to shine the brightest, the ones who heard the voices of the wild and tried their best to sing back. One by one, the kin took these people for their own and remade them. Knowledge was passed through them and down, an unending line of heralds. These heralds in turn took on others, apprentices, cartographers, adventurers. And so, the word continued to spread; the songs and enchantments and cries of the wild places melting into every fibre of humankind.

They heard these heralds, and knew it was time to reach out and take one for their own. The fisherman was not the first. He will not be the last. But whilst he still breathes, and walks the rolling decks of his ship, *she who dances on waves*, he burns the brightest. They took him up from repose, lifted him on high atop waves and called out, *He Is Mine. May He Swim As The Selkie For Many Tides.*

II.
now.

Candles.
March, 1816.
Abraxus.

The cellar was a warm reprieve from the biting wind that had blown up around them on the journey back. He hadn't taken them far: out along the coastline away from the village, and back again. The *Asherah* skimmed over the waves, her prow dipping and rising. Abraxus could feel the joy of freedom echoing through her sails, the snap of canvas and creaking of rope creating a song only he was in tune with.

Tias and Smythe had spent most of the excursion by the bowsprit, Tias leaning out over it, resting his elbows on the railing. Eli had stood with them for a moment, staring out over the waters. Abraxus could tell his mind was far away, somewhere out along the horizon. When they emerged from the shelter of the cove, Eli had taken off down the deck and scrambled into the rigging. Abraxus had to stop himself from calling a warning – Eli knew how to handle himself on a ship. Abraxus chose to ignore the look Smythe cast in his direction. He already knew.

The boy climbed about three quarters of the way up, and then looped his legs through one of the gaps, creating a somewhat precarious seat. He remained up there until Abraxus had dropped anchor once more and Smythe was in the process of shoving the gangplank back out onto the cove's wall.

'Eli?' Abraxus called up softly. He got no response, so instead he too clambered up the rigging. It was true night now, the lanterns and candles casting soft pools of light around the deck. Eli's hands were pale and stiffly holding onto the coarse rope, but still he made no effort to move. 'We are back,' Abraxus said quietly so as to not startle the boy. 'Come inside and we will talk, yes?'

'Do you know how lucky you are?' Eli said, his voice insubstantial. 'To have all that waiting for you.'

It is waiting for you too, Abraxus wanted to say, but the words lodged in his throat. Instead, he merely nodded and rested a hand on Eli's shoulder. 'We will go back out again soon, Eli. You have my word.' At last, Eli looked at him. There was such hope in his eyes that Abraxus knew immediately he would honour his word completely. Under the moonlight – the clouds not yet having veiled it tonight – Abraxus thought Eli's eyes, now made dark, had a liquid quality to them. 'Come.'

Once they had all made their way over the natural harbour wall, across the shingle and up toward the balcony, the wind had picked up into a howling gale. Below, the *Asherah* rolled up and down with the motion of the agitated waves. For a moment, Abraxus wondered if the sea knew what he was going to say next. If they were ready for him to bare it all. He turned his back to the water, and passed through the canvas doorway. He had promised answers.

Smythe was kneeling on the hearthstones, banking up the fire which had reduced itself to embers in their absence. Tias was roving through the shelves, occasionally pulling a book or scroll down to inspect. With slight amusement, Abraxus watched him heft a heavy stone tablet from one of the many stacks, cradling it in his arm as one finger felt along the engraved lines there. Behind him, Eli entered, the strange spell that seemed to have come over him lifting with every step he took back into the sculpted places of the earth. He made an immediate beeline for the suspended rowboat bed, reaching out and rocking it.

The ropes that held it aloft creaked a little, but did not give way. Seemingly to take this as a sign, Eli pulled off his boots – ones that had been kindly donated from the Selwin household after Eli's own had become so salt encrusted as to make them unusable – and unsteadily climbed in. Abraxus had pulled off his own boots and left them on the balcony. The laces needed another good soaking, so for once he found himself hoping for rain during the night.

Tias lifted his eyes from examining a long scroll of parchment that Abraxus recognised as having come from Smythe's first archive as Eli misjudged how far down the mattress portion of the rowboat bed would be and collapsed face first into the blankets. Tias snorted and returned to the scroll. One of Eli's feet was still hanging over the side as Abraxus came over.

'Comfortable?'

'Incredibly.' Eli's voice was very muffled through many layers of wool, but considering he had made no effort to roll over, Abraxus had to believe him.

'When you are ready, join us by the fire. We have a story to tell.' Not resisting the urge, Abraxus reached out and tugged one of the supporting ropes toward him and let go, making the bed swing. He heard Eli's muted laughter as he joined Smythe, now sitting in the armchair, his hands resting comfortably on his chest.

'Well, I think you made quite the impression.' Smythe eyed him, a small smile playing about his lips. 'It's not often you see a boy fall in love with the sea all over again.'

'Every time I take them out, Stooger, they will fall for it again. As I do.' Abraxus sat himself down on the hearthstones, his back almost resting against one of the carved ribs that framed it. He closed his eyes for a moment, and listened to the crackle of the fire. It was important that he got this next part of his tale right. 'Candles.'

'Come again?'

'Do you have any candles left?' Abraxus turned his gaze to the innkeeper, who was frowning in confusion.

"Course I do, but we've got enough light down 'ere.'

'Not those types of candles, Smythe.' Abraxus raised one eyebrow, waiting for his Wayfinder to cotton on.

It took a moment, but then the confusion lifted from Smythe's face as surely as a summer's sea fret burnt off under a midday sun. '*Oh*. Aye, I think I still have some.' With a low groan, he pushed himself up from the armchair and joined Tias at the shelves. Abraxus caught snippets of low muttering between the pair, and the sound of shuffling as Smythe searched. Before he could even question the sudden spur of intention, Abraxus darted up and took the armchair, settling down into the plush comforts.

'Got 'em!' Smythe's triumphant voice preceded the man as he and Tias emerged from between the shelves. He was holding a plain wooden candle box, the sort that could be mounted on a wall if so desired. 'And there's four left which is–' He broke off at the sight of Abraxus in his recently vacated chair.

Abraxus said nothing and dragged the little stool closer to him with his foot.

'You really are rather tedious.' Smythe dropped the candle box into his lap and took one of the other chairs. Tias did the same, valiantly trying not to laugh.

'Elias? Are you joining us, or are you asleep?' Abraxus called over his shoulder. All he got in response was a muffled groan. 'Try again.'

'Fine.' A minute later, Eli had wandered over and sank down into the place Abraxus himself had been before stealing Smythe's chair. 'That's unfairly comfortable, Smythe.'

'Ask Mam for one Eli, I'm sure she'll say yes.' Tias said. He still had the scroll in his hand, running his thumb over the curled edge.

'It certainly served me well when all the rooms above were full.' Abraxus said absentmindedly, sliding open the candle box.

Four, just as Smythe had said.

'You've been here *before*?' Tias' words had a hint of incredulity to them.

Abraxus paused, before saying, 'Yes, I have. On less... *pressing* business than this however.'

'We didn't see you,' Eli said suspiciously.

Abraxus snapped the candle box closed, and placed it on the floor. 'Let us just say that Old Man Morgan had not yet earned that epithet when I last visited. In fact, if I recall, he was just learning to walk.'

Smythe chuckled as both Eli and Tias started talking over each other. He held up a hand and said loudly, 'Now, *that* is not the story we have to tell you – although it is a good one.' The brothers settled down again, casting looks at one another that Abraxus now knew meant more questions would soon be coming.

'Quite.' Abraxus held up the candle. 'Smythe, if you would.'

'Don't you dare steal this chair whilst I'm up.' The innkeeper stood, and set about dowsing all the other lanterns in the room, until only the red-golden light of the fire remained. As he sat back down, Abraxus pulled his strike light from his pocket, and lit the wick of the candle. He felt, more than saw, Eli and Tias both shiver with anticipation.

'This,' he said, holding the candle aloft, 'is a Teller's Candle. They originated in the city of my birth, a town of ivy and towers and cerulean sea beyond. The woman who invented them was born blind, but loved stories and all the wildest images that came with them. So, in order to tell stories to the people of the city and have them see what she envisioned, she poured her skill into these candles. Watch.'

With that, Abraxus brought the candle to his lips, and softly blew out the flame. The wax under the wick had barely just begun to melt. From the wick, not proportionate to the candle's size at all, smoke bloomed. It was strange smoke: it had a *substantialness* to it and Abraxus found himself inhaling deeply, long sleeping memories of story-halls under a blanket of stars shifting slightly within. The smoke billowed and twisted filling the air between them with an almost pearlescent thickness.

'This is the story of voices and eyes below,' he said. The smoke rippled and, suddenly, within its curls and fronds, became a forest of kelp.

As he spoke, the Teller's Candle poured the story into the air. Disturbed beds of sand and rock, schools of fish melding into something with form, before returning to a shining whirl of scales. And then came the serpents. Long, undulating forms swam and gambolled through the air, tails and fins trailing delicately behind them. Tias gently reached up and let the tips of his fingers brush the underside of one of them as it swam by. Abraxus wove his words with the images, until his voice and the smoke seemed to have become one quivering and ephemeral tapestry.

A lone body of a fisherman crashed into the water silently, and hung suspended. A boat below raised up, the serpents swimming in figure eights around it.

'The Roaring god pulled blood from my veins and replaced it with seawater. I am a puppet with strings of kelp held by a cold hand. But I do not seek to cut them. I am given purpose in the form of a dance. They gave me scales to match the brethren, their most beloved creation, that swim in the corners of the world. I am theirs wholly.' As he spoke this, the smoke took on a different image. Eyes, many of them, made of kelp and shells and fish and wreckwood all stared out, pupilless and knowing. And just for a second, Abraxus swore they moved infinitesimally. Looking toward Eli.

'The Roaring god?' Tias asked. His voice was tiny.

Abraxus sighed and licked his thumb and forefinger, pinching out the Teller's Candle completely. 'Well, the seas go by many names, so why would not its creator and tender? The Roaring god is merely an overarching moniker we may all use without incurring any unsought wrath. They are neither 'he' nor 'she'; they are an entity unto their own creation.' Abraxus thought for a moment, untangling the threads of myth and lore he had scattered throughout his mind. 'But I suppose here, on this stretch of coast, you might call them Llŷr.'

'Llŷr?' Eli said, his expression still alight with wonder from the story and smoke. 'But... that's one of the stories that–'

'That Da told us,' Tias finished for him.

'John knew his stories well, aye,' Smythe said. 'He just didn't know what truth lay untapped beneath 'em.'

Silence fell across them all, each lost in their own thoughts.

Eventually Eli spoke up. 'So – so are you one of these 'heralds' you told us about?'

'We tend not to call ourselves 'heralds' anymore. It is a little too...grandiose for our purposes. But yes, that is what I am.'

'Can you die?' Tias blurted out, and then went pink around the ears. 'Sorry.'

'Yes. Despite it all, part of me is still... human. But I will walk for a long time yet before that day comes.' Abraxus didn't say that he had technically died once before, but that last day out on the *Asherah* before the Roaring god had found him was hazy in his memories at best.

'Are you like him?' Eli asked, pointing his question toward Smythe. The innkeeper was moving about the cellar room again, relighting the lanterns.

'Not quite.' He dropped back into his chair, taking the proffered candle box from Abraxus' hand. 'I am his Wayfinder.'

'What does that mean?' Tias said, sitting a little straighter. 'What does it actually *mean* though?'

'It means in some ways I am bound to Abraxus and he to me. Whilst he is off trailing the waters of the world, I am coastal bound. Without me, he would have no direction, no sense of what needs fixin' or helping.'

'Wayfinders are anchors,' Abraxus said. 'We find our way back to them when they call us. Smythe is my Wayfinder, and this is now his Wayfinder's inn.'

'The inn?'

'Part of the... the *order* I suppose you could call it.' Smythe said thoughtfully. 'Before I was here, I owned The Salt Shaken further north. The Five is just another one of the many inns belonging to the Roaring god's Wayfinder.'

Eli slumped back against the wall, eyes glassy. Tias was staring off into the fire, turning the scroll in his hands over and over unconsciously. Smythe looked to Abraxus, a small crease of worry lining his brow. Abraxus raised a hand to stop him from speaking further. He knew he had to give the boys time to process what he had imparted to them, and, if he was being honest with himself, he needed a moment to slow the beating of his heart. Hardly anyone in his long and brine-soaked memory had ever been told outright what he truly was, the nature of his seaweed entangled existence.

'The bones...' Eli broke the silence eventually.

'Hm?'

'They come from these serpents? The ones that Llŷr created?' Eli didn't notice Smythe wince at the naming of the god, but Abraxus made no comment. Whilst Eli might be privy to information not quite belonging on this mortal coil, it didn't mean that naming the god would bring said deity's anger down on him. Yet.

'The ribs, aye.' He looked over to Tias, 'In fact, I think you have the perfect illustration in your hands, Matthias.' Abraxus held out his hand, looking at the scroll.

'Oh, right.' Tias handed it over. 'It's why I picked it up – I had thought that maybe...' His voice trailed away. And then, 'Seems I was right.'

Smythe set a comforting hand on Tias' shoulder. Abraxus felt a twinge of guilt: it was one thing wishing to be in a story, to have an adventure confined to the pages and ink of a book. It was an entirely different feeling to actually find yourself in one.

Unrolling the scroll, Abraxus held it up facing the others. Along its length was a beautifully drawn and anatomically correct diagram of a serpent. He tapped a finger on the ribs. 'These are not within the serpents' body, but rather outside it. Whilst they are bone, they do discolour similarly as wood does when exposed to salt water. This is why you only find the ribs and spine on the beaches.'

'No skulls though?' Tias said.

'No.' Abraxus deftly wound up the scroll. 'The heads become a prize, you might say.' Now they came to it, the crux, the linchpin on which it all hung. 'When the – when *Llŷr* is angered, they seem to forget for a time their love of the serpents. They only see them as the misunderstood instruments mankind have come to rely on, and then so spurned unknowingly. In their anger, the serpents are–'

'Killed.' Smythe finished flatly. 'A cull, until the source of the anger has apologised, or else been smashed apart on the waters which will not be calm until whoever it is, is gone.' Smythe looked toward the ribs that framed the fireplace. 'It's cruel and unnecessary.'

'Stooger...' Abraxus started warningly.

'*It is*. But I also know that a god cannot be reasoned with. A primordial power must be placated.' There was derision in Smythe's words and Abraxus could not help but find himself in agreement. He had seen too many bones of gentle creatures in his lifetimes.

'The storms then, the boats not coming back... it's all because someone angered the sea?' Eli said.

'You said that at the meeting we all had,' Tias added quickly. 'No one believed you.'

'It is only going to get worse,' Abraxus said coldly. 'Llŷr will not stop until this is resolved. Until I have resolved it for them.'

'How do you anger *the sea*?' Tias asked, his voice a little higher than usual. Panic, Abraxus noted. 'How do you find that out? Sailors and fishermen curse it all the time, especially in rough weather.'

'This is an angering on a different level, lad,' Smythe said gently. He caught Abraxus' eye, and Abraxus nodded. Smythe swallowed and took a breath. 'It has to stem from an emotion that isn't fleeting. Something deep and dark with roots latched into the soul. A voice pulled from the earth and given a cursed meaning.'

'There is one in this village that has a mother tongue buried in loam and moss. There is one in this village that has lost so much to the sea, that a sea in itself has washed into her mind.' Abraxus spoke quietly, knowing that everything which had come before was about to become completely moot to the Kincarran boys. 'Your mother.'

Paper.
March 1816.
Tias.

He hated that it made sense. The knowledge rose like bile every time he thought about it. Part of him wanted to reject it entirely, to go back to Abraxus and Smythe and shout at them that they were wrong, that *his mother* would not, could not do anything to harm another. But the part of his mind that clicked over riddles and letters and how the cogs of the world fit together knew that it made sense. Tias just wasn't sure *how* it had happened.

His mother didn't often use her first language – in fact he couldn't clearly recall hearing it since those haze filled days in the upstairs rooms of The Five-Pointed Compass. There were certainly some bright and brief memories that came to him, a patina of sun and time overlaying the surface. The dancing dust of pollen. His father, on his back in the garden, gazing into the sky. His mother, planting some herbs and singing. The song offering no comprehension to Tias' young mind. But that had been so long ago, that Tias knew he couldn't fully trust his own recollections.

All that night, thoughts chased around and around Tias' head, refusing him sleep. He could tell from the near continual shifting of blankets that Eli was similarly awake. Smythe and Abraxus had escorted them from the *Gorwelion* Cellar, as it had been dubbed by Eli, and home to Roseate. The next five days had passed achingly slowly for the pair of them. Food arrived on their doorstep from Smythe, or occasionally Efa, who had dropped by to see if all was well in the Kincarran household. She did a poor job of hiding her disapproval that Ffion had remained in the forest vale, sending her sons out alone on the trek back with what she would consider a near stranger.

Neither of them left the sanctuary of the cottage or its little walled garden in that time. The world, it seemed to Tias, had suddenly grown much too large. For now, it was safer to remain with what he knew. To his surprise, Eli was also not overly enthusiastic about venturing out, despite Abraxus' promises to take another trip aboard the *Asherah*. The weather still remained patchy, but spring was now valiantly trying to break through the curtain of winter. Small green buds pushed up from the soil, and the frost on the grass each morning quickly melted into dew. On the air, Tias was sure he could smell the gentle scent of warmer things, a soft caress to chase away the cold. He spent his time mostly in the garden, a few books scattered around him that Smythe had brought up on his last food run.

He was busy with copying up the diagram of the serpent into one of his notebooks, when a shadow fell over the paper. 'Here,' it was Eli, holding out a steaming mug. 'It might be getting brighter, but there's still cold in the ground.'

'*Diolch*.' Tias took the mug and then winced. He hadn't realised how numb his fingers had become. Eli sat down beside him, cradling his own cup. The vista of *Angorfa* Harbour and the sea beyond it stretched before them. The white and specks of colour of the fishing boats had long since vanished, heading around the bay away to the north-west. Apparently, the catch was more yielding the closer to Finfolk Point the boats got.

'There's a word Abraxus used that night,' Eli started without any preamble, 'and I can't stop thinking about it.'

'You mean with Mam?'

Eli's answer surprised him. 'No. Not that.' When Tias looked at him with incredulity on his face, Eli rushed on. 'Well, I am thinking about *that* too, but this is something else.' Tias felt his heart lurch slightly. The look on Eli's face was the same one he had when he was about to suggest they do something dangerous.

'What?' Tias said slowly, hoping his less than enthusiastic response would let Eli take a minute to think properly about whatever plan he had managed to concoct. Tias half wondered if he should have insisted they go out to *Tua'r Môr* Bay, instead of giving his brother unlimited time to think and plot.

'Abraxus said "apprentices".' Eli had turned himself fully around to face Tias. 'When he was telling us what Smythe was, he said "apprentices".'

It took Tias a full ten seconds to locate that snippet of information from a tangle of other, more painful moments. 'He did,' he conceded finally. 'Where are you going with this?' He already knew of course, but he wanted to hear Eli say it.

'Well – I mean, what if we *asked*?' There was a fervour in Eli's eyes that Tias knew meant he wasn't going to be easily dissuaded. And, if he was going to be entirely honest with himself, something hot and alive beat at the inside of his ribs at the half-spoken suggestion.

'To be an apprentice?'

'It's not all that uncommon – Marcus goes to the next village over this summer to work with his cousin.'

'Eli, that's to be a *tanner*. What you're suggesting is we ask to earn ourselves a place alongside monsters and people who may or may not essentially be demi-gods.' The word had turned up in one of the books, and Tias had wondered, once he understood the description, if Smythe had brought that one on purpose.

'But I don't want to be a tanner. I don't want any of *that*–' and here he waved his arm vaguely in the direction of the village, '– and what it has to offer. That might have been enough before, to have the *Dawnsiwr y Wawr* and be content... but Tias, there's so much more out there now.'

'I know.' Tias knew his voice was small and quiet. The weight of it all pressed in over him. 'But it's just so... big.'

'And isn't that exciting? The only confines on a map are the ones you draw for yourself. This,' he tapped the forgotten notebook in Tias' lap, 'can document the world, and you can set it all out in neat words and drawings, but this,' he reached up and touched Tias' temple, 'can see it all. You can't pull the stars from the sky onto paper.'

Tias looked at his brother, and just for a second, wondered who he saw sitting beside him. To do something with his hands, Tias took another sip of the flowery tea, gazing off over the horizon. 'I do want to see it all.' The confession was soft, but it felt to Tias the hardest thing to do. 'I'm just not sure whether I'm ready to leave these pages behind.'

They sat a while in silence together, listening to the distant crash of the waves and the call of the seabirds. Out on the waters – a deep blue shot through with darkest black and green today – Tias thought he saw sails of the same colour heading over the spray. But he blinked and lost the shape. Maybe it had never been there at all, he couldn't tell.

'Bring them with you.'

'What?'

'The pages. Smythe said he was coastal bound, that he gives Abraxus direction. Maybe you could do that?'

'What, be a – a Wayfinder?' The word felt unreal on his tongue.

'Why not?' The fervour was back. 'You to Smythe and I to Abraxus. If, of course, they'll take us and that's what you want too.'

'I...' Tias let his voice trail off. Before, where there had been ceaseless winds and echoes of thought, now there was only colour. The possibilities it opened up were endless, and Tias felt that weight on his shoulders, at his back waiting to tear him asunder. But the alive thing in his chest beat newly found wings and called him on. 'Let me think about it.'

And once again, Eli surprised him. 'That's fair. I don't want to ask this without you agreeing.' He stood, stretched and set his empty mug down on the ground. 'I might go for a walk. Coming?'

'No, I'll stay here for now.' Tias held up a book that was nearly as big and thick as one of the slabs that made up their garden wall, 'I have some reading to do.'

'Knowing you, that'll be finished by the time I get back.' Eli said with a smile. 'I'll be home before dark. See if I can get anything from Owen for later on.' With that, Eli headed for the end of the garden and vaulted over the wall, completely ignoring the gate. Tias watched Eli's copper hair catch in the sunlight as he vanished behind the crest of the hill.

'Apprentices,' Tias whispered to the sky. The paper beneath his fingers was coarse, the lettering stamped there by some long ago hand. A breeze picked up, bringing with it that new spring smell again. The pages rustled, turning on their own accord. The letter arrived before the clouds dipped over the sun once more.

III
then.

Sea gifts.

When he was a child, they were oddities. Mere curios to pick up from the lapping waters, strands of seaweed hanging, beard-like, off their smooth surfaces. In a distant memory that he was now not sure was infallible, Abraxus walked the coastline of his childhood home, the bright white cliffs looming over him offering shade from the bake of the midday sun. Lapis and sapphire waters crashed gently onto the shore, rolling in crested with crushed glass. There was another beside him, a hand holding his. Large, burnt by the sun and hardened by years at sea. Abraxus only remembered the hand, and how it felt in his. It was an anchor, an insistent pull toward things that now had little bearing over his life. *Family. Home.*

Beneath the surface of the waters, something caught his eye. Pulling away from his companion, he waded a little further out, the top of the water lapping now at his knees. A call from the shingle told him not to go out too far. With a small noise that could have been an affirmative, he reached down and plucked the stone of his curiosity out and held it to the light. It was nearly perfectly circular, blunted a little at one end. But what enthralled Abraxus the most was the keyhole slit in the cream-coloured stone. It was just wide enough for him to fit his little finger through. In his palm, the stone had a comforting weight.

He held it and knew that he had found something special that day. Why, he couldn't answer.

He returned to the place that he called home later on that day, the sun slipping west below the horizon, painting the sky a riot of purple and orange. The very sea seemed aflame. The night markets were open, the crowd dense and loud. A patina of salt, unwashed bodies, spices, and something indefinable that might have been the soft green undertones of plant life rose above it all. The hand that guided his led him unwaveringly through the packed streets, under lanterns and canopies of silk.

Past the whispering arches, through the alley of close shadows and up the spine stairs they walked. The crowd thinned the deeper into the city they went, until the only people they passed were those closing the shutters and leaving out lanterns and candles for the nightwalkers. Abraxus let his free hand trail through the smoke of a Teller's Candle and watched as it took on the form of a huge bird, its eyes pinpricks of ember. A soft tug on his arm steered him away and onwards. Their door was once painted white, but it had long since flaked and chipped away, leaving rough pieces of the wooden planking exposed. From underneath the door, Abraxus watched as footsteps disturbed the soft golden glow of the candlelight from within.

That night, after he'd been left alone in the house, he climbed down from his bed and padded silently to the main room. The door was locked and bolted from the outside, his parents having taken the key after their departure for the night markets. The fire burnt low, the ashes slumbering quietly as he passed. On a nail protruding from the wall, was a bundle of twine. Clambering up onto the bench that served as both table and workspace, Abraxus snatched the twine down. Measuring out an arm's length of it, he bit at it until it snapped. Rewrapping the twine into the same complicated ship's knot it had been in before he'd disturbed it, he slipped back to his bed.

When the morning came, he was out on the streets before the sun rose. That calloused hand in his again. Beneath a watery egg-shell sky, they pulled up sails and tied off guidelines. Once the depth was suitable and the weight of the land had been left behind, nets were cast overboard, and the quiet hunt began. Abraxus spent the day running barefoot from crew member to crew member, carrying and fetching. He loved every minute of it. One of the crew, the mate, had laughed at his new necklace. He'd tugged lightly at it and called it extra weight to carry him down to the ocean floor. Abraxus had merely sidestepped him and tucked the stone back under his shirt. It had taken on the heat from his chest, and he found its solidity comforting.

Before the moon had made one complete cycle in the night sky, over a dozen stones had migrated from the shoreline to Abraxus' windowsill via his sand-lined pockets. Some were strung onto more pieces of rope and twine; worn about the wrist or neck on sailing days. Several he'd made into some sort of hanging chime. It clattered discordantly on the days when the wind raced through the narrow streets of white stone and ivy.

The sea kept offering these treasures to him, and somewhere in the buried parts of his soul, Abraxus knew that to refuse them would be a great slight. There was a world locked away inside the stones, one that was biding its time. All it took was a glance.

IV

now

Beasts.
March, 1816.
Eli.

Fy mechgyn, my boys,

I am not sure when this will reach you, as the messenger departed from here with only the name of the village. Let me start by reassuring you: I am well, as is everyone you came to care about in Dyffryn Cernunnos.

You will probably recall that on our journey toward the valley, we passed through a steep pass — the place where I told you to keep your voices low and footsteps hasty. Not too many days after your departure, and before Tudwr had returned to us, some merchants unaware of the lay of this land passed through. They brought us the news that part of the cliffside had collapsed on them as they journeyed through the gully. None of them were injured, but all were very shaken.

Tudwr only just returned to us the other night and confirmed what the merchants — now gone — had said. The pass is completely blocked, and I do not know any other road out of Dyffryn Cernunnos toward you. I am afraid that I will be away from you much longer than I had intended, but the moment the pass is cleared, I shall be on my way.

Take care of each other, cariad.

All my love,

Mam.

Eli had read the letter so many times now he could recount it almost verbatim from memory. Its edges and along the fold had gone soft, and it threatened to fall apart soon from so much handling. Inside the folded letter had been a sprig of willow leaves, still green and vibrant. Part of the parchment was stained slightly, as if the vitality of the cutting had leaked into their mother's words.

The news had arrived yesterday, the letter sitting on the table for Eli as he'd returned from his walk. Tias had bitten the inside of his thumb until it had bled, anxiety written clearly over the planes of his face, despite their mother's assurances. Eli himself didn't know what to feel. Things had been gingerly patched up, pieces of bark and caulking gapping the weakest bonds. He wanted his mother to return, but the smallest, most secret part of him discovered a profound relief that he and Tias had more time alone in Porth Tymestl. He knew he wasn't ready to ask how Ffion had angered the sea.

It had also tipped the balance in favour of his idea. With their mother away for the foreseeable future, Eli found himself daydreaming more and more often about learning everything Abraxus could tell him. Some uncaring hand had placed an obstacle on the path, and in doing so, had removed another for Eli.

The day after the letter, Eli and Tias had ventured out together to try and find Smythe. The village had been bustling that morning, the streets seemed too small to contain the noise of its people. With the promise of spring, hope seemed to have bloomed alongside the yellow sea gorse. A firm wind had sent people's scarves and hats flying, but most just commented it would make for a decent day of fast sailing. The food stores that had been so precariously low that winter were still a sorry sight: mostly bare shelves and only a few more racks of smoked fish. But it seemed that with each passing day, as they lengthened, the people of Porth Tymestl seemed to be able to subsist on good feeling.

As they'd walked, Medwyn, Aron and Thomas had passed them. Thomas resolutely ignored the pair, although he did slink a little further into his father's shadow. Eli had been content to merely nod and walk on, but Medwyn had stopped them, saying, 'Just a moment, lads.'

Aron looked down toward the harbour, clearly wanting to be off.

'Won't be just a moment, Aron, hold on.' There was a cut to Medwyn's voice that signalled to Eli that whatever Medwyn was about to say, it had been previously discussed and met with consternation.

'Everything alright?' Tias asked curiously, looking between the trio.

'Aye, we were–' At this Aron let out a huff, '*fine*, I was wondering if you both had anything to fill your days with?'

'No?' Eli said. 'Not at the moment. Mam is going to be away for a bit longer than we thought so we're just sort of–'

'Waiting,' Tias finished.

Medwyn nodded, as if he'd be expecting the answer. 'Well, in that case there is space on both mine and Aron's boats for some capable hands. I saw how well you worked with John, and it would be a shame to let any Kincarran blood go to waste on the land.'

Eli and Tias exchanged looks, a silent conversation passing between them. From his peripheral vision, Eli saw Thomas shift uncomfortably. 'I think,' Eli started, 'that we might need some time to consider?'

'It's a very gracious offer,' Tias put in.

'Nothin' gracious about it.' Aron finally spoke up. 'You have your father's make. We need all the 'elp we can get.' He looked down at Thomas. 'The young'uns need to be ready, readier sooner than we thought.'

'It's a fast boat, Da's,' Thomas blurted. 'Not as shallow on the draft as the *Dawnsiwr y Wawr* was.' He suddenly seemed to realise he was speaking aloud, and held himself back again.

Tias looked Thomas directly in the eyes, 'I've seen her. She's lovely.' He turned back to Medwyn. 'Like Eli said, may we have some time to consider? We have a few other ideas we're entertaining at the moment.'

'Of course.' Medwyn's response was drawn out, and it was clear to Eli that he was desperate to ask what sort of other ideas.

Aron huffed again and glanced in the direction of The Five.

Eli had to smother a smile.

'Well, come by and let us know what you decide.' And with that, the three passed on and headed toward the crowd at *Angorfa* Harbour.

'Why is it,' Tias asked pensively as they continued onto The Five-Pointed Compass, 'that we are given options either not at all, or far too many?'

'I have no clue. Never makes for a dull moment though.' Eli didn't say anything about Tias also asking for more time. Part of him was daring to hope that Tias had really started to consider the apprenticeship idea. So wrapped up in his thoughts, Eli didn't realise that they had already reached the inn. Tias had stopped dead, staring at the door. A piece of thick parchment had been nailed to the door. On it were the two words, "gone fishing".

'Smythe doesn't have a boat, does he?' Eli asked.

Tias looked at him like he was stupid. 'No, but Abraxus does.'

'Oh.' Half-heartedly, Eli tried the handle. The latch remained firmly locked. 'I suppose we could try again later?'

Apparently, Tias wasn't listening. 'Maybe that's why we've had more food recently. Abraxus might have been going out for the catch, Smythe with him. Remember last night's dinner?'

'That soup thing?' It had been delicious, reminiscent of the more decadent meals they'd eaten at The Five-Pointed Compass.

'Exactly. I don't think Smythe could have made that unless

he'd been given access to a fresh catch. And I keep thinking I see the *Asherah* on the horizon, but I never can tell if it's actually there, or just the sea.'

'Well, fishing or not, we still need to tell them about Mam.' Eli dropped his voice, despite the fact that there was no one close by. 'Especially if this is, you know, her fault. We can't fix it until she's back.'

'Alright, give me a minute.' Tias proceeded to pull a page from the back of his notebook and scribble a message on it, slipping it beneath the door. 'Best we can do for now.'

They spent the rest of the day down at *Angorfa* beach, watching the tireless efforts of the sailing folk docking, unloading and making sail again. Just a little after midday, Old Man Morgan came to join them, but he seemed scattered and unsteady in conversation. His eyes had clouded over of late, and his gait, always rolling as if still on the deck of his little skiff, had become even more tottering. As both Eli and Tias stood to leave, the sun beginning to touch the horizon, he finally spoke up. 'Finfolk point will be ablaze at this hour. Sunlight pouring through the arch.' He looked away to the west, the curve of the coastline hiding the natural archway.

Eli hesitated, not sure whether or not to respond. In the end, he kept silent, slipping away after Tias.

The sunset inked the sky overhead in soft oranges, a distant and unknowable landscape. Eli found himself tripping more than usual on the walk back to Roseate Cottage, keeping his eyes on the sky. The orange melted away at the rim of the world, dripping down out of sight, and leaving the sky to riot in its darker colours.

Roseate Cottage was cold when they finally pushed open the door, the hearth empty and their beds upstairs unmade. Tias doggedly began the night-time routine, stacking kindling and heading out to fill the water pail up. Eli, however, stopped in the middle of the main room, looking around. There seemed to be an invisible presence to the cottage, as if footprints had been stamped onto the floor in water, but had long since dried. He turned in a slow circle, trying to figure out what was amiss. It would have gone unnoticed, the inclusion so unobtrusive that he could have reasonably looked past it. There was a small jug on the table, a sprig of heather, gorse and early budding valerian inside. No one put flowers on the table but Ffion.

'Tias.'

'Hm?'

'Someone's been here.'

Tias whipped around, looking at his brother. 'What?'

In response, Eli pointed to the jug. 'Only Mam does that, and she isn't here.'

Tias headed for the door immediately, inspecting the lock. 'Someone's pulled this up.' Tias fiddled with the latch, before bringing out a small splinter of wood. It was the one way to cheat the latch and lock on the door: their father having shown them how to do it. 'Someone broke in... to leave flowers?'

'Maybe you have a secret admirer, Tias.' Despite the seriousness of the situation, Eli couldn't help himself.

'I am not listening to you anymore.' Tias came over to stand beside Eli at the table. He paused, frowning. 'What's that?'

Eli had spotted it too. A flat expanse of slate sat beneath the jug, unlike anything they had at Roseate. It seemed vaguely familiar, and as he reached out to take the jug, Eli recalled the stack of stones on the natural ledge that led down to the harbour where the *Asherah* was docked. 'I think Smythe must have left it.'

Tias beside him relaxed visibly. 'This is probably some form of payback, didn't you get into Abraxus' room?'

'I left him honey at least, this is some flowers and rock.' Eli flipped the slate over in his hand. 'Oh.'

'A rock with a message.' Tias leaned in closer to read.

Come see. Seaward. XII.

The handwriting was definitely not Smythe's, that much Eli knew. It was thin, with an almost sharp quality to it. '*Tua'r Môr* Bay,' Eli said.

'Midnight,' Tias added, pointing to the "XII". 'They're numerals, an 'X' means ten.'

Eli looked to his brother. 'What else could he possibly have to show us?'

That night was a clear one. The wind had swept away any cloud that might have hidden the moon's silver face. It shone down, a gleaming coin suspended in the deep of the skies. Constellations painted out in fragments of light, their stories immortalised and distant. Without the blanket of clouds, it was also bitterly cold. Tias' fingers fumbled a little on the lock, Eli shifting a little from foot to foot in a vain effort to warm himself. Tiredness itched at his eyes, and just as Tias managed to lock the door, he found himself left with nothing but the deepest desire to go back inside, scurry up the ladder and bury himself in blankets until the dawn light spilled through the shutters.

Both of them had managed to snatch an hour or so of sleep after they'd eaten – the food provided courtesy of Efa. But Eli had found it anything but refreshing. His dreams of late had gained a shocking vitality – riots of colours and half formed thoughts breaking through this strange veil that seemed to have clothed his mind. During that hour, all life beyond his dreams seemed dull and flat: the unreal had become vivid.

'Ready?' Tias tucked the spare key away, rubbing his hands together.

'For what?' Eli rejoindered. 'A mysterious midnight trip to *Tua'r Môr* based on a scratched message on seas slate?'

'...That, aye.' Tias' face was cast in silhouette, the light of the moon turning his face into hollows and angles.

'Never more, let's go.'

The night was absolute around them, broken only by the halo cast out from their father's bowsprit lantern. Frost glittered on the cobbles, an array of soft stars below their celestial cousins. Porth Tymestl lay silent: a few candles burning down to stumps left out on the doorsteps, the only indication that life still resided within the rough-stone cottages.

Somewhere behind them, a door closed softly. In the silence, it sounded like a thunderclap to Eli. Tias, holding the lantern, started, the light scattering and flickering with the motion.

'Do either of you 'ave any idea how hard it is to herd a load of rowdy fishermen out of an inn?'

'Smythe, warn a person next time!' Tias stilled the wild pendulum of the lantern. Both he and Eli had whirled around at the unexpected voice.

'My apologies.' Smythe fell into step with them unchallenged. Eli knew where he was headed.

'Busy night?' Eli asked as their feet found the softness of grass. Gravestones reared up from the misshapen ground, the snapped off teeth of the earth.

"Celebratin". A good catch out by Finfolk. You should have joined us, we ate well tonight.'

The talk stopped as they finally approached the steep path down to the beach. Vaguely, Eli wondered why he still hadn't mastered this particular traverse in the near pitch black. He'd done it enough times in the past few months. Far below, a gold and green driftwood fire glittered near the hushing wash of the shore. Cast in silhouette beside it was the tall, rangy frame of Abraxus. Unseen, the sea rolled softly against the sand, the horizon a silver-lit thread ringing the world. As the halo of the lantern met the beacon of the fire, Eli felt the insidious claws of night-ice retract. Across the impromptu fire pit, Abraxus motioned for them to sit. He had never looked more unknowable, green-golden sparks alighting for a mere second on his clothes, his hair, singeing points of soot on the staff that lay beside him.

No one broke the spell of silence as they all sat. Abraxus had clearly been here awhile. Woven blankets of wool and what appeared to be grass, thickly matted, ringed the fire pit. Eli glanced over to his brother, whose attention was firmly fixed on the battered leather satchel that lay companion to Abraxus' staff. The contents seemed oddly shaped, points and curves rucking the leather.

Over the snap of the fire, Eli eventually found his voice. 'What are we doing here?' He felt oddly timid, as if this was some sort of ritual that was not to be verbally sullied.

'Do you remember the lightningless nights?' Abraxus started. His voice rolled in over them like the tide, smooth and unstoppable.

'Aye. Thunder, but no lightning beside it,' Tias said slowly. It was obvious to Eli that his brother was trying to parse out whatever piece of the story this little curio fitted into.

'You are come here tonight to meet the ones that make that sound.' Abraxus let his fingers drift over the smoke of the fire, making it curl and billow. 'When Llŷr sacrifices his servants, those that escaped the cruel hand call out for their kin. They mourn in the deep. Those nights when Porth Tymestl seemed besieged by storm, are the nights that the cull was greatest.'

A sick feeling curled up through Eli's throat. 'We were hearing these creatures... *scream*?'

'Aye.' Abraxus' voice could have the gentlest breeze, it was so soft. 'You heard thunder, and the truth of the sound is not too far from this. But, as with the bones, the bound human mind chooses to hear something it can associate with its known parameters.' He looked between Eli and Tias, both his eyes a shadowed black. 'They see wood and hear storms: I see bones and hear screams.' He seemed to drift away for a moment, but then with a little shake, Abraxus returned to them on the sands. 'I think it is time you meet those that guard your waters so protectively.' With that, he reached for the bag, and passed it to Eli. It was lighter than Eli had expected, the object within seeming thin and delicate. He opened the bag and pulled out two circlets.

One was not unlike Abraxus', although the wire was silver and woven through the spider-web like strands were small coils of twine, dyed into all the shades of the sea. At the very back, the wire seemed to curl up in the mimicry of waves. The other was made of driftwood, bleached white and smoothed by years of salt and grit. Several pieces had been intricately locked together to create the near horseshoe-like shape, and as such, it had the appearance of a crown. Where the erratic points of wood stood up from the main circle, Abraxus had taken pains to stain with muted natural colours; ochre, red clay, seaweed. Both had a place to slot a stone in over the left eye.

'Pick.' Abraxus held out his hands, palms up toward them. A stone lay in either one. Eli recognised them as two of the trio that had been woven into the chime Abraxus had gifted them. The man must have sequestered it away from its perch in the cavern without them noticing. Tias reached for the brown one, long and narrow with the hole perfectly eroded in the middle. Eli took the slate grey, jagged at one edge with veins of purple running through rifts in the rock. There was a strange moment of heady unrealism as they figured out which circlets matched with which stone, and slotted them into place.

'Here.' Smythe had shuffled closer, and was now helping Tias adjust the driftwood crown. He twisted some elements of it, so that it was comfortably close to his head. Before Tias could look up, however, Smythe snatched the stone out of its socket. 'Not yet,' he said with a wry smile.

Then it was Eli's turn. The wire bent in whichever way Smythe's deft fingers chose, and soon enough, there was a cold, but not entirely unfamiliar, weight settled over his right ear and atop his head. Similarly, the stone was removed and placed into his hand.

'These stones,' Abraxus said, fitting his own circlet, 'have long been the centre of many stories. Witch stones, hag stones, seeing stones. They have been given many names, but only a few have figured out their true purpose.' He tapped his own white pearlescent one held by the crook of copper. 'Something that has been shaped only by the powers of land and sea can reveal to us things beyond our original sight. These are the eyes of the earth.' He stood, bringing his staff up with him. 'Are you ready?'

Together, they waded out hip deep into the surf. Eli's toes were immediately numb, sand spilling through and over them. Abraxus waited until they were both still, and then raised his staff. With the speed of a spear fisher, he plunged it into the water. Eli felt something within him lurch as a concussive thud reverberated through the water, the waves stilling for a moment as ripples cascaded outwards. 'They come.'

Tias looked at Eli, turning his stone over and over in his hand. Eli nodded, and together they reached up and slotted them into place. The sea lit up.

With a yell, Eli scrambled backward, almost overbalancing into the water. All around him were huge rippling creatures made of the same light that falls through deep water. Echoes of purple, green, blue, black shimmered upon their scales. Long spines of fins seemed insubstantial, but Eli could feel the pull and push of the powerful current they created as they swam in lazy circles around him. Some were as long as the *Angorfa* Harbour walls, others no bigger than a child's skiff. Whilst Eli had made to move away, his brother seemed locked into place, staring out at the riot of glowing colour before them. A gentle hand pushed in the small of Eli's back, and he turned to see Smythe. 'Go on. They won't hurt you.' Eli took a deep breath, and waded back in.

One of the serpents arced through the water toward him, its long spinal fins trailing kelp and the delicate bones encrusted with barnacles. This one was luminescent green, about as long as the *Asherah* was, but narrower than some of its kin. As Abraxus had described, the ribs of the creature were entrenched deeply into the scales *outside* its serpentine body. A long, blunted snout rose up from the water, slitted nostrils opening and blowing out droplets of salt water. It turned its head as it rose, looking at Eli with one swirling opalescent eye. A film passed over the eye sideways and it cocked its head, a low chittering sound vibrating in its throat. Its powerful tail swished lazily in the shallow water, keeping it in place. Eli reached up his hand, and then pulled back again. Long, needle-like teeth protruding from the upper jaw still dripped with water. The serpent, seeming to sense his hesitation, slunk back down and started to swim in figure eights around him, occasionally letting a spinal fin or its tail brush against Eli's leg. Letting his fingers trail in the water, Eli felt the serpent very gently bump its snout into them, before continuing to swim.

Looking to his brother, Eli saw that Tias had gone into the ocean even deeper and was nearly treading water as two serpents, one a deep indigo with short fins and a set of long, ornate horns, and the other a swirl of blues and whites, its tail fraying at the ends reminiscent of jellyfish tentacles, cavorted along beside him. Eli thought that they seemed to be playing, their snapping movements not unlike the ones he'd seen ports' dogs do as they chased each other. Abraxus stood sentinel between the both of them. All around him the serpents swam, a huge circle of glowing light. None of them got closer to Abraxus, and Eli wondered if it was something akin to reverence that kept them at bay.

'Bones of wood, eyes of pāua shell, scales the many shades of the sea, fins of sails and teeth of man's broken promises.' The words were almost intoned by Abraxus, and the swirling circle of serpents around him grew tighter, closer to him. And with that, he submerged himself. Amongst a mat of phosphorescence, Abraxus was a human shaped shadow imprinted atop it, his coat and hair swirling about him as he swam deeper.

Eli tried to still the beating of his heart, and looked to Tias. He was still entranced by the pair of serpents around him, letting his fingers drift out occasionally to run along the back of one, the points of the horns on the other. Before Eli could stop to fully think, he took a breath, and ducked beneath the water. It took a moment of willpower to open his eyes, at which the salt stung them furiously. He came to a cross legged sit on the sand floor, and watched the creatures around him. Once he had crossed the line fully into their element, they became less frightening. This was their domain, Eli was merely a visitor. The green serpent with the long fins came up close to him, the blunted point of its face nearly touching Eli's nose. It breathed out a thin flurry of bubbles and swam past, its body slipping by Eli's ribs. He shuddered; there was a cold slickness to the scales.

Eventually, he had to come up for air. Abraxus still had not surfaced, and Eli had lost track of him. Not long after that, the thrill began to wane, and shivers started to wrack up his body. Before an unpleasant cascade of memories could hit him, Eli turned and began to head toward the shore. Tias noticed his passing and followed. He too was trembling with the icy bite of the Celtic waters.

Smythe was waiting dutifully on the sands, two of the blankets Abraxus had put down around the fire in hand. He wore no circlet, but rather had a cream-coloured stone hanging from a piece of frayed string around his neck. 'Here,' he said, passing the blankets out. 'Get dry and come back to the fire.'

'What about -?' Tias started, rubbing the blanket fiercely up and down his arm to help warm himself up again.

'He'll be along shortly, don't worry.' Smythe looked out over the black waters. 'I think he needs some time with those that are closest to kin for 'im.'

Eli looked back as he scrubbed the sand from between his toes. With distance, the serpents were now just indefinable streaks of colour, glowing and weaving through the waves.

Abraxus had been lost entirely to view.

Huddled in their blankets, ringlets of wet hair clinging to their cheeks and necks, Eli and Tias slumped down beside the fire once more. Tias disentangled one of his hands and reached up to take off his driftwood circlet. He turned it around, bringing it close to his face to make out the minute details of it. 'It's beautiful,' he murmured.

'Abraxus spent a while making them,' Smythe said, poking at the fire absentmindedly. 'Started them even before you went off to the forest vale.'

'Give me yours, Eli, I want to see it.' Tias had settled the driftwood crown into the sand and was holding out an expectant hand. Almost immediately, Eli regretted ever submerging himself fully under the waves. His hair was a tangled mess and hopelessly knotted around the delicate strands of wire. After a few minutes of quiet cursing and suppressed laughter from Tias and Smythe, Eli pulled it loose.

Before he could fully unhook it from his right ear, however, the sound of light footsteps met his ears. Abraxus had waded from the sea and was now making his way back toward them, staff hooked around his shoulders. He seemed to carry himself a little straighter than he had done previously. Water ran in small rivulets off his coat, which he slung off and laid out near the ring of stones to dry. As he sat down, crossing his legs, Eli worked the curved wire a little looser and passed his circlet to Tias. Smythe had started to say something to Abraxus, but whatever was being said bypassed Eli entirely. The minute the stone had been removed from his line of sight, a sharp pain sliced through his head, just behind his eyes. It was gone as quickly as it had come, but Eli couldn't help the involuntary noise and subsequent flinch as it passed.

'Eli?' Tias had dropped his circlet and was looking worriedly at his brother. 'What's wrong?'

'Nothing,' Eli ground out, reaching up to press his fingers

to his temples. 'Must be the cold or something.' He knew as he said it that it wasn't true. This had been something else. Throughout his life, Eli had managed to break his arm and once, a few fingers. That break, the *snap* that reverberated through his body was a sensation he would never forget, and had no desire to experience again. And it was the closest thing he could compare to what had just happened. But this time, that snap had come from *everything* around him. The world had just cleaved itself in two, and mended not even a second later.

'It is not the cold,' Abraxus said. His own circlet had been threaded back onto his belt, the stone only just visible in his hand. 'Some, after seeing beyond what is in our usual range of sight, experience something like a disconnect.' He fixed Eli with an appraising look. 'Reality for you has just been thoroughly broken.'

'Happened to me too when I first looked,' Smythe said, gently tugging the blanket back over Eli's shoulder from where it had slipped. 'Hurt like the devil, but it won't happen again.'

'Good,' Eli said. He shuddered with the implication of what Abraxus had just said, and then resolutely put it from his mind. He could think about the confines of reality later.

Tias cast him one more concerned look, and then returned his attention to Eli's circlet. As Smythe continued to feed and tame the fire, Abraxus stretched out on the mat, lying flat on his back and gazing into the young night sky. It was still clear, although a flatter block of colour was drifting in from the west. Eli wondered if it would rain tomorrow.

No one spoke for a long time. Each was wrapped in their own thoughts. Phosphorescent streaks of colour kept dancing in Eli's mind, the feel of the wet scales against his legs. He wasn't sure at what point his thoughts wandered into the more insubstantial form of dreams, but he came to just as the sky overhead was touched with light. Underneath the blanket and curled up by the long fire, Eli felt incredibly warm and weighted. Beside him, Tias was fast asleep, one hand clutching the curve of his driftwood circlet. With little effort, Eli slipped back down into sleep again. As he fell further and further away, he comprehended soft voices conversing with one another.

'–is what she needs to see. To understand what her words did.'

'She won't come, Abraxus, there has to be–'

All meaning beyond that was entirely lost, and the words became the wash of the waves against the shoreline, the current pulling him away.

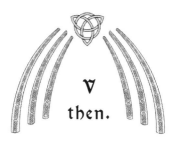

V

then.

A new sight.

He would love to claim it was thought out and carefully considered. Instead, it had been a complete accident that had left him shaking, fear crashing through his mind and body.

Some days, it felt as if he were still remembering how to breathe air. He still tasted the briny burn of the water he'd spend several hours bringing up sporadically. That first day had been unpleasant. The second had been only marginally better. He had lain on the deck of his ship, feeling the rock and swell of a patient sea beneath them. Too much had been hollowed out of him and then poured back in. The Roaring god was now with him always, a susurrating whisper in the back of his mind. He knew over time he would grow accustomed to sharing his consciousness. But for now, he lay on the deck and stared blankly into the sky.

The third and fourth days were a little more productive. The *Asherah* had sustained very little damage. The boards were a little more salt stained than they had been previously. The sails had a few more holes torn through. The ropes were, for now, crystalised with sea water that threatened to abrade his hands if he thought about grasping them. Abraxus had made what repairs he could find, moving around his ship with a ghostly step. The idea gave him pause. Why did he still walk like a dead man?

It wasn't until nine days had circled overhead that he finally gave them a heading. Despite being returned and renewed, Abraxus had come to realise he still had very human frailties. Supplies were a must if he were to embark on the voyage that the Roaring god had set out for him. He had subsisted in his convalescence on what he could find that remained below. But it was time to shake off whatever strange shock he was existing in and begin.

The accident happened the day after. Abraxus had discovered buried in the bottom of one of his old sea chests a flat, pearlescent white stone. It had a brittle quality, thin and fragile. A hole was eroded near the top, perfectly circular. Grains of sand clung inside a few cracks marring its surface. He remembered this one. He had found it on his last day. Saying farewell to the stretch of shingle beach that had been his playground had been more painful than he would care to admit. But the *pull* had been too strong to ignore. As he left, he had spotted something white glinting beneath clear water. This stone. It had been stored unthinkingly until now.

Once more, Abraxus felt that same deep instinct whilst holding the stone. Something was meant to happen. It was important somehow. He had pocketed it, and headed back out of his cabin for the wheel. The stone had remained in his coat until sundown, when he dropped anchor. In the distance, a hazy smudge told him he was nearing landfall.

Casting off his coat in the thick evening air, Abraxus heard a slightly heavier dull impact and recalled his lost find. He brought out the stone, and turned it over and over in his fingers. He headed for the bowsprit and perched himself on it, legs astride and dangling over the water. 'What are you for?' He said. His voice was still thickened with salt and disuse. And then on a whim, he brought it up to his eye.

Not a second later, Abraxus found himself in the water. With the *things* he had just seen. He fumbled with the stone, nearly dropping it. They vanished. Breaking the surface, he took in a few panicked breaths, casting about for what he had just seen. In the back of his mind, a voice drew him to the stone and away from his fear. He looked again.

After that, he never really stopped looking. In the small port town, he picked up sufficient supplies and several lengths of a copper-coloured wire. It was merely a practicality to have both hands free and to still watch the colourful ribbons of the Roaring god's servants. A few followed him as he crossed the oceans, and these he named.

It wasn't until the impulsive purchase of a mirror in a bazaar that he saw for the first time the marks on his skin. He found he could not be prouder to wear the scales of those that danced alongside the prow and stern of the *Asherah*. He set the sails for open waters and called out to those listening to follow.

VI
now.

Charts.
March, 1816.
Smythe.

Angorfa Harbour was strangely a very peaceful place to be at in an evening. The last of the sailors had cleared out, leaving behind them their ropes and tackle for the next day. Sails had been brought down, leaving the masts of ships like a forest of bare trees in the winter. Smythe sat at the end of one of the harbour walls, letting his legs dangle over the edge. He was leaning back, putting weight on complaining wrists, but he had no intention of moving anytime soon.

As the days continued to get longer, the sense of tentative hope also grew within the village. Finally, some luck seemed to be on the fishing crews' side, as they had discovered a seemingly untapped area to cast their nets overboard. The fact that it was even near Finfolk Point didn't dissuade. Smythe once again found himself marvelling a little at the hardiness of the folk of Porth Tymestl. He knew that direction was hard sailing, with hidden rip tides and currents ready to pull a ship asunder. And the lure of Finfolk Point itself was a siren call to most sailors. Smythe was only ever aware of Old Man Morgan completing the journey *through* the natural archway. Deep down, however, he suspected it might have been the last thing that John Kincarran ever attempted.

A light tread behind him brought him thankfully back to the

present. Before he could turn to see who had decided to offer him company that evening, they sat down heavily beside him. '*Nos da*,' Tias said.

'It is, isn't it?' Despite the bank of cloud that had rolled in over the land and resolutely decided to linger for several days, the weather hadn't been all too bad. Overcast was certainly better than storms, and Smythe found himself breathing out a silent thanks to whoever may be listening that the sea seemed not to roil as much of late.

'The Five's closed?' Tias phrased it like a question.

'Aye. Fancied a bit of a stretch. Not quite sure why I ended up here.'

'Well,' Tias' voice had taken on a more pedantic tone, 'I've been asked to ask you on behalf of some very thirsty fishermen when you'll be back and why you aren't there currently.'

'Ha, sendin' you with messages now are they?' Smythe said, looking over to the boy. Tias rolled his eyes, looking mildly irritated.

'It's because they've all noticed how much time I spend there. They're probably thinking I'm looking to step into your role eventually.'

'I heard Aron and Medwyn made you and Eli an offer?' Smythe said, shifting forward and shaking the cramped ache out of his wrists.

'Aye.' Tias looked out over the water. The evening was beginning to spill over the sky, already a line of darkness spanned the horizon. 'We should really give them an answer but...'

'You can't decide if that's your proper callin'?' Smythe said gently. Tias merely nodded in response.

Choosing his next words very precisely, Smythe said, 'There was a time when I thought that you'd follow your Da. The Kincarran line at the helm, sailing the waters of this bit of sea for years yet.' Tias looked at him, worrying his lip. 'But I think that if you chose to do something different–' he paused, meaning lying heavily in the minute space he'd given, 'then I think he would be very proud.'

'Really?' Tias' voice was so small and quiet Smythe could have mistaken it for the distant sound of the late breeze shifting the grass. He was looking down at his feet, and to the ebb and flow of the ocean below.

'Aye.' Smythe reached over and put a hand on Tias' shoulder. Tias glanced up at him and away again. 'He would.'

They sat together for a while after, neither speaking. It was the sort of silence that didn't need to be filled with words. Mere presence was enough.

Eventually, the sounds of raised voices met their ears. Smythe turned around in time to see a small group heading toward the harbour. 'I think they got bored waiting for your message to be answered,' he murmured conspiratorially to Tias, who grinned.

'Smythe! We got good spirits and coin, but we're missing an innkeeper!' Hywel's words carried down toward them.

'*Dwi'n dod, Dwi'n dod,*' *I'm coming, I'm coming,*' Smythe called back, getting to his feet. Tias started to laugh when the movement from the innkeeper garnered a cheer from the waiting men. They were both accepted into the fold, and made their way, now *en masse*, toward The Five-Pointed Compass. Hywel was asking after Eli and if the boots they'd lent him were suiting him. By the time they reached the inn, Smythe felt his already high spirits even further lifted. Tias appeared at ease in the large crowd, something that Smythe couldn't really remember happening before, chatting amicably back and forth with the sailors around him.

Smythe couldn't help but produce the key to the inn with a little flourish, causing another round of hearty cheers from the people assembled outside. Before too long, there was soup over the fire, crackers and cheese laid out along the bar and ale and mead flowing in plentiful supply. The inn seemed to glow from the life within, the chatter and snatches of shanties rising and falling. By his reckoning, there weren't many missing in the throng. Tias had disappeared from his side when they were swept into The Five. Smythe caught glimpses of him and his brother sitting at one of the long pews he'd liberated from Crow, seemingly deep in conversation with Aron and Medwyn. The looks of slight incredulity and a somewhat put-out expression on their faces had Smythe smiling to himself as he poured another mug.

In what had become his usual corner, sat Abraxus. The blue and yellow panels of the lantern above him cast out sparkling colour into the deeper shadows of the nook. Not many paid him much mind: he'd been in Porth Tymestl for so long now that he seemed to have become part of the scenery. And, Smythe sensed, there was more of an ease around him now on the inhabitants' part. Especially, it seemed, when no ill intentions toward the Kincarran boys had been made. Smythe had even watched Owen tentatively raise his mug in Abraxus' direction as he passed by. The baker was still pale, still haunted by the sudden loss of Gethin, but he'd been seen out more and more frequently of late, which everyone took as a good sign.

The night passed on outside, the initial furore of the gathering settling as the moon surely climbed higher, unseen between the clouds. Most had sunk low over their empty mugs and bowls, conversing in more gentle – albeit slightly slurred – tones. He'd lost track of Tias, Eli and now Abraxus. In a moment he deemed quiet enough, Smythe stole over to the table Abraxus had occupied. There was a slip of parchment propped up against an empty mug. Smythe unfolded it and huffed a laugh. All it said on it in Eli's handwriting was "downstairs". Next to it someone – he bet Tias – had doodled a little compass pointing west.

'Won't be a minute, lads,' Smythe called out to the occupants of the bar. 'You lot have nearly drunk me dry tonight!' Good natured jeers followed him down as he pulled open the trapdoor and headed for the passage. A flickering light cast orange-black shadows on the curved walls, throwing the carvings into a harsh relief. 'I open the inn at the behest of one Matthias Kincarran, and here you are, hiding.' Smythe put his hands on his hips, shaking his head.

'In my defence, I was just the messenger,' Tias said, barely visible between the stacks of shelves.

'And he's apparently a rubbish messenger, it took you ages to come back,' Eli rejoindered. He was lying on his front by the fire, the serpent scroll unfurled in front of him.

'At least I came back. Remember when you forgot you were delivering a message from Mam and went for a swim instead? I was stuck with Crow for *hours.*'

'Oh no, that was on purpose.'

'I knew it!'

Smythe looked to Abraxus, who had stolen his chair again. Abraxus just quirked an eyebrow, looking fondly exasperated. 'Did you suggest down here, or did they drag you?'

'I am inclined to say it was latter. Although, I believe that whatever is coming from them next is worth the privacy.' Abraxus' eyes flitted between the boys, who were still bickering from either ends of the room.

'Well, we'd better interrupt, this'll just devolve into name callin' and insults.' Smythe said. He raised his voice, 'Tias, come over here. Eli, stop being annoying.' Eli spluttered at that and was about to retort, but after a look from Abraxus, he sank back down, muttering a little mutinously.

Once they were settled around the hearth, Smythe spread his hands out as if to say "please, continue". Eli and Tias shared one of those looks that had an entire silent conversation in it, and seemed to reach some sort of agreement.

'Medwyn and Aron asked us to sail on their ships. Begin our work under them. Not uncommon for our age, and useful too given the catch recently.' Eli started. He was still looking at the scroll in front of him, delicately tracing the points of the sailfins on the serpent.

Smythe was relatively sure that both the boys had missed it, but at Eli's words Abraxus had locked up slightly, tensed for a blow that was about to fall.

'We refused them tonight,' Tias said.

'Mighty disappointed they were too,' Eli said distantly.

Abraxus uncoiled, the tension rolling off him. 'And why did you do that?'

Eli looked up finally from the drawing. 'Isn't it obvious?' He started slowly, looking briefly at Tias.

'We were wondering if we could apprentice to you?' Tias said it all in one breath, the words running into each other. Smythe wasn't sure if Abraxus took a moment to decipher what Tias had just said, or if it was plain shock that kept him quiet. For a man who could be so perceptive about some things, Smythe sometimes marvelled at the gaps in Abraxus' thought process. He'd been expecting the question ever since that first night in the *Gorwelion* Cellar – the name Eli had given it had irrevocably stuck.

Abraxus seemed to come out of his reverie and stared at Smythe. Smythe then decided that words weren't really necessary and shrugged. Abraxus in turn seemed to find this extremely unhelpful. He sighed and scrubbed a hand down his face. 'Yes, fine.'

A beat. '...yes?' Eli said.

'Fine?' Tias added.

'That is what I said,' Abraxus said ruefully.

Another beat. And then there was a lot of noise as both Eli and Tias shot to their feet, talking animatedly and excitedly over and to one another. Smythe started to laugh, leaning back in his chair and watching them fondly. Abraxus just seemed utterly bemused. After some minutes of incoherency from the Kincarran boys, Abraxus stood interposed himself between them. With a nod at Smythe, the innkeeper did the same. As one, they both stretched out their hands, Abraxus toward Eli and Smythe toward Tias.

'Ready?' Smythe asked.

'Aye.' Tias looked to his brother, who had already clasped Abraxus' elbow, forearms touching. 'I am.' And with that, he reached out his own hand.

'Charts!'

'Charts?'

'The best place to start if you want to be a Wayfinder.' Smythe searched through the shelves, stacking a mounting pile of scrolls into Tias' waiting arms. By the time he was satisfied with the amount he had collected, Tias could barely see where he was walking. 'We'll take 'em upstairs, there's more room to work.'

'Right.' Tias seemed to be having a little difficulty balancing the now very precarious pile. One slipped off the top and rolled open across the floor. 'Smythe–'

'I got it, don't worry.' Smythe said, a teasing lightness in his tone. Together they traipsed upstairs, Smythe finding Tias trying to navigate the short ladder into the barroom very amusing. It wasn't often he heard him curse.

The inn had been closed for the day – not that it mattered, nearly everyone was once again down on the seafront. Smythe estimated that the first people in from the sea would reach his door in no more than four or five hours. Plenty of time to start his first lesson with Tias.

'Set them down on the floor, lad.' Tias did as he was told, settling scrolls down and chasing after those that rolled away over the flagstones. 'First things first, let's get them all opened.' Soon enough the entire floor of The Five-Pointed Compass resembled a huge map, stretches of sea and broken off chunks of land creating strange new continents across the span of the room.

And so it began. Tias already had some knowledge of nautical charts, having watched his father closely as a boy. He could work out a bearing, read lines of longitude and latitude. He could have a good go at working out some meridians on the more complex charts.

The day passed in a haze of paper, compass needles and

Tias asking question after question. Outside, the sky burnished itself into copper and a light drizzle drifted in from over the sea. They stopped just as the sun set, Tias' eyes a little glazed, but his expression alight with curiosity and newly found knowledge. He leaned back against the bar, legs stretched out in front of him. One of the larger maps was spread over his knees, his fingers wandering up and down one of the lines of latitude marked there. 'Why charts?' He asked.

'Hm?' Smythe was busy rolling up the scrolls and tying string around the ones they had not had a chance to get to yet.

'Why start here?' Tias clarified, 'I'm not complaining,' he added hastily, 'but shouldn't we start with, I don't know, more details about Wayfinders?'

'You would assume correctly, lad.' Smythe dropped the scrolls in a neat stack and came to sit beside Tias. 'But you've been thoroughly inducted into this... this *outside* view, so I thought I'd start with the theory and work outwards.'

Tias considered his words, and then nodded. 'Aye, that makes sense.'

'And,' Smythe added, 'a good Wayfinder is someone who knows where they're going, but often where they are going, are places uncharted and unknown.'

'So... so you're saying that to be good at this,' Tias gestured around the inn, encompassing Smythe in the sweep of his arm, 'I have to know where I've been to know how to go where I'm going next?' He furrowed his brow. 'Wait, no that doesn't make–'

'It makes perfect sense.' Smythe said with a smile. 'You've got a knack for this already, I can tell.' He reached for the map across Tias' legs, deftly rolling it back up. 'And, I'll let you in on a secret.'

Tias leaned a little closer.

'This is much more preferable to what Abraxus will have Eli doing.'

'Why?'

Tempest.
March, 1816.
Eli.

'No!' The swell that was approaching them far too quickly for his liking was *massive*.

'Oh yes!' Abraxus stood at the helm of the *Asherah*, and if visibility hadn't been as atrocious as it was, Eli would have sworn blind that the man was grinning. 'Grab the halyard and get ready!'

'*Why?*' Eli had to shout to make himself heard over the crash and roar of the sea.

'That is an order from your captain, Elias. Haul on!' The deck of the *Asherah* rolled wildly beneath his feet, and Eli had to fight hard just to maintain his balance. The sea around them was a dark grey, churning with black shadows and broken foam. Rain lashed down from the sky and Eli had entirely given up trying to keep his hood up. He was soaked to the bone, freezing cold, a little frightened – though he would never admit that one – and completely in his element.

Reaching the line that Abraxus had directed him to, Eli waited for the next order. They crested the top of a wave and came crashing down the other side. The next that was approaching them rapidly was even larger than the last. Eli tightened his grip on the rope unconsciously.

'Ready?' Abraxus roared.

'Aye!' Eli braced himself for the shock of the soaking he knew was about to happen. As they began to climb the wave, the bowsprit pointing wildly upwards into the sky, Eli started to feel the infectious waves of delight pouring off Abraxus. He was surprised at how well the two of them had handled the *Asherah* in this tempest. Of course, he knew that there was something about the ship that was indefinably alive, but he had still had his apprehensions about going out onto a storm-tossed sea with a crew of merely two. But the *Asherah* had lived up to her name, and although the sky was occasionally lit up by streaks of lightning, and the roar of the waves and the taste of salt permeated all his senses, Eli had never felt safer aboard a ship before.

'Now!' They had nearly crested the wave. With an almighty pull, Eli put hand over hand on the halyard, the green and blue mainsail above diminishing slightly. He tied the knots off purely on instinct, catching a hold of the railing as they finally hit the peak. The bowsprit was pointing straight to the roiling sky above, and Eli felt the drop in his stomach as they began to plummet into the trough. With the impact of their descent, a huge cascade of water plumed over the deck, catching Eli squarely in its way. As was bound to happen eventually, Eli lost his footing and was sent sprawling over the deck. He heard Abraxus shout his name above the scream of the wind and crack of the ropes pulling themselves taut.

'I'm fine!' Eli yelled back, clambering back to his feet. He turned and looked up toward the quarter deck, Abraxus hanging over the wheel. 'Where are we going?'

'I have no idea!' Abraxus called back. There was slightly mad joy on his face, and Eli knew that if he looked in a mirror at that moment, he would see the same expression reflected back at him. 'Shall we find out?'

'Aye!' Eli turned back to the main deck. The next wave came on quickly, a dare from the ocean surrounding them. Eli planted his feet firmly and stared down the wall of water. 'Here we go.'

Toast.
April, 1816.
Tias.

If it hadn't been for the candle flickering, the cooling wax hissing slightly as the flame danced, Tias would not have noticed his brother's return. He reached up and cupped his hand around it, turning to look down toward the door. Eli was currently battling a little with the wind in order to close and latch the door. Eventually, he slammed it closed and just stood, leaning against it for a second. He was soaked through, his clothes dripping dismally onto the worn stones of the cottage floor.

Tias stood, the little chair he'd occupied now for most of the day scraping back with a harsh sound. It seemed to jolt Eli out of whatever stupor he was falling into. 'I see what Smythe means,' Tias said wryly.

'Huh?' Eli currently didn't seem to possess any more speech in him than that.

'That what I'm doing is preferable.' He came over to lean on the railing that guarded the balcony from the drop. 'How was it today?'

'Abraxus seems to have a hideous talent for only taking us out when the weather is truly just *foul*.' Eli lifted his arms slightly and flicked them downwards. Spatters of water sprayed over the stone. 'I am *soaked*.'

Tias fought down a smile, knowing that anything but sympathy would elicit some form of unnecessary reaction from his brother. Although it was tempting. 'There's bread and jam by the fire. Kettle's full too.'

'Excellent.' The sound of layers upon layers of wet fabric hitting the floor reached Tias as he turned back to his desk. Most of the chipped wooden surface was covered by a scroll of parchment, thick in stock and curling slightly at the edges. Where this one differed though from the previous charts and documents Smythe had shown him, that this one was still mostly blank. Picking up his pen once more, Tias started working out the nautical bearing he'd been calculating before Eli came home.

'D'you want any?' Eli called from downstairs. There was a muffled quality about his voice and Tias surmised that Eli was eating jam straight from the spoon again. The homely smell of toasting bread wafted gently through Roseate Cottage.

'Probably.' Tias called back distractedly. He honestly couldn't remember if he'd eaten today. Ever since Smythe had set him this project, it had consumed him. Every waking hour – and some of the hours that were meant to be dedicated to sleep too – Tias had debated, planned, crossed out and started again. Once, he'd even gone so far as to throw his fourth plan into the fire for the grim satisfaction of watching it go up in flames. It needed to be perfect. The main issue was that Smythe was back to his old tricks again.

'A project, something for you to work on.' Smythe had said, handing Tias a ream of blank parchment. 'Take your time. Have confidence.'

'What's it for?' Tias had asked, feeling the shiver of anticipation that a new task always gave him.

'I want a chart. Of this coastline, around Porth Tymestl. As to what it's for...' Smythe here had merely winked and said conspiratorially, 'Somethin' *important*.'

This, naturally, had not helped Tias' near obsessive levels of perfectionism. However, this attempt, he was feeling more confident about. The contours of the cliff edge and demarcations of paths seemed a lot more cohesive and clearer to him than previous tries.

He was just adding in some cross hatching to show the steep drop down to *Tua'r Môr* Bay when Eli called him down with, 'It's mostly burnt, but still good.' As Tias stood once more, he rolled his shoulders and neck, eliciting a series of cracks and crunches that he felt he should be more concerned about. Scaling the ladder, he joined Eli by the hearth and started to liberally spread jam across the 'mostly burnt' piece of toast.

'Still working on that chart?' Eli asked, licking his fingers.

'Aye.' Tias cast a glance back up to the balcony. He'd left the desk candle burning, knowing that tonight would be another late one.

'Any idea..?'

'None whatsoever.' Tias shrugged. 'There'll be a reason, there always is.'

'Well, whatever it is, just don't keep me up, I'm exhausted.' Eli finished off his toast and stood. He ruffled his hair, still damp from the lashing rain and sea spray. 'Next time, remind me to tie it back.' With that, he headed for the ladder and within two minutes Tias heard the creak of the bed frame as Eli undoubtedly fell face first onto the blankets.

After making sure Eli had latched the door properly and pulling the shutters closed, Tias slipped back upstairs and resettled himself at the desk. He'd brought another chunk of bread up to keep him going. Outside, the wind picked up its voice and began to whisper in through the windows and under the door. Rain pounded down overhead, and for a time all the world shrunk away into the small puddle of golden candlelight, haloing around the chart. Tias watched as, seemingly on its own, land and sea began to form itself over the paper.

It was well past midnight when Tias found his own bed. The rain had ceased, allowing him to hear the distant crash of the sea against the rocky coastline. Dousing the candle, Tias was asleep in seconds.

ABRAXUS ELIJAH HONEY

Moonlight.
May, 1816.
Abraxus.

Looking back on the past few weeks Abraxus had been forced to realise one indisputable truth. Before docking in Porth Tymestl, before bones and caverns, before the Kincarrans, he had been lonely. The ache that he now associated with those memories of being alone on a wide sea seemed nearly unbearable. He couldn't bring himself to fathom how he'd managed to stay sane during those isolated years. With a wry smile, he wondered if perhaps he hadn't. After all, just below him on the foredeck was Abraxus' apprentice, his Wayfinder and *his* apprentice. How the tides changed everything that he once considered normal.

Shifting his grip a little on the wheel, he let them drift further out to sea, the waves lapping at the hull with a soft, rhythmic shushing. The night was somewhat clouded, offering a little warmth and the occasional snatch of stars. The early May wind blew in off the land, now a mere dense black line behind them. After several days of seemingly non-stop storm, it was a welcome reprieve to lightly lean on the wheel and let his attention wander. He gave most of the control to the *Asherah*, knowing she would steer them right. Abraxus closed his eyes, and listened to the sounds of a world that, for the moment, was utterly perfect.

'–and so there I was, standing less than clothed in none other than the *Empress' bedroom*.'

Abraxus unwittingly made a sound that could have either been a laugh, or a huff of exasperation. Smythe's voice drifted back to him as their heading changed from west to more southerly. He knew this story inside and out. It was one of Smythe's favourites. It was also completely untrue.

'An' then from outside the door I hear this almighty thumpin' and I think to myself, well here come the guard, you're in for it now Stooger.'

Leaning forward, Abraxus watched with detached amusement as Smythe waved his hands expressively. Eli was leaning against the side of the railing, seemingly rapt. Tias, on the other hand, wore an expression of amused disbelief, fiddling with a length of rope that Abraxus had 'put away' near the mainmast.

'The guard come burstin' in, armed to the teeth, and I look around, thinking. And then it comes to me–' Smythe paused for dramatic flair. Eli leaned in closer.

'The window.' Abraxus mouthed the words as Smythe said them, shaking his head.

'The window?'

'Aye, so I run for the window and, remembering there's one of those reflecting pools beneath the chambers, I j–'

'Smythe, how much of this is actually true?' Tias broke in, clearly unable to hold himself back any longer.

'All of it!' Smythe said indignantly. He paused for a second before adding. 'Well, most of it.'

'Most of it?' Tias pressed, smiling openly now.

'He once visited an Empress' court at my behest. That is as far as the truth goes.' Abraxus had left the wheel, murmuring quietly to the *Asherah* as he did so, and was descending the stairs.

'See, that sounds more interesting than what you were just telling us,' Tias said.

'Just once,' Smythe started, whirling around to face Abraxus as he joined them. 'Just *once* I'd like to finish that story without you ruining the – the *immersion*.'

Eli raised his hand, 'I was enjoying it, Smythe.'

Smythe spread his arms in a gesture that clearly meant a sarcastic *diolch* and shot Abraxus and Tias a dirty look. 'I'll write it down for you Eli.' He spoke over the muffled sounds of laughter now coming from both Abraxus and Tias. 'At least you appreciate a good yarn.'

Abraxus closed the distance between them and clapped a good-natured hand onto Smythe's shoulder. 'No, no it is a very good story. Very distracting.' He said it with a slightly side eyed glance to Tias, who was now very clearly struggling to contain his amusement.

'Get you going. Don't you have a ship to steer?'

With a final grin to the boys, Abraxus raised his hands in mock surrender and turned back toward the quarter deck. Below, the sea was a mirror for the sky, smooth and onyx. The only disturbances came from the foaming wake they left behind them. It was tempting to take out his stone and cast around in the waters for any sign of the serpents, but ever since that night he had revealed their secrets to Eli and Tias, they seemed to have kept mostly away and in the deeper reaches of the ocean.

They were turning for their stretch of coastline when Smythe joined Abraxus by the wheel. 'I have decided to forgive you,' he said magnanimously.

'How kind.'

'How's it goin'? With Eli?'

'As well as I expected,' Abraxus said somewhat evasively.

'Perfectly then?'

'Aye.' His voice was quiet, but he knew Smythe had heard him. There was a second of blank introspection, but then he pulled himself back and looked to his Wayfinder. 'And Tias?'

'Studious to the point of concern.' Smythe said wryly. 'Look.' He pointed down to where Tias was sitting. He managed to find four different lanterns from somewhere and had arranged them in a semicircle around him. Before him were scattered papers, nautical instruments, ink, and a heavy tome or two.

'The chart?'

'Something to behold, truly.' Smythe let out a long breath, tilting his head up toward the night sky. He let the light breeze stir his hair, closing his eyes. 'When are you thinking of doin' it?'

'Soon.' Was all Abraxus offered. 'If I am honest, sooner than

I would have expected. They both have taken to this with far greater aptitude than I could have imagined.'

'Really could not have asked for better,' Smythe said. There was an odd note in his voice that made Abraxus look at him. Smythe's eyes were no longer closed, nor looking toward the unknowable sky. Instead, he was looking down toward the foredeck. 'Look.' Following his gaze, Abraxus' sight alighted on Eli, elbows resting on the railing and looking out over the water.

And there it was. Something so open and wistful in his expression. His eyes seemed to be a long way off, looking toward the shadowed horizon. A cloud slid by, revealing the pale light of the moon but for a moment. The light glanced off the water, turning the crests of waves into pure silver. Abraxus watched as an utterly unrestrained smile crossed Eli's face. He watched, and saw a mirror from many centuries ago.

VII
then.

Kith and kin.

The message arrived, as it usually did, through a half-remembered dream. Fragments of colour and shape drifted through his consciousness for the entire day, as evasive as smoke. The more he tried to grasp it, the more it eluded him. In the end, Abraxus found himself content to forget it, leave it to the erosion of memory and continue with his aimless wandering.

Before the bowsprit of the *Asherah,* the cerulean ocean spread out endlessly before him. Only the dark slash of the horizon broke the vista, and each day, Abraxus found himself willing the edge of the world to draw just that little bit closer. But instead, control was wrested from his hands and the *Asherah* was pulled by the whim of a current held fast by an ancient grip. Three nights prior, the earth deep beneath the waters had heaved and rolled. It displaced the unquiet seas and the effects were sent cascading in ever growing strength toward an inlet of unsuspecting coastline. Toward this unknown place Abraxus was headed.

Soon, stars began to climb overhead, and the day slunk down into pastels, giving way to deepest blue on that unreachable line. Leaning heavily on the wheel, steering mostly with his elbows, Abraxus gazed off into the distance, his mind – for once – beautifully blank.

The fragments coalesced into one mosaic image. A village,

decimated. Saline flood water brackish and thick with debris. The ocean recoiling in horror at what it had wrought, anger coursing through the sea currents toward the restless earth beneath. And running like a vein of gold through it all, two words. Separate, but irrevocably linked. *Another. Kin.*

Abraxus' own whims were, he felt, sometimes drowned by those of the Roaring god that now pervaded his mind on a daily basis. But his stubbornness had not been diminished, and despite this sudden rush of understanding, of something new and so tantalising, he resolutely set the wheel and started making the evening preparations for bedding down. As he dropped the anchor, he thought that the ripples prolonged themselves out over the mirror water's surface for just a little longer than they should. 'Tomorrow,' he intoned lowly. 'I will look tomorrow.'

Earthen song.

He arrived by boat. The long, rickety dock had long since been destroyed, wiped away by the waters with such a playful fury that she felt sickened by it. All that was left were the rotten wooden stumps that once held the entire structure aloft. Broken teeth, embedded into a muddy maw.

In amongst all the filth and desolation, the colours the ship sailed by seemed like a beacon. An unwarranted spark of anger flickered up to life within her marrow. Taking a breath, she cooled it to a sharp flint, and stood, ankle deep in the water that still lingered, watching the ship slow. There seemed to be no crew aboard.

The anchor splashed down, the noise muted amongst the death-heavy silence. A small rowboat followed, and its sole occupant began to pull in strong strokes toward her. She buried her toes into the loosened earth, and listened. She did not expect to hear what came next. *Another. Kin.*

As he waded his way toward her, she knew instinctively that he was not like her, but in some ways, closer than a sibling. His head was wrapped in seaweed and sea fret, salt coursing through his veins as surely as blood. She flexed her hands slightly, and felt the cracks open there. From inside her closed fist, reddish golden light seeped through the gaps in her fingers. She waited, knowing that this was the first meeting this man had had with another like them. She wondered vaguely what his manner would be.

'I have been sent to help.' A voice like the tide rolled over her, and she suppressed a shiver. *Another.*

'From the waters, or from the earth?' She questioned. Their languages were dissimilar, but they understood one another perfectly. She no longer questioned this. He seemed unaware.

'The Roaring one.' Came the reply.

She nodded, thinking. 'Welcome to both you and the Roaring god.' She pressed her hand, palm down, over her heart and inclined her head slightly. 'We – I was not aware that they had claimed another.'

'Are you...' The first bit of hesitancy that she had seen from this stranger made her smile. Unsure, but honest in his unknowing.

'I am like you, and wholly different.' She flexed her hands again, opening the cracks that had begun to slowly seal themselves again. The man's mismatched eyes widened as hot, liquid light dispelled from underneath her skin. 'I too am marked, but not by the Roaring one.' She canted her head, 'perhaps you will come to guess.'

The man stared openly for another moment, before physically seeming to shake himself back into the present. 'I thought I had seen all...' He murmured, seemingly to himself.

'The world is wider than you know, friend. There is more than salt water on this earth.' She turned, the cuffs of her salwar soaked through. 'The water is still high throughout the village. Perhaps you can send it back to where it belongs.' She knew that he was following her, and knew that the water that lapped around them let him pass easily where she had to struggle. But the earth remained firm beneath her, and she knew that they would not let her lose her footing.

They worked together until the moon crested at its midpoint in the sky. Beneath its silver shimmer, finally they sat, aching with the work done that day. Only the soft glow from the fissures in her skin permeated the inky blue world. 'The Molten god welcomes you,' she said, barely above a whisper. 'And so do I.' She did not turn to face him, but felt his gaze upon her. 'You may call me Rama.'

'Abraxus Elijah Honey.'

'There is much you have yet to see, Master Honey. Much more world to explore, and many more to meet who guard it like you and I.' Now, she turned to him, and watched the silver moonlight reflected in his right eye. She wondered how and where else he was marked by the Roaring god.

'Take me over the horizon,' he said.

'Over the edge,' Rama said, 'and then further.'

VIII
now.

Canvas.
May, 1816.
Eli.

That morning was the first where the frost didn't turn the grass and cobbles into crystalline rivers and lakes. Instead, the dew was thick, beading on the heather, gorse and grass. It caught the sun, and it seemed to Eli as if the world was suddenly more vibrant; in-focus in a way that it had not been since the onslaught of the winter. He felt the green around him pull in a deep breath, releasing the last vestiges of that sharp chill of those months in the delicate sky.

He stood barefoot by the low garden wall. The heat from the clay mug he cradled almost seemed to bite into his fingers. Despite the undoubted fineness of the morning, the sun was yet to give out its warmth. Eli smiled a little as he sipped the tea. The fragrant blossom taste seemed to mirror the budding spring around him.

Away to the east, the sky was quickly becoming a clear and brilliant blue. Like the rest of the world, it too was shaking off its winter's repose. Beyond the stout walls of *Angorfa* Harbour glittered the sea. It was as flat as water in a well, and seemed just as deep and unknowable.

This, for Eli, was a rare occasion. He was not, by admission of everyone who knew him, an early riser. There had been many a time when Eli had only just made it down to the harbour before his Da's ship weighed anchor. But since he started working with Abraxus, Eli had begun to wake with the dawn. He knew logically that it was because when he returned from a day on the waves, all he managed to do was eat something and then promptly collapse into bed. On some days the sun had barely set before he had slipped away from the land of the waking.

He'd left Tias sleeping. His brother was sprawled out over the blankets, not even seeming to have changed into his nightclothes. Ink stained his fingertips black, seeping down to the edge of his wrist where he had accidentally dragged it through words still drying. There was paper everywhere: on the floor, across the desk and some larger leaves hanging like rugs over the bannister. Eli had carefully stepped around the mess, almost overbalancing more than once. It had been even trickier to navigate the ladder one-handed, intent on not spilling Tias' mug of tea all over himself and his brother's hard work. As Eli had set the mug down beside Tias' bed, he quickly studied a few of the more visible pieces of parchment. Curves of inlets, sweeps of bay and beach, dense crosshatching for rock and harbour wall. He couldn't make too much sense of it, but knew that Tias found a perfect harmony in the chaos.

A breath of spring air cleared away some of Eli's sleep-softened thoughts. He buried his toes a little deeper into the unkempt grass, feeling the cold loam cling to the soles of his feet. From over the sea, a breeze picked up. Sailing conditions would be perfect today, and Eli found himself wondering whether he should get a head start on Abraxus and head down to the secret cove to make ready. It would also serve to impress, another thought Eli was particularly partial to.

Turning back to Roseate Cottage, a minute movement caught in the corner of his eye. Down at *Angorfa* Harbour, someone was moving. It was still early enough that all the fishing crews would be at home, pulling on woollens and portioning out copious amounts of porridge. Not only that, but the figure was small, with an unsteady roll to their gait. For a moment, Eli thought that one of the few of Porth Tymestl's younger inhabitants had slipped the watch of their parents and headed for the best place to play. But then the figure walked with purpose along the wall and knelt down slowly to unhitch a mooring line. With a rush of understanding, Eli looked on as Old Man Morgan threw the mooring rope down into his skiff, *Esgyll Gwerin*, and began the precarious climb into it. Within the minute, the single white sail unfurled and the skiff began its slow dance out into the open waters. He took a north-westerly heading, and was soon lost behind the sweep of the coastline and the increasing glare of the risen sun on the ocean.

Eli watched the horizon a little longer, waiting for the white speck to reappear. Surely Old Man Morgan wasn't going fishing? Whilst the catch had improved again lately – something Eli and Tias still suspected Abraxus had a hand in – all crew available were still pulling rope and hours to stock up for the summer smokehouses. Perhaps, he reasoned, Old Man Morgan wanted to lend his many years of expertise and return to the job he had loved during his stronger years.

Resolving to mention it to someone later, Eli turned once more for the cottage. As he pushed open the door, he caught Tias clambering down the ladder. His hair was stuck up every which way and Eli could tell that he was barely awake, functioning on a subconscious routine. 'There's tea by your bed.'

'Oh.' Tias paused on the ladder, took a full three seconds to comprehend the thought, and went back up.

'We're out of bread,' Eli called up, glancing into the clay pot where they kept supplies. 'Fancy a trip to Owen's?'

Ten minutes later found the pair of them striding down into Porth Tymestl proper. Tias kept yawning into the scarf he'd somewhat haphazardly looped around his neck. The morning rush was beginning to wash out to sea by the time Owen's bakery came into view. From the open hatch, the mouth-watering aroma of freshly baked bread drifted down through the street. Eli found himself quickening his pace.

Owen was still a noticeably paler shadow of the man he had once been. His face was thinner, his blond hair long and thrown back into a messy braid. But there was still some jovial light left in his cornflower blue eyes that not even the grief of losing Gethin could dull. '*Bore da* boys.'

'Morning Owen.' Eli dug in his pocket. The amount of coin he pulled from the slightly sand filled interior was small. 'Whatever this will get us.' He shoved the coins over the counter, scoring tracks in the flour dusted there.

'Mam still not back then?' Owen called as he turned to rummage through the shelves.

'No. We're not too sure when she'll even *be* back,' Tias said, looking toward the coastal path just past the graveyard.

A letter had arrived yesterday, alongside an openly concerned Efa. The letter had briefly stated that the pass was still blocked, but the clearing process was going well. As Tias read it aloud, Eli watched Efa's mouth grow more and more pinched. She let out a barely audible huff as Tias folded the missive and carefully placed it behind their father's lantern atop the mantlepiece.

'I am not one to speak ill of people, particularly not your mother, but I cannot pretend I'm not... *disappointed* with her efforts.' Looking between them, she continued. 'If it had been my children, or any family at all, I would have braved the edges of a map to get back. Especially if they were alone.'

'She is trying,' Eli began. 'But...' His voice trailed away. How could he explain to Efa, or anyone, that Ffion didn't *want* to be in Porth Tymestl anymore? On the nights when exhaustion crept in before sleep, Eli found himself wondering if the pass was as severely blocked, if the route around it was as uncharted as their mother had led them to believe.

Efa took his failing words, however, as emotion. 'Oh *cariad.*

She'll be back soon. You know you can always get something warm to eat and some comforts with me and Medwyn.' She came forward and cupped Eli's cheek. Her eyes seemed to study his face, before flicking to his brother and doing the same. 'Both of you, so grown up now. Whatever it is you are doing,' and here she leaned in with a conspiratorial smile, 'it's doing you the world of good. Despite however much Medwyn complains that he missed out on having Kincarran blood back on the fishing crews.' Her hand dropped, and there was a pang of something lost, sharp and sudden in Eli's chest. Efa sighed, and made to leave. As she passed the raised workbench by the door, her hand dipped into her pocket, and, in a quick motion, left a neat column of coin on the roughened wood.

With Efa's coin now spent on hopefully several days' supply of bread, Eli cast his gaze up and down the street. Smoke curled in a thin stream from The Five-Pointed Compass' chimney stack. A shadow passed by the window, and Eli wondered if that was Abraxus getting ready for the day. The man didn't particularly keep a punctual schedule. Eli could be called to sail at a moment's notice, sometimes at the break of day, sometimes as the sun lay down for the night.

'Here y'are.' Owen came back to the counter, pushing a large loaf over, followed by two thick slices of bread, topped with melting butter and a fried egg. 'From Crow's own hens this morning.'

'Owen, that's–'

'That,' Owen stated, speaking over Tias' protestations, 'is what that coin will get you.' He fixed them with a look that brooked no argument. 'We've been hungry too long. Take it, and eat it under this rare and fine sky.' Some more of that old light re-entered Owen's expression.

'*Diolch.*' Eli said earnestly. In the slowly deepening day, the taste of fresh bread with melted butter leaking through it danced on Eli's tongue. He closed his eyes, took in a deep breath and savoured every moment.

ABRAXUS ELIJAH HONEY

The planking beneath his feet had been warmed by the sun. Their colour shone out in complement to the gentle heat slumbering there. Walking with a cat-like grace that only really seemed to come to him on the water, Eli padded down the quarter deck stairs toward the mainmast. A cool wind came in over the sea, making the blue-green shot sails billow. Beneath the rush of the waves ran the creak and snap of canvas and rope. The old shanty and lullaby of his childhood, picked up and played once more. Eli turned his face to the sun. Today, the world was at peace with itself and with him.

Behind the wheel, Abraxus stood unmoveable. Only the slight rocking motion of his hands on the spokes differentiated him from a statue found in a long crumbling city. The lesson for this particular day appeared to be working on Eli's intuition. He had not been given a single direct order nor any hint of suggestion from the moment the wind took the sails and pulled them out onto open seas. At first it had been a little disconcerting; serving on his father's ship he had been precious more than a crews' hand, always at the beck and call of his father's sailors. But aboard the *Asherah*, he had apparently been promoted to first mate alongside still-learning apprentice.

All was calm. Eli turned an appraising eye over the ropes, the sails, even the deck itself – Smythe forever complaining that what it really needed was a good scrubbing – and could find nothing amiss. He cast a glance back to Abraxus. The man's expression was as unreadable as ever, but Eli could imagine that there might be a softer light in the man's mismatched eyes.

As the sun reached its zenith and passed over, staining the sky an even more unfathomable blue, their compass needle continued to steadily point north-west. The heading they picked each day seemed almost random: Abraxus would close his eyes and cant his head to the side and listen to the breath of the wind, or the sigh of the sea and then he and Eli followed it toward its unknown terminus. Leaning his elbows against the sun and salt bleached railing, Eli wondered if Abraxus knew that, if they continued this heading, they would eventually reach Finfolk Point. He was about to call out, the question half formed on his lips, when, for the second time that day, his eye was pulled to something out of place.

It took merely a second to comprehend what it was, and only another for Eli to feel his knees go weak. White-knuckled and shaking like he had been doused in icy water, Eli gripped the railing, peering below into the cerulean ocean. All his words seemed to abandon him. The waves made it – *him* – their plaything, sickeningly bobbing up and down on the water.

With one trembling hand, he pointed. It seemed to take all his strength to do so. Whether Abraxus had seen him crack, or if the *Asherah* had conveyed his distress to her captain, he would never know. 'Eli?' The question came as a sharp snap, worry pervading the words and whetting themselves into points of anger.

'In the...' Eli's voice fled once more. Distantly, the sound of quick footsteps came down the quarter deck stairs toward him.

'What–' Abraxus stopped abruptly. And before Eli could do anything more, witness this further, Abraxus had pulled him away and into a fierce embrace. Eli pressed his face into the rough leather of Abraxus' coat, gripping the back. Beneath his fingers, the worn surface had crystallised with tiny shards of salt.

'Go below. Do not look. Do not come back up until I call you.' Abraxus' voice reverberated against Eli's ear, soothing all too reminiscent of his Da. Unbidden, the aching sting of tears started in his eyes. 'Go.' He felt himself propelled away.

His feet seemed made of stone, clumsy and dragging. Behind him, the sound of a coat being shucked off, the rattle of a rope ladder thrown overboard. And the door closed, shutting out the golden blue light of the afternoon. Entombed in the narrow galley of the *Asherah*, Eli stumbled against the wall, desperate for an anchor. He should have said. A simple word would have sufficed. But he had forgotten. Why didn't he say *anything*?

Outside, a splash, then silence. Abraxus was a strong swimmer. He would reach the body quickly. Eli wondered if he would wrap Old Man Morgan in canvas for the journey home, stitch it up with kelp and give the old seafarer the burial he deserved.

Shanty.
May, 1816.
Smythe.

The crowd was three deep as Smythe pushed toward the precipice of the harbour wall. He didn't bother muttering any apologies as he employed his elbows to his favour. Now visible around the headland, the blue and green sails of the *Asherah* caused a ripple of muttering, echoing out through those gathered.

'Aron. *Aron*, let me see it.' Smythe had reached the front, the toes of his boots edging the void. Wordlessly, Aron handed over the ragged piece of parchment. His eyes were fixed on the slowly approaching ship.

Smythe ripped open the parchment, nearly tearing it along the touch softened fold. There, in a shaky hand, were the words Smythe had heard racing through Porth Tymestl as he had hurried to *Angorfa* Harbour. He hadn't wanted to believe them true, but here they were. Indelible as the words carved upon a gravestone.

The *Asherah* drifted into *Angorfa* Harbour for the first time, and Smythe knew in his very bones, it bore news. Abraxus would never give up the safety and seclusion of the hidden cove unless he absolutely must. Another cascading ripple of whispers played through the crowd, some repeating the words written on the paper now crumpled in Smythe's hand, some wondering about the ship now drawing inexorably near. Those who had arrived first to the harbour borne by the whispers of rumour were the most silent. Those who had arrived to watch an unfamiliar ship make port felt the chill, pervasive and cloying, of something terribly wrong.

Without another word, Smythe turned his back on the open ocean and headed in tandem with the ship along the harbour wall. Reaching an open mooring point, Smythe numbly worked free the coils of rope, and stood ready and waiting. After a moment, the weight of it lessened a little in his hands. Turning, Smythe saw Medwyn, Aron, Marcus and several other sailors take their positions along it. Smythe stood a little taller, lifting his chin in some unknown act of defiance.

Within minutes, the *Asherah* was docked and secured. Abraxus stepped away from the wheel and seemed to collapse in on himself. It was like watching a man return to consciousness after the blissful peace of silence and black. He walked down the stairs and kicked over the gangplank. It rattled against the stone until Edwina stilled it with her foot. Of Eli, Smythe saw no sign.

Abraxus stood at the edge of the gangplank, looking vaguely down into the people gathered there. His eyes roamed over them, settling on Smythe. There was a helplessness there that Smythe had so rarely seen. They contemplated each other, unwillingly locked into a silent and stretching conversation. And then Abraxus turned away, over the deck, to where a blanket wrapped bundle lay. With a barely audible grunt of effort, Abraxus lifted it into his arms and came back toward them. Smythe met him halfway, helping lift some of the burden. Together, they laid the body out on the harbour wall, those gathered parting and making room.

The very air seemed to have left them. All were caught in this void, breathless and grappling for reason, for understanding. The letter drifted on the late afternoon breeze, grazing people's ankles, until it quietly fell into the sea and sank. It didn't truly matter: the words were branded into the minds of those that had read it. Abraxus knelt by the body, lips moving in silent prayer or apology, Smythe didn't know. Someone, somewhere, had started to cry.

That first sound of human life, of something that was the tangible human emotion of grief, brought the air back into everyone's lungs. As one, the crowd rippled, swayed and then, inevitably, collapsed. Questions, rapid and urgent, ran like wildfire through them, some jostling closer. As the noise crescendoed, Smythe found he could stand the uncertainty no longer. With one decided movement, he pulled back the blanket.

Cynfor Morgan looked somehow younger in death. All the cares and lines of his face had smoothed. Peaceful, Smythe realised. It should have offered him some comfort, and he knew logically that later on when the hurt had faded to an ache, it would. But right now, the wound was new and raw. Another gone to the waves, to the locker of salt. It was enough to make the mass quieten again. Confirmation, it seems, stuns the very thoughts from a head. Cynfor's hair was still wet.

'Make way.' Crow appeared from the depths of the crowd. His black robes drifted behind him with the breeze, making him look more corvid like than ever. He cast one appraising eye at Abraxus, who had not yet moved, and then mirrored him in kneeling down. In his officious voice, he administered the last rites, intoning the 'amen' at the end. Several others joined in, others mouthing it silently. Crow bowed his head, and then fluidly stood once more. In a death, he had purpose. 'We shall not leave our friend here on the wall like carrion. Bring him to the church. We can proceed from there.'

Faceless and shadowed sailors did as Crow asked, and Old Man Morgan was brought home on the shoulders of those he

helped raise. The procession – for that was what it was now–
followed, heads low and whispers rife. Smythe stayed. Wordlessly,
he reached out a hand. Abraxus took it, gripping the innkeeper's
forearm to bring himself to standing. Once again, they conversed
with no words. Smythe pressed a hand into Abraxus' shoulder, as
solid and dependable as he could offer.

'Too many, Smythe.' The words were deep, and Smythe shivered
involuntarily. Abraxus continued, 'Too many have gone to the
seafloor. This must end soon.' Mismatched eyes roved over the
little village, and Smythe saw that there was a wet sheen to them.
'How can one such small place know so much *suffering*?' There
was an edge to his voice now, one that told Smythe just how tired
Abraxus was. How close he felt to despair.

'And yet,' he said softly, 'they have not given up.' Taking a
fierce lowness into his words, Smythe pressed on. 'They remain.
They stay and they fight. These people need you here, whether
they fully know or accept that. So, you stay, and you *fight*
Abraxus Elijah Honey. D'you hear me?'

Tears rolled down the ancient seafarer's face. Eyes too old
looked at Smythe. A nod, a slight setting of the shoulders. 'I
stay.' It was said barely above a whisper, but it was all Smythe
needed. He nodded, and removed his hand.

'The boy?'

'He found him, Smythe. Off the starboard side.' There was
still a hollowness to Abraxus' words.

'By the gods.' Smythe looked toward the *Asherah*. All her
magic seemed to fade amongst the other fishing vessels. Just
another ship amongst sisters awaiting their job. 'Is he–'

'Smythe!' The innkeeper felt his heart lurch in his chest at the
distressed call of his name. He wheeled around in time to all
but catch Tias as he skidded to a halt beside them. Tias gripped
his arm, Smythe trying not to wince as the boy unconsciously
dug his fingernails into the skin. 'I saw – coming up from the
harbour, and they said a ship with blue sails and – they had a

body.' Tias looked completely frantic, terror racing through his features. Smythe could feel him shaking minutely.

It took him too long to discern what Tias was thinking. In his silence, Tias' eyes looked from Abraxus to Smythe and back again, his face rapidly losing colour. 'No. Please, no.'

'No, *no* Matthias, it isn't Eli.' Smythe felt utterly sick at the implication Tias must have started believing as he ran down to the harbour. He turned imploring to Abraxus, who was now nearly as pale as Tias himself. 'Where is he, Abraxus?'

'Below. I shall fetch him.' Abraxus seemed to make a move toward Tias, but then thought differently and hurried away. The boy's legs were shaking now, and Smythe made the decision for both of them to sit, guiding Tias down into a slightly awkward slumped kneeling position.

'Who?' Tias' voice was made from spider silk and broken glass.

'Cynfor. Old Man Morgan.' Smythe felt the barest tug of a smile at his lips as he used the man's epithet. Not many of the younger ones in Porth Tymestl had actually known Old Man Morgan's first name.

'*Why?*' Tias was gazing at him now pleadingly.

'For that,' Smythe murmured, 'we don't have much of an answer.' He cast about, looking for the paper that had held Old Man Morgan's last words. Remembering it was lost to the water, Smythe closed his eyes and recounted: "I go to home as the sun rises. I go to the place that was named for my deeds. Please, do not grieve. I am at peace. I wish you all a fond farewell.' He left a note weighted down near to where his old mooring spot was.'

Tias remained still and quiet after that, staring blankly at the point where the thin band of horizon met the water. He only roused at the sound of a door closing gently from aboard the *Asherah*.

Too many, Abraxus had said. Smythe could see that sentiment now weighing on Eli's shoulders. One village could see so much death in its time: this was natural. But one boy? *Too many*, rang Abraxus' words in Smythe's head.

If it hadn't been for Abraxus' guiding arm around him, Smythe felt sure Eli would not have moved, instead becoming a macabre figurehead for the *Asherah*, bound to the ship forever. He didn't look up, his feet catching on the edge of the gangplank. Staggering slightly as the give of the plank solidified into stone, Eli merely stood, looking abandoned. Still, he did not look up to see those that waited for him. Another gentle push in the small of his back from Abraxus got him to move another few steps toward them, at which point Tias rose and caught hold of his brother. Eli made no usual motion to avoid the embrace, his arms hanging limply at his side. And it was then that Smythe knew the death of Cynfor would cause devastating ripples.

Whilst Tias pulled back and tried to get Eli to look him properly in the face, Smythe turned to Abraxus. There was that same lost expression in his eyes again as he regarded his apprentice. 'Not a sound, Smythe.' Abraxus' words were barely audible above the whisper of the wind and tide. 'Nothing except after I pulled the body from the water. And only then…'

Tias turned to look at the pair, the worry and fear that had alighted in his features back with vindication. 'I'm going to take him home.' Smythe had to marvel at the boy for a moment. Despite it all, Tias' voice was strong and steady. He suspected this was mainly for Eli's sake, but all the same. There were times when Smythe forgot there was only ten minutes between the boys' ages; times when Tias seemed so much older.

'Alright,' Smythe said gently. 'You know where people are if you need anything.' He fixed Tias with a look. 'And I mean *anything*, Tias.'

He nodded and turned away toward where the wall sloped down to meet sand and eventually cobbles. As they went, Smythe saw with a sharp pain that Tias was leading Eli by the hand.

'What did he say?' Smythe didn't turn to look at Abraxus, but instead seemed to address his question to the sky. 'After?'

"I did not say."

Old Man Morgan's remains had neither been buried nor given back to the sea. On a clear and cold night, the inhabitants of Porth Tymestl had silently walked down to *Angorfa* beach, some bearing candles, others lanterns and gathered around the driftwood and castoff pyre erected there.

Atop the pyre, lay the still canvas-wrapped body of Cynfor Morgan. No wind ruffled the feathers of the night, and the sea seemed loud in everyone's ears. One by one, those with lights stepped forward and placed them against the pyre. After a time, the wood there began to blacken and catch, until a new fire had been born. Gaining strength, it raced up the dry and salt infused wood until the entire structure was ablaze. As it burnt, Crow came forward and started to talk. Smythe didn't really pay much attention to the words, letting them ebb and flow over him. Somewhere toward the back of the crowd, lurked Abraxus.

The man had not been seen in the village for the days that followed his arrival into the harbour. The only indication that Abraxus was still amongst them was the muted light that poured from the small windows of the *Asherah*'s state room by night. Likewise, Smythe had not seen much of the Kincarrans either. Tias made some half-hearted appearances in the village, collecting charts and books from Smythe, food from the smokehouses and Owen. He had a pallor to his face that suggested he hadn't seen the light of day for a while. Whenever Smythe had seen him, only for a few minutes at a time, it seemed that there was a shadow hanging over him. The innkeeper could make a good guess as to why. Of Eli, there had been no sign.

Tonight, he had not yet caught sight of either of them, but there was a small patch of tension toward the middle of the crowd that gave Smythe some indication about where the boys might be. As the flames raced higher, adding their sparks to the stars above, those with smaller children drifted away and back toward The Five-Pointed Compass, where the wake was to be held. At first, Smythe had railed against the idea when it had been broached by Crow and a few others. He had had enough of subjecting the timbers and stone of his inn – that was in his mind and in the minds of other Wayfinders a place of sanctity – to utter sorrow. But in the end, he had relented, especially after Medwyn and his cousin Rhys had dropped into the conversation that it might bring Eli out of his self-imposed hiding.

The door had been left unlocked, the lanterns burning bright, as if their multicoloured hues could help chase away the darkness that had settled over everyone once more. Smythe lingered a while longer, trying not to breathe in too deeply. A few touched his shoulder as they passed, a silent thank you for the space he was opening to them where they could share in their grief.

It was only when a hand lingered a tad too long against his upper arm did he finally take notice of those still around him. Abraxus had moved toward the pyre, gazing into its red and black light. Smoke billowed from it now, thick and sickening. Smythe turned to look at him, watching the lines in Abraxus' face becoming substantially harsher in the flickering half-light. 'When Ffion returns,' Abraxus began, his voice low, 'I will have to do what is necessary for this to end.'

Perhaps it was the setting in which they were spoken, but a shiver passed through Smythe at the finality of the tone. Foreboding seemed to lace Abraxus' words, and Smythe could sense the roil of the man's emotions beneath the carefully blank face.

'Abraxus–' Smythe started, tense.

'I mean no harm.' Abraxus cut in. 'But sometimes harsh truths can do more damage than any weapon.'

Smythe fell silent at that. It was true that Ffion needed her eyes opened to the damage she had so unwittingly unleashed on the little village, but simultaneously Smythe felt loath to cause the woman any more pain. The night after Old Man Morgan's demise, there had been thunder accompanied by no lightning.

'The fire's burning down,' Smythe murmured eventually. There was only a handful of people left on the beach now, and Smythe guessed that most of them only lingered out of unabashed curiosity at the words passing softly between the two of them, cloistered as they were. 'Let's go.'

'To the living,' Abraxus intoned.

'Aye, to the living.' Together, they walked through Porth Tymestl. The silence rang in the dead air. Smythe felt, just for a moment, that he would have sold his soul for a breath of wind. Anything, just to stir the shroud clinging over them.

Inside, muted chatter half-heartedly rose and fell. Many already clutched mugs, foam collecting over the sides. A few raised them in greeting as Smythe entered, closing out the night behind him. Abraxus slipped into the throng and away to his usual table. It had been left empty.

No speeches were made that night. No mighty words or tall tales stretched the hours and brought ghosts back to wander through the living. Instead, there was simple peace and the sense of quiet company. An ear was there if it was needed, a shoulder ready to accept a weight. Underneath the hatchway between the bar and the rest of the inn, sat Eli and Tias. Smythe had actually tripped over them this time, not really expecting them to come up to the inn. Usually, this would bring laughter, maybe some fond comment about the boys' nature. But now, eyes were averted, flicking between the Kincarrans and Smythe and away again. A few glanced over toward the corner where Abraxus sat sequestered.

'Are you alright?' Tias asked quietly as Smythe regained his balance.

'Fine, fine, don't you worry about me.' He looked down at them. 'I have to say I didn't really think you'd be 'ere.'

Tias merely shrugged in response, his eyes grazing over Eli's face for a second, before returning his attention to the innkeeper. He kept his silence.

'I'll get you somethin' to drink.' Smythe said, 'Tias, come pick something you fancy.'

Tias was far too clever to fall for the ruse, but nonetheless he stood, shaking the cramp from his legs and came over to look at the selection of bottles and small barrels stacked behind the bar. Smythe didn't even need to speak to prompt the boy. 'He hasn't said anything for days.'

'At all?'

'Not unless it's when he's sleeping.' Tias reached out and tugged at a loose splinter of wood along one of the barrels. 'Which he also doesn't do much of.'

Smythe leaned backwards a little to look at Eli, still hunched over under the hatchway. His knees were brought close to his chest, fingers stiffly interlocked around them. Even from this distance, Smythe could see the deep circles blackening around Eli's eyes. 'And you?' Smythe pulled his attention back to Tias, who had succeeded in pulling the splinter from the barrel.

Again, Tias shrugged noncommittally. He pressed the splinter between his fingers, a barely audible hiss escaping him when it punctured the skin.

'Stop.' Smythe pulled it from him, casting it away. 'I'm going to need more than that, Matthias.'

'I can't help.'

'Say again?' Tias' words had been mouthed, just a slight exhalation of breath to give them form.

'I can't help him, nothing I do works.' Tias looked up, blinking. 'He's just... *gone*, Smythe.'

'Traumatised.' Smythe gave up all pretence of looking at the drinks and turned bodily to face Tias. 'Not gone, never gone.' Smythe, making sure that the majority of attention was not on himself and Tias, leaned in and began to speak. 'Seein' an old friend in the water with their life just pulled away is a terrible thing, Tias. I've seen it, and it doesn't let you alone for a while. But, I think, or at least I *guess* there is somethin' more to this. Remember, Eli found your Da's boat. Who knows what he'd have imagined he would find next after that.'

There was a moment of clouded confusion in Tias' face, and Smythe could see him working through the still incredibly raw pain that the mention of John had brought up. 'There was a night...' He started slowly, 'He woke himself up shouting. But not for Old Man Morgan. For–' Tias broke off, his voice catching.

'For your Da?' Smythe guessed softly.

Tias nodded once.

'The mind does strange things when we're mired in feelings that are too big to be contained. And 'aving what happened to Cynfor follow so closely what you imagine could have happened to your Da, well... just for a moment, that was *not* Cynfor in the water.'

Tias turned haunted eyes back toward his brother. 'I didn't think of that,' he whispered.

'It shouldn't be your place *to* think of that.' Smythe pulled Tias in close. He felt the brittle tension in the boy's shoulders and back leech out a little under the embrace. Abraxus words rang through his mind once more, but now they had mutated themselves. *Too much.*

'And now that I do know that, what should I do?' Tias asked. In an unconscious childlike motion, he scrubbed the cuff of his shirt across his eyes.

'You do nothing.' Smythe straightened as best he could to his full height. 'You leave this to Abraxus and me.' So caught up in their own turbulent emotions over the past days, Smythe now tasted the bitter tang of shame. Despite it all, despite watching them both grow and flourish under his and Abraxus' tutelage, Eli and Tias were still *boys*. Still finding their footing in a world that at times could be so callously cruel it made Smythe want to pack a bag and never stop running. With more force, he stated, 'You leave it to us.'

As the pale sliver of moon rode high overhead, and mugs returned empty to the bar for another filling, someone deep in the crowd started to hum. Low and rough, the tune trailing away only to find itself again, picked up around the barroom. With a slight scrape against the flagstone floor, one sailor, then another and another pushed back their chairs and stood.

It was an old shanty, one that had lain dormant in the minds of the people of Porth Tymestl for generations. Smythe remembered every word. More and more voices filled the space, the higher tones of the women seeping in underneath the salt-coarse sounds of the men.

"Tend to the lantern as it gutters and dims,
Over the blue depths on westerly winds.
Gull overhead, pay no heed to its shrieking,
Empty boots set the planks a-creaking.

Gone away, pulled, and took by the tide,
Beneath the horizon there's no place to hide.
Sail under stars and moon and the sun,
Turn back for home when the work it is done.

Drowned down below in the briny blue,
Lovers and brothers sing out to you.
Wrapped in sails and stitched with weed,
Roughened hands shall no longer bleed.

Gather ye round, and take a sip of mead,
And listen to stories of which to take heed.
Those that are lost are not forgotten,
Drift below with their souls salt-sodden.

Tend to the lantern as it goes out once more,
And see shadows around the cabin's door.
The sun sets down, away to the west,
Come, close your eyes, lay yourself to rest."

Beneath the hatchway, Tias sat beside his brother, his voice adding to the multitude. Eli curled upon himself further, and Smythe watched as his shoulders began to shake.

IX
then.

The final moments - part one.

Although he did not know it at the time, John Kincarran's last days broke with fog hanging low over the water. In the pale light of the dawn, Porth Tymestl seemed to have been transported overnight to a world coated in specks of crystalline light. Glimmering drops of dew hung, poised and ready to fall, from the rough wood of windowsills and lintels. As the early winter sun finally struggled over the black crest of the moors and vales to the east, its golden light saturated the mist until it seemed to John that he walked through a dream.

The home he had left behind was silent and still; the peace within only broken by the rhythmic breathing of three inhabitants. He rubbed his thumb and forefinger together absentmindedly as he walked through the streets, the silken texture of Ffion's hair a lingering spectre on the roughened pads of his fingers. Half-light falling through the ajar shutters had cast her face and hair in colour he knew he could never name. She had turned away from his touch, seeking the lonely reprieve of dreams. John had smiled, pulled on his boots and left. Above, hidden from sight, Eli shifted and muttered something unintelligible.

John stood a moment on the well-worn doorstep, looking back into the home he had carved from salt and wood and sea. Then, shouldering his bag a little higher, quietly closed the door. '*Mi fydda'i adre reit fuan.*' *I'll be home soon.*

The cobbles beneath the thin tread of his boots were slick with the morning's dew, layered over the steadily melting frost laid on the ground by the sweep of night. His breath plumed gently into the fragile air. John felt that if he were to raise his hand and pass it forcefully down, it would all shatter about him. He walked with no men by his side, no chatter or well-meaning jibes. No shanty was lifted to the scraped sky that morning. Over the sea, the fog rolled in ever closer, drawn to the land by some great pull. John felt himself pulled in the opposite direction, working against the solid current of the land. Underneath that veil of fog, the ocean murmured and stirred fitfully. He could only guess at its colour.

As the sounds of its breathing grew steadily louder in his ears, vague and smoke-like memories began to pour into his mind. It was the reason for the itch in his eyes, the slow, melancholy ache in his limbs. Undisturbed sleep, recently, had become a rarity. Each night, his thoughts became more and more salt-soaked, the cascade of the sea forcing his thoughts down into the depths where the light did not penetrate. And underneath it all, whispers. Unceasing and voiceless. John had first thought it the wash of the tides on the shore, the sound to which he had lived most of his life. But then, after waking a little before dawn several mornings ago, he came to the realisation that the sounds he heard weren't rhythmic enough; they followed the cadence of a voice, its inflections up and down. After that realisation, the dreams stopped being beautiful intangible things. After that, John was loath to lay down each night and hear their call again. They unsettled him in a way he could not give voice to.

The *Dawnsiwr y Wawr* was waiting, nestled in close to the walls of *Angorfa* Harbour. Her masts bare, ropes hanging slack. She had not seen the open waters in a little over a week. Persistent fog and no real need for a catch had kept her there, cornered. John dropped his bag down onto the pocked deck and followed it, cringing a little at the hollow thud his boots made on the planking. For reasons he could not begin to fathom, he did not want to be discovered nor stopped. The silence of the morning returned blanket-like around him, and he straightened. He didn't bother properly stowing his bag, but rather kicked it into a nook at the stern-end. Walking the length of his ship, John made ready. The movements were ingrained into his calloused skin, allowing his mind to wander ever further away.

It seemed, at least to John, that if he took to the seas alone, even just for a few hours, the sea-whispers would stop. *Pacified*, was the word John felt drifting through his mind. That was all he intended: out of the harbour, lose the line of the land and return to step foot on the doorstep just as the first night lanterns were lit along the village paths. Part of him acknowledged that to go out alone was dangerous, but surely. A few hours. He could handle a few hours alongside the steadfast *Dawnsiwr y Wawr*.

Beneath the burning red rim of the sun, the canvas of the *Dawnsiwr y Wawr* unfurled. John put hand over hand on the halyard, tied it off and looked up to the harbour wall. Only one length of rope lay coiled and knotted between him, his ship and the waves. Usually, one of the dock workers would cast it off for him. John clambered back up onto the stout stone wall, unwound the mooring line and dropped it to the deck. Taking the hand-smoothed wood of the rudder, John turned back once more to look at Porth Tymestl just awakening behind him. The walls of *Angorfa* Harbour dropped away, spray from the sea beating miniscule patterns on the stone. Letting the *Dawnsiwr y Wawr* drift a moment, John walked to the bowsprit. At the end of a pulley swung the lantern he had been given by Stooger Smythe.

Pulling it toward him, John gingerly opened the little hinged door and lit the candle inside. It guttered momentarily, and then the flame took. He sent it back out to the end of the bowsprit, a tiny beacon of gold upon the water. The fog closed in around him, and soon, from the shore, all signs of John Kincarran's passing was lost to white.

X

now.

Truths.
May, 1816.
Ffion.

Her sons so rarely asked her for anything. Even when queried about birthdays, celebrations, Christmas day, there would be no satisfying response. Eli had once spent almost an entire winter wearing boots a size too small for him because he hadn't wanted to cause trouble for her in the efforts of procuring a new pair.

But when the letter arrived, alongside a tired and travel-weary messenger, it came with a very open plea. Tudwr had delivered it to her door early one morning, just after the birds had finished their dawn song and were spreading their wings for the day. Pink touched the sky, cresting into gentle blue beneath a veil of wispy clouds. Her letters had mostly gone without a reply returning from Porth Tymestl, but this hadn't upset Ffion, as she knew that if any letter did arrive, it would more than likely contain something important. It also meant that someone at home had gone to the effort of seeking out someone who knew part of the way toward the forest vale. Silence from the sea-edged village meant all was well.

Tudwr, seeming to sense her apprehension heightening the moment he handed over the folded parchment, stayed discreetly by her side in the Sycamore Hut. The letter was written, to her surprise, in two hands. The first was the cramped script of her eldest.

Mam,

Cynfor Morgan is dead. He took his skiff out in the early morning. Eli spotted him from the Asherah *– that's Abraxus' ship. A lot has happened since we came home. It's too much to write here, and I do not think I could do it justice. I know you wanted to stay in* Dyffryn Cernunnos *for as long as possible, and I understand that. But we need you to come home now. I need you here.*

Eli isn't... it's hard to explain. He isn't the same anymore. He doesn't speak. He barely sleeps. And I don't know what to do. Smythe said he would help, but I think what would help the most is you. Just being here.

I'm writing this at the bar of The Five. Smythe has asked if Abraxus can add something to the end of the letter. I don't know what he wants to say, but I'm not going to ask.

I think I already know.

Please, come home. We need you here in more ways than one.

Tias.

Ffion was glad of Tudwr's company. Especially when her knees decided to buckle and send her toward the earth. Cynfor. Another gone to the seas. But, according to Tias, by his own accord. Tudwr's arm wrapped gently around her waist, and guided her into a slumped kneeling position on the hard packed dirt floor. '*Bad news?*' The sounds of her mother tongue felt like a balm to the whirl of her thoughts. She sniffed, and looked back down toward the letter. She would have to relay the news to him; Tudwr never learnt to read in the common language.

'*One of our elders is dead.*' This was the best way she could impart the magnitude of news. It must have worked, Tudwr's arm, now around her shoulders, tightened comfortingly. '*My sons need me home.*'

'*Of course. The pass will be cleared enough for your journey to begin tomorrow.*' He appraised her for a moment before adding, '*Will you need accompaniment?'*

Ffion managed a fragile smile for him, shaking her head. *'Thank you.'* She patted his hand lightly, and he removed it immediately. *'I need to make ready.'*

'As you wish.' Without needing to be asked, Tudwr started to help her gather supplies, piling them neatly by the door or else on the scarred table. He did not ask about the second half of the letter. The part that Ffion knew he would be able to read. Abraxus had revealed to her that he could speak her native tongue as well as someone born to it. Apparently, he could also write in the old script as well. The vertical lines crosshatched with diagonals covered the second half of the page, as well as the back.

They worked in companionable silence for a time, until everything that was needed was expertly stowed into her travel pack. Tudwr, never one for superfluous words, nodded once at her and made for the doorway. He lingered a moment on the threshold, seeming to think over something. But instead, he turned away, and with a slight setting of his shoulders, strode off into the forest.

Alone, Ffion sat down at the table, and pulled the letter once more from her pocket. It took longer than she would like to admit to gather the courage to reopen it. Eyes flicking over Tias' words again, and feeling fresh pain at them, she at last turned her attention to the second half.

Ffion.

I will not echo what Matthias has already spoken about. The pain of hearing it once is enough.

However, I shall repeat one sentiment expressed by your son. You need to come back. There is more at work in Porth Tymestl than you can fully understand. Your sons are on the edges of it, and even that feels still too incomprehensible to them.

There is a wrong here that needs to be rectified. And this wrong, this slight*, can only be corrected by you. Because you caused it. Not advertently, not out of malice or cruelty. But out of that deep sea of pain that is grief.*

Words cannot encompass what I hope to impart to you here. I shall speak more of this with you in person. But if you desire any hope for the future of the place you once loved and called home, the birthplace of your sons, then you will do this for them. For all living here.

There will be great pain on the horizon for you. And would that I could take it from you. But I cannot, and you must face this alone. For this, I am sorry.

Come home.

A.E.H.

Ffion could not pretend to understand Abraxus' cryptic words. But they rang with a truth that she knew in her soul to be irrefutable. Something was rotten in Porth Tymestl, and had been slowly spreading its insidious blackness ever since John died. Inside, the whispering black sea stirred. It had never been still nor silent, not even as she spent more and more time burying herself in moss and loam. It had been left unchecked, unlooked at for too long. Ffion knew she would give anything to be rid of it, and knew that nothing she could ever do in her lifetime would make it recede. These words that Abraxus had taken pains to scribe in her own language, had a promise of peace in them. She longed to put down the pain, pack it away neatly and only look at it when memory began to fail and find, perhaps, that it had softened into merely an ache. Something bittersweet to float in, not drown beneath.

Tomorrow, she would begin the journey back. Looking toward her pack, resting ready by the door, Ffion found herself speaking out into the green silence of the hut. The words surprised her, but she knew that they were true, no matter how much she tried to deny it to herself. 'Homeward bound.'

ELLA RUBY SELF

Returns.
May, 1816.
Tias.

Light cascaded through the windows. He must have forgotten to pull the shutters to last night. Patches of golden warmth made the flagstones of the floor gleam, smoothed by generations of feet. In the hearth, an old ember still smouldered, asleep in a bed of ashes. Beyond the warped glass, the birds and the sea built up a distant rhythm. Above all, the dome of the sky arched.

Tias had pulled open the door and stepped out onto the doorstep before he was even fully awake. Turning his face toward the sky, he felt something that had been so absent from their lives for too long. *Warmth.* Undisturbed by any wind, not laced with the clinging cut of the deep winter. Pure, it came down onto him from a sky that was an unbreakable sapphire. Rising over the meadows, the sun gleamed a bright yellow-white. A jewel held in a setting of velvet. Reaching out his arms, Tias let the loose sleeves of his nightshirt fall back, exposing his forearms. The sensation of the sun on his skin was utter bliss. He let out a long sigh, merely basking for a few moments.

The idea that came to him was nearly as perfect as the day laid out before him. He knew that Smythe and Abraxus had resolutely resolved to take some of the responsibility off his own shoulders, and to them he was very grateful. But Tias knew that old habits die hard, and for as long as he could remember, he had been his brother's watcher almost as much as he'd been his accomplice.

Since Old Man Morgan's wake at The Five, Smythe and Abraxus had been by Roseate Cottage nearly every day. Either to drop things off; books, food or merely a story or two told in the shelter of the garden, or to bring them both to the *Gorwelion* Cellar. Whilst Tias had continued to work with Smythe, poring over dusty and forgotten records and tomes, Abraxus had seemed content to just sit and be with Eli, occasionally starting some menial task that he would try and engage Eli's interest in. And, much to everyone's relief, it had started to work. Eli seemed less haunted as each day dawned anew. He had yet to say more than a few words, but his sleep was less disturbed. The black circles under his eyes seemed to diminish slightly, leaving the skin there bruised, but no longer shadowed.

For this idea to come to fruition, however, Tias needed a head start on Abraxus and his Wayfinder. He turned back into the shade of Roseate Cottage, leaving the door open, inviting the early summer warmth inside. He slipped back up the ladder, got changed and then dithered for a while beside his brother's bed. Eli was mostly buried in blankets, one hand hanging limply over the side. Tias was loath to disturb him, knowing that all the rest Eli could get at the moment would do him good. The other alternative was going ahead and informing Smythe and Abraxus of his plans for the day, but if Eli woke and was seemingly alone...

'Eli,' Tias called quietly, reaching out and gently shaking his brother's shoulder. 'Eli, you need to come see this.'

'Hmm.' The blankets shifted, and a half of Eli's face was revealed. He blinked slowly up at Tias, his features shifting from a sleep-imposed calm to a slight crease of worry at his brows. He sat up. 'What?'

Tias tried and failed to fight the smile spreading across his face. Any words his brother spoke currently he counted as a personal victory. 'Just come and see.' He turned and headed back down the ladder, hearing the creak of the floorboards as Eli followed him. 'Outside.'

Eli looked at Tias, bemusement plain on his features, but

nonetheless, stepped out of the open door. Tias followed, and as soon as the sun's light hit Eli, he heard a sharp intake of breath. He watched as Eli tipped his head back, eyes closed and seemed to drink in the warmth that Tias knew was permeating every bone in his body. Eli turned back to Tias eventually, and there was something akin to shock on his face.

'It's *warm*,' Tias said. Eli nodded, the same giddy excitement that Tias felt illuminating his features. 'I have an idea for today. Get ready, and then we'll go down to The Five.'

Not needing to be told twice, Eli hurriedly disappeared inside. Wandering over to the low stone wall, Tias leaned on it with his elbows, looking down into the village below. Noise cascaded up to him from *Angorfa* Harbour. Sails had been opened out, and there was more white between the stout walls than the blue of the water. Bursts of laughter, and once, a snatch of shanty, reached him. The arrival of true summer seemed to bring with it good cheer, and more importantly, hope. Porth Tymestl would be near empty today.

Behind him, Tias heard the latch of the door click shut. He turned as Eli came to toward him, tucking the spare key into a pocket. He was barefoot. 'Boots?' Tias questioned wryly, wondering if in his excitement to be off and out, Eli had just completely forgotten them. It wouldn't be the first time.

In response, Eli just shook his head.

'Ah,' understanding came to Tias. 'A bit early on, isn't it?' In the height of summer, Eli often forewent his boots altogether, preferring to go everywhere barefoot until the leaves turned from green to gold and the frost crept in once more. It was a constant source of amused annoyance to their mother, as the soles of Eli's feet would often be black by the end of the week and trekking sand, grass and seaweed around the floors of Roseate Cottage.

'It's warm,' Eli said quietly, gesturing around. The fact that he had echoed Tias' own words wasn't lost on him, but Tias hadn't been expecting a response, and he suddenly found that the day around them was just a bit brighter. It didn't matter that Eli's voice was rough from disuse. It was *there*.

'Fair enough,' Tias said, grinning. 'Ready?'

Apparently, hope wasn't the only thing that had re-emerged with the sun. Halfway down toward the village, Tias looked slyly over at his brother, and then back down the path they were taking. 'Last one to The Five-Pointed Compass,' he started conversationally, 'has to scrub the foredeck of the *Asherah* without being asked.' And before Eli could fully process what Tias had just said, Tias broke into a run toward the cobbled streets of Porth Tymestl. A moment later, he heard the beat of Eli close behind him, and there trailing behind them on the wind they made for themselves as they ran, the faintest trace of a laugh.

Neck and neck they careened into Porth Tymestl proper and then immediately split up, both heading for the route they thought was fastest toward the inn. Between the gaps of cottages and buildings, Tias caught glimpses of Eli, leaping over the rain gutters cut into the streets. He was thoroughly out of breath by the time The Five-Pointed Compass came into view, but then that was all but forgotten when Tias saw Eli skid around a corner in front of him and put on a dead sprint for the last leg of the impromptu race.

'*Damn ei fod*!' Eli had reached the door and was standing in the porch space, one hand resting triumphantly against the lintel, chest heaving. A genuine smile split his face, and Tias decided he wouldn't begrudge his brother winning. And in any case, Eli was the one apprenticed to Abraxus. He would likely have to scrub the decks anyway at some point in his tuition. 'Well, knock then,' Tias said, still fighting a little to catch his breath. Eli raised an eyebrow slightly and turned away, rapping smartly on the door.

As they both waited for Smythe to unlock the door, Tias gazed down toward the harbour and the thoroughfare that led to its stout walls and captured pool of ocean. Those who were still making ready for the day had their shirt sleeves rolled up, flashes of weathered brown amongst the off-white. Most of the fleet was gone. He hadn't much inclination of the time; there was no timepiece adorning the mantle of Roseate Cottage. It must be late, no fisherman worth his proverbial salt would waste such a day like this on the shoreline.

The latch clicked open from inside The Five-Pointed Compass, the door creaking ever so slightly as it was pulled ajar. 'Bit early for a dr–' Smythe's words broke off as he caught sight of who was standing on his doorstep.

'*Bore da.*' Tias didn't wait to be invited in, but gently pushed the door out of the innkeeper's loose grip and stepped inside. The temperature dropped significantly and Tias felt the hairs on his arms rise. Thick walls and small windows meant excellent insulation come winter – something that had served everyone well over the past few months – but in the hotter months it was liable to make even the cosiest places feel like an icehouse. What sunlight did make it through the small square windows reflected on the worn stone floors and made the lanterns above shine out their colours.

'To what do I owe the pleasure?' Smythe said, smoothing down his hair. It was relatively clear that the man had himself only just risen, a long ankle length robe hastily tied at his waist. It was covered in what seemed to be exquisite embroidery and Tias found himself itching to ask where Smythe had procured it, but for now, he flattened the curiosity. Smythe kept surreptitiously glancing toward Eli.

'Have you been outside today?' Tias asked innocuously.

'No... why?' Smythe's eyes flitted over both their heads toward the door, still open a little. 'What's happened?' It was testament to how the strings of their lives had been taut for too long that Tias didn't even question the suspicious and even slightly frightened note in Smythe's voice.

Before Tias could respond however, Eli had backtracked to the door, opened it fully and beckoned. Smythe looked to Tias, who nodded. 'Go on.' He watched as the innkeeper stepped out, looked into the deep sky above, and saw all the tension along Smythe's back and shoulders cascade off of him and into the mellow breeze that had stirred itself from sleep.

'Smythe, where do you keep the spare blankets, I need to–' Abraxus' voice preceded him down the inn's stairs. Unlike the innkeeper, Abraxus appeared to have been up for hours. 'Ah. I did not expect we would have visitors.' Tias could see Abraxus trying to piece together what was going on, his mismatched eyes roving around the room and their faces. Both were an intensely bright blue today.

'Abraxus, my old friend,' Smythe called from the porch. He had yet to move.

'Aye?'

'Come and see what Porth Tymestl is truly like.'

Abraxus stepped toward the door, casting a confused look at both Tias and Eli as he passed. He stood shoulder to shoulder with Smythe on the doorstep, and like Tias had done in the garden of Roseate Cottage, lifted his arms before him, palms and forearms exposed to the sun and sky.

'I had a suggestion,' Tias called to the pair. 'About what we could do today.'

Both Abraxus and Smythe as one turned back to him. 'By all means, do tell.' Abraxus' mellifluous voice had something deeper in it, almost as if it had become more resonant in the exposure to sunlight.

'Smythe, have you got any spare rugs and a basket?'

'Elias, where are your boots.' Abraxus' voice didn't contain any inflection whatsoever, and Tias had to pick up his pace to make sure his brother didn't see him grinning. Smythe seemed to also share in his amusement, catching Tias' eye and then hurriedly looking away again just as they were both about to break into laughter.

The walk to *Tua'r Môr* Bay felt almost entirely new to Tias, despite having made the trek countless times. The breeze, stronger up on the exposed edge of the sea cliff, rippled the long summer grasses and sent spiralling motes of pollen into the air. The uncut meadows were vibrant underneath the singularly blue sky, sparks of wildflowers mixed in with a haze of verdant green and soft flaxen gold. Across over the sea, the birds wheeled and sang. A few gannets swept off the cliffs, their black wings shadows in the air only but for a moment before they plunged straight into the waters below.

'You won't be seein' Eli's boots again for a while now,' Smythe called over his shoulder. 'He's decided today is the day 'e stops needing 'em.' From his left hand swung the laden basket he'd managed to unearth from behind the bar. A large slightly moth-eaten rug covered the top.

'Summer tradition.' Tias added, pre-empting Abraxus' confused questions.

'Hm.' Abraxus turned his attention back to the expanse of blue-green to their left. His fingers drifted down to the copper circlet strung on his belt, tracing the curve for the seeing stone to slot into. In his other hand was the staff, the small pieces of sea glass braided into the hanging threads swinging and catching the light.

Together, they made their way down the steep cliff path, Smythe holding out the basket to one side almost comically to keep his balance on the precarious slope. Tias was the first to reach the sands, jumping down from the ledge and reaching up to help Smythe down. The man swatted irritably at him, muttering that he wasn't '*that* old yet, Matthias.'

Eli was the last down onto the beach. Tias had already set off with Smythe towards the water, the familiar saline tang filling his lungs, but he glanced back. Abraxus almost seemed to be dithering in indecisiveness as he watched Eli side-step down the last part of the path. It had been a little bit of a concern for Tias, and so it seemed, for Abraxus too, how Eli would be when faced with the ocean again. After all the destruction it had caused to their lives, how many ghosts it now held captured in its salt, Tias would not have been surprised to see his brother resolutely turn away from it, just like Ffion had done.

There was the slightest moment of hesitation before Eli cleared the jump onto *Tua'r Môr* Bay proper. Lost to the roar of the waves, Tias couldn't make out the words spoken to Eli by Abraxus; the man had come closer, seeming to have come to a decision, and had gently placed his hand on Eli's shoulder.

'C'mon.' Smythe had caught his sleeve and was tugging it lightly. Tias realised he had stopped and was staring back toward the pair. 'Leave 'em be.' He allowed Smythe to turn him away, and looked into the man's weathered face. Smythe was staring directly ahead, but Tias knew where his attention really was.

'*Diolch.*' Tias said it so quietly that Smythe could have reasonably pretended not to hear him.

'We said we'd do more. Today is for the *both* of you.' Smythe left it at that, and continued to walk on.

Along the beach, strung out in irregular patterns, bones still lingered. It seemed to Tias to be considerably less in number than the dead of winter, Abraxus having clearly been coming down to the bay to do some midnight work. But now knowing what creatures they had once belonged to, to have *seen* them so alive and iridescent in the waters, Tias felt a sharp pang in his chest. He looked back over to the sea; he had always known it

434

was cruel, but to sacrifice the serpents wantonly – he couldn't fathom how Llŷr could do such a thing, all in the name of a perceived insult. A thought came to him then. He had moved from trying to figure out what the mysterious posts were on a beach, to trying to comprehend the infinite thought processes of an ancient primordial force. A slow smile crept onto his face. How strangely wonderful it had all become.

Smythe was currently trying to fight a blanket into submission. Every time he lifted it up into the air to try and spread it flat against the sand, the sea wind took it, making it ripple and flap. At one point a large quantity of sand was thrown up too, and, consequently, into Smythe's face. Chuckling to himself, Tias hurried over and grabbed the opposite corners. He weighted the corners down with rocks, sat, and kicked off his own boots. Above, the sun had steadily climbed to its zenith, warm air beating down against the reviving wind. Beneath the horizon, specks of white sails danced lazily atop the crests of waves. Canvas became indistinguishable from the graceful flick and spin of the gull's wings above, until it seemed to Tias that the sea and sky were one and the same; both populated with things borne on feathered or fabric wings.

Abraxus and Eli joined them a moment later, settling themselves down on the blanket. Abraxus thrust the end of his staff into the sand, so it stood upright, the strings swaying. It felt almost like a sentinel to Tias, standing guard over them and the day. As Smythe distributed whatever food he could find at such short notice, Abraxus slung off the small shoulder bag he'd been carrying. Amidst the small portions of dried fish, fresh bread from Owen's and canteens of water, he laid out, almost in reverie, Eli and Tias' circlets. They had been taken back from them after the night of the serpents, Abraxus wanting to make some adjustments to the fit of them. The seeing stones that fit their respective circlets, they had kept. Tias had taken to carrying his around alongside his notebook in the bag Ffion had gifted him at Christmas. The leather was already battered, small lighter marks gathering at the corners and clasp. He knew that Eli kept his in his pocket, and would often see him clutching it in his palm, running a finger idly over the grey-purple surface. The chime they had come from now hung over their mother's bed, a singular stone turning from its fishing net snare.

'For later, perhaps,' Abraxus said quietly, pushing the driftwood crown a little closer to Tias.

'The serpents...' Tias began, lifting the circlet and letting its weight feel familiar again to his hands. 'Are they only active at night?'

'No.' Abraxus didn't say any more, cutting up the dried fish into four portions.

'When?' It was almost amusing how quickly Smythe and Abraxus looked up to Eli as he spoke.

'They are here always,' Abraxus said, turning deliberately back to his task. 'They prefer the crepuscular hours, and often will keep time with the tides.'

'But that's not to say they all act the same,' Smythe cut in. 'Some of the bigger ones stay right out to sea. The ones you saw are the tide timin' ones.'

As they all ate, Abraxus and Smythe regaled them with stories about the creatures; Abraxus recounting the first time he'd seen a serpent, the variety of patterns and colourations he'd seen them display. It transpired that one of the serpents that had been amongst the group Tias had seen that night was an avid tracker of the *Asherah*, and would often turn up in the shallows of wherever Abraxus made port.

'LongFin.' Eli had quietly broken in there.

'LongFin?' Tias said confusedly.

Eli seemed to consider his next words, the pause gentle. 'The green one. I named it.'

Vaguely, Tias recalled a spark of seaweed green in the water swimming close to his brother. It had submerged itself fully when Eli had. He would have taken more notice, but the two serpents, one with horns and the other with fins reminiscent of a jellyfish had captured his attention so fully, there was little room for anything else.

'A fitting name, I think,' Abraxus said musingly, clearly picturing the serpent in question in his mind's eye.

Around them, the day grew steadily warmer, the heat lingering against Tias' skin. Closing his eyes, the world turned a burnt orange, the occasional ripple of deepest red passing over as a wisp of cloud crossed the sun's path. Only the wash of the waves permeated the gentle quiet that fell over them all. From within his bag, packed neatly alongside his notebook, Tias withdrew his chart. It was becoming softer at the folds, and as such he handled it with a care that seemed more fitting to an archaic tome. It was essentially complete, but Tias couldn't help but add in some small details within the largely blank space that denoted the sea. By the spit of land that signified Finfolk Point, he delicately traced in the outline of Old Man Morgan's skiff.

He surfaced from his reverie of pen strokes sometime later; looking around he noted Abraxus knee deep in the water, a little closer to them now as the tide drifted its way inward. Smythe was buried in a book, eyes flicking down the lines of words with a speed that Tias could only hope to one day emulate. By the innkeeper's side was Eli, curled up and fast asleep. Rolling up the chart and carefully stowing it away, Tias stood and stretched for a moment before setting off in Abraxus' direction. Smythe didn't even notice him go.

'What're you doing?' The water, as it always was along this stretch of coast, was bitterly cold. Tias didn't bother rolling up his trousers, the late mid-afternoon sun would dry them quick enough.

'Why do I have to be *doing* anything?' Abraxus didn't turn to him, keeping his gaze fixed out over the ocean. 'I am simply being.'

'Oh.' Tias stood at the man's side, scanning the horizon. 'How do you do that?'

Abraxus sighed, but there was no real irritation in it. He

looked toward Tias. The staff was held close to him, the edges of the foam crested waves darkening the colours of the beads and sea glass. 'The chart?'

'Finished, I think. What do you want it for?'

Abraxus thought, seeming to measure his next words. Immediately, Tias knew he was about to get half an answer, if that. 'Let us say... it's for an induction.'

Tias didn't press the issue. Instead, he looked back out over the water. It seemed easier to say what he wanted to without looking into Abraxus' piercing eyes. 'When Mam comes back...' He trailed off.

'Go on.' There was a quiet sympathy in Abraxus' tone now.

'I heard a little of what you said that night with the serpents.' A distant white sail came into view, heading home. 'I didn't catch all of it, but I think you said something about her needing to see?'

'I did,' Abraxus said simply, waiting for Tias to continue.

'You meant the serpents, seeing them alive?'

'Aye.' Abraxus' hand landed softly on Tias' shoulder, forcing him to look at the man. 'I think seeing the beauty of the world to remind her that we are still alive and not yet gone, will begin to heal what is broken here.' And with that, Abraxus guided his hand down and tapped lightly just below Tias' collarbone.

'You won't get her down here,' Tias said.

'Smythe told me the same.' A pause; Tias listening to the shush and whisper of the tide. 'It will not be a perfect healing, nor an easy one. But broken and mended with gold is better than in pieces.'

Tias had nothing to say to that. He merely stood and, for a while, tried to figure out how to just *be*. It seemed peaceful. When he felt a little more clear-headed, he turned back toward the beach. The long expanse of sand was thinning now as the tide crept in higher. It wouldn't cut them off completely, the winds were low and Smythe had picked a spot nearer the cliff path, rather than around the slight bend where the cavern lay. 'Come and see what's in the rockpools.' The request was spoken before Tias could snatch it back. He cringed slightly, thinking he sounded childish.

But before he could hastily renege on his offer, Abraxus smiled and nodded. 'Fetch your notebook, lad.'

As Tias and Abraxus made their way through the shallow surf toward the rock pools at the far end of the beach, Smythe set down his book and followed them at a little distance. He slipped in and out of the bones that still lay in the sand, letting his fingers trail over their barnacle encrusted surface. Further down the bay still, Eli lay peacefully under the sun.

Evening touched the rim of the world, trails of salmon-skin clouds stretching over the pastel sky, deepening to a rich blue-black at the distant place where sky touched sea. Tias had filled six pages of his book with all the long and complicated names Abraxus had reeled off endlessly at the rockpools. Smythe was leaning against one of the larger bones, watching them and Eli concurrently.

His brother had woken just as the sun began to lose its heat. Now, he'd taken up Abraxus' place in the water, the sun catching on the silver threading through his hair. Abraxus himself had lifted his stone up to his eye when he'd spotted Eli out in the water. 'It seems your brother has made a friend.'

He passed the ivory-white stone over to Tias. A long, thin luminescent band of bright kelp green wove itself around Eli's legs. 'LongFin.'

'Go and join him, if you wish.'

Tias nodded, handed back the stone and began scrambling over the craggy rocks toward the sand. Before he picked up his own driftwood circlet, he rummaged through the basket Smythe had brought down. If they were planning to stay longer, someone would need to do a supply run back to the village. Hunger was beginning to make itself known.

After what was perhaps an hour in the shallows with Eli watching the serpents, Abraxus and Smythe called them back in. Eli had somehow managed to drench himself from head to toe, although Tias reflected, perhaps some of that was LongFin's fault. The serpent seemed to have the temperament of a young child, splashing and weaving through the water in a streak of emerald. 'They'll be people houndin' at my door soon enough.' Smythe said, reaching down to roll up the blanket.

'A cloudless sky means a bitter night.' Abraxus added a little distantly. Above them, the first glitter of the stars began to show themselves in the deepening blue. Ink seemed now to stain the horizon, tendrils creeping ever higher as the moon pulled itself up over the land.

'We've no food at home,' Tias said with a jolt of realisation. 'Or at least, nothing substantial.' He shuffled a little uncomfortably as he spoke. The feeling of debt to Smythe and the warmth of The Five only seemed stack up, but as usual, Smythe was having none of it.

'I'm sure I can rustle you somethin' warm up.'

'Where's the *Asherah*?' Eli's voice just behind Tias' shoulder made him jump, lurching slightly into Abraxus. The man steadied him.

'Still in *Angorfa* Harbour.' There was a light tone of disgruntlement to Abraxus' words, as if the village harbour was not a befitting place to house his ship. 'Why?'

Eli shrugged and then looked back out over the sea, placid as a mill pond now.

It clicked together in Tias' mind what Eli was thinking then. 'You want to go out and... fish?'

Eli nodded. 'For the others too.' He gestured back toward Porth Tymestl.

A thoughtful expression was cast over Smythe's face. 'It's not too bad an idea...' He turned to Abraxus, who seemed reluctant. 'You've been helpin' with the catch on the quiet. This would be no different, 'cept people here would finally see you as an ally.' Abraxus still seemed doubtful, but looking toward the water, something softened slightly in the darkening eyes.

'I suppose allies within the village may come in useful in case —' He trailed off. The unspoken *this happens again* hung between them all, uncomfortably filling the silence.

'Well, if that's what we're doing, we'd better get back up to the village. We're losing the light.' Smythe rallied them all once more, throwing the inelegantly folded blanket at Abraxus. 'Let's go.'

Nets.
May, 1816.
Abraxus.

With the dim eyes of Porth Tymestl upon him, Abraxus pulled the gangplank back and nodded to Smythe. As the gentle evening wind played around the sails, he watched the walls of *Angorfa* Harbour slide away leaving only the open waters before them. The people ranged along the walls – still packing away the detritus from the busy day – stopped to watch them pass. Abraxus felt their gazes prickle up the back of his neck, and resolutely turned to face the horizon. He understood the reasoning behind their continued mistrust, but sensed deep within his bones that perhaps a change was coming. A fresh new wind easing out the old and swirling something young over the cobbles.

By the bowsprit, leaning lazily on the railing, were Smythe and Tias. They seemed to be in deep conversation, Tias sketching with his fingers images in the air something that only he could see. Once or twice, he saw Smythe gesture lightly to the little leather bag that Abraxus knew contained the chart. With a sudden clarity of mind, he decided that it was time. Tomorrow, or perhaps the day after. There was little point in waiting any longer. The uncomfortable prickle that had lingered with him long after the walls of *Angorfa* Harbour were lost from view changed, and now the heady anticipation of excitement filled him. When they made port again later this night, he would tell the boys what he had planned.

His eyes wandered away from their distant stare toward the horizon and down to the deck below. Eli was just visible around the curve of the mainmast, sitting with his back to it. From this angle, it was difficult for Abraxus to see what the lad was looking at; it could have been the sea, it could have been the polished planking beneath him. But thus far there had been no adversity to being back aboard the *Asherah*, which Abraxus took as a very good sign. The resilience of Elias Kincarran seemed boundless. Murmuring a gentle word to the *Asherah*, he left the wheel and padded soundless down the stairs to the main deck.

'A good night.' Without waiting for a response, he sank down beside his apprentice, crossing his legs. 'The serpents will be following our wake, no doubt.' He left the phrase open ended, an offer. What he got in return, however, was not what he had expected. If he had to be entirely honest with himself, he had truly been anticipating silence once more.

'D'you have spare netting?'

'...Aye.' Abraxus looked down at Eli. Now, being at his level, he could see what he was looking so intently at. The bowsprit. 'Ah.'

'Can I..?'

'I do not see why you could not.' Abraxus said wryly. 'Tell me. Did your father's ship have such netting?'

'No.' Abraxus waited patiently, knowing there was more Eli could choose to say. 'I'd hoped he would add it though.' A small grin flickered over his face. 'I must have asked a thousand times.'

'If we are not too tired by the time we return to port,' Abraxus said, 'I shall help you tonight.' He looked up into the sky, now fully overtaken by the wing of the night. 'It would be an enchanting place to watch the stars.'

'*Diolch.*'

Abraxus responded in his own long dead mother tongue, watching the intrigue light up the hazel of Eli's eyes. 'Now, however, I think we shall do what we came out here to do.' He stood, offering a hand down to Eli, who took it. 'Fetch the nets,

Elias. I will put these two stowaways to work.'

'Aye.' With that, Eli disappeared below whilst Abraxus drew himself up and marched over to Smythe and Tias.

'–No, you'd need to take into account the westerly, here look–' They had actually gotten the chart out now.

'Gentlemen.'

Tias started slightly, whilst Smythe just turned toward him, a belligerent expression already firmly on his face. 'Yes?'

'To work with you, I will have no idle chatter aboard *my* vessel.' Abraxus felt that the effect of his words were lost slightly by the smile that kept fighting its way onto his lips. 'Raise the sails, let her drift.'

Smythe rolled his eyes good naturedly and pulled Tias around by the shoulders. 'Right away.' Abraxus suspected he would have saluted, or some such nonsense, had Tias not immediately headed for the halyard lines.

Amongst the golden glow of the night lanterns strung about the ship, the netting was cast over the side by the well-trained hands of Eli and Tias. Theirs was a technique that Abraxus had seen little of, and he took a moment to stand back and watch the boys at work. 'Porth Tymestl and John's boys through and through,' Smythe had whispered, more to himself than Abraxus.

In surprising time – Abraxus suspected that some unseen serpents of Llŷr worked below to aid them – all four of them aboard the gently rolling *Asherah* were heaving up the netting, the coarse and salt-roughened rope abrading their hands as they did so. It wasn't the best catch Abraxus had ever seen, but for people who had looked over the precipice into the depths of starvation, it was a feast. As he turned them toward home, Smythe, Eli and Tias sat by the prow of the *Asherah* and sorted through the catch. At one point, Abraxus was sure he caught a few notes of a softly hummed shanty, though who it emanated from he could not tell.

Two large oil lanterns had been left burning to signal the entrance to *Angorfa* Harbour. Abraxus still chafed at the idea of leaving his ship within the manmade confines of its walls, rather than the natural harbour that lay around the cove.

Smythe disembarked first, and made headway for The Five-Pointed Compass, ready to let those inevitably gathered there know that a hot meal and supplies were awaiting them at *Angorfa* beach. Tias drifted away to begin building a fire down on the sand, leaving Eli and Abraxus alone to clean up the mess of silver scales littered over the golden planking.

No words passed between them as they worked. In fact, the quiet wasn't broken at all, not even when they stowed the gangplank and headed toward the young, pale-yellow flame that had sprung up on the beach below. From up the long cobbled street, the distant strains of curious chatter wound down to Abraxus. It was all he could do to vaguely hope that they had enough, and try and remember to thank the serpents properly when the moon had reached its highest point.

Just before they reached the ring of light cascading outward from the fire, Abraxus felt a solid force hit him against his chest. It was Eli. The lad's arms were wrapped close across Abraxus' back, his shirt pressing to the scales hidden there.

'Thank you. For everything.' His words were so quiet Abraxus could pretend to not have heard them if needed. And before he could even try to react, Eli had slipped away and toward his brother, settling a hand to Tias' shoulder. Tias looked over in surprise, and then smiled.

The crowd of lurkers descending from Smythe's inn was getting ever nearer. Abraxus turned to meet them; a black mass of noise edging closer. A few carried covered lanterns or open candles, lighting up their faces and slivers of those closest to them.

At the very back of the crowd, one lone figure carried a familiar lantern. It did not give off as much light as the others, the candle inside appeared to be nearly spent. But Abraxus saw in its softly swinging pendulum the glow dance off golden hair, a long, travel-worn cloak. Ffion had returned to the village by the sea.

XI
then.

The final moments - part two.

There was an indefinable peace in the face of the unknown. Whatever happened next *would* happen, come fog or rain or tide. Breakwater lapped gently at the hull of his ship as John passed quietly onwards, toward some undeterminable destination. The whispers of salt-stung voices had faded, now barely distinguishable from the waves.

The fog had thickened into a true sea-fret: it would roll off the back of the ocean and consume the land by nightfall. Its whiteness was reflected in the waters, and John found himself wondering if he had somehow slipped into the sky and begun to sail toward the world's brittle edge. Strangely, the colours of the *Dawnsiwr y Wawr* seemed blurred, muted, rather than vibrant against the blankness he found himself surrounded by. Canvas held beads of water at its roughened edges and John found that the *drip, drip, drip* was setting his teeth on edge. It broke the silence that seemed to him to be almost holy.

It did not take long to fold the sails and slacken the ropes and knots. Something deep within the twine of his fishing net soul called and begged for him to stop, that if he were faced with a sudden weather front... he pushed it all away.

Out over the water, swaying gently to and fro, the light within the bowsprit lantern flickered weakly. The candle was burning itself out. He would need to replace it soon, but John found himself entirely unwilling to move. Cold bit at his fingers; the chill beginning to settle in his chest. John had not moved all night. He had sailed into the next day after his leaving without feeling the need to sleep, nor for that matter, eat. His back to the stern edge, changing the course of his direction based on the whims of the current beneath him, John had merely sat and listened to the world around him.

The candle had burnt out not long after the twilight of the next day began to stain the fog a deep red. John found himself missing its fragile company. Still, he did not move. As the crepuscular hours deepened into true night, the wind began to pick up. Ropes creaked as it flew, unbidden, over the seas and around the little ship. And then, from deep below, grating on every fibre of his being, the voice returned to his mind.

You Hesitate. You Wait.

'Wait?' John wasn't entirely too sure if he'd spoken out loud, or was merely thinking. The silence afforded him no answer, his words – or thoughts – deadened by the mist.

Come Below. There was something coldly beckoning in the voice now; it had taken on a clarity John had not yet heard from it. The salt of the sea seemed to give it vitality.

'No.' John stood, bracing himself on the rail, staring down into the grey, unquiet waters.

But I Will Love You, This I Promise. Come Below. It was in the sails now, in the creak of the rope. The startling call of a gull made him jump, wheeling around and desperately trying to catch sight of the phantom as it disappeared into the fog on spectral wings.

'Love...' John turned the word over and over in his mind. No, it didn't feel like the call of a lover, a summons to a warm embrace. It felt like a command, a desire to possess without long lasting care. 'No.' He said it with more force. For a moment, John Kincarran wondered if he was losing his mind. Talking, or not talking, he still wasn't sure, to a voice carried to him on the tides.

Come, My Love. Be One With Me.

Anger sparked suddenly in John's chest. The voice, whilst still insubstantial, still twisting its way through nature, had taken on an unbearably familiar cadence. 'How *dare* you use her voice!' John whirled around, trying to find a corporeal form to focus his sudden rage on.

Come To The Seabed.

The mist tangled around him, seeming to snag momentarily on his wrists, tying him into the cold, blank sky. Night had settled in truly now. The waves lapped at the hull of *Dawnsiwr y Wawr*, a rhythmic beat that set his teeth on edge. 'Please, just – just *stop*.' John didn't know where to look to address his plea, and ended up pacing to the bowsprit, leaning over it and looking into the slate grey waters below. His lantern hung, cold and empty over the unquiet ocean.

You Will Not Come Below? Not Even With The Promise Of My Eternal Embrace?

'No, no I will not. Leave me *be*, I just want to sleep again, and be with my... my...' He trailed off, looking around as a sleepwalker waking and finding themselves away from the soft warmth of their bed. 'Why did I come here.' It was not a question, he realised, but a flat realisation of where he was, what he was doing.

You Are Here Because You Love Me. You Are Here Because You Let Me In. This Is Not A Lie, Master Kincarran, And To Deny It Would Be Another Falsehood. Still, lying beneath the rasping sediment of the voice, was Ffion's sunlight and honey-rich tones. John reached up and clasped his hands over his ears.

'I do.' He was not sure who, *what*, the whisper was directed to. It tasted like sweet poison on his lips. 'I do love you.' He straightened: he was not about to be cowed by the element he spent his life by. 'But I am not yours.' And with that, he turned and began to loosen the sails. They furled downward, limp and heavy with the clinging mist.

Come Below, the sea murmured, resolute.

A name stirred in John's mind, a name remembered alongside hands as big as the paddle of an oar, a voice of oak and bellow of thunder. A name spoken alongside the music of a winter's fire, smoke twisting through a chimney and into a blindingly white sky beyond.

Grasping the rudder, John swung the *Dawnsiwr y Wawr* in the direction of home.

Master Kincarran. Come Below.

'You may have me, Llŷr, when it is time.' Feeling steadier with the familiar smoothed rudder in his hands, John took a steadying breath, and began to press homeward.

The voice spoke one more time, in a hiss of strangling kelp against barnacle sharp rocks. *And What If I Decide That The Time Is Now?*

XII
now

Light.
May, 1816.
Ffion.

As supple May drifted ever onwards, Ffion watched lily-of-the-valley and yarrow push their way through the tilled earth and toward the pale blue sky above. Her garden had been left too long untended, but now under her careful ministrations it was flourishing once more.

She leaned forwards, resting her elbows and forearms on the uneven line of the dry stone wall that demarcated her own little world of tamed greenery. Beyond, the sea washed onto the shores, gently breathing in and out, its softly undulating surface rolling the ships upon its crest into a slow, graceful dance. Closing her eyes, she breathed in the salty air, letting it fill her chest and filter through the moss and lichen that was thickly growing there. And for the first time in what felt like many years, the salt was not abrasive. It held a sting, but it was the same sting of a slowly closing wound. The itch of something, finally, healing.

Ffion could feel the brittle folds of the letter in her pocket, alongside the stone that had been delivered this morning. It was almost as if the ink from the letter had bled through into the coarse cotton lining, and was spreading in black veins through her slip, her dress and onto her skin. She had read and reread the side in the vertical hand of Abraxus over and over again, by the candlelight before sleep, by the early morning rise of dawn. Now, her fingers brushed the edges of the paper, and she resisted the urge to read it by the late afternoon sun. There was a truth in the words that she had not yet entirely fathomed, but knew in her bones was hidden within the cryptic words the seafarer had given her. A first step was needed, a blind beginning into something unknown, but Ffion knew she'd need a guiding hand to make that first step. So, for now, she contented herself with her garden, the sea and her sons.

The first night back in Porth Tymestl had felt strained, but in a way that was bearable. Emotions ran high and too deep for Ffion to fully comprehend, so she simply allowed herself to hold Eli and Tias close and let the rest of the world drop away. They sat, a quiet three, just inside the ring of firelight on *Angorfa* Beach. The smell of baking fish and tangy dried seaweed permeated the air around them, punctuated by laughter, gentle chatter and the occasional hum of a shanty. It was then that Ffion knew something was *good* in Porth Tymestl. People were starting to sing again.

As the evening wore on into young night, Ffion disentangled herself from her sons and picked her way through the crowd to find Efa. Tias had mentioned in passing he and Eli had her and her family to thank for several nights of company and food. Efa had looked Ffion up and down, sympathy warring with disappointment on her face. Ffion held her breath: Efa had been a dear friend to her and to lose that bond would be another devastating blow. But then Efa's face softened, and she pulled Ffion in close, pressing her cheek to cheek. 'It's good to have you back,' Efa had murmured, pulling away and observing her closely at arm's length. As Ffion had begun to stammer her thanks, Efa had waved them away, pulled her into another quick embrace, and hurried off back toward Medwyn, who raised a tentative hand in Ffion's direction. Ffion reciprocated. She knew, instinctively, that somewhere in the crowd, Abraxus was watching her with his mismatched eyes. But tonight was not for him; tonight was for her sons.

Upon arriving home to Roseate Cottage, the tentative peacefulness had been broken. Eli had stood still in the middle of the room, seeming to Ffion small and scared. His shoulders stood in a tight line of anxiety, eyes cast downwards to the polished stones below. Tias had quietly brushed past her, circling around to face Eli, murmuring words Ffion could not make out. Her eldest had looked up at her, over his brother's shoulder. And Ffion knew then with an incredibly sharp pang of sadness, that she had missed Matthias growing up. The knowledge splintered through her very body, shattering her – and making her whole. Without thinking, Ffion crossed the space that stood between her and her boys and pulled them close to her. They ended up together on the floor, arms wrapped close, and faces buried in hair, the crook of an arm, the curve of a neck. The only light in Roseate Cottage came from John's bowsprit lantern, the constellation pinpricks of light dancing around them.

A chill wind had picked up from over the sea. Ffion drew her shawl closer to herself, standing straight and rubbing the reddened indents the wall had left on her forearms. She had busied herself for most the day, mending what needed to be mended, sweeping out the fireplace and winter's dust from the rafters. New bundles of dried herbs hung from them now, their vibrant greens beginning to fade into softer, darker colours. The smell of wild garlic, cowslips and dried nettle seeped out into the cottage – an unusual combination, wild and verdantly dissonant. It reminded Ffion of her childhood.

Eli and Tias had left that morning at sunrise. Ffion had already been awake, watching the sky through the open shutters lighten gradually from inkiest blue to blue tinged with pastel pinks, night clinging to the salmon-skin clouds in wisps of grey at their edges. Opening the door to let the thick air of sleep dissipate from the house and to let the already warm morning in, Ffion had heard the soft clink of rock against stone. Behind her, Eli and Tias had stopped preparing for whatever it was they were doing today. A flat piece of slate, ragged and sharp at the edges, lay on the doorstep. She lifted it, turning it over in her fingers. On it, etched in a scratchy white, were the words, '*Welcome home. The Five, III.*' Underneath the words, a small picture of a ship had been scratched, tiny and flying over heaving waves.

'It's not for us,' Tias said, startling Ffion. He was peering over her shoulder at the message. 'It's for you.'

'The inn? Why?' Ffion asked.

'I think it might have something to do with the letter Abraxus sent you.' Tias mused. Before she could ask, he pre-empted her question. 'No, I didn't read it. But I think I can guess.' He pointed to the three vertical lines. 'This means three – so, late in the afternoon.'

'Where are you going?' Ffion stowed the stone in her pocket and turned to face her eldest. Tias shifted slightly.

'Uh...'

'With Abraxus.' Eli said softly, looking to Ffion as if trying to judge her reaction. 'Or, I will be at least.'

'And you?' This to Tias.

'With Smythe. Or we might all be together.' Tias looked past her out into the clear day that held so much promise. He was clearly ready to be off and out.

'I think,' Eli said, 'that whatever you want explained will be at The Five.' He looked Ffion straight in the eyes as he spoke, a gravity to his words that Ffion felt ripple frostily up and down her spine.

'Alright,' she found herself saying. 'I trust the pair of you.' She reached up, cupping the back of Tias' neck and placed a kiss on his forehead. 'I shall perhaps see you at The Five-Pointed Compass?'

'Very possibly,' Tias said, smiling a little. She stood aside for them, letting them pass, catching Eli's shoulder in a comforting squeeze as he went by. She found it encouraging that, according to Tias, he had spoken a lot more since her return home merely the night before.

The sun had now passed its highest point, beginning to dip gracefully down toward the west once more. Whilst the day had been warm, the nights still swept over the coast with a chill blanket clutched in its claws. Sea fret was starting to form in the distance, rolling quietly toward the land, ready to make port the next morning. Ffion turned to look back at Roseate Cottage – the door was locked, the fire slumbering down into soft ashes. There was nothing now between her and this meeting at The Five-Pointed Compass. Resolutely, she had pushed the key under the door, leaving only the merest sliver of string by which she could hook it out again upon her return. There was to be no more hiding.

In one hand, the letter. In the other, the stone. Ffion squared her shoulders and pulled back to the surface the woman who had walked so tall and strong through Porth Tymestl's streets less than a year ago.

Hands.
May, 1816.
Smythe.

Ffion Kincarran arrived like a storm on a heavy summer's day. Her hair had long since come unbound from the loose braid she pulled it into and it danced wildly about her face and shoulders in the wind. The late afternoon sun poured liquid gold into it, coating her face and glinting deep within the woody brown of her eyes. Smythe shuffled his feet slightly on the doorstep to The Five. He glanced up and down the street, feeling the merest hint of relief at seeing it was relatively clear of passers-by. Most were down at the harbour, or else out to sea. He could expect the first wanderers at his door within four hours. They had time.

'*Prynhawn*, Ffion.'

She held up the stone Abraxus had left on the Kincarrans' doorstep by the pale light of the late moon. 'It's a good thing Eli and Tias hadn't left yet when I found this.' She turned it over in her fingers, 'I wouldn't have known what you wanted.'

'Ah.' Smythe beckoned her over the threshold of the inn, closing the door against the wind behind them. 'Aye, I'm afraid that's Abraxus preferred way of gettin' word to folks.'

'Hmm.' Smythe looked quickly behind him at Ffion's murmur, wondering if he'd catch derision or annoyance on her features. Instead, all he saw was a young playfulness there, curiosity kindling within her eyes. Turning back toward the bar and lifting the hatchway, Smythe had to smile to himself. Ffion was as much a part of her boys' mannerisms as John had been.

'Smythe, I appreciate the gesture, but really it's a little too early for a drink.' Ffion dropped the stone onto the wood of the bar and leaned over it, facing Smythe directly.

'You insult my fine stock, *cariad*,' Smythe said with a wink. Then he sobered. 'But no, that wasn't the reason why I called for you. Will you follow me?' He indicated the still open hatchway. Ffion canted her head slightly to the side, brows furrowing.

'Is there much point in me asking why?' Before he could answer her, Ffion added, 'Or should I say is there much point in me asking *yet*?'

In response, Smythe just held out his hand.

Ffion hesitated for one infinitesimal moment, and then rounded the bar. Smythe leaned over and pulled up the trapdoor to the cellar. 'I will say this now – you won't get all the answers yet. Some, yes. If you're happy to know a little and then walk away, then...' He trailed off, gesturing to the darkness below.

Ffion thought and then resolutely nodded. Smythe turned and descended the ladder into The Five-Pointed Compass' actual liquor cellar. As Ffion herself came down into the half-light, Smythe once more held out his hand. 'Come with me.'

Ffion's fingers gently brushed his own, before she seemed to come to a decision. Smythe felt some weight drop out of the air as Ffion's slender, yet work roughened hand, clasped his own firmly. Turning toward the deeper rectangle of black in the small space, Smythe led Ffion down the twisting passageway to the *Gorwelion* Cellar. As they went, Smythe murmured into the thick quiet, 'Feel along the wall as we go.'

The soft rasp of fingertips on uneven stone told him she had done so. There was a little gasp as Ffion traced the scales and ridged backs of the serpents carved there. 'What is it?'

'Soon.' Was all Smythe said.

They had come to an agreement, he and Abraxus, the night Ffion had returned to Porth Tymestl, not to tell Ffion all straight away. It was, they both had felt, the surest way to get her to turn tail and run for the woods again. Step by step, piece by piece Abraxus had said was the best way to approach this. And Smythe agreed – the weather had been kind for a while now, the sea less antagonised when he gazed out from the harbour wall. The catch was still on the sparse side, but by now the people of Porth Tymestl had become accustomed to less food: a sad truth but one that had stopped them from feeling the pangs of hunger from a less than clement spring's catch so sharply. The first thing to do for Ffion, Smythe had put in, was to inform her of her sons' positions with them.

'She will not like this,' Abraxus had muttered, a tad mutinously.

'It's her right as their mother,' Smythe had countered. 'And, even if it ain't the answer you want to hear, if she says a flat no to it all, then we 'ave to respect that.'

Abraxus' eyes had found Ffion in the crowd then, breaking away from an embrace with Efa. 'Tomorrow. Tell her tomorrow.' He turned to look at Smythe and said earnestly, 'The charts are done. Eli knows enough and Tias is ready to guide him.'

Smythe found an instinctive protestation rising to his lips, but after a moment of introspection, he knew that Abraxus was correct. 'Alright,' he said simply. 'Write a message for her tonight, and I'll see her in the afternoon. Take Tias out with you for a little while – it would be wise to give us some breathin' room.'

They rounded the corner from the passageway into the Cellar. Abraxus had left that morning from here to the hidden cove where the *Asherah* had been docked in the night, once the crowds on *Angorfa* Beach had dissipated. The candles dripped wax onto the floor, and the fire was beginning to sputter. Smythe disentangled his hand from Ffion's and hurried over to it, pulling a chunk of driftwood from the stack leaning against one of the rib-bones framing the hearth and mantle. As he prodded it into place, sending a shower of green tinged sparks flying upward, he heard Ffion's cautious footsteps move throughout the room.

'Welcome,' he said, turning and standing with a muffled groan, 'to the *Gorwelion* Cellar. Name courtesy of your youngest.' He lost sight of Ffion for a moment as she wandered between the shelves, her fingers reaching out and ghosting along the spines of books, the uneven wood of the stacks themselves.

'Smythe...' She breathed, rounding the corner and taking in the hanging rowboat bed.

Smythe chuckled lightly. 'It does tend to have this effect on people.' He gestured to one of the chairs by the fireside. 'Whenever you are ready, we'll talk.'

He settled himself into his favourite battered armchair and pulled the footstool closer, childishly thanking whatever powers that may be that Abraxus was not around to steal it again. Ffion wandered the Cellar a little longer, gazing at the lichen and moss growing in the drystone wall separating them from the cliffside and ocean beyond. Eventually, she drew nearer to the rib-bones and settled a tentative hand against one of them. 'Will I get to...' Her voice trailed off as she took in the height, the solidity of the bone.

'You will. But first things first.' Smythe waited patiently as Ffion settled herself opposite him, still looking around the room the way a young child looks at the world. 'I expect you'll be wonderin' where those boys of yours have gotten to.'

'Y-es,' Ffion said slowly, clearly wondering where this was leading.

'I make it no secret that both Abraxus and I did act on our intentions without consultin' you first. And perhaps that was a mistake, or a – a breach of trust, if you like. I'm hoping you'll be able to forgive us this.'

'Smythe, I haven't been the most attentive mother recently.' Ffion shifted in her chair, as if trying to shake off the guilt she clearly felt. 'Anyone who was there for them when I could not be will forever be in my gratitude.'

'We did what we thought might be best for them,' Smythe continued, feeling a slight prickle behind his eyes at the earnestness Ffion was looking at him with. 'Late March, I think it was.' Smythe paused, wondering how best to carry on without sounding like a man who had lost his sanity. 'You were still at the forest vale, and we'd had news by then that the pass was closed.' He paused again, and this time Ffion broke into his thoughts.

'Whatever you have to say, Smythe, you can just say it.' She spoke gently, but there was a taut line of metal in her voice: she wanted to know.

'Abraxus and I are a little... different from most other men.' Smythe began at last. 'Abraxus more so than me. And I promise we'll get into *that* later, but for now let's just say that people like Abraxus and I, well, we're sometimes known to take on apprentices. Not often, and not anyone either.' He looked meaningfully at Ffion, who looked back at him, measured and waiting. 'In the end, we didn't even ask, it was the boys who asked us. They turned down a position on Aron's boat that very same evenin' and came to us instead. I won't say I was disappointed hearin' that,' Smythe chuckled, 'I know Aron was sore about the whole thing.'

Ffion mulled this over for a moment before saying, 'So, if my interpretation of that is correct, Eli and Tias were offered steady work aboard Aron Gillet's boat, turned it down, and came to you and Abraxus to... apprentice?'

Cold water crept up Smythe's neck. 'When you say it like that...' He said balefully, not quite meeting Ffion's eye.

'And, of course, you said yes.'

'We did. Tias to me and Eli to Abraxus.'

'Naturally.' Something slid into Ffion's voice then, and Smythe was forced to look up to try and figure out what it was. After a moment, he realised it was *amusement*. At his clearly shocked look, Ffion raised an eyebrow and said, 'Well I suppose it's a good thing – Eli would have been thrown off the crew in less than a week for fighting; Tias wouldn't stand for that and would probably have joined in too.'

'You aren't... angry?' Smythe cursed himself internally for fishing for feelings that might not even be there.

'No. A little concerned about what apprenticeship to 'people like you' might mean. But no, not angry.' Ffion relaxed back into her chair and Smythe found himself mirroring her. 'Like I said Smythe, you were there for them. I was not.' She gave a little derisive laugh, sadness settling into her frame. 'In some ways you've been more of a parent than I have since John–'

'Stop that thought right there.' Smythe said firmly. 'Ffion, you must never, ever think you stopped bein' a mother to those boys. You lost a part of your world in a matter of days, with no warning. It would tear anyone apart. And you did what you needed to heal, or start healing, and perhaps that's not the way that everyone else would heal or tell you *how* to heal. But it was not *their* world that was ripped apart. This grief is your own, no one else's. You would never abandon those boys, and I know you would pull the sun from the sky if it would make 'em happy. But you needed time, and time was one thing that we could give you. Abraxus and I – although he would never admit it – love those boys like they're our own, but they aren't our own, they're yours. And they will always see you as the person who stood tall in the face of a black sea and tried to wrap them closer to your heart. So, no more of that, Ffion. You will always be a mother. Nothin' can take that away from you.'

Ffion had tears streaming down her face as Smythe finished. He wasn't entirely too sure where that had all poured from, but it felt good in the air – the same way a sea breeze on a fearfully hot summer's day does. Smythe leaned forward again in his chair and caught Ffion's lightly trembling hands in his own. 'They are yours,' he repeated. 'But will you let us teach them?'

'Yes, yes of course.' Ffion came forward out of her chair until she was kneeling on the ground, pulling Smythe down with her. They sat together by the fire, Ffion holding onto Smythe's shoulders and crying quietly. '*Diolch.*'

'You are always welcome.' Smythe whispered. They stayed like that until Smythe's knees began to protest at the stone floor.

'One little step,' Ffion's voice was so soft Smythe could barely discern it above the crackle of the fire and the distant crash of the waves outside. He smiled secretly into her hair, knowing what she meant.

Eventually, Ffion let go of his shoulders and smiled. It was wavering, barely there, but it felt like the first real smile from Ffion that Smythe had seen for a while. Smythe gently helped Ffion from the floor and took her around the shelves, pulling down tomes and scrolls and tablets he thought would interest her. They spoke about nothing more important than what language was used, or when an ancient hand had etched their words onto rock and parchment.

Smythe reflected that Abraxus had been utterly correct in his approach with Ffion and the truth. The man had centuries of understanding behind him, and not only of the sea. The people and the waters were intrinsically linked and would always be.

Beyond the canvas hanging, brushing lightly against the floor with the wind, evening dropped over the coast. Smythe had pulled aside the canvas to allow Ffion a view of the hidden cove and at the first sprinkling of stars dotting the purple velvet of the crepuscular hours. He took it as a small, and yet good, sign that she hadn't baulked at stepping out onto the cliff to be face to face with the sea.

Lights, golden and burning, rounded the headland. The point of a bowsprit, a tiny lantern hanging from its end emerged, followed by the glorious blue-green of the *Asherah*'s sails. Ffion's breath caught in her chest, and Smythe knew that, like Eli and Tias before her, she had thought it was John's downed ship.

As the *Asherah* made her slow way into the safety of the natural harbour, from their vantage point Smythe spied a figure perched atop the yard of the main mast. His feet kicked lightly against the canvas as the ship beneath him rolled, one hand wrapped tightly in rope. Beneath the figure, another sat with his back to the mast, lanterns arranged about him weighing down pieces of rough parchment. Ffion gave a little gasp at the sight of her sons, tremulous fingers pressed unconsciously to her lips. At the wheel, the strong and dark frame of Abraxus stood, rolling gently to and fro with the motion of the waves. Before Smythe could suggest they meet the others, Ffion had all but flown to the steep stairs and down to the shingle beach. Smythe followed.

As he hurried to catch her up along the rocky wall of the cove, Smythe spotted Eli stand and, cat-like, walk along the yardarm and toward the rigging, finding ropes to hang onto as he passed. Tias stood, stretched, and looked over to the harbour wall. 'Mam?' His voice was just discernible over the creak and snap of canvas and rope, the rushing of the evening's tide. Ffion smiled broadly, tears glinting in her eyes once more and waved.

'Eli!' Tias ran to the rail, leaning over it toward them. 'Eli, Mam's here!'

'What?' Eli was halfway down the rigging by now, but stopped and scanned the wall for his mother. He spotted her, and waved back.

'Both hands, Elias!' Ffion called back, no true bite to her words.

The *Asherah* came to a wavering halt, the rattle of the windlass telling Smythe that Abraxus was done for the day. Before too long, the gangplank had been roughly shoved over the side and came clattering down at their feet. Abraxus stood there, one hand resting on the railing of his ship. 'Ffion. It is good to see you by the water.' His voice was deep, caution held within. He made no move to step onto the land and, Smythe noticed, no move to let Eli and Tias past him.

Ffion met his gaze steadily. 'Smythe has filled me in on what I need to know.' She inclined her head ever so slightly. 'I pass on my full permission to teach them what you can.'

Abraxus' hand relaxed against the rail. He seemed to shrug off a cloak of sea fret and salt as he gestured, palm open, behind him. 'We invite you aboard.' Stepping back, he revealed Eli and Tias standing just behind him. Both seemed apprehensive. Eli's eyes were wide, as if seeing his mother out on a seawall was something he could not even reconcile with his wildest dreams. Ffion glanced back to Smythe, a question and the dark light of fear in her eyes. Smythe nodded and once more took her hand. He led them both over the gangplank and onto the shining deck of the *Asherah*.

Abraxus reached out and took her other hand as she hesitated, her head warring with her heart. Together, they led her toward Eli and Tias, still gathered by the mainmast. Smythe looked to Abraxus as Ffion seemed to finally find her feet and moved ahead of them. Her fingers whispered through theirs, leaving them behind.

'Whatever you said,' Abraxus muttered, watching Ffion greet and embrace her sons, 'was clearly the right thing. My thanks.'

Smythe nodded, a smile curling his lips as he saw Tias and then Eli begin to talk to their mother animatedly. 'The tide always eventually changes. Sometimes it just has to come in and wash away the old footprints in the sand first.'

Cove.
May, 1816.
Eli.

As he rummaged through the detritus Abraxus seemed to have collected in the dank hull of the *Asherah*, Eli wondered if he could really hear the light footsteps of his mother still walking the golden planks above him, or if it was simply a figment of his imagination.

Seeing her waving to them from the hidden cove's harbour wall had felt simultaneously like a punch to the gut and warm embrace. There seemed to be something *lighter* about her too, he noticed. She waved to them like a child welcoming home her family from a day's work. Both he and Tias had drawn her into overlapping and most likely incomprehensible chatter the minute she had stepped aboard the *Asherah*. Their mother was finally reuniting herself with a part of their world that had become all-encompassing over the past few months. Eli had felt his words pour back into his throat, his breath. After so long feeling like he was choking on them, uttering monosyllables and trying to untangle thoughts from gordian knots into strings of sentences, he felt the stopper in his throat dissolve. His voice was still a little rough from disuse, but he could make do.

Unearthing a mess of thick ship's rope and old netting from beneath several piles of what seemed to be tapestries, Eli weighed them in his hands. His fingers unconsciously rolled their way down each line of rope, checking for imperfections or thinning to the woven cords. That morning, he'd been alone with Abraxus on the deck of the *Asherah*, merely working through some routine checks of the knots, sails and ropes. Abraxus had then disappeared up to the *Gorwelion* Cellar, returning with Tias in tow. They had taken the ship out onto the waves – a calm grey-green today – and Eli had informed Tias of his request that Abraxus had agreed to honour.

The bowsprit was ready; thick and stout iron nails protruding from it at intervals marked in Tias' careful hand with chalk. All that was left to do was to sling the ropes and netting from the nails and hope it didn't all drop into the sea when Eli tested it.

He made his way back to the deck, ropes and netting slung haphazardly over his shoulders, listening. As he reached the gridded trapdoor, Eli paused, his fingers curled in the wooden lattice. His mother's voice, lilting over the lap of the waves, mingled in with Smythe's animated one and huffs of laughter from Tias and Abraxus. Smythe was apparently telling Ffion his Empress' bedroom-window story. Eli joined them on the deck, watching as Tias caught his eye with a wry smile. Leaving the others to talk, or rather for Smythe to regale Ffion with tall tales, Eli headed for the bowsprit. The light pad of feet behind him spoke of his brother trailing after.

Together, they clambered onto the long beam of the bowsprit, Eli passing back some of the rope and nets to Tias, and turned to face him, legs swinging either side. Occasionally, a little more forceful wave would collide with the *Asherah*'s hull, sending icy droplets of water up against the soles of his feet. As they knotted and tied off and cut sections of rope, Tias leaned forward a little and murmured, 'I didn't think we'd be able to do it. She seemed so set...'

'We aren't there yet,' Eli returned, keeping his own voice low. He noted the little triumphant flash in his brother's eyes as he spoke up. 'Apprenticeship, she knows about.'

'But not everything else.' Tias pulled a knot tight. 'Can you reach the lantern? This one is fraying.'

Eli inched himself backwards along the bowsprit, feeling a tad comical, and stretched to reach the lantern still burning at the end of the beam. The metal handle bit into his fingers with a sharp heat, making him hiss. 'Quickly.'

Tias opened the little latch and carefully extracted the candle, cupping his free hand around the wick to keep the flame from dying. Eli hung the lantern back as Tias held the candle against the frayed rope.

'How do we tell Mam about the serpents?' Eli asked, wrinkling his nose at the smell of burning rope. 'Or Llŷr.'

'Smythe says you should call them the Roaring god,' Tias said distractedly. 'It's polite.'

'I'm not really sure if they mind that much,' Eli said, grinning. He sobered. 'But really, how?'

'I think,' Tias started, his eyes distant and in thought, 'we leave that to Abraxus and Smythe.'

Eli was about to respond, but then he caught a glimpse of the trio on the deck. Ffion and Smythe were leaning over the railing, staring out over the sea toward the horizon. The gentle susurration of the waves remained even beyond the shelter of the cove. Above them, the sky was veiled in stars. Abraxus was nearby, absentmindedly fiddling with the first chime Eli had seen him place in the rigging. He spun one of the stones and, as Eli watched his mentor closely, swore he could see a flicker of a smile as the eroded hole lined up for a moment with Abraxus' eye. Eli brought his focus back to Tias, who was regarding him knowingly.

'It's up to them,' he said. 'We've done our bit.'

'Alright.' It was all Eli could manage in response. He knew Tias was right; Abraxus could soothe the seas and in turn soothe Ffion, and Smythe had his caring words and guiding hands.

The hour was late by the time they'd finished rigging up the net. Tiredness itched at Eli's eyes, but he wanted to see the job through. A sloping, triangular cross hatching of ropes and net now waited for them, slung beneath the bowsprit. It would certainly hold the two of them, although Eli was tempted to let Tias get in first, just in case their knot tying skills were lacklustre. Ffion had wandered over to them just as Eli was burning off the last frayed end of rope. She eyed the net a little dubiously.

'It'll *work*,' Tias said exasperatedly. It was almost as if he could hear Eli's intentions.

'After you, then.'

Muttering darkly and making them swear to fish him out of the sea if something did snap, Tias dropped into the net. It held. 'Told you,' he said sanctimoniously.

'Move over then.' The ropes were not the most comfortable thing to lie on, and Eli pondered if he could take some of the blankets and cushions that littered Abraxus' cabin to pad it out a little for longer excursions. He stretched out, pillowing his head on his arms and stared up into the night sky, expansive and serene above him. Below, the water murmured and rolled over in its slumber.

The net dipped once more, and both Eli and Tias looked up to see their mother place a tentative foot down onto one of the ropes. She looked at them, as if asking permission. Eli shuffled over to one side to make room. Ffion settled herself between them, reaching out to card her hand through Eli's hair, the other wrapped around Tias' shoulders. 'This ship...' She started, her voice pitched low. 'It feels...'

'Alive?' Eli supplied.

'Yes, *alive*,' Ffion said, wonder suffusing her words.

'Memory walks here like a stowaway.' Tias said. 'It's in the salt stains and smoothed wood.'

Their mother let out a little sigh. 'I have always wondered how you two see the world, how it works in its mysteries for you.' She looked back into the night sky, her hand still comfortingly atop Eli's head. 'I think I am beginning to understand.'

Landmark.
May, 1816.
Tias.

Despite it being late spring, the night air took on a chill as the moon passed overhead and toward the west. Tias had managed to rouse himself from what would have been the edges of sleep as he felt the first numbing nip in his fingers and toes. Beside him, Eli *was* asleep, curled onto his side. Tias rolled his eyes at that: his brother had the amazing knack of being able to sleep literally anywhere. Their mother had left them at some point, probably seeking out warmth.

Warring between the sibling temptation to just leave Eli and wanting him to be warm, Tias dithered a moment, looking out toward the gap in the cove. The night was still deep there, but the first very faint streaks of dawn were creeping their way from over the headland east. He wondered idly if there were any serpents spiralling below them. Making up his mind, Tias clambered out of the net and then reached over the edge and shook Eli's leg. 'Come inside.'

'Hmm?'

'Come inside Eli, it's cold and nearly dawn anyway.' Watching his brother trying to navigate getting out of the bowsprit net was worth waking him up; Eli was very uncoordinated, continually putting his feet through the gaps and swearing.

Once a now thoroughly grumpy Eli had found the deck, Tias headed for Abraxus' cabin, the tiny window set into the door expelling a tender golden light. He swung it open, finding Abraxus seated behind his desk, Smythe collapsed into a chair, mouth open and snoring, and his mother laying, somewhat gingerly, on the edge of Abraxus' bed.

Abraxus greeted them with a nod of his head, gestured silently to the bed and stood, stretching. Tias heard a rolling crack travel down the man's spine. Then, without a word, he left the cabin altogether. Tias looked at Eli, who seemed just as bemused as he did, but nonetheless shrugged and edged around Ffion toward the back wall of the cabin bed. Tias followed suit, reminded forcibly of those anxiety-stricken days in The Five-Pointed Compass, top and tailing with his feverish brother. As if sensing the rise of unpleasant memories in her eldest child, his mother turned to face him as he settled next to her. She reached out and ran her finger down between his eyebrows and nose. It was an old motion, lost, Tias had thought, to the nostalgia of childhood. But he found it still had the same effect; his eyes began to close of their own accord, as he slipped down into salt-tinted dreams.

The lamenting cry of a gull brought him back to wakefulness. Tias looked over toward the windows set into the stern of the *Asherah* and watched its solitary progress through a cornflower blue sky. He then realised he was alone in the cabin, the candles having burnt out and the door left propped ajar. A cool wind swept into the room, it's refreshing coldness hanging against the floor. On it, there was the smell of burgeoning summer; green and mulchy, sweet pollen underlying it all.

Opening the door fully, Tias saw the rest of his family –

blood and chosen – sitting by the mainmast. They seemed to be having breakfast.

'*Bore da*, lad,' Smythe said, noticing Tias' approach. He held out a slice of bread, liberally spread with jam. 'Get that in you, and then–' he looked slyly to Abraxus, 'we've got somethin' to tell you.'

'I've tried,' Eli said, looking a little put out. 'But they were insistent I wasn't to know without you and *nor* was I allowed to wake you up.'

'Patience is a virtue,' Smythe said succinctly, laughing when Eli threw him a dirty look.

'And not one you seem to practise, m'boy.' Abraxus added, lifting a mug of something steaming to hide his smile.

Tias let the chatter wash over him, content to just listen and be amongst them all. It seemed to him that notes of summer were everywhere this morning; in the musical calls of the birds overhead, in the bursts of yellow from the gorse that clung stubbornly to the cliffside, in the sweet stickiness of jam. He tilted his head back, leaning on the palms of his hands and felt the morning sun ripple over his face, sunbursts of red and orange flickering behind his closed eyes.

'Can we know *now*?' Eli's voice brought him back to the present. Ffion was smiling exasperatedly at him, although Tias did note a hint of well concealed curiosity on her own features too.

'What do you think, Abraxus?' Smythe said, clearly drawing it out for his own amusement.

'Stop torturing the boy Smythe.' Abraxus looked to Tias, 'You have your chart with you, yes?'

'I... think so?' Tias said, 'I left it in the cabin.'

Abraxus looked at him with an expression that said, *well go on then*, and Tias scrambled to his feet. Retrieving the chart from one of the diamond recesses in the starboard side, Tias took a chance to unfurl it before he laid it before the eyes of the others. He had to admit, he was proud of it. Perhaps not as nautically professional as some of Smythe's, but, it was his first attempt. He'd been adding little sketches to the sides, more for his own entertainment than anything else. A long, coiling serpent with trailing fins swam in the shallow waters of *Tua'r Môr* Bay. The *Asherah*, sails unfurled, danced by the compass he'd drawn in the top left corner.

There was a small amount of apprehension as he laid it out on the deck, Eli helping him weight down the corners with detritus from breakfast. What if it wasn't what Smythe had been looking for?

'Tias...' His mother breathed. 'You made this?'

'Aye,' Tias' voice caught a little in his throat as he watched Smythe cautiously.

'It's beautiful.' Ffion's fingers traced the marker for the lighthouse further down the coast, which Tias had rendered as his father's bowsprit lantern.

Smythe finally looked up and caught Tias' eye. 'Your mother has a good eye.' That was all the confirmation he needed. Tias sat back down, feeling his shoulders relax a little.

'This,' Abraxus tapped the chart, 'is what comes next in your learning with us.' He looked between the pair of them, his eyes both a piercing blue today. 'I have taught Eli how to handle the *Asherah*, and his prior knowledge has only strengthened this. The evidence of how you, Matthias, are faring under Smythe is proof enough here.'

Tias felt himself flush slightly and resorted to fiddling with the hem of his shirt. He abruptly stopped and looked up at Abraxus' next words, however.

'Which is why the next thing I will ask you to do is to set a course, by this chart, and sail it.'

Silence met his announcement.

Then, 'Wait, what?'

'Alone? Just us two?'

Tias and his brother spoke at the same time, voices confused.

Panic shot through Tias like lightning. He'd sailed on his father's ship, and even on this one, but had never shared command of its destination, nor of how it was run. He looked to Eli, and was not entirely too surprised to see the eagerness and anticipation already begin to set into his features.

'We will be with you,' Smythe said, his tone calming. 'But you will be in relative command, aye.' He glanced at Ffion as he spoke. She looked as anxious as Tias felt, but seemed to keep her words back.

'When?' Eli said, sitting forward on his heels.

Abraxus laughed openly, reaching over to cuff Eli around the head. '*Patience*.' The man's ease somehow soothed Tias' panic. He found himself looking at his chart, factoring in currents, tide times and prevailing winds.

'Soon, we reckon,' Smythe said, answering Eli. 'The weather has held nicely, and the longer days will 'elp too.'

Tias felt Eli's hands on his arm, shaking him in his excitement. 'Find us a good route!'

He batted away his brother. 'Let me think first.' Leaning closer to the chart, Tias began to lose himself in the lines he was so intimately familiar with. Distantly, he was aware of Eli dragging Abraxus up to the quarter deck and of Smythe reassuring his mother that they would be perfectly safe. His eyes kept travelling up to one landmark further up the coast, north-west from their position now. He'd drawn a small figure amongst the waves there, beside Old Man Morgan's skiff, scales flowing over her face and down her chest. Unconsciously, he tapped the marker, tracing the arch there. From the corner of his eye, Tias saw Smythe begin to smile.

XIII
then.

The final moments - part three.

Gulls wheel overhead, crying onto the wind. He watches gannets dive down into the froth and foam. They become ghosts, deep down under that ceaseless blue, flecks of white that mingle with the breakwater.

He was pulled here as if by a current, to where the land gives way and all is water and salt and desolation. The current is strong. It has to pull him under.

As the moon rises and the tide lowers, the vessel is cast out onto the mercy of the open seas. Red sails fill with wind, beckoning the ship onward, to splinters. Beyond him, is nothing. His consciousness is now defined by the tides, the voice of silt and salt, the creatures that belong on the edges of maps, the ceaseless wheel of weather.

Seabirds circle overhead, calling. They circle the empty ship too. They are bewildered by the lack of carrion aboard. Someone not-quite-departed seems to walk the deck.

He watches the night pour over the world. How long has he been below? Watching the mirrored sky slip over him, dizzying. Does he rest within the sea, or void? The water here is colder, deeper. Claws and teeth of bluest sapphire; they grind and yawn in their long sleep, restless but not waking.

It is dark, it is cold. These are the only two things he is aware of. It is dark. And he is so very, crushingly, cold. He is not sure what has happened. He had turned for home, set his mind against the weight of sea. And then, the next, the sea rose up from its glass-bed and pulled him in. Under.

He is not gone, surely? He is merely below. John Maredudd Kincarran, the sailor, his fall like that of Icarus, opens frost-tinted lips. There is no breath in his lungs. No voice remaining in his throat.

Held in the icy embrace, a thought. *I wanted to go home. I was going home.*

A reply. *You Are Home.*

XIV
now.

Belonging.
June, 1816.
Eli.

A warm summer breeze had leapt over the past hour, dancing in over the sea and rippling through the uncut meadows. The golden grasses and bursts of wildflowers rippled and swayed at its touch; its own sea of roots and seeds.

Eli had been awake with the dawn, lying in bed and watching the sun burnish everything copper through the open shutters. The night had been thick with heat, air cloying and blankets discarded. His mother had even left the door propped open all night, trying to entice the cooler darkness inside. The steady breathing of his mother and brother had done nothing to quell the beating of his heart. Today was the day. The first day of middle summer, as Abraxus had said. He and Tias had spent the rest of the slow march of May working aboard the *Asherah*, learning everything they possibly could before command was handed over to them alone. The layout of the ship seemed branded into Eli's mind – every rope and its knot, every crevice with counterbalance, how the sails hung furled and how they billowed when set free to the winds. Tias' hands and forearms seemed to be perpetually covered in ink, juggling stacks of paper and a few books as he walked from prow to stern, measuring and thinking. And today was *the day*, and Eli would be lying to himself if he said he wasn't feeling a little bit sick.

Ffion had passed along her blessing for them to take the *Asherah* out, anxiety lacing her tone but her hands steady and gaze meeting Abraxus'. It hadn't missed Eli's noticing that his mother seemed to meet them more and more regularly at the hidden cove, stepping aboard the ship and settling into comfortable night talk with its motley crew. Smythe had gently suggested that they take walks together whilst Tias was not under his care, and much to his and Tias' amazement, she had tentatively agreed. Where they went, or what they discussed was never shared; not that Eli begrudged this. His mother needed that time alone in order to begin to reconcile with their oldest and most changeable neighbour, provider and kin.

As the burning rim of the sun broke over the world truly, Eli could stand it no longer. He threw back the thin sheet that replaced their winter blankets and padded quietly over the ladder. Slipping through the door, he relished the sensation of the dew between his toes, the slick grass still clinging to the dirt and night's chill. Beyond him stretched the sea. The dawn light made embers out of the peaks of the waves, the white foam becoming roiling ash. At the horizon, a golden thread laced the fiery sea and the candescent sky together. There was already a warmth to the air. Eli turned his face toward it, and once more tried to still the beating of his heart.

A solitary hour passed, Eli losing himself to the whisper of the far-off shore and the dawn chorus breaking over the land. He started slightly when a hand closed over his own. Ffion stood beside him, staring at the water. Eli looked into her face and saw nothing there but a contemplative peace. No words were needed, they merely stood together at the breaking of a new day.

It was Tias crashing through the door that broke their reverie. He was trying to pull on a shirt whilst keeping a tight grip on his furled up chart. When he finally emerged, his hair was tousled and there was a look of naked fear on his face that Eli could only remember seeing a few times. Their mother beckoned Tias over, looping an arm around his shoulders as he drew level. Eli looked past her to his brother. Catching Tias' eye, he nodded once and managed a half grin. Tias tried his best to return it.

'Make the sea remember the Kincarran name,' Ffion whispered in Eli's ear before he closed the gate between them. She pressed a quick kiss to his temple and watched them out of sight.

Now, as the warm wind drifted over the meadows and the sea birds called and pinwheeled above, Eli and Tias strode along the cliff paths toward the gap in the broken stonewall that eventually led to the hidden cove. They hadn't even tried the inn and down into the *Gorwelion* Cellar; it was likely locked up, Smythe making preparations with Abraxus down at the *Asherah*. Finding the secreted path Eli, followed by Tias, traversed the treacherously steep way, clinging onto the cliff face at the hairpin bend. Soft rock flaked off in his grip, settling beneath his nails. Eli had foregone boots again that day, and was now glad of the extra grip his bare feet could afford him. He had to reach back and steady Tias a few times, his brother's hands full.

Over the sickeningly swaying rope bridge, the sea churning beneath them in whorls and sprays of mischievousness, and finally through the natural arch onto the shingle beach of the hidden cove. The *Asherah* was waiting for them, the figures of Smythe and Abraxus just visible on deck. The sails were furled and Eli felt a thrill run through the entirety of his body: the ship was theirs – albeit only for a day – to command. He looked to Tias, feeling all apprehension melt away.

'Ready?'

'No.'

Eli grinned. 'Me neither. Let's do it.'

At a shout from Eli, the three others below on the main deck sprang to and began untying knots, loosening ropes and, eventually, letting the green and blue sails unfurl in a ripple of canvas. The mid-morning sun shone through them, painting those on the deck the colours of the underwater. Eli shielded his eyes for a moment, gauging what to do next. In the end, it didn't matter what decision he came to; the *Asherah* began to drift out of the confines of the cove. Eli laid a gentle hand on one of the spokes of the wheel, almost asking permission. The first lurching slam of the open waves cascading against the prow was all the confirmation he needed.

All too soon, the natural cove dissipated into what would only be seen as jagged rocks to the untrained eye. The wind caught in the sails, billowing them and irrevocably drawing them out into the wild blue places of the world. Eli felt the rock of the *Asherah* beneath his feet as the wind pulled at the loose strands of hair he'd not managed to catch in the tail he'd tied it into. He pulled the air into his lungs and *breathed*.

Tias appeared next to him, scanning the horizon and occasionally glancing down to the compass held fast in his hand. Abraxus and Smythe waited on the main deck, ready to take instruction as necessary.

'North-west!'

Tias' call broke him from the reverie he had slipped into. Looking at his brother, Eli did some quick mental orientation. 'What? But that'll take us—'

'I *know*.' Tias was finally smiling now too, the wind whipping his overlong hair about his face.

'Tias there's no way—'

'We *can*.' Tias looked solemnly at him. 'Let's try.'

Smythe and Abraxus had joined them on the quarter deck now that they were properly underway. Already, Porth Tymestl seemed like a toy village in the distance, the line of the coast bobbing up and down as they sped across the waves. 'Where is your boy leading us, Smythe?' Abraxus called, eyes alight.

'North-west... that would take us...' Smythe muttered a little, sketching little abstract shapes in the air with his fingers. He broke off abruptly as they began to round the headland, Eli having taken Tias' directions despite thinking they were madness.

'Finfolk Point,' Tias said.

An arm of land, reaching out into the seas and seeking the chaotic touch of the waves. Finfolk Point was a cathedral of rock and salt and earth, precariously clinging to the land from which it had been excommunicated and left to hollow ruin. Where the sea lapped at the two spines of rock, a green tinge crept up from beneath the water; slick seaweed inching its way toward the sky, reclaiming the lost land. Within the arch itself, the breakwater was known to be fierce. Two tides met each other beneath Finfolk, dissuading any who might try and sail through. It had stood for as long as Eli could remember, and was said to be the place where merfolk and selkies met under the light of a hunter's moon. Their Da had told them countless stories of men who had sailed through it and have never come out from the other side. Old Man Morgan had been the only person in their living memory who had sailed through and come home again. As they drew steadily closer, Eli caught the call of a seabird – the rare, high-pitched shriek of an osprey – and spotted it swooping low beneath the arch, hunting. The lamentable cry could have been an omen, a plea to turn back. He took it as a waymark. *Follow me*, whispered the thundering tide. Onward, the bird curled and swooped into the endless depth of sky. 'Onward,' he murmured.

Seeming to hear him, Abraxus' face split into the widest smile

Eli had yet seen. He laughed, brought a hand down on Tias' shoulder and locked eyes with Eli. 'Take us in, m'boy.' His voice was full of delight, the wave and spray crashing alongside it.

Eli took a steadying breath, and brought the wheel around to point the bowsprit toward the archway. 'Like threading a needle...' He muttered to himself, trying to keep his hands from shaking too much lest that affect the course they were so clearly set on. As Finfolk Point grew steadily closer, Abraxus and Smythe hurried back down the main deck at his call. He wondered briefly if passing through would have the same effect as putting on his circlet – what was Finfolk Point, if not one of the world's biggest seeing stones?

'Hold her steady, Elias!' Abraxus' words brought his attention solely back to the task in hand. Finding his footing once more on the deck of the ship, Eli gazed down the arch as the bowsprit passed through. Tias ran to the railing, leaning over it. The sun was blotted out suddenly, the zenith of the arch directly overhead. Shadow fell over all of them, muting the colours of the sails. And then they were through, the mainmast clearing the gap and the colours reigniting themselves under the midday sun. A roar from below met his ears and Eli could feel the elation welling up inside of him too. It was quickly overtaken, however, by a lurch, both of panic and from the *Asherah*. The winds had changed a little, causing the two tides that met here as unlikely friends to break unevenly against the port side instead of the prow cleanly cutting through them.

Eli grappled with the wheel, putting hand over hand on the spokes. Something then took over, instinct, memory, or something more inexplicable he didn't know. Letting the tide roll into his own voice, he called down to the others, giving command after command. As one, they jumped to his calls and hurried about the deck. Turning his gaze to the horizon, Eli planted his feet firmly on the quarter deck of Abraxus' ship and let the sea call them out and away. The spray dancing up from their passing and above the song of the tide and the wind, Eli could just pick out the seabirds crying out, marking their passage away from land, away from Finfolk Point. He relished it, pulled it all into his soul and held it there. He felt, briefly, the unquiet ghost of his Da at his shoulder. Something deep within him slotted, finally, back into place.

Faerie tale.
June, 1816.
Abraxus.

He paused. His knuckles were barely inches from the wooden door, discoloured from years of keeping the weather locked out. It would be so easy, such a tiny movement to announce their presence. To begin to put an end to this all. And yet, he hesitated. It had been one thing to let Eli and Tias in, so ready and willing as they were to accept, to *believe*, that there was more magic in this world than what was already in front of them. The boys had been followers, adventurers – Ffion was another story entirely. She was written in green inks that smelt of mulch and a gentle summer. Perhaps there were stains of enchantment left in those long-ago written letters; he wondered how much of it was left. But her story had not yet ended, Abraxus had to make sure of that. If it did, it would mean penning the end of Porth Tymestl in what was to be an indelible hand.

Beside him, Smythe nudged him in the ribs, not unkindly, not with impatience. A simple touch to let him know he had a friend at his side, and that things with Ffion might not be so difficult. After all, she had begun to let the sea in more and more, willing to meet it at the breakwater. But Abraxus needed her to go further, to wade in deeper. Which would not happen if he didn't collect himself and *knock*.

Three hollow thumps matched the sudden beating of his heart, and, as they waited for an answer within Roseate Cottage, Abraxus idly wondered when the last time was he had felt this nervous. Perhaps when faced with the first meeting of all the other Heralds of the world.

The door swung open, and Ffion stood framed within, wiping her hands on her apron front. The smell of bread settled about them, drifting into the summer's air.

'Smythe, Abraxus. I wasn't expecting company.' Whilst there was welcome in her voice, he couldn't help but hear the slight undercurrent of apprehension there too. A silent second stretched between them, until Ffion stood aside in the doorway and allowed them entry. This was only the second time Abraxus had been inside the Kincarran household, and he still found himself looking around like a curious child. John Kincarran's bowsprit lantern adorned the mantlepiece, the edges of the rough metal gathering a patina of dust. There were no sounds of twin brothers annoying one another emanating from the balcony space, so all Abraxus could do was assume they were out.

Gesturing for them to sit, Ffion busied herself by the fire, still lit despite the heat that was slowly baking the fields outside a golden yellow. 'If you're wanting Eli and Tias, they're down on *Angorfa* Beach. A big catch came in this morning and they volunteered to help gut and sort it.'

Smythe caught Abraxus' eye at the mention of a catch. The Roaring god, it seemed, was beginning to be placated. Whether it was from the boredom of not seeing a coastal town crumbling as easily as they would have liked, or if they had sensed Ffion's presence near to their waters, Abraxus was not sure. At least there had been no more lightningless nights for weeks now: the bones that had littered *Tua'r Môr* Bay were growing less in number by the day, Abraxus sending them to rest on the seabed whenever he had a more peaceful moment to himself.

An insidious thought crept into his thoughts – how long would this delicate truce last? All it might take for the Roaring god to unleash all their fury and chaos onto the land was Ffion failing to meet them one night aboard the *Asherah*.

She was still talking, filling the quiet between them with a slightly anxious chatter about the smokehouses and how it was good for Eli and Tias to spend a little more time amongst the village rather than on the periphery.

'Ffion.' Abraxus broke through softly. She stopped abruptly, her shoulders rising a little. 'We have come here to talk. I think you know this.'

'I... suspected.' Ffion straightened herself and turned. 'I knew there had to be something to discuss.' She reached into the pocket of her skirts, withdrawing a crumpled and soft-edged letter. Letting the fold open itself, Abraxus caught a snatch of long vertical lines, crossed with diagonals. The epilogue he himself had written to Tias' missive several months ago.

'Will you sit, *cariad*?' Smythe said gently, pulling out one of the chairs for her. Ffion sat wordlessly, setting the letter out in the middle of the table. Abraxus scanned the words there, reminding himself of what needed to be said.

"On the edges of it',' Ffion murmured, also reading the letter – although Abraxus suspected she had read it to the point of remembrance. 'I think they are now thoroughly *in it*, am I correct?'

'Eli and Tias? Yes. I told them all and they accepted it.' Abraxus levelled Ffion with a look. 'If you are willing, I would like to tell you too.'

'Will this help fix whatever wrong I caused?' Ffion asked, a slightly helpless note entering her tone.

Smythe reached over and caught her hands in his. 'It's just one more step down this path, *cariad*. You've done the hard bit, now you've just got to trust your feet.'

Abraxus waited patiently for Ffion's answer. In truth, he was not sure what he would do if she baulked now. He had, he recalled with an inner wince, threatened with possible violent intention to make Ffion see the damage caused. But now, having placed himself in her life, in her sons' lives, he had no such intention. With sudden clarity, Abraxus realised he would wait for however long he had to and keep the wilds of the sea at bay with the last of his breath if it came to it.

'Alright.' Ffion's voice was so small in the cottage. She looked up and met Abraxus' eyes. 'Tell me.'

A breath before the plunge. 'The day of John's funeral. You do not need to tell me what occurred precisely. May I guess – you cried out over the sea? The graveyard is so beautifully placed here, where generations may rest deep within the chalk and clay of the cliff by the thunder of the waves. But I think, for you, there was only malice in this decision. For the memory of your husband to be laid to sleep next to his murderer.' Abraxus looked to Ffion for any sign of confirmation and got it in the shining of her eyes. Casting a glance to Smythe to make sure he had not said something insensitive, and seeing no reproach on the Wayfinder's face, he continued.

'I wonder, Ffion, if you are like your sons. If I took you to *Tua'r Môr* Bay, I wonder what you would see. If you listened on storm filled nights, would you hear thunder, but note the absence of the lightning? Would you hear screams, or would you merely hear the tempest pulling apart the sky? They see bones where others see wood. They watch the horizon like they watch the fire, waiting to pull a story from it, thinking about what shapes they might catch in it between waking and dreams. I imagine that you could not keep them close to you in the forest either, how could you? When you know what slumbering magic lies in the green places of the earth. Your childhood, Ffion, was steeped in moss and under the eye of a watchful, Quiet god. And you grew to be a woman who loved in the salt and found peace in the roar of the tides. So, I think yes, you are like your sons. Which is why this is not yet the ramblings of a very old man, but words that speak to your soul.'

'I...' She seemed to grapple to find the right word. 'I... *hear* you.' Ffion said as Abraxus regarded her. 'There was always something in... in the woods...' Her gaze became unfocused, remembering whatever enchantment had been planted within her from being raised in *Dyffryn Cernunnos*.

'When you called out over the ocean, I think you knew what you were doing. Why else would you do it in a tongue that had long since been dormant? In a language that held weight and the ire of centuries?' The last part had been a small amount of guesswork on his part, but it made sense to Abraxus that Ffion had spit her vitriol in her mother tongue. Seeing how easily she had slipped into conversation with him on those long nights in The Five-Pointed Compass had told him that it wasn't dead within the recesses of her memory.

'We live in a world full of things that are alive, Ffion. From ourselves going about our daily business as the sun and moon march overhead to the smallest insect weaving through a labyrinth of grasses. But there exist things that are alive in ways we do not expect. Watch how the wind plays with hair, how it runs over the fields. How the forests sway, brighten, die over and over again. In places where the sun is hot and the rain is scarce, how the sands there dance and sing in golden tones.' He looked out through one of the windows, towards the sea. Toward home. 'How the waves rush toward the land, only to whisper onto shore in lengths of blue and green and pearl. It is all alive, Ffion. And a very long time ago, before the people walked and the insect lost its way, these places, already so vibrant and breathing became something *more*. Voice worked its way into the sand, touch into the bark and thought into the sea. When man came along, we named them, some worshipped them. And some, like me, still serve them today.'

Abraxus stood then, watching Ffion's face set alight with

wonder, curiosity, the edges of apprehension. 'I speak for the Roaring god, or who will be named Llŷr in this part of the world. They marked me as their own a very long time ago, and I am theirs entirely.' He reached down and pulled the hem of his shirt up to beneath his shoulder blades, turning to show Ffion his back and the scales that ran the length of his spine. She gasped audibly, and perhaps made some abortive movement away from him, as Abraxus heard Smythe murmuring reassuringly to her. 'I am part of the sea, one of the oldest entities on this earth. Llŷr heard you that day on the cliffs. They rolled in the deep and listened to your grief turned to wrath and took offence.'

He let his shirt drop, retaking his seat. Ffion was wide-eyed, a hand pressed shakily to her mouth. 'What – what *are* you?'

'I am the Herald of the Roaring god. I do their work and am their voice.' Abraxus intoned, 'I am here to set things right.'

'Offence?'

'Aye. It may seem a fickle thing, the word of one woman offending the might of the sea, an ageless power. But Ffion, you do not know the power you hold inside *yourself*. Perhaps it was a matter of feeling threatened, perhaps it was the power of one of the old tongues. I cannot profess to understand Llŷr's inner workings. I think you are now beginning to understand how this tale will unfold?'

It was true; Abraxus could see the comprehension dawn on Ffion's face. 'The catch? The bad weather, the storms? All of it because I...'

'Unknowingly.' Smythe jumped in here, seeing Ffion beginning to collapse into distress. 'Grief is not somethin' that is to be taken lightly. How could you have known? Abraxus may be right, maybe you are like your boys, raised in magic that others don't see. But remember what I said to you, *cariad*. Your world had shattered.'

'Smythe is not wrong. I am not here to act as divine punishment or enact some poorly justified revenge. I am here to make amends between you and the sea.' Abraxus leaned forward across the table, placing his own dark hand over Smythe and Ffion's pale ones.

'Bones?' At the slight non-sequitur from Ffion, she hastened to elaborate. 'You said Eli and Tias saw bones on the beach?'

'Serpents,' Abraxus said. 'The bones of the servants of Llŷr, washed up on the beaches as warning or merely as a result of their anger.'

'I've stepped into a faerie tale.' Ffion looked a little faint: Smythe stood up and began to collect things for tea around the cottage. Abraxus took up his vacated seat, closer to Ffion, who he could see now was trembling.

'The world has always been a faerie tale, it is just that some people choose to close the book.' He smiled gently at her as she met his gaze. 'I would like for you to see them, the serpents. Eli and Tias were quite enchanted with them.'

Ffion seemed to think for a while, before eventually saying tremulously, 'And if I go and – and see the *serpents*,' here, with a little quirk of her lips and exhalation on the word, Abraxus watched the wonder being rekindled, 'will that... *count* as an apology? Will it all stop? Will the boats come home safely again?' She looked at him earnestly and Abraxus met her eyes evenly. 'You don't know, do you?'

'No,' he said simply. 'It is easy to say sorry after the wound is already bleeding.'

'Oh.' A clay mug appeared in front of Abraxus, Smythe setting another in front of Ffion. She stared into the swirling tea, steam rising in coils from its surface.

'But,' said his Wayfinder, sitting down and blowing on his own tea to cool it, "there's no harm in tryin".'

'Ffion.' Abraxus noted the hint of desperation that entered his voice. 'Please, for this village, the place you once called home, that *is* home to your sons. Will you try?'

'Why did it take John away from me?' This was not what he had been expecting, but Abraxus would not renege on his earlier promise: he would wait.

'I do not know.' Abraxus glanced at the dusty bowsprit lantern on the mantlepiece. For the first time, he noticed how battered it was. 'The Roaring god would not have taken him lightly, not to cause sorrow. I can guess, but I will never have a true answer for you.'

'Guess,' Ffion said a little wildly. 'You might be the closest thing I get to answers.'

'From all the stories I have heard, John Kincarran was as fearsome as the sea itself, master at the helm. It seems that there was no doubt he loved you and your sons as much as he loved the waters. Llŷr would have felt that love and devotion, and would have sought to make John Kincarran part of themself forever. Gods are selfish things, Ffion. And I am sorry for it.'

Ffion was openly crying now, silent tears tracking their way down her face. 'But I loved him more.' Her voice cracked right down the middle and Abraxus felt an answering crack in his own heart.

'I know.' It was all he could say. On a whim, Abraxus leaned in closer and pulled her shaking frame to him. 'I know.'

'He's still 'ere, *cariad*. In the stories we tell and the songs we sing. He's everywhere in your boys – the way Tias laughs, how Eli walks on a ship.' Smythe spoke gently, softly. Abraxus felt Ffion shift a little against him and released her, placing hands on her shoulders. Something weighty fell into the air between them.

'I will try.' When she spoke, the words were tear stained, cracked but not broken. Ffion drew herself straighter beneath Abraxus' hands, and repeated, 'I will try. For John, and Eli and Tias.' She looked through the window down to the sea and the village beyond. 'For home.'

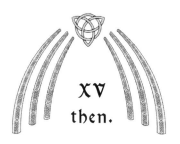

XV
then.

A Roaring.

It Will Not Take Long For Bones To Settle To The Seafloor. Held Under, Pushed Down, Drowned, Asleep. Gone. Or Perhaps Merely Departed. A Fleeting Mind Exhumed From Flesh And Brought Into Caustic Salt, Hold It, Treasure It. He Loved You, He Knew That By The End.

Home Is Such A Finite Concept. He Wanted To Go Home, He Is Home, I Am Home. Fragile And Wounded, Clinging To A Soul That Needed To Be Unburdened, Brought Into The Blue Places Of The World. There Is Peace Here, Gentle, Unending Deep. Quiet.

Roll Of The Tides And Pull Of The Moon Tell Of Days Past, Passing, Gone. All Days End In A Wash Of Fire, Extinguished By The Edge Of The World, A Bathing Of The Day's Troubles In Salt And Waves. Lay Them To Rest, Your Work Is Done. I Will Hold You Now.

Does He Dream? He Falls, Cascades Of History, Of Stories And Myth, Legend, Death, Triumph Lap Over Him. Yet He Falls, Silently. He Will Not Be Kept, There Is No Reason For Another. My Voice Is Beholden To Me, And Breathes Again.

The Ship. Small, Breakable. Well Loved. Painted In Colours Of The Sunset, The Death, The Dying Of The Day, The March Toward The Night. He Should Have Known. He Flew The Colours Of Finality. Upon The Beach, It Splinters. On The Rocks, It Breaks. Is It Still Loved, This Broken And Gone Thing?

There Is A Boy. Will He Love This Broken And Gone Thing?

There Is A Woman. She Lived Within The Very Fabric Of His Being. I Borrowed Her Voice, For He Was Mine, Not Hers. That Voice

Now Tears Through The Sky. Tears Through My Dreams, My Peace, My Deep, Endless Quiet.

There Are Bones On The Seafloor. The Roll With The Abyssal Current. They Become Sand With The Void Of Time. They Are Mine.

I Heard.

I Awoke In The Depths Below.

XVI

now.

Forgiveness.
June, 1816.
Ffion.

There was to be a party in the village that night; starting the minute the sun touched the horizon, with intention to end when she reappeared in the east. Thus far, it had been a balmy summer. After the storms and the struggle of the winter months, the people of Porth Tymestl felt cossetted by the long days, the soft sail-making breeze. Less lanterns and candles lit up the streets at night, and everyone's doors were continually unlocked. Open windows and boots by the doorstep were an unspoken invitation. *Come in,* they said, *you are welcome here, come and share the honey of the summer.*

Midsummer was not a tradition usually celebrated with this much affair. It was marked with a late night at The Five-Pointed Compass, perhaps, and some uproarious singing of shanties. But nothing more. This year, however, the people of Porth Tymestl were unknowingly emulating the preparations for the solstice with the same bustle and cheer that the folk of *Dyffryn Cernnunos* would be. A pang of homesickness hit her at every corner as Ffion turned down the cobbled streets. Someone – Efa she would bet – had decided that the narrow lanes needed flags and hanging decorations adorning them, strung from cottage to shop to cottage again. The effect, Ffion had to admit, was quite magical. Not being a village of arts and crafts, the sailors and fishermen had made do with old lengths of ships' rope, bowsprit lanterns and bells, garlands of seaweed and wreathes of spiked, butter yellow gorse.

She had woken that morning to the deliberately quiet click of the door closing. Ffion would have been able to find sleep again, if the sound of one of her boys tripping over the loose stones toward the gate and subsequent laughter hadn't jolted her out of the muzzy half-space between sleeping and waking. Pulling her quilt around her shoulders like a child, she had opened the door in time to see Eli and Tias pull shut the garden gate. The sun had only just risen; the birds beginning their chorus.

They had forewarned her that they would be leaving early that morning over their evening meal the night before. Abraxus wanted them out on the waters before true daybreak.

'Why?' Ffion had asked, bumping the door open with her hip, holding two plates. They had taken to eating their evening meal in the garden, both of her boys usually exhausted from their days' work with Abraxus and Smythe, but both unwilling to come inside just yet.

'Something to do with the eve of the solstice,' Eli had said, accepting his plate with a nod of thanks.

'Apparently–' Tias started, and then faltered. He cast a glance between Eli and Ffion, as if looking for something that would allow him to continue.

Ffion settled herself cross-legged between them, looking out over toward the sea. She had told Eli and Tias about her conversation with Abraxus and Smythe about what she now knew – even if part of her mind, the part tied resolutely to logic, denied it at all turns. Tias had seemed a little guarded, almost as if he disbelieved her ability *to* believe. Eli had immediately started chatting, his thoughts flying off in all directions, telling her about the serpents he had somehow managed to *befriend*, about the first night they had snuck down to *Tua'r Môr* Bay and how Abraxus had berated them.

For a moment, Ffion had stopped listening to what exactly he was saying, merely just watching her youngest speak with such animation. Eli was practically back to his old self, and it was with sharp realisation that Ffion knew she meant Eli's old self *before* John had died. It didn't mean that Eli had forgotten his Da, on the contrary, she had seen him dust off and collect the lantern on the days he was out for the night aboard the *Asherah*. But, perhaps like herself, Eli was finding a solace that he would be able to live with for the rest of his life. Tias was more of a puzzle to her. But within Tias she knew there was a metal strength that not many saw, and that if he began to slip, he would always turn to her.

'Go on, Tias,' Ffion said warmly, trying to encourage him to gap that distance she felt a little too keenly between them.

'Apparently,' Tias started again, 'the serpents are far more active around this point in the year.'

'And on the winter solstice too,' Eli said, a little thickly through a mouthful of bread.

'Smythe said it was because that's when "the world all begins to slip in and out of alignment between things seen and unseen".' Tias quoted Smythe's words to them, brow furrowed as he made sure to get them correct.

'What on earth does that mean?' Ffion laughed, shaking her head at the ways of the enigmatic innkeeper.

'No idea.' Eli shrugged. 'Tias likes it though because it sounds *mysterious*.' He grinned and nudged his brother.

'That's not true!' Tias said, flushing a little.

Ffion laughed again and reached out to ruffle his hair. 'You can like it even if you don't understand it, *cariad*. Look at me with Eli.'

'Hey!' Her youngest looked scandalised. Tias collapsed into laughter, all embarrassment forgotten.

They had spent the rest of that evening ribbing one another and swapping stories. As the quiet night closed in and the stars began to wake up in the velvet sky overhead, Ffion, lying back in the grass whilst Tias pointed out all the constellations he had learned with Smythe, had a sudden realisation. This felt *normal*. It felt *right*. There had been no normality since John had left them behind. Blinking away the sting of tears, Ffion brought herself back to the present, nestled between her two sons; one turned toward the stars, the other sleeping to the deep music of the world.

Now, as she wended through the streets towards the hub of *Angorfa* Harbour watching the decorations fly up and preparations made, Ffion thought of her *Nain*. She was long since entombed in the earth, having died not too long after Ffion had left. John had continually reassured her that it was coincidence that her death coincided with Ffion's leaving. Watching her boys go this morning, Ffion wondered if that was how her *Nain* felt as she traversed her way out of the valley and up. But Ffion knew that her grandmother would have felt betrayal, love and anxiety all mixed into a spiteful potion. She only felt proud.

Turning the corner, the vista toward the sea opened up, the stout walls of *Angorfa* Harbour busy and loud. On the horizon, the sails of the fishing fleet were dancing over the cascading waves. The number seemed lessened, but with no cause of anxiety – Ffion knew that the waters around Finfolk Point seemed to be more plentiful at the moment. The children of Porth Tymestl were clustered on *Angorfa* Beach, a small knot of giggling and high-pitched shrieks. Many had been given chunks of sea-chalk to draw on the walls of the harbour, where they began to rise from the sand. A few of the older ones were swimming, the waters calm and glittering.

Ffion had no purpose here aside from lending a hand to whatever work needed doing. After her conversation with Abraxus and Smythe, she had decided that it was time to try and reintegrate herself amongst these people who had accepted her as one of their own. Isolation was a comforting blanket over the shards of grief and anger she had felt, but now that chest full of broken glass seemed to be grinding down back into sand.

A flare of pride rippled through her as she stepped onto the harbour wall without recoiling. A ship was just pulling into dock, the sails dropping and chatter increasing. She recognised it as Aron Gillet's boat, *Y Hwrdd*. It was a battered and well-loved ship, large chunks taken out from the railing and the sails running ragged at the seams. It was Porth Tymestl's sturdiest boat: solid and heavy, able to cope with a storm and cleave a path unerringly through waves threatening to capsize a smaller vessel. Ffion spotted Thomas helping gather in the nets, and was surprised to see a new found ease in the boy. His shoulders were relaxed, an openness to his face that belied no malice. His father walked past him, clapping a hand onto his shoulder. Thomas ducked his head to hide his smile.

Rolling up her sleeves, Ffion joined the small crowd assembled along the edge of the wall, waiting for the toss of the mooring line. Several of them gathered there gave her openly curious stares, as if they had forgotten that anyone but Eli and Tias actually inhabited Roseate Cottage. A prickle of discomfort rolled down her spine, but nonetheless she straightened her back and, when the mooring line came through the air, trailing strings of kelp and droplets of water, she caught it alongside the others. Expertly helping to hitch the knot, Ffion felt her fingers remember the intricate twists of ships' rope, knots made for sailing. *It's not just the men that hold the Kincarran name*, she thought to herself fiercely.

Once over the initial shock of seeing her out, the others gathered along *Angorfa* Harbour brought her into their ranks and she spent the rest of the late morning and afternoon pulling in the catch, mooring ships and running messages between the sea and the salthouses. At one point Ffion even joined in with one of the shanties that picked up along the wall, most of the voices the high, heather-course tones of women.

'Shall we sail 'til days' breaking
and watch the dawn sun rise,
as we all shake sleep from our bones.
There is wind in the canvas
and horizon in our eyes,
we sail to return us home.

'Listen all, to call of our people
oh homeward, homewards,
to the waves we go.
Through long times we have waited,
an arrow to the bow,
oh homeward, homewards we go.

As we gather, nets and rope and sails
for the way,
and leave weighted anchors all 'lone,
our voices they carry
far over salty spray,
we sail to return us home.

'Tis our song, the cry of our people,
oh homeward, homewards,
to the waves we go.
Many days we have waited,
an arrow to the bow,
oh homeward, homewards we go.''

It was an old song, one that Ffion had heard sung at The Five-Pointed Compass, often accompanied with the strains of a fiddle. When the workers on *Angorfa* Harbour reached the point where the fiddle took over the tune, the singers turned to whistling, humming or even attempting to mimic the instrument. The final verse and chorus became punctuated with uncontrollable laughter. Below on the beach, the younger children who had never heard the song before looked up to their parents and elder siblings as if they had lost their minds.

The good mood was seemingly infectious; those leaving the serenity of the harbour departed singing their own songs, the ones coming into dock watched bemusedly before picking up the tune as they passed by. As the air became burnished, the copper coin of the sun steadily beginning to descend, Ffion felt the first stirrings of anxiety. If she was honest with herself, part of the reason she had decided to help with the work today was to distract herself from what was to come later.

A few days after the conversation with Abraxus and Smythe, Abraxus had come back to Roseate Cottage. She had appreciated that he had clearly been trying to give her space after all of the revelations she was still grappling with.

'I do not wish to rush you.' He had said, standing on the doorstep. 'But perhaps it would be wise to... *do* what needs to be done sooner rather than later.' Abraxus seemed a little nervous as he spoke, shuffling on the spot.

'Why?' Ffion had asked sharply. 'Is there something else happening?'

'No, not at all.' Abraxus winced and ran a hand through his hair. 'I will stay here until you feel you can face the waters...'

Ffion waited, knowing there was more.

'But... Porth Tymestl is only–'

'A small piece of the world?' Ffion finished for him, her voice softening kindly. '*Traed aflonydd*, *restless feet*, her *Nain* would call it.

'The sea is immense, and I will admit to being restive.'

'You sound like John and Eli.' She smiled at the almost startled expression that crossed Abraxus' face at her words. 'I understand, and I appreciate the sentiment to wait for me. I wonder though, if you'd be waiting nearer to forever if you *didn't* rush me.'

'Are you certain?' Abraxus asked earnestly.

'Aye. I'll need a little more time, though,' Ffion rushed to add. 'I don't think I could do it tonight.'

'No, no of course.' Abraxus thought, his eyes vibrant green shot through with deepest indigo, and pastel blue today. 'The eve of the summer solstice. Would that suit you?'

Ffion did a quick mental calculation. Taking a deep breath, she nodded. 'Aye, the eve of the summer solstice.' Abraxus put out his hand, and Ffion grasped it just below the elbow.

'An accord, then.' He nodded, seemingly satisfied, if not a little relieved.

As another shanty started up along the harbour, Ffion watched the sunset paint the sky, work forgotten at her feet. It was time.

The path to *Tua'r Môr* Bay was one that she would have once wished she could forget. Now, it seemed to stretch endlessly for miles. She hadn't traversed this path for an age, not frequenting the secluded bay when John was alive. Unbidden, the memory of her first day in Porth Tymestl arose. The susurration of the waves around her, the way her dress drifted in the current and dried later to a salty stiffness. John's strong and scarred arms, tight and safe around her. Glancing over the precipice, she noted a ship, lanterns ablaze and sails proudly green and blue running parallel to her on the sea. It could have been a flight of her imagination, but Ffion wondered if she saw four miniscule figures there on the deck. If she heard a snatch of well-loved laughter.

She would be on the bay first, she realised. Whilst the *Asherah* was docking, and her crew made their way to her through a series of paths she hadn't quite yet uncovered. She would be alone.

Ffion paused at the entrance way to the cliff path, remembering how steeply treacherous it was. The thought of her boys doing this alone, several times in the dark, had her stomach lurching. Stepping sideways on her feet, Ffion gritted her teeth as she descended. It was time, she *knew* this. It was wrong to keep a man so bound to the tides and current, as Abraxus was, in one small corner of the world for far longer than she guessed he usually would. That knowledge only gave her the stubbornness to continue, not the will. What came next, what would happen in the next few hours, no-one could guess. Even Abraxus didn't know.

Tua'r Môr Bay was exactly as she remembered it. Long, lonely and beautiful. The tide was drifting in, but not so much that all of the sands would be swallowed by the water. The *Asherah* swept around the gently curving headland and disappeared from sight. All she had to do now was wait. Sitting still was not an option, and before she could question the unconscious intention, Ffion had stripped off her boots and stockings. Cold, grainy sand pressed into the soles of her feet and made her shiver. Resolutely, refusing to shy away from it all, she dug her toes in deeper, feeling the briny damp that clung there.

It was merely one step in front of the other, literally this time. Flashes of thought about Eli finding splinters of his Da's ship passed through her mind, hideously coloured and too real. Ffion pulled in a shallow chest full of air and focused. John's strong arms wrapped around her waist, keeping her safe. Nights spent with a green burning fire, stories and the soft warmth of a love she knew would never quite burn out.

There was a slit in the cliffs ahead. Jagged and narrow, Ffion peered into it. It opened into a cavern. The more she looked, the more she saw of her sons' passing. The ledge at the back was padded with rudimentary bits of sacking and old fabric. Above her, the clack of wood against rock brought her attention to a store of driftwood. Discomfort forgotten, she edged deeper into the den Eli and Tias had made for themselves when they needed to hide away from the world entirely. A few chunks of chalk rested on the shelf and Ffion saw small drawings on the back wall – tiny undulating serpents, a ship, kelp fronds. She pressed her hand to the picture of the serpent nearest to her and fought the sudden urge to cry.

Leaving behind the cavern and continuing her trek along the bay, she came upon what could only be the bones Abraxus had mentioned. Ffion had plagued herself with thoughts of not being able to see them for what they truly were, like so many in the village seemed to do. It was tied to a deeper fear that she had outgrown the magic that childhood lays gently over the eyes, whispering that just around this corner is something new and undiscovered. But they *were* bones. Long, curved and white. Barnacles clung in odd clusters to them, pitting their surface. Looking up and down the beach, Ffion realised this was the only set of them here. She didn't know if she should take comfort from that, or find sorrow in the fact that whatever damage had been caused, was still ongoing.

'I never meant...' she whispered, pressing her forehead to the nearest rib.

Voices caught on the wind. Turning, Ffion saw four figures making their way toward her. Her heart hammered suddenly in the cage of her chest. She looked up at the bone, a stark white spike against the evening sky. 'I will make this right.' Her voice was firm.

'You will need this.' Abraxus said, holding out what appeared to be a copper crown to her.

'What is it?' Ffion asked, taking it and turning it over in her fingers.

'Somethin' that will help you see the serpents.' Smythe said. He lifted a stone strung on a cord out from under his jacket.

'You'll need one o' these too.'

'Alright...' Ffion said, perplexed.

'Trust him, Mam,' Tias said. He was holding what seemed to be a circlet of similar design, albeit made of salt smoothed wood, slotting a stone into a gap.

Ffion lifted the circlet to her head and slipped it on, looking to Abraxus for silent permission to bend the delicate wire in ways that would fit to her head. He nodded, turning away and then sighing exasperatedly at Eli who was snarling at his own circlet, one of the wires caught in his over-long tangle of hair.

'Do you have a spare... stone?' Ffion asked, gesturing helplessly at the one slotted into Tias' circlet.

'Here.' Abraxus held out a hand, a pearly white stone nestled there, a hole eroded near the centre top. 'Use mine.'

'Wait 'til you're in the water, Mam.' Eli said, having disentangled himself. 'It'll make it easier.'

'I have to get in the water?' Distress was now creeping into her voice; she could feel the deep, black ocean lapping at her mind again.

'We'll be right behind you.' Smythe said, clasping her cold hands in his warm ones. He added quietly, 'This is what bravery looks like, Ffion.'

The sun was only half visible behind the rim of the world as Ffion stepped into the ocean. Beyond, the sky edged toward deep blue, salmon-skin clouds scudding over the mainland. Umber and ochre drifted into the air, grasping at the lighter blue valiantly trying to retain the day. There was barely any breakwater, merely the soft shush of the waves rolling to shore, only to be subsumed once more into the expanse of water beyond. Ffion didn't bother to tie up her skirts. She let the water soak them, the cold climbing higher as she walked forward. Knee deep in the surf, she turned back to look at Eli, Tias, Smythe and Abraxus gathered behind her. Abraxus had his hand on Eli's shoulder.

Turning back to the ocean, Ffion took the stone and slotted it into the gap in the circlet. Then, her very perception of reality changed. For in the water, circling her ankles in the shallows, their long fins protruding from the waves, were the serpents. No longer in control, Ffion dropped to her knees. The cold rushed up to her waist. She had never truly doubted Abraxus, but spoken word and seeing were two very different things. It was one thing to pick up a book. It was another to be within the ink. A long, lithe green serpent swam past her. Its trailing fins looked like strings of kelp. Ffion could not put into words, nor thought, how beautiful they were. *And she had helped to kill them.*

'I'm sorry,' she said, her voice cracking as she felt the warmth of tears on her cheeks. 'I am so sorry, I didn't...'

The green serpent, as if it heeded her words, passed by her again, letting its fins trail against her leg. She didn't shudder. 'I'm sorry.' It seemed to be all she could say, over and over again, her hands clutched to her chest where she could feel her heart breaking.

There was a ripple, far out to sea from where she knelt, surrounded by the peaceful luminescence of the serpents. It spread out in unerring circles, never quite fading until it reached the shoreline alongside the breakwater. Ffion looked up, wondering what was happening. The air around her seemed charged. From the shore, there was nothing but silence.

And then John, *her John*, rose up from the water, only submerged to his ankles. Ffion gasped raggedly, her whole body shaking. He looked toward her, the sun catching in the auburn of his hair, his beard. Step by step, he walked toward her, no ripples or wake left in his wake. All Ffion could do was stare. *John.* He reached her and slipped down into the water, kneeling, holding out his hands.

My Love. He said.

Ffion broke down entirely. She reached for him, trying to pull him closer to her; the sea would not take him again, no more would she be alone in this world. He was cold to her touch.

I Have Missed You. His voice echoed, muffled and distant, like it was emanating from the very bed of the sea.

'I missed you too,' Ffion said, sobs and laughter all mixed up in her words. 'I missed you so much it *hurt*. Every day. Every single day.'

I Know. I Was Here All This Time. A well known and loved hand reached out and pressed against her heart. There was something wrong with his eyes.

'Come back?' Ffion tried to rise, to pull John with her to shore. 'Come back with me. Our sons, John, you'd be so proud of them–'

Love. It was all Ffion needed to hear to know.

'No, please. *Please.* You can't go again.'

I Will Never Be Far From You. I Am Here In The Waves, In The Gorse, In The Sails On A Summer Morning. I Am Here In Your Heart, Your Mind. Your Dreams. Love Is Not Something That Dies Easily.

'I don't know how to do this without you.' Ffion sobbed, resting her head on John's chest. It was stirred with no breath.

Oh, But Of Course You Do. Because Look, Here You Are Still Breathing. Still Feeling. Still Living, Ffion. He caught her face in his hands, raising her eyes to meet his. *You Are Strong My Love. Pain Is Just A Part Of Being Alive. It Is Never Far From You. But, Shall I Tell You A Secret?*

Ffion felt that laugh again in her throat, made sad and heavy by grief. The playful glint in John's eyes was all too familiar. 'You can tell me anything.'

I Am Also Never Far From You. And, with his hand under her chin, he bent to kiss her. His arms wrapped around her waist, pulling her closer. There was no warmth to them, and the sensation made Ffion ache. She tasted salt on his lips, closing her eyes and letting the tears continue to fall. John's kisses were always salt-stung.

She kept her eyes closed as she felt him pull away, felt those hands settle on her shoulder, run down her arms. She kept her eyes closed as she felt a sea breeze from the west pick up, felt a soft spray of mist pass over her face, her eyelids, her lips. Ffion kept her eyes closed, for she could not bear to watch John slip away from her again.

The mist swirling about her began to fade, spectral tendrils of it lingering a mere moment longer than was natural on her cheek. And then it was gone, and Ffion was left cold in the ocean. She clasped her hands to her chest, feeling that roar of a black monster within her soul. She willed it to be still and silent; anger was not the answer here. Instead, she bent double at the waist, covered her face and cried. She felt her hair take up the weight of water. The sobs wracked her, pain pulsing through her being like a thousand wounds.

At the end of it all, Ffion looked up to a world broken and beautiful.

She sat in the water.

Pulled in sea air. Watched the sun go down.

Grief.
June, 1816.
Eli.

Eli watched his mother in the water with the spectre of his father. Heard her sobs and felt his own eyes sting. In the shelter of Smythe's arm, Tias buried his face into the innkeeper's shoulder. His own shoulders were shaking.

Abraxus' hand was a comforting weight. Eli reached up and clumsily held onto it. He felt it tighten beneath his hand. As the sun disappeared from the sky, Eli watched the figure of his Da dissipate into sea mist, drifting out toward the empty horizon.

He heard his Mam break, her sobs finally breaking his own will.

'That wasn't our Da.' It felt right to speak the words. To utter the truth he wanted so badly to reject. Eli looked up at Abraxus, watching the sunset mirrored in the man's eyes. 'Our Da didn't have eyes the colour of the sea.'

Abraxus cast his gaze to him, sorrow swimming there. Then, so quietly it could have been the tide. 'Dead men tell no tales.'

XVII
then.

Dawn and dusk.

The first night in Porth Tymestl was quiet. Deceptively so. No storm rocked the little village, no wind pulled at the grass and made the shutters rattle. He noted the lanterns and candles left on the doorsteps, lighting his way down the cobbled streets, tiny pinpricks of warmth that belied a possible welcome. Whether that welcome would be mirrored in the faces of the village's occupants was another matter and one he'd leave for the pale brush of dawn.

The threads that hung from his staff swung as he walked, their many beads, shells and the ring clicking against each other. Idly, Abraxus wondered what people might think if tired eyes were to glance from the darkened windows. The figure of some unquiet, drowned soul; whispering through the small hours leaving but the drifting tint of salt in its wake.

The village was not large, but the paths he walked were labyrinthine in their construction – a palimpsest of generations shaped from cobble and stone. It left him feeling a little disoriented in the near dark. Closing his eyes, Abraxus listened to the roar of the sea, away to his left. Swinging back around, he made his way back toward the inn.

His Wayfinder had not felt the need to greet him from the seas: at first the distinct lack of the genial figure of Smythe in the cellar had perturbed him. But upon his approach to the cellar

505

trapdoor, and hearing the clamour of ale-fuelled voices, Abraxus had reasoned that Smythe's absence was justified. He had loitered in the bar's actual cellar for some time, waiting to see if Smythe would duck down for a fresh cask. No such opportunity presented itself, so he waited until the noise of life above him had sunk away into a murmur and then eased the trapdoor open.

Feeling like some sort of thief, Abraxus set the trapdoor down quietly and made a quick pass of the room. Most of the sailors were so deep in their cups, they seemed halfway into the arms of sleep. One of them shifted toward the bar, regarding him with bleary eyes. Abraxus stared back, challenging the man to say something, or else dismiss him as a figment of an ale addled mind. Eventually, the man reacquainted his forehead with the chipped surface of the table and Abraxus let out a breath he hadn't realised he'd been holding. Then he cursed softly as he spotted the familiar silhouette of Smythe disappearing up the stairs. And so, Abraxus had taken to the night furled streets with nothing but the stars for company.

Upon his return, the inn's door had been left unlocked, although the lightless windows signalled it was closed to patrons. Smythe must have pre-empted his wanderings. The fire had burned low in the hearth, reduced to slumbering embers. On the bar, propped up by a full mug of ale, was a flat piece of sea-slate. Taking the mug, Abraxus held the slate to the meagre light emitting from the hearth, and let out a huff of laughter. All that was drawn upon its smooth surface was an arrow, pointing downwards.

'Glad to see you got my thoroughly encrypted message.' Smythe was warming his feet by the fire in the cellar, a book resting open against his chest. He made no move to greet Abraxus, merely inclined his head. Abraxus saw the momentary flare of relief flash through the innkeeper's eyes.

'A cipher indeed,' Abraxus said dryly. Then, because he saw no point in wasting time. 'The work?'

Smythe sighed, sat up and stretched. The book dropped to the floor with a dull thud. 'Storms. Bones, lightningless nights.' A pensive look came over his features. 'We've lost a few of our own, recently.'

'I will do what I can.' Abraxus sipped from the mug he'd brought down with him, gazing at the two ribs that framed the hearth.

'All stowed?' Smythe asked briskly.

In response, Abraxus canted his head toward the sea chest he'd brought up with him.

'I'll get a room ready for you upstairs, folk might ask questions about the strange man appearing and disappearin' from behind my bar.'

The talk after that turned to Abraxus' recent travels, where he'd hailed from when the message reached the hull of the *Asherah*. Smythe in turn spoke about the village, its people. Abraxus was a little surprised to hear that Cynfor Morgan was still alive. A few names were mentioned that Abraxus made a note of; the Griffiths, Owen, the Kincarrans, Aron Gillet. He would learn their faces in due course.

As the small hours of the night gave way to dawn, he felt the gritty itch of sleep in his eyes. He sank lower into his chair, letting the fire warm his salt-soaked bones. Smythe must have noticed his travel-weariness and left, resting a hand on Abraxus' shoulder before making his way toward his own bed. 'I'm glad you're here.'

The bed sequestered in the old rowboat was divine. Cosseted in blankets, Abraxus gently touched one bare foot to the cold floor and set the ropes swinging lightly. The sensation was not too different from sleeping in his cabin aboard the *Asherah*. Homesickness would not plague him this night.

Before sleep could pull him under, he distantly heard waves tumble onto the shingle of the beach below. The sea seemed agitated to his mind, perhaps casting about for where their Herald had vanished too, beyond their reach. Abraxus sighed, turned over and let the sway of the rowboat bed displace all thoughts for a while. He could only hope that his dreams would be gentle. After all, there was work to be done.

XVIII
now.

Paths.
July, 1816.
Tias.

Summer wandered on over Porth Tymestl. They were treated one night to a spectacular storm, roiling black clouds turning the early evening to deepest wintry night in a matter of hours. There was both thunder and lightning, but this time, they came as a pair.

As the days drew longer still and the mornings were permeated with sea-frets that filled the streets with saline spectres, Tias spent his time wandering the beaches, the cliff paths, even the lesser traversed alleys and footpaths in and around Porth Tymestl. He stared down the rutted dirt road that led out of the village and inland, the mud there baked dry and cracked. He wondered where it led to, where it ended.

There was a broken peace within him now; the acknowledgement that things were not right in his life, and nor would they be again. And yet, there was comfort and solace in the way the wind rippled through the coarse grasses of the cliff-top meadows. There *was* peace in looking at the broken shards and seeing the way they refracted the light.

After midsummer's eve, they had all drifted a little from one another, needing the time and solitude to begin to collect whatever fragments each wanted to retain and which to discard. Eli meandered in and out of his company, content to be quiet at Tias' side as he wrote in his notebook, or simply vanishing for hours at a time. He always came back before they could worry.

Their mother had risen out of the sea that night and walked, as if in a dream, back to the beach, stopping only to pass Abraxus back his circlet and stone. Then, she had slipped back up the cliff path and into the gathering dark. Tias, unable to truly form a cohesive thought, had tried to scramble away from Smythe and after her.

'Stay here.' It had not been Smythe or even Abraxus' voice. He had turned and came face to face with his brother. 'Stay by the sea for a while.'

Shaken, Tias nodded and reached up to dash the tears away from his cheeks. His mother needed the time alone. It was only when the driftwood fire was sending sparks of emerald flame into the night that a thought came to Tias. The voice Eli had spoken to him in, the cadence to his tone. He had sounded almost like his mentor.

It had been just before dawn when Smythe had pulled him aside and asked.

Ffion had spent her days sitting quietly in a chair pulled outside into the garden, facing the water. Sometimes there was a book in her hand, or some other busywork. Mostly, she sat. Occasionally, Tias sat with her, neither of them speaking, their silence almost sacred and unbreakable. Before he had wandered out today, he had watched Eli disappear down the path toward the village at his mother's side. Almost imperceptibly, she sighed and reached out to card her hand through his hair. It was almost to his shoulders now, and unlike Eli, Tias didn't bother to bind his back. He liked the way it hid him from the world when his head was bent over some tome of Smythe's.

'Would you like me to stay?' He asked quietly.

'No, *cariad*. You go.' Ffion ran her thumb and index finger down a strand of his hair and looked down at him. She smiled, a little sadly, but still the emotion of it reached her eyes.

The words felt like they were lodged in his throat. Tias thought a little, wondering whether he should ask. If he had the *courage* to ask. 'Mam... are you going to – to stay?'

His mother blinked, and then looked back over the sea. It was mirror smooth today, no wind rippled its cerulean surface. 'No, I don't think I will.' She said it thoughtfully, as if by voicing the intention she had suddenly made it a definite decision. Tias took in a deep breath and scanned his eyes over the descent to the village and the ocean. He had thought that would be her answer, and what surprised him more than anything else was the level of calmness he felt. It made his own choice easier.

He stood, feeling for the first time since that night, solid on the earth. His bare feet pressed into the soil, leaving marks that told the world of his passing, no matter how briefly those prints lasted. Looking down at his mother and then back out over the small corner of the world he had known his whole life, he knew.

You go. His mother's words, an answer to an innocuous question. And also a blessing in disguise. Tias stooped and embraced Ffion, who's arms rose up to latch onto his own. '*Caru ti.*' *Love you.*

'*Rwy'n dy garu di mwy.*' *I love you more.* She released him. 'Eli..?'

'I don't know,' Tias said honestly. 'Although...' He tried to think of a way to put his brother's possible intentions into words. At last he settled simply on, 'It's Eli.'

Ffion smiled a tad more broadly. She closed her eyes, tilting her face back to catch the mid-morning sun. Tias sensed that same broken peace surrounding her, softened by the warmth of the day.

'I'll be at The Five.' Tias collected his bag from the dew-damp grass and slung it over his shoulder. 'I'll be back before sundown.' He promised, pausing by the gate and looking back into the pastoral confines of the garden. One last question, just to make sure. 'Are you–'

'Go, Tias.' She turned to face him. 'Go and see it all.' There were tears in her eyes, but in the sun, they shimmered like miniature drops of crystal. He nodded, opened the gate and stepped out. Tias couldn't help but wonder where the road might take him.

Keys.
July, 1816.
Smythe.

The room was emptied. All of the detritus Abraxus had managed to collect during his time in Porth Tymestl had been unceremoniously shoved into a large sea-chest and dragged into the hall. With a rather copious amount of swearing and grumbling on Smythe's part.

Through the little open window, Smythe caught the sound of chatter from the streets below. Several days ago, a handful of folk had dug out and repaired the old cart, yoked it to a rather obstinate horse belonging to Crow and travelled inland to the villages nestled in woods and valleys. They had returned today, the cart overflowing with supplies. The people of Porth Tymestl had certainly learnt their lessons in being prepared with surplus, and had dug deep into the collective coffers and materials to trade alike in order to return home with what amounted to a bounty. Smythe was well pleased with the three small casks of fine honey mead that had been rolled through his open door that morning.

Sweeping away the last cobweb stubbornly clinging to a corner, Smythe wiped his brow and looked around the room. It was almost as if it had never been occupied. The only things that now remained to tell of Abraxus' passing was the staff leaning in the corner and his long leather coat draped over the back of the chair. Smythe reached into his pocket and pulled out a sprig of purple heather. Removing the slightly shrivelled stem of lavender from the small glass bottle nestled into the box windowsill, Smythe put the heather in its stead.

From below, a call. 'Smythe?'

'Upstairs, lad, be with you in a moment!' Smythe called down to Tias. Gathering up Abraxus' coat and, with some reverence, his staff, Smythe backed out of the room. The latch clicked shut and Smythe turned the key resting there. There was an odd sense of melancholy as the lock slid into place.

Tias was leaning on the bar, tracing abstract patterns on the wood with a little spilled water. Smythe deposited the staff and coat by the unlit hearth and turned to face him. When Tias caught his eye, Smythe knew exactly what he was here to say. Unable to help himself, a broad grin broke out over his face. 'I assume you've discussed?'

'Not really, no.' Tias said ruefully. 'She just sort of *knew*.'

'Of course she did,' Smythe said with a chuckle. 'She's a canny woman, your mother.'

'Will Abraxus ask Eli?'

'I would imagine so, although, he won't do it in as many words, nor as eloquently as I did.' Smythe rolled his eyes fondly as he spoke, coming to settle against the bar alongside his apprentice. For the first time, Smythe noticed that Tias now stood a little taller than him.

The night Ffion had walked into the sea and the shape of John Kincarran had walked out, the night where there had been quiet and tears and a sorrow so deep Smythe couldn't help but feel its blackness pull on his very soul, he had asked Tias a question. Not one to be answered immediately. He wasn't even sure if he should *have* asked that night, it felt almost unfair to tug even more on the lad's taut and frayed emotions. But asked he had.

It didn't matter to him what Abraxus' intentions were for Eli. Smythe could guess, and guess with more accuracy than most, but to him the other man's choices were moot in this issue.

Smythe had tutored a damn good apprentice, and he wasn't about to leave him behind.

He studied Tias a little more closely, trying to catch any apprehension or anxiety in the boy's expression. But the more he looked, the more Smythe saw only the anticipation, the willingness. 'Are you sure this is what you want?' He asked carefully.

'Aye.' Tias looked him full in the eyes, a determined set to his jaw. 'I'm ready to see more.' A smile flickered at the edges of his lips. 'To see it all.'

'And of course,' Smythe said, leaning over the bar to produce two quarter-mugs, 'we can come back anytime.' He slid one over to Tias and then rounded the bar. 'Since we're leavin', then, I'd quite like a chance to taste this before I have to leave it behind.' He poured some of the honey mead into his own mug and reached for Tias'.

'Will you lock up The Five?' Tias asked, sipping his mead. 'This is *really* good, are you sure we can't take it with us?'

Smythe laughed, savouring the sweet roundness the drink left in its wake. 'Quite sure, we're to be travellin' light.' He looked around the barroom, taking in the lanterns, the battered tables, the blackened hearth. It had been home for so long, shelter to so many lost and weary.

'Smythe?' Tias asked gently.

'Sorry, lad. I won't deny it, it'll be hard leaving. But what is a home, if not a place to return to? The Five will stay open, I can't take that away from the folks here. The keys I'll give to Efa. If anyone can make an inn welcoming, it's her. Who knows? Perhaps another Wayfinder will take up residence.' He winked as he spoke, watching the curiosity kindle in Tias' eyes.

'When do we leave?' Tias asked, seemingly satisfied with Smythe's choice of successor.

'As soon as we know what Abraxus and Eli are doing. Get packed, we'll want to make the best of the day.' Smythe raised his mug, Tias matching the movement. They brought them together with a dull clunk.

'To the road,' Tias said.

'Onwards.' Smythe replied.

Eyes.
July, 1816.
Eli.

The voice of the wind whirled around him. Below, the sea crashed endlessly against the inlet, white spray casting itself into the air and then re-joining the water as salt-laden rain. It was an odd thought that this place used to frighten him, that he traversed the bridge as quickly as possible, desperate to reach the other side and the promised safety of solid land. Now, Eli sat, suspended above the ocean, framed by the land.

He had been on his way down to hidden cove, traversing the cliff path and bridge down rather than taking the less wild route through The Five-Pointed Compass and down into the *Gorvelion* Cellar. The dusk was coming on fast, the sky already stained pink at the edges. Abraxus had said to be with him before nightfall, and whilst the sweep of feathery black was a little way off, Eli had no desire to hurry. Instead, he sat on the rickety bridge, the cold dampness of the wooden slats slowly chilling him. Occasionally, a wave would break with so much force that he would feel the sharp coldness of the spray hit his ankles.

Beyond the whirl of the inlet, the wider sea was beautifully flat. Only the gentlest undulation stirred its vast, mirror-like surface. The colour of the sky leached into it, giving the water a soft patina of gold, pink and fiery orange along the horizon line. Yes, it was odd that he had once hurried over this void.

There was a tranquillity here, a liminal space which he could occupy – neither land, nor sea, nor air. Above and under and in all at once. To the west, the wind picked up, sending its caresses over his cheeks, through his hair.

He had not spoken the words he had uttered to Abraxus that day to his mother or Tias. He wasn't sure if Tias had reached the same realisation on his own and was merely keeping it to himself, much the same way Eli was. He knew with certainty that his mother hadn't noticed. Fleetingly, Eli wondered if that was because she had been so desperate for it to be his Da that she had just ruled it out. Or if it was the fact that, even though he hadn't been gone for long, Eli found himself starting to struggle to recall details about John Kincarran. Either way, he had kept his silence. The knowledge rested a little heavy within him, but it was a weight he knew he could bear.

Eli stood, the cuffs of his trousers patterned now with darker marks where the sea had tried to reach up and catch him within its grasp. The bridge beneath his feet swayed, but he paid it no mind. Really, it was no different to the deck of a ship.

As the path curved downward toward the hidden cove, Eli found himself wondering what Abraxus had planned for them. They had kept company over the past weeks, albeit a little quietly, but there had been nothing out of the ordinary – mostly making sure that the *Asherah* was fit and ready for what Eli began to suspect might be a long journey. The notion whispered through his thoughts, curling up and making him feel slightly sick every time he paid it the least bit of attention. Faced with what might be the ending of the story, Eli wasn't sure if he had it in him to close the book.

Abraxus appraised him with a critical eye as he boarded the *Asherah*, raising an eyebrow at his wind-bedraggled appearance. 'Are you ready?'

'Where are we going?' Eli said, slipping immediately into his now well-worn routine before they left the comforts of a harbour.

'Out into the open waters. There is something we have to see.' Abraxus' answer was a little short and Eli looked to the knots he was fiddling with, making sure that they were tied in the manner Abraxus preferred. Seeing nothing amiss there, he looked back to his mentor, but Abraxus had already climbed to the quarter deck and situated himself behind the wheel. Moving over to the halyard, Eli waited, casting glances up at Abraxus. *He's getting ready to leave you behind. It's easier for him this way.* The sick feeling was back. A lurch from the prow told him that he'd missed his mark on putting hand over hand on the halyard, and he jumped to it, letting the green-blue sails unfurl overhead and catch the wind.

Their exit from the hidden cove was slow and stately that night, the wind gentle, curbing the *Asherah*'s usual gleeful dance into a light waltz. Checking that everything was how it needed to be, Eli headed for the rigging, ready to take his usual perch on the yardarm. It was an entirely unsafe place for him to be, particularly whilst out on the open seas, but there was something delightfully dizzying to Eli about being in amongst the canvas, looking down on the decks below. Abraxus had given up trying to lecture him on it, instead merely resigning himself to asking Eli to carry a guideline with him.

'Elias.'

'I've got the guideline, see?' He held up the length of rope to show Abraxus.

'You will need this too.' Mirroring Eli's movement, Abraxus lifted his arm, something delicate and silver catching the light of the lanterns and setting sun. His circlet.

'Why?' Eli asked, quickly ascending the stairs to join Abraxus at the wheel. Abraxus didn't answer, merely looked into the distance with a half-smile. 'Do I need to stay down here?' Eli tried again, adjusting the metal filigree behind his ear.

'No, I imagine that the view will be more spectacular on the yardarm.' Abraxus said, finally looking at Eli. He shivered; there was the same sort of light in his mismatched gaze that a squall brought on. 'Come down when I call.'

Eli nodded his agreement and rushed down to the rigging, scrambling up the intricate lattice to the crossbeam that supported the canvas of one of the sails. Once settled with one arm wrapped around the mainmast for support, Eli slipped his seeing stone into the socket and scanned the sea.

The serpents were following. But unlike the serpents Eli had managed to befriend in the shallows of *Tua'r Môr* Bay, these were creatures of the deep. Long, sinuous bodies trailed behind them, a ripple of luminescence. They seemed to cut the sea: fins cascading behind them, bony sails adorning a few backs slicing the water with each undulation. Several of them were utterly immense, their trailing tails lost to the deep and out of sight. One came alongside the *Asherah*, gracefully rolled over in the water and dived, a streak of glowing navy blue disappearing and reappearing from beneath the hull. They had a delicateness that belied their size and Eli couldn't help but remember the whales he and Tias had seen from the deck of their Da's ship.

As the sun set and the night pulled the stars into focus, the serpents in the water beneath only seemed to glow brighter. Amongst the serpentine coils, Eli saw a flash of quicker, lithe seaweed green. It seemed that LongFin had also joined them on this moonlight trek.

'Eli.' Abraxus didn't even have to raise his voice to be heard – everything around them was still, as if the very world was holding its breath in the face of a display of such otherworldly beauty. Eli walked across the yardarm, trying to split his focus on not plummeting to the deck below and keeping a watchful eye on the serpents.

'Is this what we came out here to see?' He asked, three-quarters down the rigging and leaning backwards away from the *Asherah*, still looking into the ocean.

'In a sense. Come down.' Abraxus had shucked off his coat

and boots, his own circlet secured into his hair. As Eli's feet found the deck, he turned to the railing and a bundle of rope stashed there. Unfurling it, Eli realised it was a ladder. And then with complete certainty of what was coming next, he watched Abraxus throw it over the side. Suddenly, his heartbeat was very loud in his ears.

'Abraxus...' He looked over the railing and, no longer at his vantage point, fully appreciated how large these serpents were.

'Elias, do you trust me?' Abraxus' hand landed on his shoulder. Eli turned to face him, seeing the openness in Abraxus' expression.

'Of course.' The reply was easy to give.

'Then trust me when I say that they will do you no harm. You are well acquainted with the serpents of the shallows, of the ones that guide your catch into port. But you must also meet with the denizens of the deep.' Removing his hand, Abraxus leapt lightly onto the railing, gripping the rigging to keep his balance. He turned, holding out his hand. After an infinitesimal pause, Eli took it. 'It is time to see if the Roaring god is in our favour once more.'

Eli took in a deep breath: he hadn't known that this was something Abraxus needed to check, he had just assumed that everything would be righted. The serpents swirled lazily below.

'Shall I count?' Abraxus asked.

Eli nodded, a little numbly, facing what he was about to do. Abraxus started counting backwards from ten, Eli's heartbeat mirroring each number.

And then, all too soon, 'Three...'

The stars seemed drowned in the sea, a sheet of sky rippling with the weight of the cold celestial fires.

'Two...'

A serpent swam alongside the *Asherah*, its swirling opalescent eye staring up at them languidly.

'One.'

Eli exhaled, closing his eyes.

'Dive.'

Taking in a chest full of air, he leapt. He seemed to dive straight into the sky. The cold wrapped around him, clinging quickly to his bones and making his head ache. And then he forced his eyes open, and all discomfort was forgotten. The serpents had spiralled around him, an ever-shifting mass of light and colour. LongFin swept up to him, turning dizzyingly around him before swimming upward. Eli followed, gasping for breath he had nearly forgotten he was holding.

Treading water, he watched as the serpents seemed to drift away from him. Eli just caught sight of Abraxus' head descending beneath the water; he must have dived whilst Eli was enraptured by the underwater display. He submerged himself once more, following Abraxus' shadow, stark against the luminescence of the creatures. Abraxus swam deeper, angling himself downward in broad, strong strokes. Through the stone, Eli caught a glimpse of the man's back – Abraxus seemingly having discarded his shirt before entering the water. It glowed in silvers, purples and deepest blues. It had never truly occurred to Eli that when Abraxus referred to the serpents as being kin, he was being literal.

Still, Abraxus swam. Eli was forced to stop, looking down at the serpents who had now formed a tight weave around Abraxus. LongFin stayed nearby, moving in lazy figure eights around Eli. Then, echoing around them, a deep, concussive thud to the water. Eli felt the pressure of it slam into his chest, felt his heart stumble a beat at it. Shaking off the shock of it, he looked back down. Bubbles escaped his mouth as he opened it, either to yell or to gasp he wasn't sure.

The serpents had spread out now, several of the longer bodied ones forming a downward curving semi-circle. Abraxus was lost to the black depths. More joined above the others, now creating a slightly flattened circle, pointed at either end. LongFin suddenly dived, the swiftness of the motion sending

Eli tumbling slightly in the water. He righted himself, seeing that more serpents had risen from the depths, their colourings deeper and darker. They swirled in a perfect circle in the middle of their companions.

Abraxus was in the dead centre of the circle, a black mark. LongFin joined the congregation and sank behind Abraxus as a seaweed green outline.

Eli stared into the eye of Llŷr, Abraxus at their pupil. Llŷr stared back. The eye blinked, the serpents beginning to dissipate, sliding back down into the depths.

Eli watched, transfixed as the sea around them faded back into a void of endless black. A speck of glowing colour remained: Abraxus was coming back up to the surface. He passed Eli, not slowing, and Eli followed. Together they broke the surface and struck out for the *Asherah*, a golden sanctuary waiting for them.

Dripping and shivering, Eli made immediately for Abraxus' cabin once aboard. He grabbed as many quilts as he could manage and dragged them back out, slinging one around his shoulders as he went. Abraxus was lying at full length on his back in the middle of the deck, gazing into the sky. Eli threw some blankets over him and sat down, huddling into his own.

'We are forgiven,' Abraxus said quietly, and there was a relief so heady to his words that Eli felt tears prick at his eyes. Abraxus turned his head to look at him completely. 'We are *forgiven*.'

'It's really over.' Eli murmured. He looked around the deck, almost as if he was trying to memorise it. For the first time, he noticed a large sea chest by the companionway, its lid open and Abraxus' possessions almost spilling out of it. 'You're really going.' He said quietly. He felt that prickle at his eyes again, and pulled the quilt up higher around him.

'Eli...' Abraxus' voice was soft, gentle.

'M'fine,' Eli said shortly, looking away.

'Eli, did you honestly think I would leave without you, m'boy?' Abraxus had sat up, an arm looping around Eli's shoulders, pulling him close. 'Just because the sea is my home, does not mean that home cannot be lonely.' Eli looked up into Abraxus' face and saw nothing but love there. 'What do you say?'

Eli tried to think of something to say, some answer that managed to convey everything he was feeling. 'Tias... Mam...'

'Smythe has already asked Matthias to accompany him inland, and as for your mother – I believe there is a house in the woods waiting for her.' Abraxus gazed back over the sea and sky again. 'And even if they were to stay, I would still offer you the same.' He shifted a little, perhaps a little uncomfortable with how much he had just exposed to Eli. 'Besides, the *Asherah* is rather fond of you.'

Eli laughed a little incredulously, a little through tears. He didn't speak, but instead reached out and hugged Abraxus. Abraxus stilled for a moment and then relaxed, returning the embrace. It was all the answer Eli needed to give.

Onwards.
August, 1816.
Abraxus.

In the end, Porth Tymestl could not be home to any of them. At least, for now. There was too much sadness attached to the buildings, the streets, lurking in the shadows of night and memories. Love still resided here, but it walked with unquiet, salt sodden footsteps.

They celebrated the twins' seventeenth birthday under the burnished summer sun, visitors coming and going from Roseate Cottage to bring well wishes and to see if the flying rumours were true. Those that ventured inside the walls of the cottage saw a sea chest, two battered travelling packs on the table and a house stripped bare. The spare key had been handed over to

Tias, who wore it on a string around his neck. In the morning, they would depart.

On their last night in Roseate Cottage, Abraxus and Smythe joined the Kincarrans for a drink and to watch the sunset over *Angorfa* Beach. Below, the village of Porth Tymestl was loud – The Five-Pointed Compass doing roaring trade under the stout and watchful form of Efa. Few words passed between them, silence was company enough. Ffion sat in between her two sons, holding them close. Occasionally, she would sniff and press a kiss into Tias' hair, pull Eli a little closer. But there was no true sorrow in her actions, only a fond acceptance of what was to come. Abraxus sat beside Eli, braiding fronds of grass as he had done all those months ago to calm Tias' mind in a lonely sea meadow. Smythe, a thick book on his lap, closed his eyes and hummed gentle strains of sea shanties. Abraxus caught the tune of one and joined in, a poignant one of leaving things behind and turning for new paths.

When the moths began to swoop in and out of the open door, chasing the light of the candles still lit, they retired inside. Bedrolls for Smythe and Abraxus had been laid out on the floor. It was to be an early start, and there was little point delaying. To while away the hours before sleep overcame them, Ffion unrolled the fabric that allowed Eli and Tias some privacy on their balcony bedroom, requested several candles, and proceeded to tell stories from her childhood accompanied by an incredible array of shadow puppetry.

That night, Abraxus slept peacefully, surrounded by family.

The morning came, bright and glassy. Last preparations were made, Eli's sea chest locked and latched, Tias trying to cram one more book from the *Gorwelion* Cellar into his pack. Ffion stepped over the threshold of Roseate Cottage into the morning sun, her own pack slung over one shoulder. One by one, they all exited. Ffion closed the door, pressed her hand against it for the briefest moment, and then turned the key.

Roseate Cottage was to remain empty until one of them had need of it again.

The path diverged before they reached Porth Tymestl. One road ran out into the vales beyond, to the heather and trees and quiet places of the world. The other, to the salt paths of the sea. Abraxus turned toward the sea, Smythe toward the green. There were no words needed between them; this was not their first parting and nor would it be their last. Smythe winked and grinned. Abraxus canted his head, pressing a hand over his heart.

Ffion brought in her boys for one last embrace. With a wince, as if disentangling herself brought her physical pain, she let them go, tears shimmering in her eyes but not falling. She cupped Tias' face, bringing him down to kiss his forehead, repeating the gesture with Eli a moment later. 'Your Da would be so proud of you. *I* am so proud of you both. Be safe. Write, if you can. Come and visit me.' She gazed up into their faces. 'And most importantly, remember, you are so loved.' She smiled, and it was like a ray of sun on a grey winter's day, breaking through the clouds and making the world afresh.

Tias nodded, seemingly unable to trust his voice. Eli reached out and held his mother's hand for a moment, before letting her go. Ffion nodded to herself, straightening her shoulders resolutely, and turned toward Porth Tymestl. For the first time since John had died, the coastal village was venturing inland to rekindle their old trade alliance. Ffion had a promised spot on the cart leaving. Before she dipped below the crest of the hill, Ffion Kincarran turned, lifted her hand, waved and was gone.

Abraxus waited for Eli on the path towards the sea. He watched as Eli turned to his brother, wondering what was going to pass between them.

'Well... don't drown,' Tias said.

Eli stared at him before breaking into laughter. 'And you remember that there's a world *outside* of your books.'

'I'll try,' Tias said ruefully. He regarded his brother. 'I hope it's all we ever dreamed of.'

'It will be,' Eli said. 'And more.' He held out his hand. Tias took it in the grasp Abraxus and Smythe adopted, forearm to forearm.

'I'll see you soon,' Tias said, letting go. He turned to look at Smythe and the open road.

'Watch the tides,' Eli replied.

Matthias joined Smythe's side, took in a deep breath of the rich air, his eyes closed. Abraxus noticed his fingers stray down to the battered leather shoulder bag, feeling along the ridges of several, new notebooks nestled there. Smythe gestured before him, and Tias took a step out onto the path, and then another, strides growing longer and more confident as he was beckoned onwards and away. Smythe nodded one last time to Eli and Abraxus, before following Tias.

'Fare thee well,' Abraxus murmured over the sound of the breeze susurrating through the grass.

From the *Asherah*'s bowsprit, a lantern hung. It was battered, rusting a little in places, with pinpricks cut into its surface to emulate the light of the stars. He would light it when the night came on.

Eli was waiting for him at the wheel, barefooted, hair bound back. Ready. Behind them, the armchair bay of Porth Tymestl was sinking into the hazy distance, the white sails of its fleet becoming nothing more than the swift wing of gull seen high above.

Abraxus grasped the wheel, feeling the unbound joy of his ship thrill through the spokes. *Somewhere new.* He looked back to Eli. 'Where to, Master Kincarran?'

Eli gazed out over the prow, watching the dip and rise of the bowsprit. In his hand, a small pocketknife, the handle made of antler. A reminder of home and what waited for him there.

'How about... the horizon?'

'Aye, I think we can do that. Do you hear the song of the sea, m'boy?' Abraxus span the wheel, swinging the sails overhead in a sweep of verdant green and blue. The sun shone down through them, staining the deck in all the colours of the world.

Eli glanced at him, and then back to the sea. A smile worked its way onto his lips. 'Aye.' A deep breath before the plunge. 'Here we go.'

part four

the horizon

I
later.

September, 1818.

The midmorning sun made the motes of dust swirling around the casement look like miniature snow fall. They drifted gracefully down, alighting on a scatter of papers, the ink still drying in small pools of black. A lax hand settled atop the papers twitched slightly, as if trying to grip the pen that rested in its palm. Ink was spattered here too; up the wrist and darkening beneath bitten nails.

Matthias shifted, eyes flickering behind closed lids and dimly began to register the crick in his neck and ache settling along his back. Slowly, inch by inch, he pulled himself toward wakefulness, aided by the golden light streaming through the large window opposite the desk. His first coherent thought of the day was *this is not my bed*.

Finally succeeding on getting his eyes open and shaking away the last gossamer thread of a dream long forgotten, Tias took in the landscape of his desk. It truly was a mess from this low, intimate angle. From above, he could just about justify the clutter, knowing where everything was. He watched the dust motes fall in the shaft of light, wondering if Smythe would be annoyed that he had – accidentally – skipped another night in a proper bed.

The lodgings they had procured a little over two months ago were, in his opinion, lavish. A whole separate room for study, his own bedroom. It certainly was a contrast to the dingy inns and roadside hedges they had found themselves in over the past two years. Although, and he was sure Smythe knew of this, Tias would much prefer to be in said roadside hedge or thicket than under a roof for too long. Not that this wasn't pleasant. '*Traed aflonydd.*' His mother's voice whispered in his mind.

A knock sounded at his door. Tias sat bolt upright, stifling a groan as his back protested and called a little incoherently, 'I'm awake! Working on–' He was cut off by a laugh and the door swinging open, revealing Smythe. The erstwhile innkeeper's laughter only grew louder upon seeing his ward: Tias had failed to realise that, in his rush to look awake and presentable, there was a piece of paper stuck to his cheek. He batted it away irritably.

'Do you see that door, down the hall?' Smythe asked, pulling the study door wider and gesturing. 'It has a room and there's a bed in it. I wonder if you've tried it?'

'Very good,' Tias grumbled, stretching and then wincing at the series of cracks that rolled down his spine. 'What do you want?'

Smythe raised an amused eyebrow and then held up a handful of letters. 'Post.'

'Anything from Olsen?' Tias asked, turning back toward the window as Smythe joined him, placing the letters on his desk.

'Not yet, no,' Smythe replied. 'He'll be busy, lad. Give it time.'

Tias had to bite back a tired retort to that – he'd been desperate to meet another Wayfinder since the night Smythe had sat him down beneath a winter's sky and laid out all the different Heralds, their names and respective Wayfinders. And now, Olsen wasn't responding. Their letter had been sent on to his inn, *Det Stille Vannet* – The Silent Water – just as they had arrived at this current set of lodgings.

Smythe rested a hand on his shoulder, looking down into the bustling street below. A cart went by, the coachman sitting proudly at the front, long whip in hand. A city had been something Tias would've had very little time acclimatising to. The noise and the people were one thing, but the fact that a lot of them seemed to lack *green* really took him by surprise. He'd spoken to a young woman in the previous city who had confided in him that she had never once seen a true forest, living most of her life by the murky canal that had bisected the place.

'Write, or wander?' Smythe asked, still looking below into the street.

'Wander. I want to see the sky for a while.' Tias stood, stretched once more and began casting about for his coat. The summer was still resolutely clinging on, the heat cresting with the sun at midday, but there was an undeniable nip to the wind that now blew through the paved streets.

'Open those first, an' then we'll get going.' Smythe pointed to the letters and turned to leave the room. 'Breakfast is on the table!' He called as he descended to the shared dining room below.

Snatching up his letter opener – another unnecessary luxury, but Tias was too pleased with this one to truly care – he slit open the first letter. Scanning over it, he quickly tossed it to one side, deeming it of little importance. The same happened to the next two letters, simply stories of things people had 'seen' out beyond the sprawl of the city, responding to Tias' notice on a board just beyond the church. He would read them thoroughly later, and then deem if they were worthy enough claims to fully look into.

The last envelope was heavy, and something slid within its confines. Tias tipped the contents onto his palm and felt his heart lurch. A perfectly flat slate stone rested heavy in his hand. Feeling his breath shallow in his chest, Tias flipped it over. There, scratched onto the opposite side, a message.

"Seaward".

Beside it, several numerals that Tias took a moment to puzzle out into a date. Three days from now. 'Smythe.' Tias called over his shoulder,

'Aye?' Smythe's voice drifted up through the stairwell.

'We're going to be wandering a little farther than normal today.'

The landscape around him was becoming more and more familiar. Tias found himself recognising the curve of a path, the shape of a crooked tree. They felt like good friends, greeting him and calling him onwards toward something old and well loved.

In the air was a definite clean salt tint, the haziness to the under-edge of the sky that grew with each crest of a hill telling him that what he sought was just a little further down the road. The horse beneath him nickered as he guided it into a canter and then, unable to contain himself any longer, a gallop. It had been the quickest way out of the city, and since travelling with Smythe, he had gained some experience riding them. Their long stride and strength was something he found exhilarating in ways he couldn't describe.

They crested the ridge, and there below him was the achingly familiar roll and buckle of the land, an armchair bay and a small cluster of stout houses nestled within its shelter. Smythe caught up and gazed down into Porth Tymestl.

'Two years,' he said reverently.

'Do you think The Five is still running?'

'I should hope so. Whether or not they've discovered the cellar is another matter.' Smythe winked at Tias, who saw the barely concealed longing and excitement warring over his expression.

'Shall we?' Without waiting for an answer, Tias took off down the hill toward Porth Tymestl.

They careened into the village, the hooves of their horses beating fast and wild along the cobbles. People started and leapt out of their way, staring at the unusual sight. As the wind streaked past Tias' head, he caught shocked voices intermingled with the whirl of the air itself.

'Ought to slow down–'

'Is that *Matthias*?'

'–the Kincarran boy, and *Smythe* too–'

'Someone fetch Medwyn–'

Neither Smythe nor Tias slowed down to stop and greet anyone after their time away, but merely thundered on toward the churchyard and the cliff path that awaited them there. There would be time for lesser reunions later.

Tua'r Môr Bay stretched desolate and striking around them. The tide had slunk out, leaving the beach exposed, a thin film of crystalline water coating the sands. They had travelled swiftly, making it to the beach the day before the one etched into the message stone. Now, as the sun set, Tias stood calf-deep in the surf, hands in his pockets, feeling in some ways that no time had passed at all.

He had visited the cavern the moment they had reached the bay, running his hand gently over one of the walls as he ventured inside, the touch of the rough stone intimate. Some storm or other had washed away the canvas that lined the back shelf, and their driftwood supply was long gone. Tias had pulled a chunk of chalk from his bag, hoisted himself up onto the shelf and scrawled on the back wall: *The cavern. Matthias and Elias Kincarran. Shelter here from the storm. – 1818*

'Do you think they'll actually come?' Tias asked, not taking his eyes off the setting sun.

"Course they will.' Smythe stood nearby, skimming stones against the waves. 'We've had direct word from 'em.'

Tias didn't respond, letting the wash of the waves around his legs soothe him. Of course, during his time with Smythe they had been to the coast, to wild expanses of stones and torrents of waves. But none of them had settled into his soul the way *Tua'r Môr* Bay did now.

They lit a fire to keep the night's chill at bay. An unspoken agreement had passed between them that they would sleep on the beach tonight, rather than try to acquire rooms at The Five-Pointed Compass. In any case, Tias felt that staying there as a patron might be a little bitter-sweet for Smythe, and was much more content with the quiet company of the stars. That night, with the sand as his bed and the sky as his roof, Tias dreamed of the serpents and of a ship with sails made of the sea.

'Tias. Tias, wake up.' A rough hand on his side, shaking him slightly. The murmur of the tide, the dawn call of a gull. Gritty sand itching his eyes, in his hair. The sensation of being *home*. 'Tias, there's a ship.'

Dawn was pulling back the curtain of night, pastel hues inking the sky and chasing the blue-black away. Framed by the rocky cliffs of the bay, out to sea, a ship, at this distance no bigger than a child's toy, rocked peacefully up and down on a restful ocean. It was silhouetted, its colours reduced to shadow. He sat up, his blanket falling away from his shoulders. A small shape detached from the ship and was inching its way toward them on the bay. It took him only a second to realise it was a rowboat.

Both he and Smythe were on their feet in an instant, wading out into the shockingly cold water. They watched the rowboat's progress, neither one of them wanting to voice the question, until Tias could stand it no longer. 'Do you think..?' He trailed off. Closer the boat came, until he could see that there were two people occupying it.

And then a shout went up from over the water, and one of the occupants stood up and waved, making the little vessel rock wildly. Another shout of annoyance followed it; Tias and Smythe exchanging glances and identical smiles beginning to break out across their faces.

'That is most *definitely* Eli.' Tias said. If he needed any further proof, he was given it immediately, as the person standing then proceeded to dive head-first *off* the boat and into the water.

From out of the Celtic sea walked his brother. He was dripping wet, grinning and seemed to have truly inhabited the role as a ship's hand; everything about him now told Tias of a life at sea. Eli waded toward them, until he stood facing Tias. 'Abraxus is going to shout at me when he catches up.'

Tias let out an incredulous laugh. Clearly, not much truly changed in two years. He reached and grabbed his brother, pulling him into a hug. 'I see you haven't drowned yet,' he said, voice muffled slightly by Eli's shoulder.

'Not for lack of trying on Abraxus' part, the man's insane.' Eli whacked him on the back to get Tias to release him, and then levelled a look at Smythe. 'You could have warned me that he would steer us *deliberately* into every storm he could find.'

'Good to see you too, lad.' Smythe held Eli at arm's length, as if assessing him. He nodded, seemingly pleased with what he saw.

'Elias, you nearly capsized the damned boat!'

Eli shot Tias and Smythe a look that said, *told you*, and then turned to his mentor. 'I didn't want to wait anymore.' He waded back out to help pull the rowboat up onto the sand.

Abraxus left him to it and came to greet them. 'Can we swap.' He said to Smythe, dead-panned. There was a beat, and then Abraxus' lips twitched. Tias found himself in a three-way embrace between the other two men, clutching the back of Abraxus' coat.

'It is good to see you again, Matthias.' Abraxus said quietly. Tias just held on a little tighter.

'Ready?' Eli called, still standing by the boat.

'What for?' Tias said, disentangling himself. The dawn was steadily growing stronger, the sky sharpening its colours from muted pastels to a cutting arctic-blue.

'Well, we didn't come all this way to stand on the shore.'

A serpent, huge and lithe, crested the water in an arc, its tail flicking spray across the deck as it dived once more. Tias hung over the railing, letting some of the droplets collect in his outstretched palm.

They danced over the waves, the *Asherah*'s prow mimicking the arc and dip of the serpents as she flew across the ocean. The wind picked up, filling the canvas and driving them onward. Tias' hair whipped around his face, and he heard a laugh emanate from the wheel above him. Perched in the rigging, leaning outstretched and backwards to the water, Eli watched the serpents cavort alongside them.

He looked over to Tias, catching his eye. Tias could already see what his brother was planning. He began to shuck his boots off, and then joined Eli in the rigging. 'Ready?' Eli roared over the call of the sea. He didn't wait for an answer, merely let go of the ropes and let himself fall backward into a perfectly straight dive. Tias looked to Smythe and Abraxus, steady and alive under the sun. He followed.

Swept up into a whirl of colour, made part of the sea, Tias watched Eli catch one of the serpent's horns and hold on. In a streak of scales and fins, it came barrelling past, and Tias felt Eli's hand pull on his wrist. Together, they flew through the water, the serpent leaping once above the waves, allowing them to catch a breath. The *Asherah* followed behind their wake, her colours singing.

Cresting the waves once more, Tias caught a glimpse of the horizon, the thin ridge that ran around their world. They echoed under the deep sky, that faintest thread of blue calling them on.

Acknowledgements

This is really difficult, I think as I stare down the header of this page. 'Acknowledgements'. What if I miss someone? I've made a list, and it is long, but still. What if? I'll do my best.

To my Mum and Dad: thank you for listening to me ramble aimlessly for hours to work out plot points. Thank you for being my first readers, my first editors and spellcheckers. Mum, thank you for pointing out 'leant' and 'leaned' are two different words. Dad, thank you for telling everyone you meet that your child has written a book. Thank you for just being there. Love you.

To my Grandma: thank you for your support, being my second ever reader and letting me ask countless questions about who your favourite character was, what worked and what didn't, and which was your favourite bit. Answers to those questions are invaluable to a writer.

To Granddad: even though you aren't here, thank you for being inspiration. You're everywhere in this story. I think you would have liked it.

To James, Amy and Ted: thank you for inviting me into your amazing world of Northodox Press. I couldn't have done half of this without you, and all your advice and input has been so valued. Thank you for making little eight-year-old me dreams come true.

To Dr Dyfrig Hughes: thank you for all your amazing work on the Welsh translations, they really add authenticity to the novel. It's a language I'd love to learn, so maybe I'll be coming to you for some lessons.

To Laura Joyce: hi Laura! Remember my MA dissertation?

This is it, all grown up and in book form! Thank you for being the first person to set academic eyes on my writing and telling me to go for it.

To The Vixere: yes, I've written that in the back of my book. Thank you for the best years of my university life (and adult life, we aren't stopping any time soon) and letting me, once again, talk for hours about my imaginary friends. You gave me countless ideas, and when I wasn't writing this, I was writing with you.

To the Blakeney people: thank you for late night kitchen readings, sudden inspiration strikes on my behalf and the incredible illustrations you drew for me. I have them printed out in and in my notebook.

To the DnD group: honestly, I am sorry for all the messages you all got about this book. But what can I say aside from you're all amazing storytellers in your own right and sometimes a writer on their own just needs to yell into a void about their ideas. Thank you for all the chaos, plot moments that made us scream, and being found family.

To the axe-throwing gang: thank you for gin in the afternoons and letting me imagine my plot holes were attached to the target board. You have no ideas how much that helped.

Finally, for the people to thank, actual blood family – Nan, Bampy, cousins – and anyone who I told were chosen family, that have loved and supported this book and my wacky daydreams, that told me to keep going. This one is for you too. You know who you are.

Now for the quirkier ones: thanks to my playlist which has been my carefully curated daydreaming soundtrack for the past four years of my life. I absolutely spent way too much time listening and not writing. Thanks to my Pinterest board, which is currently topping out at 2,692 pins. Sorting character art into little boxes gave me unreasonable amounts of joy. Thanks to Mr. Michael Sheen for living rent-free in my head every time I came to write anything about Smythe (imagine Staged era

Michael Sheen here, not Good Omens era).

And lastly, thanks to you, reader. You make all this possible. I hope you enjoyed my tall tale. Rest assured: there is more to come. You have my word.

Printed in Great Britain
by Amazon